TEEN
WIL

10/10/23

Wilde, Rhiannon

Where you left us

Where You
LEFT US

Where You
LEFT US

Rhiannon Wilde

2023 First US edition
Text copyright © 2023 by Rhiannon Wilde
Jacket illustrations copyright © 2023 by Christopher Cyr

At the time of publication, all URLs printed in this book were accurate and
active. Charlesbridge, the author, and the illustrator are not responsible for
the content or accessibility of any website.

Published by Charlesbridge Teen,
an imprint of Charlesbridge Publishing
9 Galen Street
Watertown, MA 02472
(617) 926-0329
www.charlesbridge.com

First published in Australia by University of Queensland Press, 2022.

Library of Congress Cataloging-in-Publication Data
Names: Wilde, Rhiannon, author.
Title: Where you left us / Rhiannon Wilde.
Description: First US edition. | Watertown, MA: Charlesbridge, 2023. |
    Audience: Ages 14 and older. | Audience: Grades 10–12. | Summary: The
    Prince sisters, Cinnamon and Scarlett, struggle with family dynamics,
    queer identities, and mental health while their great aunt's secrets begin
    to unravel around them.
Identifiers: LCCN 2022031327 (print) | LCCN 2022031328 (ebook) |
    ISBN 9781623544232 (hardcover) | ISBN 9781632893840 (ebook)
Subjects: LCSH: Sisters—Juvenile fiction. | Fathers and daughters—Juvenile
    fiction. | Depression, Mental—Juvenile fiction. | Lesbians—Juvenile
    fiction. | Interpersonal relations—Juvenile fiction. | Secrecy—Juvenile
    fiction. | CYAC: Sisters—Fiction. | Fathers and daughters—Fiction.
    | Depression, Mental—Fiction. | Lesbians—Fiction. | Interpersonal
    relations—Fiction. | Secrets—Fiction.
Classification: LCC PZ7.1.W5335 Wh 2023 (print) | LCC PZ7.1.W5335 (ebook)
    | DDC 823.92 [Fic]—dc23/eng/20220809
LC record available at https://lccn.loc.gov/2022031327
LC ebook record available at https://lccn.loc.gov/2022031328

Printed in the United States of America
(hc) 10 9 8 7 6 5 4 3 2 1

Jacket illustrations done in digital media
Display type hand lettered by Jon Simeon and set in Bon Vivant Serif by
    Nicky Laatz
Text type set in Freight Text Pro by Joshua Darden
Printed by Maple Press in York, Pennsylvania
Production supervision by Nicole Turner
Designed by Jon Simeon

For my sisters

For my sisters

Prologue

Princes Beach, 1968

The white house sits on a cliff in an Australian seaside town that's just like all the others and also a world of its own. Just close enough to watch the waves lap at the rocks below and hear them hiss-crash over each other onto wet sand. It's bright tonight, the ocean a greenish hue—as if a flashlight is shining from underneath.

You are supposed to be leaving on this night, and only your family will ever know why.

You're walking out toward the ocean, just to look. You stand cloaked in night on the sandy-ghostly edge of the cliff. Wind plays with your cropped-short hair, and you tuck it behind one ear.

Your father walks like the important man he is toward where you're standing on the edge of the world. He speaks like an important man too, over the top of you sometimes without properly listening to your reply.

"Have you got everything?" he asks briskly.

"Yes, I think so." Your voice is sullen. You pin him with your eyes.

"You know why it has to be this way," he says, or perhaps he just stares back. You won't remember exactly later—your mind will go blank in places the way memories do. You'll give it your best guess.

You fold your arms across the floral sweater-vest you're wearing, a favorite knitted by your dearest friend. "I don't, actually."

"It's just the way things are. The way they've always been."

"And that's a good reason for doing something, is it? Because it's what has *always* been done?"

He says your first and middle names, the ones your mother gave you just before she died, and then, "Be reasonable." You won't let him off the hook that easily.

"I won't go," you say. "There, that's reasonable."

The one you love is waiting for you too, at the edge of the fence near the edge of the world. He steps into the starlight, his shoes crunching on rocks. You look at him. Your father sees him too and rushes forward. The one you love startles. Slips.

You run to grab his hand.

Someone is watching from down on the beach. But you won't know that until later, when you no longer care. It'll be a dazzler of a story—what they think they saw—long after you're gone.

What is a history
told by those who hated you?

1.

Cinnamon Prince is running away from home.

Not properly or for good—just literally running along the scraggy stretch of beach below her family's house.

The water is blue as far as her eyes can see, and she breathes in as much as her chest can hold. She does this a lot—running. She likes her brain best when it goes almost blank. There's not as much blue in the sky as she'd like today, though, not as much as she needs. White clouds scud across her vision. Clouds that, if she squints, look like shapes of her life.

Her dad.

Uni offers.

Her sister.

All the stuff left behind by her (dead) grandmother,
if she stares for too long.

Cinnamon inhales deeper and runs until the clouds start to float hazily away. If all the thoughts she's imagined as clouds, or whatever her free mindfulness app tells her to envision, ever became corporeal, this sky would be as full of garbage as the Pacific Ocean.

Halcyon House looms over her the whole run back, white with a steep gabled roof and rows of windows like empty eye sockets. Its faded face peers toward the edge of the cliff, casting soft shadows over the sand and sea. Cinnamon used to think that Halcyon stretched toward the ocean the way plants do toward the sun. Or as though it's determined to drown itself and everyone in it.

The Prince family have lived in this tumbledown residence for generations. There have been many of them—Princes—over the years who've grown up here and moved on. But something always pulls them back.

Home.

Notorious is one of the words locals use to describe the house and its occupants. Mostly because it can be imbued with more nastiness than *infamous*. Her family is, Cinnamon supposes, famous. At least, her dad, Ian, is. *Was*.

Her dad's band, the Princelings, were an almost-big deal in the nineties music scene. Something about the tone (dark and dulcet) and Plathic metaphors gifted Ian Prince (poet and lead singer) with, among other things, three number-one albums, a cluster of intense fans, and a wife (and then two daughters).

For a while.

He was the most famous Prince since Arthur, who built the house years and years ago after making a fortune selling wine. But fame didn't stop the thing that fueled Ian from also eating away at him. The muse. The moods. They existed as a ragtag pair until one of them won.

This is why Cinnamon is stuck in this town where people are afraid of her family. She's nineteen and sans life direction, with sand in her socks, and listening to her dad singing in her headphones because he won't talk to her. Because of him, because the rest of her family is gone, because someone finally had to take some goddamn responsibility.

At least that's why she thinks she's still here.

She jogs up the private stairway cut into the sand dunes, gripping the hands of sad-looking lillypillies for support. The stairs have no railings and are stupidly steep—to deter enemy intruders, her grandmother Maggie always jokingly said—and climbing them without paying attention has been known to be fatal.

The front gate to Halcyon sighs when Cinnamon kicks it open with her sand-crusted Nike. Inside she puts the kettle on, wiping the sweat off her forehead with an annoyingly cheery rabbit dish towel. If her dad were consciously here, he'd call her a heathen for doing that. It feels rebellious for a second. Then it just feels like everything else.

Her dad is in a Very Tired All the Time phase. Nobody knows how long it'll last.

They never do.

When the water is almost boiled, Cinnamon walks down the hallway to check on him.

He's lying on the couch by the blinds-closed window, exactly where he was an hour ago.

If he moves from the bed to the couch, it's a good day.

Ian Prince has faded red hair and gray eyes and a soft sort of face that people like Cinnamon often cause to fall. He's blinking now like he's remembering her, even though she's right here.

"Hi, Bug," he says. "You go for a run?"

"Just a short one," Cinnamon says. She hasn't enjoyed being called Bug since she was four. She feels squirmingly defensive about it. About having gone running at all. About the fact that sometimes she daydreams that she could keep going and never stop.

"That's good."

"Do you want tea?"

3

Ian smiles faintly, shakes his head, and looks toward the TV.

Meeting adjourned.

Back in the kitchen, Cinnamon spoons tea leaves into a strainer while idly scrolling on her phone. She checks her email, but there's nothing. Several weeks ago she labeled any mail that came from the uni she deferred as spam. She puts her phone back on the counter, and it immediately vibrates.

Message from ~Scarface~:

my train gets in at 6:10.
Are you picking me up, or shall I get the bus?

Cinnamon thinks in a flare about texting back: *Shall you remove thy stick from thine butt?* She isn't precisely sure what it is about her sister that inspires love and hate at the same time. Her dad used to call them *chalk and cheese*, but really, Cinnamon thinks, they're not even as similar as that.

Scarlett is younger, with red hair to Cinnamon's blond, freshly finished with her last year at boarding school in the city. Scarlett is clever and snobby and wears girly things. Scarlett looks like their mother—*is* like their mother. She was Cinnamon's best friend when they were very small, but there's something different and walled about her now. Something Cinnamon can't hold on to.

Scarlett doesn't know about the day their dad collapsed after the tour and the funeral or the trip to the doctor's office after. Scarlett left all that behind—left them behind—when she went to school.

Cinnamon's looking out the window now at the surfers dotted far out near the break, and then her eyes follow the jagged lines of waves toward town. People are walking along the beach: locals starting their day, tourists starting summer holidays on the early side. Sometimes they shield their eyes to look up at Halcyon or take pictures of it. Sometimes they wonder who lives in it; sometimes they know.

She slams the window shut.

2.

Scarlett Prince is coming home.

Unwillingly. *Highly* unwillingly. And just for the summer. Just between the end of school and the rest of her life.

Scarlett loved school. The routine and certainty of it, structured days sliding into quiet nights: homework, read, bed. She doesn't feel remotely ready to Make a Mark on The Real World now that school is done. She doesn't even know how to make more than one type of sandwich. She refused, denied, pretended it wasn't happening for as long as she could. But the holidays are here, unavoidable as summer heat.

Graduation was two weeks ago. Her dad and sister came and clapped for Scarlett in her blazer as she stood arm in arm with girls from homeroom whom her family doesn't know because she doesn't want them to. (Her mother was away for work and couldn't come, which was fine because Scarlett didn't want her to.) Ian wore a blue button-up shirt and looked pale; Cinnamon wore Docs and a strappy black dress and looked pissed off.

Cinnamon generally looks pissed off, at least to Scarlett. She's just an angry sort of person. Dark. Maybe that's what reading too much Pablo Neruda etcetera does to a person. Scarlett (re)reads classic novels because it gives her the illusion of calm. She is rarely calm.

After Cinnamon and Ian went home, Scarlett went to one and

a half end-of-school parties and gave herself a modest pat on the back about finishing exams. Her roommate, Niamh, left as soon as she could. Scarlett stayed as long as she could, slowly packing up her school life: three framed photographs of her parents and grandparents, her laptop, her uniforms and weekend outfits, and her favorite books she couldn't live without. That was it—her whole entire life packed in three medium-sized boxes she shipped ahead express.

Now she's on a train. Outside the window, the sun slips into bruises on the horizon. The next station is home—*except it's not, not anymore*. She doesn't know how that feels exactly.

Definitely uncomfortable, but manageable if she stays focused on staying focused. Scarlett has a system on trains. She takes no chances. Beside her she has the following:

- one bottle of water, still slightly cold, purchased from the vending machine before she left;
- one foil packet of Tylenol, in case of sudden headache that could potentially cause nausea;
- ginger tablets, in case of nausea (she's never actually *been* travel sick, but you never know);
- an apple, in case of low blood sugar (which could cause both headache and nausea);
- her phone, currently playing a soothing BBC podcast about British queens;
- a copy of *Pride and Prejudice*, orange and worn, which she brings most places in case she has to sit or wait and doesn't know what to do with herself.

She swallows a ginger tablet, just to be safe.

She reads Cinnamon's text again:

yas I know i'll be there.

She flips open the pink compact mirror roommate Niamh semi-passive-aggressively gave her for Christmas. Most things Niamh did were passive-aggressive, since she discovered Ian had been in *that* nineties band and Scarlett was his disappointingly ordinary progeny.

Niamh was big on makeup in a YouTube, contouring, Sephora sort of way. Scarlett is currently doing the thing where she looks at her own outward expression to prevent obsessive awareness of her insides. All she has on are mascara and lip gloss, and both are melting off.

Scarlett's face annoys her somewhat. It's not ugly, but it's easy to skim over in a way she worries makes her easy to ignore. Pale eyes that are too big and too gray blue—buggy, really—give her a look of perpetually being afraid. She'd like to be able to hide that better.

She closes the mirror with a snap. Holding her phone away from her face to avoid eyestrain, she quickly scans Google alerts of her dad. ROCK LEGEND IAN PRINCE CANCELS RESCHEDULED REUNION TOUR, CONFESSES ONGOING STRUGGLE WITH MENTAL HEALTH is still the latest from a while ago. She doesn't like the "confesses" or "struggle." (*Just say depression*, Cinnamon snapped when she first saw it.) Scarlett swipes the browser window closed.

The train passes through one last cluster of trees and then rolls to a stop at the familiar old station. Its yellow paint is still peeling in the same places, and the sign that hasn't been updated since the sixties declares in faded block letters she is actually, definitively back in the place she ran away from. Scarlett jumps up just before the doors close and drags her bag onto the platform.

It's a balmy sort of night, the air thick with the green-grass, blue-ocean smell she can never remember until she has it in her nose and mouth again.

The old Jeep is parked under a slowly dying jacaranda tree, purple petals alternating between hanging on and slipping to the ground. Cinnamon stands beside it with one burgundy-booted foot crossed over the other. Cinnamon is striking in a conventional way that Scarlett knows annoys her (though Scarlett has never understood why). Button nose, brown eyes, and blond hair—bobbed short now, blunt and bright just below her ears. At least, Scarlett remembers it used to annoy Cinnamon.

Scarlett feels vaguely fraudulent assuming anything about Cinnamon anymore. She looks good, anyway—tall and tanned in a plaid shirt and shorts. But she also looks pissed off. Per usual.

Scarlett sighs.

Cinnamon silently uncrosses her legs and hauls Scarlett's bag into the Jeep. Scarlett then hauls herself up into the passenger seat. No hugs.

"Good trip?" Cinnamon asks when their seat belts are buckled.

Scarlett nods. "Fine."

The car coughs loudly into life, as though it knows this is the last of the welcomey words they have for each other.

There's salt breeze leaking through the open windows; it wraps summer-cold arms around them both. Scarlett shivers. "Can you put the windows up?"

Cinnamon frowns at her like it's the most outlandish thing anyone's ever said. "No? I like the fresh air."

They wind through the sleepy town with its salted shop faces, then up the hillside in fast-dropping dark. Scarlett hugs herself, watching the lights splay out below. Cinnamon rolls her eyes.

Halcyon House sits where it always has—hunched on its cliff staring out to sea. The Jeep jerks to a stop in the driveway, tires crunching on gravel. Cinnamon kicks the front door open, and then they're in the scuffed-hardwood entryway. An echo of a smell wafts over them—sage and salt, and under that, dust.

It's pitch-black and dead silent. Cinnamon flicks a switch and yellow-tinged lights bring the familiar grand Victorian house into view, dotted everywhere with things that people in town would call *bohemian*. Or maybe *weird*.

There are bookshelves crammed with cracking-apart volumes, plants trailing leaves along the walls and around doorways, abstract paintings in heavy gold frames, dusty dark-wood *Downton Abbey* furniture, altars with statues of saints, altars with music awards, altars with candles and tarot cards left facedown in a spread. An echo of Princes past who (bar three) are long gone.

Scarlett swallows, looking down the wallpapered hallway. It's so quiet that she can hear every wave hitting the distant shore. "It's like nobody lives here anymore," she says. She regrets it straightaway, sees from the twitch in her sister's jaw that it was exactly the wrong thing to say. But it's too late.

"He's probably *asleep*," Cinnamon says sharply, flicking on more lights in the wood-and-marble kitchen. It's clean. Cinnamon must clean now.

"He's been really tired, since . . ."

Scarlett forces her brain to stay focused on the moment and not heavy-fall back into the past. *Here, now, look around you.* "But it's only eight-thirty," she says.

"Yeah, well." Cinnamon shrugs without making eye contact. "He goes to bed early now."

Once upon a time, Ian would have been the one waiting at the station, eyes bright with mischief, hug warm and comfortingly too tight.

To the east of the kitchen is their grandparents' wing: their bedroom, the sunroom with the glass framing dark by now, and two checked chairs facing out.

Now. Don't think about then.

This is even worse than Scarlett worried it would be, and she's worried about it *a lot.*

She feels overwhelmed—a great sudden sweep of it, all the oxygen sucked out of her blood.

This hallway tapers off into the drawing room; she follows its winding path rather than her thoughts.

The drawing room is stuffy velvet, and the windows are all closed. She pushes one open and breathes in the summer night—flowers and rain and a strange something else—until it fills up her lungs.

Cinnamon appears in the doorway. They look at the boxes at the same time, Scarlett breathing in and Cinnamon frowning.

"Is that . . . Is that all her stuff?" Scarlett asks.

This is the wrong thing to say too. Even more so. They haven't talked about Grandma Maggie since the funeral. *You're just talking about her things, though. It's fine. Easy.*

Cinnamon rounds on her. "Most of it. Someone's got to go through it. You could do that, if you want to actually be useful."

Scarlett blinks. "Now?"

"No, not *now.* Just at some point."

" . . . Okay. If you want."

"I don't know what you expected coming back," Cinnamon says. "It hasn't exactly been sunshine and roses around here since you left."

"I know that," Scarlett replies, trying to keep her voice even. She doesn't like the anger rising in her. It's the Cinnamon kind—hot and congealing in her chest. She wants to massage her temples or find the Tylenol in her bag—there is a ghost of headache, she's sure of it—but feels that's probably rude.

"*Do* you?" Cinnamon throws at her like a punch. "Do you know?"

A wave crashes down on the beach, so hard that Scarlett almost jumps. She hates this: the explosive part of living near the ocean, of being in her family.

"Yes," she says quietly. It sounds like a question.

"You don't know anything," Cinnamon spits and stalks out.

3.

Cinnamon and Scarlett's mother always says that everything looks better in the morning, but really, Cinnamon thinks as she makes toast the next day, that has to be the biggest scam. She's still just as furious.

More so, if anything.

She moves through the house quietly, so as not to risk waking Scarlett, who is an even lighter night-sleeper than Ian. She showers downstairs and throws on clothes straight out of the dryer. She checks once on Ian. She doesn't check on Scarlett.

Part of the fermenting fury in Cinnamon's chest is that things were going fine. Not great, sure—but fine. Watching Scarlett take everything in yesterday made everything look worse.

Cinnamon turns her thoughts to the person she cares most about in the world besides her dad: Will Taylor.

Blue-eyed, clever, *Star Wars* tragic, best friend. Will goes to the local uni. It wasn't his plan, originally. They were supposed to go to the city together, with their other best friend, Phe. But Cinnamon stayed, and Will stayed with her. He invited her to morning coffee today, sensing from her increasingly livid texts last night that it would probably be safest if they met outdoors.

Will lives in a redbrick house down the road, opposite the beach. He's waiting for her on the front steps, squinting under morning sun that's almost as bright as his hair. "Well, hey." He falls into step beside her. "You look very angry with a capital V."

"Coffee," Cinnamon grunts.

The two of them walk toward town covered in summer heat that's sticky like tape. Cinnamon used to avoid hanging out in town where older locals would whisper about the oddness of her family in the shops or the street. The Mad Princes, they used to call them. It's been different since her grandparents died and it's just been her and Ian, though. Not like the gossips are sorry, exactly, but at least they're more subdued.

"I'm only saying," Will says when they're about halfway to the café, "a king being buried under a parking lot *fairly recently* should make us a bit more discerning in how we treat landmark locations."

"*Mmm*," Cinnamon agrees, not really listening. She's mostly thinking about coffee.

Will doesn't notice. "I was watching this documentary about how the woman who excavated Richard the Third was, like, a trainee! And she thought she was totally going to mess it up and lose her job or whatever because she dinged a bit of his skull before she knew what it was, as in properly put a literal hole in his head, but it was fine and they . . ."

Cinnamon closes her eyes and tips her face up, feeling the sunlight defrost her cold dead heart. She loves this about Will. The way he fills silences before you even notice you're in one, warm and quick as a hug. She just doesn't always know how to match it. Sometimes Cinnamon thinks and feels in pictures. She joked to him once that his mind is like a book with a movie tie-in, and hers is like a version of Pac-Man. She stands by that, but still can't say for sure whether her thoughts are Pac-Man or the void.

"Wait, did you say she put a hole in his head?" she asks now.

"*Right?*" Will smiles because he has her now. He always gets her, eventually.

They get to the spot where Main Street splits off from the path by the sea and walk wordlessly toward the café. They always go to the minimalist one on the corner because the owners are from Italy and therefore not here, and so therefore don't know Cinnamon's entire family history— plus, there's a ten-dollar lemon pancake special they can split.

When they sit down, last night hits Cinnamon again like a kick to the shin. She went to bed early to try to avoid this feeling, but it was still there all morning at home. *Is* still there now. She sighs.

"So," Will prompts. He's doing the thing where he waits for her to be ready to talk about all the things, which would be annoying if she didn't rely on it so damn much.

Cinnamon screws up her face, trying to find the right piece of the home-situation garbage-inferno crap festival to describe to him first so he doesn't try to get her to be nice.

"Oh wow," he says, reading her expression. "I was expecting the anger, but this is—"

"Justified, given my recent change in circumstances?" Cinnamon scrunches the menu between her fingers.

"I was gonna say homicidal, but yeah. Sure." Will's eyes crinkle, his buttery blond hair curling over his forehead.

Will goes over to order for them, grinning at Frank, the owner, about something Cinnamon can't hear. He always gets an iced latte with almond milk, and a long black for her. They're quiet for a while when he sits back down. Cinnamon feels almost soothed, looking at the familiar lines of him.

Almost.

Will's phone vibrates with a text, but he doesn't pick it up.

"Is she still saved as 'Hannah from uni'?" Cinnamon teases to change the subject, referring to the latest of Will's attempts at a rolled-r *romance*. Talking about the girls Will dates usually makes her feel a weird combination of proud-jealous. Before Hannah there was Ella, who called Cinnamon *a piece of work*. Also Zoë, who was desperate to be Cinnamon's friend and then left with no warning. Before *that* there was Felicity, who was so much of an angel it gave Cinnamon a stomachache. Cinnamon still follows her on Instagram. Every single story.

"Shut up," Will says. "She's Hannah F., if you must know."

"There was *another* Hannah? Why didn't I know this?"

Will shrugs suggestively. "Maybe I have mystery. Maybe I'm secretly a gigolo."

"*Are* there gigolos who study history, do we think?"

"Totally. We go off."

"Ew."

Their coffees arrive with neat matte-black saucers.

"Wait!" she exclaims when they're alone again. "Hot Cousin Hannah! *That's* the other one. You sneaky little snake."

Will wrinkles his nose. "Who calls her that?"

"Um, everyone, because she is hot. Her brother is too, actually. Almost as hot as yours. Do you not see it?"

"Ollie's not that hot, is he?"

"For a guy? Yes. That's why he only dates other hot guys. As stated—hotter than Hot Cousin Hannah's brother."

Will sips his drink and looks put out, frowning under the halogen light swinging from the ceiling. "Right, well. Excuse me if the whole shared-genes thing impedes my judgment."

Cinnamon snorts. "I can't help that you could fry eggs on several of your relatives. It's just facts."

"*Speaking of*," Will says. "How goes it on the home front?"

"Ugh. Don't say 'how goes it.'" Cinnamon spends a long time giving her drink a stir it doesn't need before answering.

Will waits.

"I just," she starts, tucking her hair behind her ears, "hate her?"

Will is unmoved. *Hate* is a word she throws around often. Too often, probably. "I'm sure it isn't that bad."

Cinnamon sips her coffee. "I think we were inside for like three seconds before we were screaming at each other."

"Scarlett screamed?" Will asks with interest.

"Fine. Before *I* was screaming at *her*. Like the banshee bitch I am."

"You're not a banshee."

"I am a bitch, though." Cinnamon sighs faux-heavily. "I'm just so *good* at it."

Will shakes his head. "You probably should try and give her a shot. It's gotta be weird. Graduating, coming home to . . . You know. All of the everything."

Will knows most of Situation Dad. He's sage and supportive, and also (sometimes) quietly disapproving of how much Cinnamon's taken it on as her own personal crusade. Also sometimes he just doesn't *get it*. His parents are both academic types. So steady and similar they could be related.

"*Mmph*," she grumbles. "Maybe. If we don't kill each other first. I don't know how I'm going to survive the entire summer with her."

Will twists his mouth sympathetically. "What can I do?"

Their pancakes arrive. Cinnamon cuts off a giant bite—butter and lemon and sugar dissolving on her tongue—chews, and pretends to consider. "I need . . . for you to show me all the soppy sadboi stuff you've been sending to Hannah."

"No can do, because there is no soppy stuff."

"Look at your face! There so is."

"There is *not*."

"Come on. Show me! I need it."

"No. I'm keeping my dignity. I don't care how great your need is."

"It's totally *Star Wars* themed, right?"

"No comment."

"Oh, come on. Now you have to show me." She plucks the phone out of his hand and starts scrolling through his thread with Hannah F.

"Cin—Give it back! It's *private*!"

"I see a gif of Princess Leia. And . . . a lot of Xs and Os. Like a lot. God, we need to rein in that runaway horse, babe. Stat."

"Piss off."

"I just want you to be happy! You . . . scruffy-looking, Nerf-herding—oh my god."

"Piss *off*!" he says again, snatching the phone back.

Cinnamon swears back at him, extremely grateful for a minute that if Scarlett has to be at home, at least she has Will out here.

Scarlett knows she's objectively boring.

She also knows she probably comes across as fairly annoying, with the books and the quirks and the clothes and whatnot. Cool people don't say whatnot. She's thinking about these things—among many others—as she wakes up at Halcyon House, so late that it takes her a minute to remember wherewhywho she is.

She stares up at the yellowed ceiling above her childhood bed for a long time, listening to the house wheeze. Light moves across the cracked plaster. The sound of the sea swells even with the windows closed.

Her mind floats to her end-of-school results like it's been doing often since graduation, all her maybe-futures flowing through her limbs in a hot nervous flare. She knows she probably has the marks she needs for what she *thinks* she wants to do. It's a waiting room cliff's edge, being here.

Everything in her life may feel different, but this room is oppressively the same. Scarlett feels like an interloper sitting among the debris of someone else's life. Their floral sheets, their old perfume bottles and participation trophies, their tacky Polaroids all over the walls.

She huffs and swings her legs out of bed with one hand on her chest as her lungs squeeze. *Nope. Don't go there.* Her bag is still open on the floor from when she ravaged it after a freezing shower last night. She pries free three things:

- a forest-green shift dress with a wide collar;
- a matching scrunchie, to pile up the carrot mess that is her hair;
- mustard knee socks in case of a chill (it's cloudyish outside, but here that can mean anything).

Before Scarlett left town, she used to agonize over what she looked like, what she wore. This place has a strict dress code, dictated like everything else by the beach. Linen, surf brands, bikinis, and denim. Not that it matters much what you wear if you are a Prince, since people whisper anyway, but following codes always makes Scarlett *feel* better.

Cinnamon doesn't care about codes. Scarlett loves them. She'd stuck religiously to denim shorts and linen, but when she turned fifteen, her hips and chest burgeoned—just *everywhere*—and it also became apparent the closest she'd get to a tan was freckles and bronzer.

At boarding school, her textiles teacher was all about slow fashion and vintage. She had this thing that *clothes should love your body*. Scarlett figured somebody had to, so she switched her clothes to a style that actually fit. Fit her. She likes expressing herself without having to talk to anyone.

Once dressed, she makes her way downstairs in search of coffee. At her mum's apartment in the city, there's a French press and an espresso machine. Instant too, in case of weird visitors who prefer it. They were supposed to live together after The Divorce but Scarlett said it was fine, that she preferred boarding. Scarlett says a lot of things are fine.

Amy Banks-Prince was twenty-two when she got pregnant with Cinnamon. *Twenty-too-young*, she used to joke. When Scarlett said this was potentially a bit mean, Cinnamon had snapped, *Women don't owe the world motherhood.*

Scarlett should call her. Amy. *Mum.* She should remember to call her that—people always think it's weird when she doesn't. Scarlett unlocks her phone. Her thumb hovers over the Contacts app as she breathes in and out. She hits Instagram instead and navigates to AimesAimes78.

Mum gardening. Mum strumming an acoustic guitar. Mum under pulsing blue lights with sharp black wings on both eyes. Mum with her arm around a man, laughing—that image was uploaded eleven hours ago. Scarlett knows it isn't normal to keep tabs on your mother this way, but it is easy. Enough. Not enough. More, probably, than what she'd get from a phone call.

Her head twinges. Probably caffeine withdrawal. *Coffee.* Fancy machine here. But no beans. Her dad's door is firmly closed, so she leaves it that way and steps outside. She makes her way down to the front gate, looking out at overcast Princes Beach. There are thick lilac clouds on the horizon, but the sun's still peeking through, and the water is flat and welcoming.

Scarlett misses the city. She loved its burnt-coffee smell, the way it looked different in crisp winter light or when it held heat in its palm for days. But the sea—*this* sea, the tiny bay that holds her whole childhood—is in her blood. *Like memory. Like history*, she thinks to herself as she looks at the beach.

Her feet follow the familiar sloping path. Past the lillypillies and the goat's foot and the banksias that don't always bloom anymore.

Along the weathered fence. Down the steep staircase toward the sand.

At the bottom of the stairs, she pulls off her shoes and socks, feeling the powdery sand between her toes, then starts walking north toward town.

A cargo ship is plodding slowly along the horizon. Scarlett remembers watching ships pass with Cinnamon years ago. They'd pretend each one was the *Titanic*, when their lives hadn't happened yet, because none of it had. All that possibility. Thinking about Cinnamon pinches her chest: *You don't know anything.* She stares hard at the sea until her chest starts to loosen again.

There's a coffee shop on Main Street somewhere, she thinks when the shop fronts come into view over the sand dunes fifteen minutes later—she does know that much. She puts her shoes and socks back on, wincing at the sand still stuck to her heels. It's been a while since she's been in town. Worry flashes through her, the Prince kind, like she should put on sunglasses or something, even as she reasons with herself that people probably won't recognize her or care if they do. She puts them on anyway, just in case.

"Scarlett Prince!" says the man at the coffee shop when she asks for a cappuccino. He has brown hair pulled into a bun and a wide, open face.

So much for the sunglasses. Scarlett pulls them off. "Um. Yes?"

"I know your mum," he says in a thick accent, handing over her change. "You look just like her, apart from the hair. Don't you think?"

"Sometime—"

"And of course I know your sister," the man continues, raising his voice. "But only because she's here almost every day. Even though caffeine STUNTS YOUR GROWTH."

"Shut your face, Frank!" a voice calls. "You're a *café owner*. It hurts us all to hear you blaspheme." Cinnamon's face pops up from a table by the window. "What the hell are you doing here?" she demands before Scarlett can make herself disappear.

Frank's eyes widen. He moves over to the coffee machine and does something that releases a spectacular grinding sound, which buys Scarlett some time.

"Coffee," is what comes out of her mouth, strangled, when the grinding finally stops. "Sorry. I'll go."

"Cin, what are you . . . Scarlett! Oh my god, hey." Will Taylor appears next to Cinnamon, struggling upright like she's trying to pull him down.

Something explodes in Scarlett's chest. Ink, she imagines, while she's trying to breathe through where it's bubbling up her throat. That's what looking at him feels like: watery ink blooming out from under her ribs and spilling its way through everything.

Will is visually contradictory: His hair is fair, but his eyebrows are ashy. There's corded muscle in his arms, but his collarbones jut out. One of his eyes is dark blue, the other ocean blue green. Altogether, the effect is sort of fragile, like if she glances away and then back again it'll be a completely different view.

When she was young, Scarlett thought he looked like a textbook nerd. Now she's looking at his morning-wet hair and:

- accidentally imagining him with no shirt on;
- trying to remember how to hold an expression on her face that makes her look human;
- wondering how, for the literal years she's known him, she's never noticed how good-looking he is;
- Will Taylor is looking at her too.

23

5.

When Cinnamon and Will first broke up, he bit his lip and said he was *sorry, so sorry*. She just said *no*.

It was the very end of high school, both of them sitting under the curved hand of a fig tree. She'd known for a while: they'd fallen out of it with each other, whatever they'd had, the same slipping and unfathomable way they'd fallen in.

He cried and she didn't. They hugged. She remembers how the light looked on his face when they pulled away, though: lovely.

That was the end of them, and also the beginning. Tonight Will is blotchy-faced and in her bedroom. After dinner he'd texted:

SOS

And she'd replied:

door unlocked come up

"Two times in one day. What's up?" Cinnamon asks. If it sounds like a joke, he's more likely to answer.

He's quiet, and he rubs his sweater sleeve over his eye. Once to actually dry it. Two more times for luck.

Will fiddles with her bedspread for an immeasurable length of time, colored squares pinched in his long fingers. Her stomach twists like origami as she watches him, because maybe you never totally fall out of it with anyone.

"Hannah broke up with me."

"Oh," Cinnamon says. "Shit."

"Via text. An hour ago. I'm kind of . . . I don't know." His bottom lip twitches. "She said she doesn't want to talk."

All the good feelings Cinnamon ever had about Hannah evaporate in a mist. "Jesus god. She didn't *seem* like the devil incarnate."

Will makes a *ha* sort of expression, but it's sad. "She's not. She's great. It was my complete lack of charm and/or restraint that did it, as per usual."

"Don't." She frowns. "You're adorable."

Will rubs at his hair agitatedly. "Yeah, cheers. That's the problem. I'm too available, or something. No *spark*. She wants *spark* in this phase of her life."

"Ew. Who talks like that?" Cinnamon's mother made her take a vow when she was younger to never call another woman what she phrased as *rhymes-with-witch*. Sometimes that vow is very hard to honor.

Will just shrugs. "She's right, though—that's what sucks about it. I can't even be like, *Yeah, because I was really really into you* without totally proving the point."

"Hmm."

"All I want to do is, like, rock up to her work with a boom box or something. Or write her a letter."

"I think not."

"No, I *know*. But I want to. Still, you know?"

Cinnamon nods sympathetically. She does know. One of the

things that used to annoy her when they were together was how easily Will cried. She distrusted it, envied it, accused him of trying to manipulate her with it. Eventually she realized that the tears weren't the point, not at all—Will is quick to feel.

"Don't pity me," he orders her now, but his eyes are shiny and his face is redder than it was when they first sat down. "I'm not there yet."

"Oh, I could never pity you." Cinnamon squeezes his fingers, feels the familiar hard line of boy knuckles. "You're a straight white man. I'm humoring you, but my fucks given are actually zero."

He laughs at that. Only once, but it's there, and she feels a burst of crushing gladness for making him do it. His laugh makes him sound younger, the way he did when they were in school. She imagines his heart for a second, like she used to do sometimes back then. All permeable cotton-candy pink.

Will rubs his eyes again. "I genuinely feel like pure shit. I forgot how bad this is."

"It's okay to be sad," Cinnamon says carefully. "Like—it's good that you are. It means it was real."

Will spends a while nodding and blinking. Then he takes a giant breath like he's just woken up and lets go of her hand. "God, I'm sorry to dump all this on you. I know you have more important stuff going on right now."

"No, I don't," she reprimands dismissively. "You're my BFF. My number-one problematic fave."

"Am I?" he asks, like he's surprised or doesn't believe her. "Even if I'm clinically unlovable?"

Cinnamon stares at him, lining up their faces until his different-blue eyes hold on to hers just like he's holding her hand. "You know she's mistaken, right? *Sorely.* And probably at home right now, cry-wanking and thinking about how she just chucked out the best gift of her life."

Will rolls his eyes. "Thanks."

"And also, I love you," she adds with a shrug. "So you're just wrong on all counts, really. As per usual."

He smiles. "As per usj."

Cinnamon drums her thighs and stands up. "What are we thinking? Hot chocolate? Movie? Go up to the bay headland and silently sit on your Sadness Cliff?"

"Tough call." Will sighs as she hauls him to his feet. "Is all of the above an option?"

"Nope." She leads him downstairs. Rain is threatening outside, low rumbles sounding from across the horizon. They look out the staircase sash window for a minute at the heaving black sea. The house is mostly dark, so Cinnamon flicks lights on as she goes.

Her dad is in the kitchen. His back makes an arched C as he bends over the coffee machine. His hair is too long, she realizes suddenly. It trails down his back, coiled and grayish red. She also realizes from his hard jabbing at the grinder button that this is a Bad Day.

"Mr. Prince!" Will wipes his shocked-wide eyes. "Hello."

Ian blinks for a beat at Will's enthusiasm, then turns to Cinnamon. "The machine's broken," he says flatly.

Will's eyes widen further at the lack of acknowledgment.

Cinnamon doesn't want the falling feeling moving from her throat through her ribs. "No," she says slowly. "It's new, remember? Fancier. But we're out of beans. I'll make you a tea."

"How was your day?" she asks with her back to both of them.

"Fine," says Ian in his same flat tone.

She doesn't want to feel angry with him, but it rises sticky in her throat. "Did you see Scarface yet?" she tries, pouring milk into the tea.

Ian's eyes grow lighter for a second. "Tell her I'll see her in the morning, okay? I'm gonna go to bed." He takes the mug out of Cinnamon's hands, pats her on the shoulder, and retreats upstairs.

Will waits until the bedroom door clicks shut before turning to her.

"Don't," Cinnamon warns. She doesn't want to have this sense she always has now, of standing on a rock alone while waves crash hard around her.

"How long's he been that bad?" Will asks.

"He's not. . . . He's just tired. There's been a lot going on over the last year, with everything after the . . . you know. Maggie. That's all."

Will leans against the counter and folds his arms. "*Cin*. Come on. You said he was getting better."

She grits her teeth. "He is. I'm handling it."

"You shouldn't have to handle it. Can't your moth—"

"I am not calling her." Cinnamon enunciates each word metal hard. "Okay? It's fine. We're fine."

Will frowns at her, but he doesn't push it. He just pulls mugs down from the cupboard and scoops chocolate powder out of the jar while Cinnamon boils the water again.

Scarlett comes home a few minutes later, easing the front door open so carefully that she almost doesn't make a sound. It's only outside that gives her away—the storm is finally hissing into being, wind running rough hands through the tree branches and rain landing in fat drops on the roof. Scarlett's soaked cardigan hits the floor with a wet slap when she pulls it off.

"Oi," Cinnamon says. "Make sure you mop that up later."

"Obviously I will." Scarlett's voice is soft. "Since when do you care about cleaning?"

"Uh, since there's only me to do it," Cinnamon retorts, setting her mug down on the counter with a muted thud.

Even though she knows it's stupid, for a minute Cinnamon waits for Ian to hear the noise and come running back down. "And shut the door," she snaps at her sister when he doesn't. "It's gonna storm."

6.

Scarlett spent the day walking all around the sea-edge of town. Between Ian not touring anymore and her having been gone so long, and Cinnamon generally not caring what anyone says, she felt weirdly okay doing it. Exposed, but okay. Like there's a piece of this place buried in her that stops hurting only when she's here, even if being here hurts.

She sat on a bench and read for a while too—*Sad Girls*, by Lang Leav, her last purchase from the bookstore near school that she's been carrying around in her bag. Now she's home and it's raining and Will Taylor is here, eating marshmallows in the dark-wood Halcyon kitchen.

"You can have one if you want," Cinnamon says as she sips her hot chocolate. "But I'm not making it."

Will frowns at her, and Cinnamon pulls a face at him like, *What?*

Scarlett is shivering. Her wet clothes are stuck to her like a green second skin. She starts gathering the ingredients for hot chocolate uncertainly, thinking she'll just take one back to her room.

Then Will says, "Hey, maybe Scarlett has some insight into my predicament."

Scarlett's stomach flips. When she looks up, Will's gaze is blue-blue-blue.

"I wouldn't exactly call it a predicament," Cinnamon says, her voice relaxing again now that she's talking to Will.

"What *would* you call it, then? I'm, like, the opposite of a serial monogamist. I am a serial three-dates-and-then-dumped."

Scarlett pulls the milk carton out of the fridge. She isn't cold anymore. Her cheeks feel hot-hot-hot.

"Because you like girls who aren't interested in you," Cinnamon declares. "That's, like, your thing."

"Untrue," Will cries indignantly, with a mouthful of marshmallows. He looks at Scarlett. "That's not true."

"It is a universally acknowledged truth," Cinnamon corrects him. "It's the eighth wonder of the world."

"Okay," Will cuts her off, laughing. "Thanks for that." He waves at Scarlett like he did in the café, soft and awkward. "Hi, by the way. Good to see you again. I promise I'm less of a hot mess than it sounds."

"Lies!" Cinnamon booms. "Burn the liar!"

Scarlett cradles her mug and chews her lip. Words are suddenly not a thing she knows. Thunder cracks over their heads so hard the windows rattle. She opens her mouth, then closes it again.

Will is still looking at her. Waiting.

"Um. Hi. So I'd better . . . ," she says. Then she walks very quickly toward her room.

Once inside she shuts the door and leans back against it, squeezing her eyes closed and sliding down until both she and a splash of her hot chocolate hit the floor. "Oh my *god*," she whispers into the dark while the rain picks up outside.

This is how it generally goes with boys. Generally it goes even worse.

Scarlett breathes and looks down at her right hand until her drink goes cold, studying every pore and freckle and reminding herself that

she exists she exists she exists she exists she exists she exists she exists she exists she exists she exists
she exists she exists she exists she exists she exists she exists she exists she exists she exists she exists
she exists she exists she exists she exists she exists she exists she exists she exists she exists she exists
she exists she exists she exists she exists she exists she exists she   exists she exists she exists
she exists she exists she exists   she exists she exists she   exists she exists she exists
she exists she exists she exists   she exists she exists she   exists she exists she exists
she exists she exists she exists   she exists she exists   she exists she exists she
exists she exists   she exists she   exists she exists she   exists she   exists
she   exists   she exists she   exists she exists she   exists she   e x i s t s
she   exists   she exists she exists she exists she exists   s h e   exists
she   exists   she exists she exists she exists she   e x i s t s   s h e
exists she   exists she exists she exists she exists   she   exists   s h e
exists she   exists she exists she exists she exists   she exists she exists she
e x i s t s   she exists she exists she exists she exists she exists she exists she exists she
e x i s t s   she exists she exists she exists she exists she exists she exists she exists she
e x i s t s   she exists she exists she exists she exists she exists she exists she exists she
exists she   she exists she exists she exists she exists she exists she exists she exists
she exists she   exists she exists she exists   she exists she exists she exists she exists she exists
she exists she exists she exists she exists she   exists she exists she exists   she exists she exists
she exists she exists she exists she exists   she exists she exists   she exists she exists
she exists she exists she exists she exists   she exists she exists   she exists she exists
she exists she exists she exists she exists   she exists she exists she   exists she exists she
she exists she exists she exists she exists she exists she exists she exists she exists she exists she exists she
she exists she exists she exists she exists she exists she exists she exists she exists she exists she exists she
she exists she exists she exists she exists she exists she exists she exists she exists she exists she   exists she
exists she exists she   exists she exists she exists she exists she exists she exists   s h e
exists she exists she   exists she exists she exists   she exists she exists she   e x i s t s
she exists she exists   she exists she exists she   exists she exists she   e x i s t s
she exists she exists   she exists she exists   she exists she exists she   exists she
exists   she exists she exists she exists she exists she   exists she exists she exists she exists
she exists   she exists she exists she exists she   exists she exists she exists she exists
she exists   she exists she exists she exists   she exists she exists she exists she
e x i s t s   she exists she exists she exists   she exists she   exists she exists
s h e   exists she exists she exists   she   exists   she exists she
e x i s t s   she exists she exists she exists she exists she exists   she exists she
e x i s t s   she exists she exists she exists she exists she exists   she exists she
e x i s t s   she exists she exists she exists she exists she exists   she   exists
s h e   exists she exists she exists she exists she exists she   exists   she
exists she exists she exists she exists she exists she exists she exists she   exists   she
exists she exists she exists   she exists she exists she exists she exists   she   exists
she exists she exists she   exists she exists she exists she exists   she   exists
she   exists she   exists   she exists she exists she exists she   exists she
exists   she   e x i s t s   she exists she exists she exists she exists   she exists she
exists she   exists   she exists she exists she exists she exists she exists she exists she
exists she   e x i s t s   she exists she exists she   exists she exists she exists she exists
s h e   exists she exists she exists she exists   she exists she exists she   e x i s t s
s h e   exists she exists she exists she   exists she exists she   exists
s h e   exists she exists she exists she   exists she exists   s h e
exists   she exists she exists she exists   she   exists   she   exists
s h e   exists she exists she exists   she   exists   she   exists
exists   she exists she exists she she   she exists she exists   s h e
exists   she exists she exists she exists   exists she exists she exists she
e x i s t s   she exists she exists she exists she   exists she exists she exists she exists
she exists she exists she exists she exists she exists she exists she exists she exists she exists she exists
she exists she exists she exists she exists she exists she exists she exists she exists she exists she exists
she exists she exists she exists she exists she exists she exists she exists she exists she exists she exists
she exists she exists she exists she exists she exists she exists she exists she exists she exists she exists

Cinnamon's laughter floats in from the front TV room, along with protests from Will and more laughter. Sometimes Scarlett goes weeks without laughing, even when something's truly funny.

She reaches for her phone to text Niamh, but what would she say? Niamh doesn't know about the Scarlett who lived here. Scarlett clicks her phone asleep and then awake again, hovering her thumb over the Instagram icon. She finds Will's profile just as the storm properly starts.

Sheets of gray rain slap at the windows, building momentum: *Let me in*, bash-bash-bash. *I'm coming. I'm here.*

Scarlett stays huddled on the floor, trying to fill her brain with the hundred or so posts on @wheretheresawill2187.

Things she learns:

- Will works at the library.
- Will likes history memes.
- Will doesn't post photos of himself.
- Will doesn't delete photos of girls he's dated.
- She likes the way he sees the world too much to let herself follow him.

The world outside becomes a darkened moan. Scarlett's chest starts to feel like knotted fabric—every sound too close, too loud, too much. The windows shake harder, and she holds on to her knees. Living on a cliff like this is pretty only in theory, she thinks, because she can *hear* it now—how easy it would be to just fall.

After a while, she lies down on the rug and closes her eyes. Breathes in and out.

Breathes. Breathes. Breathes.

Trees scream and scratch at the roof. *Howl*, she thinks, is the word. The world is a howl. Then it's over—the drumming rain dies like a light switched off.

Scarlett opens her eyes. Looks for a minute at the quiet drip of water on the window.

The world is calm again, and then so is she, and after a while she carefully sits up.

There's a sound from outside. An almighty crash, like everything is splitting apart. Like the house has let go of the cliff after all, and they're about to be swallowed by the sea.

She jumps up, and her legs carry her to the kitchen. One hand flies up to her chest. "Hello?" Scarlett says.

"Stop screeching," her sister's voice snaps. Cinnamon wanders in, wearing dark pajamas.

Scarlett's throat is thick. There's a searing comfort in the sight of Cinnamon's bare face. Embarrassingly, her eyes fill with tears. "N-nothing. I was just . . ."

"It's only a storm," Cinnamon says, in the slightly singsong voice she used to use when Scarlett panicked as a child, and no one understood. It feels patronizing now in a way it didn't then.

"It was awful," Scarlett insists.

"It's summer. It happens."

"I thought I heard something crash, though," Scarlett presses. "Outside."

Cinnamon moves through the unlit room. Scarlett watches the blurred outline of her as she peers out at the gloaming through the big arched window above the sink.

"There's nothing out there. It was probably thunder," Cinnamon surmises. There are smudges of black under her eyes that makes them look ghoulish in the dark.

"Are you sure? It sounded like something fell."

"Well, you can go out there and check if you want," Cinnamon says with a couldn't-care-less hand gesture. "I'm going back to my room."

Scarlett flicks a cautionary glance at the backyard. The light is weird—too bright for nighttime. She can see all of it: the patio stained black and the grass too violent a green. She hesitates for a minute. Then she pads across the floorboards to the back door and eases it open. Her legs are still jellyish, but she manages to get down the wet steps and across the grass.

Dripping plants poke her bare legs as she makes her way deeper into the garden. It's as overgrown and untamable as ever, roots exposed and flowerless bushes looming over the . . . graveyard.

Scarlett chews her lip and turns toward Halcyon. She wonders, for the thousandth time, what the house thinks about being a home for both the living and the dead.

When she looks back at the garden graveyard, she notices something off: a tree, toppled over by the far fence. She holds her chest again, thumb on her collarbone, and moves closer. The roots are ripped at an unnatural angle—pulled up in a mess of dirt and bark. She touches the trunk. Follows the lines of it speared into the earth like the hand of God herself.

Underneath it is a stone slab cracked clean in half. Scarlett screams, "CINNAMON!"

It takes a minute, but a bobbed head pops out of her sister's bedroom window.

"WHAT?"

"COME HERE!"

"WHY?"

"JUST COME!"

When Cinnamon appears silhouetted in Halcyon's back door—a frown and the bright of her hair—Scarlett points with a shaky index finger at the collapsed hollow underneath the grave that reads *SADIE GRACE PRINCE.*

The sea slaps against the foot of the cliff below. Like it's saying *See? See?*

"Sadie's grave. It's empty. There's nothing in there."

7.

The Mad Princes started with Sadie.

Allegedly.

When the Prince girls were six and seven-and-three-quarters respectively, a girl at school told them Sadie was a murderer, and so Amy sat them down and told them the story. Scarlett remembers it, or remembers remembering it. The earthy smell of rain through an open window, her hair wet from a bath and Cinnamon's fingers pulling at the knotty ends of it until she yelped. Amy waiting for them to be quiet, both of them tiny and transfixed.

"Your great-aunt Sadie was a legend," was all Grandma Maggie would say whenever they asked *her*. Her blue eyes would go distant in a way they sometimes did, because Maggie saw the best in everything, which meant she saw stories everywhere. "And sometimes that's the worst thing a person can be."

Amy told them that Sadie Prince was born after the Second World War. She was the apple of her father's and brother's eye. Great-Aunt Sadie was a different sort of child, as children in legends often are. Smart. Sensitive. She played outside less than other children, her nerves were many and fragile, and seaside life was hard on her. (This is the part Scarlett found most difficult to hear, because she *knew* it.)

The townsfolk didn't understand Sadie, Amy said solemnly. Quick to cry and quick to scream, and uncommonly good at playing piano. So they speculated as to what might be "wrong" with her. She was of a contrarian disposition not befitting a serious musician, and her skills were far too great for one so very moody.

Sometimes Sadie needed the dark. Plagued by episodes of sadness or headaches or visions or voices that took hold of her for days or weeks and left her too ill to leave her bed.

Grandpa Charlie, her brother, spoke to Cinnamon and Scarlett about Sadie only once, and said that in her youth she played piano, and it was a joy to hear her. A joy.

One day Sadie vanished.

The locals developed their own version of events, as locals do. She'd been seen the day before, up on the cliff and arguing with her father and a boy—Robert Hammond. She was nineteen and long-limbed and shouting in a way that did not become a well-raised girl.

Sadie Prince played piano, "suffered from moods," and was interested in politics and books and the concept of death.

Sadie Prince had gray eyes and mahogany hair and a face like a secret.

Sadie Prince killed Robert Hammond up on Princes Cliff, and then she disappeared.

"Except that she didn't," Maggie said when she walked into the room at the end of the story, surprisingly firmly.

"Then why do people say that?" the Prince girls cried.

Maggie smiled her secret smile that was full of stories while the wind blew gusts of her rosy perfume through the almost-dark room. "Nobody knows."

After the first time hearing the legend from Amy, Scarlett and Cinnamon were both a little bit in love with Sadie.

There's a portrait of her painted by her brother hanging in the drawing room at Halcyon, surrounded by hard-backed chairs and gold-fringed curtains and wallpaper that smells like the past. She's on the wall opposite the window, forever looking out to sea, her thoughts a mystery. Like a shrine. Or a warning.

Scarlett and Cinnamon used to sneak in at night to look at her. Though technically off-limits to sticky-handed children when Maggie was living in the house, the drawing room held a kind of dark fascination for Scarlett, in the way things she was afraid of almost always did.

She'd drag Cinnamon down the hall while the adults sat at the table talking after dinner, the two of them slipping through the heavy polished-wood door and giggling. It always smelled like Grandpa Charlie in there, even after he died when Scarlett was twelve— tobacco pipe smoke and garlic and cut grass. As if this room held the last bits of him.

In his painting, Sadie is in her late teens. She wears a white blouse tucked into polka-dot cigarette pants, her hair cut to her shoulders and her pale eyes staring dead at the viewer. It's this expression, calm and frank and staring out of the frame, that always fascinated Scarlett.

When they asked Grandpa Charlie whether Sadie died the day on the cliff with Robert Hammond, his eyes grew very soft and he said, "In a sense," and then nothing else, no matter how much Scarlett or Cinnamon begged to know.

All they had to go on was the grim legend in town and the spark of a different story, lit on the night with the baths and the rain. And so the Prince girls dreamed up other lives for Sadie in the drawing room. They'd sit side by side, night by night on the carpet with their crossed legs touching at the knee and whisper while the sea listened outside, and Sadie watched from her wall. Childish things at first.

"She left town on a horse and married a pirate," Scarlett said breathlessly when she was nine. "A handsome Captain Hook."

"She jumped off the cliff and swam to one of the islands," Cinnamon countered when she was eleven. "And now she's their queen."

As they got older, which took ages and no time at all, their visits to the drawing room grew less frequent and more serious. And Sadie gradually became present tense—living the sparkling outside lives they worried they never would.

"She's a doctor who lives in an apartment that's really high up and has a view of the ocean, with a dog and three kids, and all her patients love her."

"She's an artist who travels the world and never settles down."

"She was the first woman valedictorian at her university, and she still lectures there."

"She's a celebrated poet in Tasmania."

"She's famous under a different name."

"She's got floor-to-ceiling bookshelves filled with books, and she's read them all."

"She drinks black coffee and drives a giant Jeep."

"In the new town she moved to, they still talk about how beautiful she was when she was young."

"She's so nice that she tells everyone she's forgiven the town she left."

"She's been in love five times."

"She's been married five times but didn't love any of them."

Cinnamon lost interest in Sadie first. Scarlett remembers how she knocked on Cinnamon's door the first night of summer holidays when she was thirteen and Cinnamon was fifteen, and Cinnamon hollered at her to go away. Cinnamon is a present-tense person and had decided Sadie wasn't anymore. Scarlett cried a lot that night, sitting on the floor staring up at Sadie.

When Scarlett moved away, she thought of Sadie as past tense again. History. Forgot about her completely sometimes when she was buried in schoolwork and routine. But on the rare occasions she was at home after that, she'd still go to the drawing room to look at Sadie's portrait and think, *Do you think—from wherever you are—about where you left us?* Because Scarlett sees stories in everything too. Especially in her family. The Mad Princes started with a story, even if the main character exists now only in ripples that fan out in low waves to wrap around and cover them all. Still.

8.

Cinnamon wakes up late the next morning. She watches Will sprawled asleep on her floor for a while before nudging him with her foot. "Hey, Sleeping Beauty. Get up. I have work."

Will groans and covers his eyes.

Cinnamon steps out of bed and smooths down her sleep-matted hair. She's fairly sure there was a weird moment last night when they almost kissed, a bright look between them that made her go, *Oh*. This happens sometimes. One of them accidentally puts their head on the other's shoulder or holds their hand, and the months of Broken Up collapse inward like wet paper.

That's not normal, is it?

She exhales the thought out and starts rifling through the piles of dirty clothes on the floor, looking for her (also still dirty) work uniform.

"What was that last night?" Will asks, his voice morning-thick.

Cinnamon successfully pries her work pants free from the pile, but no blouse. The empty grave flashes through her mind for a second—the Prince-ness of burying things so well there's nothing there—but thinking about Sadie makes her think of Maggie, which remains unthinkable. "What?"

Will frowns sleepily. "There was, like, screaming."

Cinnamon makes another frustrated sound, both at her lack of blouse and at the memory of last night, standing with Scarlett in wet dark, looking down into emptiness.

Maggie smiling when they asked about Sadie.

"That was just Scarlett being a drama queen."

"About what, though?"

Maggie in that graveyard, dead.

"One of the graves collapsed in the rain," Cinnamon answers impatiently. She needs to get out of this conversation. "Down back near the fence. We *think*, anyway. It was kind of hard to see, but it was . . . hollowish underneath. I dunno, maybe it was always just, like, a memorial thing." Cinnamon's fingers finally snag on white starchy fabric. She triumphantly pulls out the wrinkly work blouse and slings it over one arm. She thinks of telling him the rest about the grave: the nothing underneath and how looking at it felt like being entangled in it, like being lied to, like being buried too.

Will props himself up on his elbows. He took his shirt off to sleep. The graceful-pale twin brackets of his collarbones catch the sunlight. They distract Cinnamon for a second before she shakes that thought away too.

"Seriously?" Will frowns again. "How does a grave collapse?"

"I don't know!" Cinnamon throws up her hands, pushing her thoughts back to the familiar workday stretching out ahead of her and not Will or gravestones or Sadie. "Why don't you ask Scarlett, if you're so fascinated?"

Will covers his eyes again with the bend of his elbow. "Maybe I will."

Cinnamon thinks about it for a second, then decides to get dressed in the bathroom.

A year ago (was it that recently? that long ago?) was their end-of-school dance, and he was standing in her front yard with a smile on his face like an open door, the sea spread out to infinity behind him. "You look wow," he had said.

She wore a white minidress and had straightened her hair. He put flowers around her wrist, and she held it out to inspect them. "Thanks. I hate it."

"Aw. Is this how you're gonna be on our wedding day?"

This is how Will says most things—grinning, quick, unthought—but around Cinnamon it was especially pronounced. As though he didn't need to think first, because she'd never judge him. Which was true. But also a lot of responsibility.

"You look good too," she said. And he did, in his black suit with the cuff links winking in afternoon light that haloed his hair. Will drove her down the winding cliff road while the sun set fire to everything over her shoulder. Pink and orange painting on the sky in giant, gorgeous strokes.

A very slow song she only half liked started playing on the radio, and Cinnamon had a feeling she'd had a handful of times before, of being inside a moment she was going to remember. A weird kind of fluttery, stabbing sorrow. Because it was so *good*. Because she knew there was nothing she could do to make it last. When they got to school, Will opened her door, and his familiar hand wrapped around hers to pull her toward the auditorium.

"Wait," she said. "Can we wait a second?"

He frowned, bringing her hand up to hold it with both of his. "You okay?"

"Yeah, I just . . . Listen . . ."

"What?" Will's eyes flicked down, worried and glittering. His hands moved to cup her waist the way they always did, like she was made of glass even though she was not.

"Nothing," she said, and stood up tall to kiss him as long and hard as she could.

Now she's coming out of the bathroom dressed for work, and Will moves his arm away from his eyes to pull an ironic *What are you staring at?* sort of face and throws a pillow at her. The room smells like his clothes and his breath—coffee and sugar and boy.

"Are you gonna leave for work on time?" he prompts. "You can't get fired. Literally all we do is work and go out for pancakes."

Sometimes she thinks that missing him
is her favorite feeling in the world.

Cinnamon has waitressed at the town's falling-down beachside pub for one entire tumbleweed year. She initially took the job as a temporary thing because Will works holidays at the library down the road.

It felt exciting last year, both of them just turning eighteen. Illicit and adult to work somewhere made of sandstone and beer and ghosts. It was all there was going for someone who wasn't going anywhere.

The pub is owned by Tony Stark, whose real name is Anthony Westbrook, whose father bought him the pub when its last owner died so, Cinnamon suspects, Tone would have a job from which he couldn't be fired. Tone is a self-described Creative Type in his late thirties whose various quote-unquote *visions* for the place (café, late-night bar, brunch spot, sports-screening venue, karaoke den, and once, a nightclub) all somehow crowd together to keep business thriving.

The pub has given Cinnamon a pretty healthy savings account, though she has no idea what she'll use the money for; knowledge of obscure party cocktails that occasionally comes in handy; blisters, definitely; ringworm, probably, from the time she took her shoe off in the bathroom to prod one of said blisters.

Plus hours of focusing on her hands and not having to think.

It's not necessarily advancing the greater direction of her life, but she likes the colorful routine of it all. Days bleeding together. Her regulars make her laugh, Tone is almost never in, sometimes he gives bonuses in cash, and she can run there along the beach.

She likes it best in winter when the place is mostly empty and she can just stand on the balcony upstairs breathing in the weather, not measuring time. The way faces flash in the flames of the old fireplace. It's summer now, though, which means vicious sunshine interspersed with sea storms and summer seasonal workers.

And summer seasonals this year means Daisy Leung.

Daisy started working at the pub a month and a half ago and is generally agreed, even by Cinnamon, to be doing a much better job than Cinnamon. She smiles a lot. Smells nice. Her hands are quick and sure, never spilling things on herself, or customers, or the floor.

Daisy has heavy bangs, and her hair is bleached and then dyed pale pink at the ends. She wears lipstick that never smudges off. She studies art and is working toward a trip at the end of the summer to see some of it up close.

They're friendly but not friends. Cordial but distant. Occupying the same physical space and shifts, but never the same capital-*S* Space.

There's something that's unknowable about Daisy. She's *good* (Cinnamon's never heard her bitch about anyone), in a moral sort of way that's not annoying. She actually likes people. She's warm with customers in a way that's equal parts irritating and, if you shook it out of Cinnamon, low-key kind of fascinating.

That she's so beautiful it almost makes Cinnamon softly sad definitely has no bearing on the matter.

She's watching Daisy now as she gets ready for her shift. Standing behind the bar in her button-up shirt with a camisole underneath. Tapered pants that hug her waist as she pours soda water into glasses from the gun.

Daisy flicks her gaze up. Brown. A singular, strange color that has the audacity to also throw gold. Dark, but somehow transparent in its depth.

Cinnamon quickly looks away, tying her apron too tight around her hips and picking up the scummy dishcloth to do a round of the tables, sidestepping and ignoring Daisy Leung, which she's gotten very, very good at it.

But then.

"Hi." Daisy's voice is another annoying thing. Heart-shaped faces shouldn't produce voices that . . . strong. Disarming.

"Um," Cinnamon says, thinking, *Not today, Satan. I cannot handle Perfect Daisy today.* "Hey." She's rarely intimidated, but she is now. Unforgivably so. The sudden shock of it runs hot down her spine.

"Er. Your apron's on backward."

Daisy gives a tinkly laugh, and Cinnamon isn't sure whether she wants to kill her or die. She quickly yanks her apron off, rearranging it with much difficulty.

"I wasn't gonna say anything," Daisy says ironically with her chin tipped up. "Thought it might be a *look*."

Cinnamon spins around. Banter is not a thing they do. "Ha. Yeah. The apron models in our employment manual could never. I personally do not trust them." In her head it was a good enough joke to regain the high ground, but coming out it just sounds dumb.

Daisy laughs properly, smiling, all neat little teeth. "Whatever you need to tell yourself."

"Yep." Cinnamon nods stiffly and walks out.

This is what's happened the few times they've talked. Push-pull, then Cinnamon storming away in a huff and feeling mixed-up and weird for the rest of the shift.

She's not even *jealous* of Daisy—that would actually be easier to take.

She's thought about it . . . a lot.

Not like *a lot* a lot, but more than she'd ever admit. And what she suspects—maybe—is this: Daisy is one of those people who make you forget who you are and then remember again, but more, all in the same second.

Dangerous.

9.

Scarlett hasn't slept. She tried for a few hours at some point. Then peach dawn flared out on the slice of horizon through her bedroom window, and she gave up and reread *Frankenstein* until it was morning for real.

Scarlett loves the classic novels with a random outsider narrator best. It's why *Wuthering Heights* is her favorite Brontë, narrowly trumping *Jane Eyre*. (Whenever she calls them "the Brontës" aloud, Cinnamon rolls her eyes and says she sounds like a pretentious "I READ, y'all; *I'm a READER*" character in an early 2000s teen drama.)

Scarlett likes the Brontës and their narrators because she likes the idea that someone could watch other people's stories without ever having any real ones of their own and still matter. Kind of. She told Niamh a version of this thought once, and her roommate said, "That's literally the most depressing thing I've ever heard."

It's eight o'clock now. Scarlett bookmarks her page and gets out of bed, throwing on a yellow T-shirt and high-waisted shorts in a red, white, and green check. The shorts are knee-length and possibly some of the weirder ones she owns. She made them herself when shorts came back in, but not the kind that suited legs like hers.

She decides to go for another walk but stops to look in on her dad before leaving. She saw him briefly last night and the one before that, but now he's still asleep. Ian's room at the end of the hallway is muffled dark with the curtains tightly closed. She stands at the door and squints into the darkness, her eyes adjusting and taking mental stock.

His TV flickers mutely on the far wall, black wires bleeding from underneath. Food wrappers form tiny silver constellations dotted across the floor.

Scarlett's skin feels tight. She looks at Ian's face, wondering when she last looked at it properly. He looks exactly like an aging rock star—still. Both his ears are pierced, tattoos bloom on his arms and fingers. His pajamas are black silk. But were the hollows under his eyes there at graduation, and she just didn't see?

Is this going to be okay? How do you know if not?

Do you just . . . wait?

Ian's eyelids flutter open. "Scar?"

Scarlett tucks her hair behind her ears and tries to smile. "Hi, Daddy."

His eyes are gray. Watery now, red-rimmed and tired around the edges. "You okay?"

She wants to tell him: *I miss you. I love you.*

She wants to ask: *Where do you go when you're not really here?*

"Shh," she whispers instead, backing out of the room. "Go back to sleep."

Will Taylor is sitting in the kitchen again when she gets downstairs. He's pale and overly blond, hair falling to one side and into his vivid blue eyes, like an Arthurian legend brought to life.

"Oh! You're still here," Scarlett says. Her heart is a hammer.

"Hey to you too." He grins. He's holding a ceramic mug, also blue. Scarlett stares and wonders rapidly whether Cinnamon gave it to him. If she's still here. Where Will *slept*.

"We stayed up too late watching *Chernobyl*. She's at work," Will says, seemingly reading her mind.

Scarlett lets out a breath, trying to pull herself into the moment. "Right. Good. I mean, no, not *good*, I wasn't—"

Will sets his drink down and tips his head to the side. "Relax. I get it."

Scarlett's brow furrows. "You do?"

"Sure. No one knows how much it sucks having her mad at you better than me."

Scarlett laughs, breathless and involuntary, remembering various shouted fights between them over the years. "True."

Will slides down from the bar stool and rinses his mug in the sink. When he turns around, he's chewing his lip, one red corner of it caught in white teeth. "She kind of mentioned you saw something last night."

"Oh. Yeah." Scarlett's voice is too high. "A tree collapsed down the back. It was pretty freaky."

Will is watching her carefully. "She said something weird happened, though. With one of the graves."

His eyes might be glittery, but they're also smart and sure. She *trusts* him, Scarlett realizes. She has no idea why.

"I could show you," she says quickly, before she can think too hard about it. "If you want."

Will Taylor smiles again, slow as dawn this morning. "I definitely want."

She leads him outside into the gray day and across the dripping deck, still trying not to think too hard about the fact that they're alone together. Something about walking away from how it felt in Ian's room, with Will, feels nice. The grass squelches under their bare feet, but he follows easily. It doesn't take them long to reach the spot by the back of the fence.

"Holy shit," Will says. "Yeah."

It looks worse than it did in the dark. Deep fissures run the entire length of the pale headstone, almost obscuring the writing completely—save for the name. Under the bright silvery light, Sadie's open grave looks especially wrong. A sacred thing, smashed.

Will's eyes are scanning it rapidly, as if analyzing many things at once. "Sadie Prince . . . Was she the piano prodigy?"

Scarlett nods. She forgets, sometimes, that this is the other thing people remember Sadie for.

"The one who—"

"Allegedly went mad and killed a guy. Yep," she finishes for Will, and he flushes.

They haven't mentioned the fact that the grave is empty, but they're both staring anxiously down. Scarlett feels it zap-zap between them, unsaid. The weight of it.

"God. I don't get how a tree could even do this," Will muses. "Unless, like . . ." He takes a step closer to the cavernous hole in the ground, stepping around fractured pieces of stone. He rests his fingertips on the trunk of the tree, tracing them lightly down the gnarled bark in a way that would raise goose bumps.

"Cinnamon said it could be—"

"Moisture in the rock, maybe from the roots," Will finishes, casting his eyes back into the empty space. "Yeah. There could've just been water under here for ages."

Because there's nothing in there to stop it. Because the grave is empty. Because the fact that there's a hole at all means it is probably-definitely a grave. Her eyes follow his again, down down down—into the black.

"Did you know Mary Shelley allegedly had her first kiss in a graveyard?" she hears herself ask, just to drown out her fast-moving thoughts.

Will is quiet for a beat, stands and swallows before answering. "Oh yeah?"

Scarlett nods, fixing her eyes on the mossy scratch of Sadie's birth date in the white stone.

Her pulse is still too loud. Has been since Ian's room, or maybe since she saw Will in the kitchen. *Keep it together.* "Yeah!" she says. "It was with her future husband, though, so it's romantic-ish. Not just . . ."

"Creepy?"

She smiles. "Hmm. Especially if you believe the story that they did more than kiss."

Will's eyes go wider for a second, long hands getting lost in his pockets. "I mean, that is undeniably a good story."

"I always thought so. But maybe it is creepy that people made it into a story?"

"Yeah. Practicality-wise, I have . . . questions."

"Right?" Scarlett laughs, grateful for the momentary lift in atmosphere. "Like, *on* the graves?"

"*Around* them?" Will adds.

"At the intermission of a funeral?"

Will's mouth twitches. "In front of all the mourners?"

"I'm kind of jealous, though," Scarlett admits, her thoughts changing tack again by accident. Lack of sleep always scrambles her.

Then Will says, "Why, where was your first kiss?"

The sea roars suddenly beyond the fence, below them; it thuds through her. Scarlett stares at her shoes. "Um."

When she finally looks at him, Will's cheeks bloom pink. "God, sorry." He takes his hands back out of his pockets and they flutter awkwardly up under his chin. "That was weird. You don't have to answer."

"No, it wasn't. It's just . . . My answer's not interesting," she finishes. No way is she telling Will Taylor that she's never kissed anyone ever at all. She did not wake up today and choose humiliation.

Will gives her a good-natured frown. "I don't believe that."

She wants to ask him what he does believe—of her. Of anything. Instead she just says, "Ha. Well, it's true."

"Mine isn't either," he says after another weighty pause, during which she wonders whether they're talking about the same thing. "School parking lot. Cinnamon. Unsurprising. I'm a cliché and a disgrace."

Scarlett does a weird smile to hide the flash of feeling that goes through her. "You really are."

"Ouch. Agree a bit faster, why don't you."

She blushes slightly and checks his face to see that he's not really offended. "Oh well. We can't all be Mary Shelley."

"True."

"So, what do you think?" Scarlett asks, gesturing to the grave so she has an excuse to stop looking at him.

Will chews his lip. "Honestly?"

"Yeah."

He looks at the other headstones scattered around them. "I think this kinda doesn't look like a grave from the sixties."

Scarlett feels her eyebrows lift. *This family. Is having a graveyard at the house not enough of a thing that doesn't make sense?* "So, what . . . Do you think they, like, replaced it?"

Will looks, Scarlett thinks, fleetingly impressed by this reasoning, but he shakes his head. "It would've been really hard to dig up existing stone and then put this here."

"'This' being . . ."

Will bends down to goose-bump-trace his fingertips along Sadie's name. "Granite," he says. "Which is fine. But"—he points to the smooth stone edge running flush with the lip of the grave and the ground—"it's, like, *fully* granite. And a grave, or even a memorial, from back then would've probably had concrete in it—at least in the foundation."

Scarlett stares at him. "What does that mean?"

Will stands up again, his eyes bright. "Potentially, it means this grave can't be as old as it says it is."

"But that's when she *died*! Right? In the sixties. It says so right there!"

It doesn't, though. What it actually says, etched into pale full granite, is:

In Loving Memory of SADIE GRACE PRINCE
who lived here 1949–1968

Grandpa Charlie was extremely literal. Scarlett and Cinnamon always assumed that was the reason for the (admittedly) odd wording.

But looking at it now . . . Oh.

Oh.

A seagull screams shrill sweetly above them, and Scarlett jolts out of her thoughts.

Will pulls out his phone and snaps a photo of the scene in front of them, squinting at the screen to get all the details in frame. "So, I can look into this at work, if you want."

Scarlett blinks. "Work?"

"At the library." Will smiles. "I work there."

Scarlett tries very hard to look like she didn't know that already.

"In archives. I'm actually doing history at uni," Will explains further. "Basically I have the incredibly cool life goal of secretly wanting to be the David Attenborough of history."

Scarlett blinks again in genuine surprise. "That's . . . That's kind of amazing, actually."

"I mean, it really isn't." Will laughs. "But in this case it's potentially useful."

Scarlett looks again at the date etched in maybe-too-modern stone. "Okay." She nods, as fast as her heart. "See what you can find out."

10.

That weekend is the second one in December, and Christmas—Cinnamon's least favorite time of year, for both political and aesthetic reasons—feels properly on the horizon.

Tourists flood the town seemingly overnight, their shiny cars parked everywhere and their bundles of *stuff* cluttering up the beach. Sleepy shops become overwhelmingly busy, the baking heat inside and outside like a hug from an overzealous relative. Red and green banners cascade from the palm trees lining Main Street, their glittering font spelling out *JOY*, *MERRY*, and *PEACE*.

Also flooding into town are various runaway children who left for study or work or to do anything besides sit by the beach. Among them, thank the gods, is Phoebe Mendis.

"Honey!" she shouts when she meets Cinnamon outside the café, already holding two iced coffees. "You look awful. What's wrong? Come here."

Even fresh from a two-hour drive, Phe is immaculate in red lipstick, a fluoro-purple dress with cap sleeves, thick curled hair, and bright-yellow sneakers. *A. Lot.* was her chosen self-descriptor when they were in school, besides *Sri Lankan Australian* and *intersectional feminist* and *just so gay.*

Cinnamon, Will, and Phe all attended the only private school in the area—Will and Phe for the quote-unquote education, and

Cinnamon because it was two towns over, where she could (mostly) be Cinnamon Prince and not *a Prince*. There was also maybe an incident where she pushed a girl at the public high school quite hard into a shrub for calling her sister and father "fucking psychopaths."

She met Phe in year ten sex ed, when the school had a consultant come who asked them to sign heteronormative abstinence pledges, and they were among those who flatly refused. During next period, Phe messaged her on Instagram:

so you're queer too right? x

Cinnamon didn't reply for over a week.

They've been friends ever since.

"Thanks," she grumbles now, pulling away from Phe's sticky hug. She hates hugging—a fact respected by everyone except Phe. "I try."

"I truth-tell out of love." Phe laughs, handing Cinnamon her drink. She looks at her again, scrutinizing. "Oof. Your vibe right now! So much *stress*."

"That's what I was going for."

They start walking toward the beach.

"Tell me everything that's happened in your life since I last saw you." Phe's arm slips around Cinnamon's shoulders.

After a minute Cinnamon leans into it. "You know me. Nothing changes."

Phe purses her lips. "William told me your estranged sister's back."

Cinnamon sips her coffee. "God, he's a gossip."

Phe nods. "Truly can't resist, bless him. How's it going, though?"

"It's . . . going."

"Uh-oh."

"We're just not close." Cinnamon shakes her cup, clunking ice around. "That's it. We're not magically gonna get that way just because she's back. I don't know why everyone's trying to make it a thing."

"Is your mum back for the holidays? Mine'll ask me."

"No clue."

Phe pouts in sympathy. "Come to mine! It'll be a proper Lankan Christmas, carols and all. Two of the cousin groups canceled, so it'll just be me, Dad, and Rav and the aunties, but Mum's still gonna cook for a hundred."

"Mmm, maybe," Cinnamon says. Christmas at Phe's house is always warm and busy, plates of food and her mum inviting every-one. But then she thinks about that close-knit group seeing the dysfunction that is her own family these days.

"Bring Scarlett," Phe jokes. "Mum'll have you two healed and together as one in no time."

"Maybe," Cinnamon says again, knowing it sounds like *no*.

When they reach the sand dunes, Phe dumps her giant canvas tote bag with a thud and sits down, pulling Cinnamon with her. The two of them watch the waves churning for a beat, dappled sunlight dancing across the blue edge of the sea. The sky looks almost violet on top of it, beautiful in a way that feels vaguely unreal.

"How's Mattie?" Cinnamon asks.

Phe crinkles her nose and lets out a long dramatic sigh. "Oh. I feel like we're about to break up."

Mattie is the sagacious shaved-head blonde Phe met on a dating app during O-Week at uni. She says they fell in love accidentally. They both needed a roommate, and living together proved to be a petri dish for intimacy. Cinnamon has visited their shared house in the city a few times, snug with Phe's photos on the walls and fridge poetry spelling things that make Cinnamon cringe and also jealous.

Cinnamon raises her eyebrows. "Has she said something?"

Phe shakes her head. "Just a feeling. She's been hanging out with her DJ friends a lot. Uni's really busy. We keep missing each other." She shrugs. "Ah well! I've been living on borrowed time anyway. She's way out of my league."

"I object," Cinnamon says, "most strongly. And none of that means you're gonna break up."

Phe bumps their shoulders together, slurping the dregs of her drink and crunching ice between her teeth.

"Seriously," Cinnamon says. Phe is the best person she knows—the only person who doesn't see it is Phe. "What makes you think that?"

"I have a feeling," Phe repeats, hitching the grandma underwear she always wears over her stomach with a snap of elastic and a frown. "Sometimes you just know. You know?"

"Are your feelings always accurate, though, do we think?" Cinnamon asks, trying to steer Phe toward a joke to smooth out her frown. "Like, remember when you had a feeling about Beth Fisher?"

Beth Fisher was Cinnamon's first girlfriend. She was also Phe's *ex*-girlfriend, but after they broke up, Phe "thought they'd get along." Cinnamon did, but Beth . . . was in love with Phe. Probably *still* loves Phe.

"Oh my god! *Beth!*" Phe cracks up immediately. The fact that they share an ex-girlfriend used to be her favorite icebreaker at parties. "Look—true. *That* feeling was wrong-town. But I was only trying to help!"

Cinnamon rolls her eyes. "Just so wrong. I am never making the first move again."

"*Usually* my feelings are right."

"You reckon?"

"I was right about you."

"Which part?"

"All the parts. The beautiful, dark and twisty, layered being that is you."

"God. I need more coffee if you're going to start being spiritual."

"Speaking of!" Phe says. "Tell me about *your* love life. Anyone on the scene at the moment?"

Cinnamon stretches her legs out in front of her, feeling the spill of displaced sand under her calves. For some reason Will's collarbones pop into her head, gleaming graceful. "Hard, hard no on that front," she says.

Phe shakes her head in mock devastation. "What a waste."

"I feel as though most people would disagree with you there."

"But you're not like most people, my grumpy little honeybee."

"Yeah," Cinnamon says, "I'm a hazard, especially to myself."

After leaving Phe, Cinnamon lingers in town for a while. She feels melancholy in an immediate sort of way—fed up with herself in this moment.

She thinks about Beth. About Mattie. Seeing Phe always reminds her that they *don't* really see each other anymore. She has friends, but they're constantly living and leaving, while she stands still. This past year feels like it's gone in a blink without clarifying or changing anything.

She briefly considers visiting Will at the library, as if it'll clear the fog in her brain. Then she thinks of his collarbones again, and texts him instead.

> Working hard or hardly working?
>
> Working, would u believe! I think I'ma
>
> help S look into your empty grave

Cinnamon makes a face at her phone. She thinks again of the hole in the backyard. It makes her feel strange and hot. It feels like when she saw ghosts in her dreams when she was a kid, and the murky possibility of an unsureness of everything.

Of course, Scarlett would chase this. But Cinnamon won't.

> Ugh. I thought we agreed it
>
> must just be a weird memorial??
>
> Can't just leave a mystery like that unsolved,
>
> Princey!! It goes against my creed.
>
> Loser.
>
> Ly too x

She throws her coffee cup in the recycling and changes direction, walking back toward the promenade. It's quiet this time of day, even this time of year, the wood planks bleached by the fiery midday sunlight. She takes the path to the grassy top of the headland, where dark blue stretches to the paler horizon, sits on a bench and looks down at the rippling rectangle of the ocean baths carved near the shore.

Cinnamon often watches people swimming in the sea because she won't do it anymore.

Maggie used to go to the baths sometimes in the afternoons—freestyle even if it was freezing, never bothering to wear a cap, just rinsed her hair in the outdoor showers afterward while toothpaste-in-your-mouth cold water splashed the rocks at her feet. Cinnamon used to swim with her right until they couldn't anymore, both here and at Princes Beach, the two of them racing and the sea-cold unfurling her.

She hasn't swum since.

She stares at the figures cutting through the water in straight lines. People move past her: families heading to the beach, older couples walking, surfers carrying boards, committed joggers trading sunburn for fitness. She tries to feel part of it for a minute.

Then she decides to just go to work.

Since the pub started doing what Tone calls "Semi-Bottomless Brunch," there's always one waitstaff member scheduled with the chef and barista at lunchtime. It's not Cinnamon's day, but she figures if she shows up, Tone will probably let her help out too.

She walks past the baths and over the hill to the front entrance and *ugh*. Perfect Daisy is already there, of course, setting up umbrellas on the tables outside. Cinnamon notices her hair first: that shock of pastel pink shot through with bleach and dark-dark brown, tweaked in every direction by the salty breeze. Then Daisy pushes her multicolored hair behind her ears and looks up, one hand shielding her face. She waves at Cinnamon in surprise.

"Hi!" she says. "Did I mess up the schedule? I thought it was my semi-bottomless day."

Perfect Daisy looks different, caught by surprise in the sun. There's a slight dip in the center of her top lip over her teeth when she smiles properly like that. Her lipstick is a color Cinnamon hasn't seen before, like a rose-pink red.

"No, it is," Cinnamon says. It seems like a supremely stupid plan all of a sudden, rocking up to work on her day off, but she has to commit to it now. She swallows. "Just thought I'd see if you needed backup, now that it's school holidays."

"Oh." Daisy smiles softly and nods. "Okay. Cool."

Just as well too, because they get—to use a Tonyism Cinnamon despises but must admit in this instance is true—fully sick slammed. She doesn't even have time to put on her uniform. She's glad the shoes she threw on with her linen sundress this morning are her lace-up Docs.

Two big family groups arrive and take up the entire outdoor seating area, ordering generously and leaving a path of destruction in their wake. Daisy and Cinnamon become a team for a while, methodically taking plates and cutlery to the sink in unison. Then happy hour starts, and Cinnamon barely sees Daisy, except in brief blurs of her smile when they pass each other in the kitchen.

That's new.

That's weird.

That's fine.

Cinnamon feels totally normal and fine.

After the last family group pays and leaves, Cinnamon starts wiping the tables.

"God, I'm glad you were here," Daisy says, blowing her hair back off her face. "Since when is this place actually busy? I think that's the most customers I've ever seen."

"Wait till New Year's." Cinnamon smirks.

"What happens on New Year's?"

"Tone always throws a massive party. Always dress-up. Always a really specific theme."

"Like what?"

"Last year it was . . ." Cinnamon squints, remembering. "Shrek the Halls."

Daisy's mouth drops open in a laugh. "The movie, or as a general theme?"

"Both. Yes. All of the above."

Daisy laughs again. Her lipstick's faded to a stain and her bangs are the tiniest bit sweaty.

Cinnamon turns back to wiping table eight.

They both fall quiet.

Then Daisy asks, "Why aren't we friends?"

Cinnamon bites down on her tongue.

Daisy is watching her when she looks back up. Her face looks like the words she's just said. Not angry, but curious.

"What?" Cinnamon says. "We're friends."

It's a lie,

but she doesn't know why.

Daisy has the grace to let that one slide. "It's just . . . We've worked together for nearly two months, and I realized the other day I know nothing about you."

Something about the open look on her face makes Cinnamon unable to meet Daisy's eyes when she jokes, "Yeah, that's kind of my brand." Then she feels inexplicably shitty for saying that, so she adds, "What do you wanna know?"

"Umm . . ." Daisy considers for a second. "The basics, I guess. Siblings?"

"One," Cinnamon says.

"Life ambitions?"

"Zero."

Daisy smiles and *tsks*.

"What about you?" Cinnamon flips the conversation neatly.

Friends or not, she doesn't want Daisy to think she's a deadbeat, even if it's true. "Only child, right?"

Daisy inspects one of the wineglasses. "Uh . . . yeah."

"Yeah. Jealous," Cinnamon jokes.

Daisy smiles faintly. "I mean, I kind of think my parents really wanted more kids? But they couldn't."

"Oh. Shit."

"Like, we're super close!" Daisy says, drying the glass. "But I do worry a lot about disappointing them, given I'm the one great hope and everything. Even though I know that's stupid."

"It is!" Cinnamon agrees rapidly, before realizing she said it too emphatically. Is she undersocialized after so long with Will and Phe? How do you even make new friends? She dials it down. "I mean, no, it's not."

"Hmm." Daisy stares up at the ceiling, not elaborating on what about her could ever be disappointing. It takes a minute for her eyes to come back down.

Cinnamon can't think of anything remotely helpful to add except, "I mean, I get that."

The soft skin under Daisy's chin has two freckles on it.

Beautiful, Cinnamon thinks suddenly.

Not helpful.

They're both quiet again. Daisy hoists herself onto the bar next to Cinnamon with her legs dangling, her white Converse banging against the wood.

Cinnamon looks outside at Main Street, trees and shop fronts lit by the gold dying sun. She doesn't know what it would be like to be born guilty, but she knows what it is to question why and how you exist.

"Also, you know you're, like, a properly good person," she says, ignoring her cardiac-arrest-level beating heart. "Literally everyone thinks so. It's kind of annoying."

Daisy isn't impressed by this the way most people would be.

Cinnamon pushes on. "I'm serious."

"But am I like this because I feel like I have to be, though? Or because I *am*?" Daisy says with her face matter-of-fact. "And how do you tell which is which?"

Cinnamon has a theory about getting to know someone: There's a few seconds, when it first happens, that feels like being inside a speeding car. She's in that now, can feel the unstoppable holding-on-to-the-seat flip in her stomach of being let in. She doesn't linger on the fact that it's happening with Daisy Leung.

"I don't think anyone's properly good just 'cause they have to be," she says.

"What *do* you think?" Daisy asks. Curious again.

Something changes when they look at each other, the mood shifting like a breeze. Like the light of outside is inside. Illuminating Daisy's freckles, heating Cinnamon up. "Um."

"Sorry!" Daisy bursts out after a beat, staring down at her swinging shoes. "I'm being a downer. It's just something I think about a lot."

"Please. You could never be a downer. You're, like, total high-visibility." Cinnamon points to Daisy's Christmas blouse—they're meant to wear something red, but hers is a dark, riotous hot pink.

In terms of lightening the mood, it works. Daisy snorts softly. "Excuse me. This is silk, and it's twenty years older than you are. Have some respect."

That dimple in her left cheek should be illegal. It's a flammability hazard. And Cinnamon's the work fire warden.

"So what about you?"

Cinnamon coughs. "What about me, what? Do you mean my dad?"

Daisy shakes her head. "Just, like, your family."

Cinnamon sighs in relief. "Um. Parents are divorced, and then, you know—one younger sister. Boring stuff."

Daisy leans back on her hands. "That, Cinnamon Prince"—she gives her a liminal sort of look—"is what people say when there's a story."

Cinnamon feels hot in her throat again. "Nah. Just boring stuff."

11.

Amy Banks-Prince comes home on Monday.

Scarlett hears her car pull up outside. The noise of her modified engine echoes over the cliff like a shout. She tries to remember if there was a warning text and whether Cinnamon is home tonight.

It's already been what Niamh would call "a day"—Ian didn't get up, and the heat was itchy. As Scarlett walks past Cinnamon's room, she sees light leaking from under the door. She feels tired and edgy and not ready for this fight.

"Helloo?" her mum calls, knocking once-twice-three-times in quick succession. "Girls? Ian?"

Cinnamon's door flies open. Her face is hard and angry red—a brick wall. "What the fu—"

"I didn't know!" Scarlett whisper-hisses defensively. "I swear!" There's a faint clattering sound, and then the front door puffs open to reveal Amy, brandishing her key. She's wearing what she always does: everything and not enough. A paisley skirt that touches the tops of her feet. A tiny crop top. A trailing coral-colored shawl hugging her arms like a spiderweb. Her hair is dyed very dark and cut very short—not like always. It washes her out, Scarlett thinks. In the waning light, she looks impossibly young.

The three of them haven't been alone together in the same room for almost a year.

"Hi, Mum!" Scarlett trills to fill the silence, rushing down the stairs to hug her, awkward and stiff.

Amy's eyes (big, brown) crinkle at Scarlett before finding their way to where Cinnamon stands by the banister with her arms folded and one foot propped on the wall behind her.

"What're you doing here?" Cinnamon asks, squeezing her arms tighter across her chest.

"I wanted to see you, darling," Amy says, her forehead creasing at Cinnamon's tone. "It's Christmas! And your sister said that Ian . . ."

Something hot and hard rolls up into Scarlett's throat as her sister's head whips around. "One text—"

Cinnamon's eyes flash hotter than the outside sun. "God, you would. Four fucking *days*! That's how long it took you to snitch."

"Sweet darling," Amy tries to intervene, stretching out one bronze-rings-decorated hand. "Let's just talk for a minute, all right? Scar—"

"I'm actually all good, thanks, Amy," Cinnamon snaps, and then she spins on her heel, and the back door slams, and she's gone.

Amy looks at Scarlett. She shrugs and pulls a funny sort of sad face. Cinnamon's temper never gets to Amy the way it does Scarlett. Probably because she gave it to her.

They both go quiet. Scarlett thinks immediately of telling Amy about Sadie's grave. Out of everyone in the family, her mother is most likely to understand. She loves Halcyon's graveyard—she's the one who, along with Maggie, decorated it with good-vibes plants so the spirits would have something to hang on to or help them go.

Something stops Scarlett from saying it, though. Either because it's been so long between them or because it feels as if the grave's between her and Will, and it hasn't been long enough yet.

"Let's do the cards," Amy says after a while.

Scarlett used to love her mother's tarot deck when she was younger. It's old-fashioned—the real deal, no guidebook in sight—and each card is adorned with a hand-painted portrait of a woman. This always felt like a perfect metaphor for being raised by Amy. Even the Hanged Man, the Magician, and Death are women, and every twisting strand of fate belongs to them.

"Maybe later," Scarlett says. It's been a while since she's wanted to know for sure about the future—longer since she properly believed in one at all.

"All right, darling." Amy nods. She crosses the floorboards and hugs Scarlett again—hard, floral-smelling, pressing kisses into her hair. When they both step back, she finally looks chagrined. "Where is he?"

"Upstairs." Scarlett points to the staircase. "In bed."

Amy drops her bag from her shoulder. Lipstick and organic deodorant roll out onto the floor, but she doesn't move to pick them up.

Scarlett watches her until the cropped dark hair disappears through the doorway at the top of the stairs.

Dinner that night is bad with a side of worse.

Ian comes down, at least. He always does when Amy's home. In the three years since the divorce, Scarlett has remained perplexed by how *amicable* it all was—*is*. The two of them sit next to each other in companionable silence, her mother spreading bright-green pesto onto her father's bread and handing it to him absently. They talk easily, like old friends—or old lovers, Scarlett guesses, though applying that word to her parents is certified gross.

Enter Cinnamon. She sits at the head of the table, silent-savagely scraping her cutlery on the plate and throwing flammable glances in Amy's direction.

Amy asks Ian about things like gardening and avoids talk of the canceled tour or the press or the funeral. Scarlett mostly tunes out the mess that is all of her family together—has to, in order to stay Controlled and Calm—until her dad addresses her directly.

"You still thinking of doing psychology, Scar?" he asks.

Amy puts her fork down. "*Are* you, darling?"

No. The teachers wanted her to aim as high as she could, but she can't see herself doing what her therapist does, any more than she can see herself at all. "Um. Maybe, if I get the marks."

"You'll find out soon." Amy smiles. "How exciting."

Is it? Scarlett wants to ask her. Instead, she just chews the food in her mouth, over and over.

"You'll get them," Ian says with certainty. "You've always been smart, ever since you were tiny." His eyes on hers are tired, but urgent, like *sorry.* Then he winks once, and it lances through Scarlett.

She watches Cinnamon wince too. Hope is a knife.

"*Mmm,*" Scarlett says, swallowing her mouthful of food. Top of her list is a BA in literature, but she hasn't told anyone—it's never felt like the right time. Cinnamon deferred a BA last year. "Hopefully."

Amy clears the plates when they're done, dropping them in the sink with a careless clatter that makes Ian flinch. "We should go for ice cream!" she says. "Who's with me?"

Ian rubs his temple. "No thanks, love. I'm just gonna crawl into bed."

Both girls wince again: at his *no*, at his *love*.

Cinnamon follows upstairs almost immediately after him. Scarlett hears the locks click on their bedroom doors.

"Come on," she says to her deflated mother. "I'll help with the dishes."

Scarlett turns on the faucet hard, filling the sink with scalding water and pulling Maggie's old rubber gloves up to her elbows. She hands Amy a dish towel, and they work quietly for a while.

"It'll be all right, you know," Amy says, when almost everything is scrubbed clean. "He will be."

How do you know? Scarlett wants to hurl at her. "Okay," she says instead, and when they're done, she goes upstairs to get ready for bed.

The house smells different is her last proper thought of the day as she's brushing her teeth and looking at the sharp strip of light under Cinnamon's closed door.

Things Amy Banks-Prince smells like:

- dirt, from the many plant babies she tends and talks to;
- wet, from the sea;
- roses, extra-strongly because she refuses to replace her perfume, bought in bulk by Ian in the nineties;
- shampoo, travel-sized.

12.

Since the day of their First Proper Conversation, Cinnamon has been finding herself fixated on little things about Daisy Leung.

It's probably nothing.

It's just easier than thinking about Amy, and the fact that she's chosen not to—can't, won't ever—speak to her for an entire tense-meal week.

It's just the way Daisy arranges and rearranges her hair in the last half hour of their weeknight shift. Flipping it from a center part to a side one, then twisting it into a fast-collapsing bun. She settles on pulling it into a high ponytail, scraping the dark and sugary-pink strands back with a band from her wrist tugged into place by careful fingers.

It's just that her nails are long but kind of uneven, their jagged edges somehow . . . *dear*. As though she's been too busy actually living to care about such things.

It's just that the color of her lipstick changes depending on her mood (Cinnamon thinks, anyway). Red when she laughs a lot. Or purple and serious. Quiet and nude. Dark carnation pink. Peach. Once, blue.

Who wouldn't wonder about *blue*?

Cinnamon notices a tug in her chest, empty but warm, looking at tonight's matte raspberry.

It's probably nothing.

"What's up?" Daisy asks suddenly.

"What? Nothing," Cinnamon says.

Maybe it's not nothing.

Cinnamon glances at the clock. It's almost time to go, but she doesn't want to. Her Amy rage roars at the thought of heading home. She opens her mouth to say something—anything—to Perfect Daisy, but then Tone bursts through the door with his gelled blond hair brushed back, wearing (inexplicably) a leather jacket printed with the American flag. It doesn't close up, and a large swath of soft stomach pokes out the bottom.

"My *gurls!*" he says. "How goes it? You two've been working around the clock. You're keeping me in furs! Figuratively, obviously. I love animals. *J'adore.*"

Cinnamon resists the urge to screw up her face. Tone is always like this when he comes in. "We're fine, Tone," she says. "How are you?"

"Oh, I'm swell, Cinnabon. Swell. How's the newbie doing? Eh, Daisonator? Cin been treating you okay? Bit of a prickle-prick, this one. But we love her!"

Cinnamon grits her teeth at everything that was wrong with that diatribe.

"She's been great," Daisy says. She looks shy saying it for some reason, and lets her bangs fall forward to hide her face.

"Great! Ooh." Tony grins and walks over to read the night's total on the computer. "What a night, Cinno. Keep up the good work!"

Cinnamon scratches the back of her head and nods.

When he goes out back to talk to the chef, Daisy rests her dish towel–wrapped hand on a table for a second in what looks like disbelief. "Are you Cinnabon or Cinno? That part was kind of unclear."

"Oh, they're not even the best ones," Cinnamon says, stepping behind the till to close it again, fizzing with energy that they're talking, and she didn't have to initiate it. "When I first started here, he called me 'Jessica Biel is *The Cinna*' for three months."

"No!"

"I mean, to be fair, *The Sinner* is an okay show, and Jessica Biel's hot."

Daisy laughs softly, like night air through the trees outside. She sprays disinfectant on table seven and starts wiping. They lapse into silence again, both waving to Tony when he eventually leaves properly, stepping back outside in his weather- and life-inappropriate jacket.

The fizzing and their talking have almost stopped by the time Daisy sprays disinfectant on the last table and says, "What are you doing tonight?"

Daisy's smile is even worse than her nails—all that light coming from a single point.

"Uh." Cinnamon fidgets with the knot on her apron where it's double-tied at the front, desperately trying to think of something to say that isn't *Wander the streets because my life's a mess.* "I was gonna maybe go to the carols thing. Down at the beach."

This isn't strictly true. Strictly, Phe invited her this morning, and she texted back:

over my ded body.

Daisy looks surprised. "Ooh. Interesting."

"I mean, it's stupid, but we kind of do it every year."

"We?"

"Just me and friends from school." Cinnamon still feels vaguely wrong-footed.

"Can I come?"

"What?"

Daisy is leaning against table one now, with her white-high-top-Conversed feet stretched out in front of her and her arms flung back.

Who wears white shoes to a restaurant job?

"My parents are renovating our garage. It's driving me up the nonexistent walls. I desperately need a distraction."

Cinnamon looks at the soft crooks of Daisy's elbows. She hears herself say, "Sure."

"Great! You're a lifesaver." Daisy beams, pushing herself back upright and pulling her apron over her head. "Let me just get changed."

"Yep," Cinnamon manages, though her voice still feels far away.

She looks for the giant set of keys behind the counter. Working with Daisy is one thing. Thinking about her is—well . . . But *hanging out*? What will they talk about—the frigging weather? Cinnamon has sudden visions of them sitting in horrific silence until the fireworks go off at the end of the carols. Potentially *in front of other people*, including . . . She yanks her phone out of her back pocket.

William. Emergency.

What???

Perf. Daisy from work coming to carols thing.!!!!!!! How did this happennn She asked if she could come aggggh

Wow!!! Yes!!!! Godspeed.
What are you gonna do??

Dieeeeeeeeeeee

Princess or Lady??

Cinnamon growls impatiently and shoves the phone away.

"Ready," Daisy says. She's standing in the doorway to the break room wearing black-denim overalls and her hair down again, fanned out brilliantly over her shoulders.

"Great," says Cinnamon. "Um. Me too."

"You are?" Daisy stares at Cinnamon's work blouse.

Shit. Cinnamon pulls off her apron and starts unbuttoning the blouse. She always wears a plain T-shirt underneath. Forest green this time. She untucks it with a flourish. "Ta-da," she says. "Fashion."

"Impressive." Daisy smiles. "Here I was making an effort."

They look at each other for a second, wondering what that means (in Cinnamon's case). She inspects Daisy's outfit again. The overalls are cool—faded and ripped at the knees, polar opposite of her work slacks. Underneath them is a black lacy bra-top thing that stops at the ribs—and then bare skin.

That part Cinnamon can't think about for too long.

She wrestles with the dead bolt on the front door to lock up. It sticks like always, but that's fine—good, actually—because she seems to need a hot minute to remember how to breathe. After shaking it one last time to check it's locked, they step into soft syrupy night. Cinnamon takes out her phone again and texts Will to keep her hands busy.

Am *I* the male gaze?? Have I become that which I hate?

She and Daisy walk quickly, Cinnamon watching their shadows as they weave close and then farther apart. There was a sun-shower this afternoon. Everything is still glinting, all wet but not soaked, puddles catching sparkles of light and washing the footpath momentarily free of sand.

Carols echo over their heads before they get to the beach—an off-key rendition of "Silent Night" clearly sung by the junior choir that makes Daisy laugh and Cinnamon feel braver.

"Told you it was bad," she apologizes.

Daisy just shakes her head and walks on.

Will and Phe are sitting in their usual spot in front of the rented stage. Cinnamon feels a rush of relief, seeing their familiar faces crowned with Phe's Christmas-craft paraphernalia. Then panic.

"Are those your friends?" Daisy asks when they start waving, all exaggerated.

"Yep," Cinnamon says, glaring at the fact that Will is nudging Phe in the ribs and winking.

"Cinnamon Prince!" Phe booms, clambering to stand to hug her as though they didn't just see each other. She releases her but keeps their cheeks squished together and one arm around Cinnamon's waist. "And who's this? A newcomer?"

Cinnamon nudges Phe's leg with her own, injecting warning daggers into her expression.

Phe ignores her. "Hello, newcomer! You look *hot*! I'm Phoebe Mendis. You can call me Phe. This is Will. And you are?"

Jesus.

Cinnamon nudges Phe's leg harder.

"Daisy," Daisy says, blushing slightly. "Cinnamon's, um, work friend. It's nice to meet you guys."

"It is," Will says from where he's sitting cross-legged on the sand holding his phone, his teasing blue eyes on Cinnamon. "*So* nice."

"Cinnamon never makes friends who aren't us!" Phe quips, sitting back down. "She hates everyone. Don't you, babe?"

Phe has never had a filter. Cinnamon loves this about her always, but not now.

Daisy tips her head to look at Cinnamon. "Wow. I'm honored."

"You should be," Will jokes. "She really does hate everyone. That's not even exaggerating."

Cinnamon gives him an *Okay, stop it now* thump on the shoulder.

"I can definitely see it," Daisy says. "So then, you guys are exceptions too?"

"Can we—" Cinnamon starts.

"Cinnamon and I go way back," Phe cuts her off, flicking her glossy black hair behind her shoulders. She points at Will. "And he's her favorite ex."

Jesus god.

Will chokes a bit on his can of Coke. Cinnamon shakes her head, wide-eyed, behind Daisy's back.

"Also, I love your hair more than life," Phe continues, ignoring Cinnamon again. "Is it bleached? Did you do it yourself? Why haven't I met you before?"

Daisy laughs, shifting into People Mode like she does at work. "Yes to the bleach. My school forbade it, so I did it as soon as I graduated. I'm scared to wash it too often in case I end up bald. And we just moved here."

Cinnamon's skin prickles with jealousy. Trust Phe to glean more information in five minutes than she has in two months.

"That is amazing! Here, sit with me," Phe commands Daisy, pulling her onto the sand by the wrist and passing her a pair of red-sequined reindeer antlers. "They're just about to do 'Baby Please Come Home'!"

Cinnamon sits on Daisy's other side. "You don't have to put those on," she mutters under her breath as soon as the ramshackle choir starts singing. "Phe is . . ."

Daisy looks at her for a beat too long, smirking with her eyes dancing, then slips the antlers into place behind her bangs. The dodgy spotlight from the stage splashes across her face.

Cinnamon swallows hard and turns to watch the chorus.

Will and Phe banter back and forth about things Cinnamon can't hear, then they pull popcorn and Maltesers out of a bag and offer them around. Cinnamon shakes her head, pulling her knees up to her chest.

Blessedly there's no way for her and Daisy to really *talk* to each other with all the noise around them.

When the carolers start rearranging cardboard props for the next song, Daisy looks up again.

She's even brighter in the dark.

Cinnamon drops her eyes fast, stretching her legs out restlessly.

After a beat, Daisy does the same thing. Then she shifts sideways, sitting half on her knees.

Night breeze rolls over them. Daisy shivers, then shifts again, slowly, and tucks both her feet underneath Cinnamon's thigh. Her eyes stay turned toward the stage.

Cinnamon holds completely still and stares straight ahead at the sparkly carolers too. People huddled in groups on the beach wave their orange battery-operated candles. The opaque night sea with its froth of white foam kisses the sand.

Will looks up from his phone a bit later to ask Daisy if she lives in town or out of it. Daisy answers "in it" in a perfectly even voice.

Phe says they should all get coffee sometime, and Daisy agrees. Then her shoes start to dig into Cinnamon's skin.

Just enough to leave a mark.

13.

Scarlett can't stop imagining that she can *feel* the open grave in the backyard.

It sits like a bug bite on her skin: itchy, wrong, slightly painful, something amiss. The not-knowing is unbearable. It's keeping her awake. She needs to do something to figure it out, to stop the itch. To know.

She needs to go through her grandmother's things. If anyone had answers in Halcyon House, it was always Maggie. But Scarlett wants to sound out Ian first.

Her dad's doing better. Having her mum here helps. It always does. (That's the problem.) Scarlett's plan to ask him about it is three-pronged. First she makes Ian and herself tea. She puts it with his breakfast on the tray left outside his door. There's a little white pill on the tray too. Scarlett tries not to think about it. She instead imagines his relief once she's figured it out—all of it—for all of them.

Prong two is Amy. Scarlett finds her mother eating burned toast over the sink when she gets back to the kitchen. Her dark hair is still jarring, but there's a strip of pale blond at the roots: Cinnamon-blond, threaded through with gray. Scarlett focuses on it to keep her breathing even.

"I think I actually do want to do the cards now," she says in a rush. It's technically not a lie—she needs to gather all the information she can, and surely real mysteries aren't that different from the mysteries of the universe—but it feels like one.

Amy puts down her toast and smiles, misinterpreting Scarlett's frantic air. "All right, darling. Let's see what we can find."

Scarlett sits at the kitchen table while Amy brings out the silk drawstring pouch she's had forever. It lives in her handbag, and Scarlett is struck for a second by how strangely brave it is, to carry all those futures around.

Amy sits down opposite her, the legs of her chair squeaking on the wood floor. She shuffles the cards expertly: once, twice, bending them in on themselves, separate and then back together. After two rounds of this, she puts the pile on the tabletop and spreads them out in a long line. Each card has the same design printed on its glossy back: red roses on black. Scarlett runs the tips of her fingers over them.

"Choose three, and think about whatever you want to know," Amy instructs in her familiar way.

Once upon a time, they did this every week. Once upon a time, Ian sat here too, good-naturedly laughing at them. His witches. Scarlett couldn't live in this house without Amy, couldn't live with her in the city either.

Scarlett plucks the first card at random, from the far-left side of the pile. Her head is too full to focus on a question. She tries to visualize the open grave instead, picturing its shape and its entirely granite edges. The shards scattered across green earth, and the question underneath. *Sadie Prince was here. Also—she isn't. Where did she go?* She pulls two more cards.

"Wonderful." Amy sweeps the rest of the cards back into a pile and sets it aside. "Now . . ."

Scarlett licks her lips, watching as her mother flips over the first card. A figure tumbling down into a bed of roses, falling from a giant height while getting hit by lightning: the Tower.

"*Hmm.*" Amy frowns. She flips over the second card. Two cherub-looking figures holding hands under a beaming sun: the Lovers.

Scarlett holds her breath.

Amy flips the last card. A skeleton in a white gown waving a black flag: Death.

"Well," Amy starts, "this is very interesting, darling."

Scarlett stares down at the spread. "What does it mean?"

Amy pulls the three cards toward her with her thumbs so they sit in a straight line. She clicks her tongue. "The Tower is upheaval. Great revelations. Tragedy. Change." She runs her finger over the falling figure. "Often too, a significant event that wipes out old ways of being. I'm seeing the lightning quite clearly. That's important, I think."

Scarlett's arms prickle. "Right. What about the next one?"

Amy smiles as they both look at the Lovers. "Relationships, darling. Romance. Deep feelings of love or attraction."

Scarlett exhales in relief. *There. Sometimes the cards are wrong.*

"It can mean a choice sometimes too. Some sort of romantic decision."

Scarlett is barely listening. *Sure, right.* "And Death?" she prompts. "It doesn't mean actual death, right? I remember you saying it didn't."

"You're right," Amy says in her otherworldly voice. "Death rarely means physical death, but it does mean an *end*. Endings and new beginnings. Spiritual transformation, grief, and loss. Heartbreak. But ultimately it's positive. It's life, really—leading you to something new."

Scarlett is embarrassed to find that she has goose bumps.

Amy smiles at her knowingly, gathering the three cards up and cutting them back into the deck. "Lots happening, darling," she says. "But it's all subjective. Only *you* can make your path—remember that." She squeezes Scarlett's shoulder and walks back into the kitchen.

Scarlett's mind is moving fast, thoughts like wispy clouds on a clear day. Tragedy and revelations—is that Sadie? Does that mean Scarlett will find her? That whatever happened to Sadie was very, very bad?

The Lovers stuff is funny. She thinks of texting Niamh about that, the irony, then she remembers Death and the lightning thing. That part is, undeniably, almost too creepy to contemplate. *The plan*, she instructs herself when her eyes start to burn from thinking too hard. *Focus on the plan.*

Prong three clicks into place after lunch.

Amy has been taking Ian for daily walks to the pier and back. Every afternoon she wraps him in ratty cardigans and history while he blinks, newborn-like, at the sea. She looks so pleased when Scarlett asks, "Can I go with him today?" that Scarlett feels violently guilty, until she remembers her mother is the best liar she knows.

She pulls on leggings and an arty T-shirt, white logoed and navy blue, that Cinnamon bought years ago, then handed down because it was too big. Takes her phone with her. Just in case.

She doesn't let herself worry about being alone together until they are. Her dad quietly links his arm with hers on the stairs.

They walk along the sand barefoot for a while, clouds forming draped curtains atop the gray ribbon of sea. The tourists aren't out in as much force today; only a few of them dot the beach with their wet suit–clad kids. Tiny waves lap at the shoreline. Ian lets them cover his feet and darken the cuffs of his jeans.

In a flash, Scarlett pictures him crying harder than she's ever seen anyone cry. Holding her hand tight enough to break it.

"Can I ask you something?" she says, cutting off her brain.

Ian blinks in the overcast light. "Of course."

"It's kind of . . . a family-history type of question."

Ian's face darkens like the sea today. She was expecting it, but her heart still flips into her throat. They can do this without getting lost in it, she counsels herself the way Doctor Marnie, her therapist (ex-therapist?), would. She can keep things neutral.

"You know how we had that damage to the graveyard? In the storm?"

Ian nods. "I saw."

Scarlett's thoughts snag for a second. *How did you not hear it? Where do you go, when you're not here?* "Right," she says, breathing in and looking at the water. "Well, the thing is—one of the graves got pretty much destroyed. One of the old ones, up the back."

"Your mum told me."

"Not that old," Scarlett qualifies. "Like, sixties old."

Ian frowns.

"It was Great-Aunt Sadie's," Scarlett says quickly, losing her nerve and deciding to forgo the details. "And, um, it just got me thinking about Maggie. Cinnamon asked me to go through her stuff, but I wanted to check with you first."

They've walked farther than they were supposed to—the pier looks tiny from here, people dotted on it like ants.

Ian hesitates, but recovers quickly.

"I think Mum would like that."

They look at each other for a minute, secrets and the sound of the sea hissing in the space between them.

The traces of Maggie left at Halcyon are all in the drawing room, packed loosely into boxes in front of the portrait of Sadie. Scarlett closes and locks the door behind her, and her heart thuds. She wonders whether Maggie packed these boxes herself, knowing they'd need them, or whether it was Ian or Cinnamon. She can't picture any of them doing it. It feels like the saddest thing—save going through them and deciding what to keep.

Scarlett sighs and sits down on the floor, pulling the closest box toward her. It's full of books. Her eyes fill with tears, and she feels sick. But she takes a breath and picks one up. She can do this. Even if it hurts.

The box holds paperbacks, hardbacks, leather-bound books with yellowed pages that smell like years gone by. She pulls out a handful of tiny *Reader's Digest* volumes and starts a neat pile on the floor. Then another pile for the vintage hardback illustrated cookbooks.

Maggie's meticulous looped penmanship pokes out on sticky notes in those: *meat loaf, Charlie's Meringue Pie, add 30g chopped garlic and simmer first.* It's a pinprick shock each time, seeing her handwriting. There are a couple of photo albums of trips Scarlett's grandparents took, carefully preserved. She sets those aside.

Scarlett checks her phone. It's been twenty minutes, and she's avoided reading the titles of any of the fiction books. She's not sure if she can. Books were her Thing with Maggie, the way swimming was always Cinnamon's. Scarlett and her grandmother would chat for hours about books over endless cups of tea. She doesn't want to see the stories Maggie read and not be able to ask her about them.

But that's exactly why she's here. Maybe packing up people's lives after they die goes some way toward helping you believe the unbelievable. They were here reading, swimming, talking, taking trips, drinking tea, holding these exact objects, and now they're forever-can't-talk-to-them-again gone.

Scarlett wipes her eyes and feels around the worn leather books at the bottom of the box. Maggie loved romances, but complicated ones—accused witches falling for Puritan farmers or loves that endured after death. Her worn *Wuthering Heights* is already on Scarlett's bookshelf upstairs. These books are more obscure, and most of the titles are at least partially worn away. She picks one up and flips to the copyright page. Then another and another and another.

A piece of paper flutters out of a falling-apart blue-and-yellow copy of *Ariel*, by Sylvia Plath. The paper is thin and covered in tiny typewriter letters punched officially coal-black into the page. Scarlett frowns. At the top it says *Admission and Discharge Record* with a long number, then:

PRINCE, SADIE GRACE

Scarlett freezes and stares at it, eyes rapidly scanning the rest of the typed text. Her heart is a rolling wave. Without thinking about it, she grabs her phone and opens Instagram. She and Will follow each other now. Innocently.

Her thumb hesitantly hovers over the Message icon. Hovers again when she types his name into the search bar, and again when she presses Message and the screen stares white and empty back at her. Waiting.

She looks at the paper again, at *Ariel*, inhales, and types.

> Hi Will—I hope you're good!
> Um . . . remember when you said
> to tell you if I found anything re: Sadie P?

At school, the girls around Scarlett talked a lot about messaging boys. They complained or agonized or bragged about it—the way some boys texted back straightaway, some hours later, some not at all. She always secretly thought boys couldn't be *that* different as to warrant their own reply-speed categories, but now wonders/worries for a thudding moment what kind of replier Will is.

Her phone buzzes immediately on the floor beside her.

> !!!!
> What is it?!

Scarlett's lips press together in a stressed-grateful squish for the Reply Gods smiling on her.

She looks down at her phone. Will is typing again.

> . . . i am so intrigued

Scarlett snaps a quick picture of the document. It takes a second to send. She zooms in on the corner to make sure all the text is visible, her phone blaring the letterhead:

Will does a shocked react, then:

This has made my day, and I am at WORK

Scarlett smiles despite herself.

also, look at that DATE omg
this means . . .

Scarlett swallows.

She definitely didn't die when the gravestone said she did.

The drawing room feels even hotter suddenly. It's there in old typeface, as clear as the day outside. Sadie was admitted at the end of 1968, then:

Discharged August 5, 1969

God!!!

Scarlett can't think of what else to say, and also her hands are kind of vibrating or maybe they're just shaking because, What does this mean?

Will is already replying:

this is a proper discovery of historical evidence
u are like Sherlock Holmes

Scarlett's whole body is buzzing now from talking to Will, or maybe from finding Sadie's name on this document from a hospital *after* her official death date, or possibly from the rabbit-fast beat of her heart.

> Hardly! You're the one who does this for a living. I just stumbled upon some old paper

. . .

you are!! You just cracked where she went!
You're Sherlock & I'm Watson
but not even a Lucy Liu Watson
I'm just, like, the one in that new movie with Henry Cavill

> . . .

> Does that mean I'm Henry Cavill?

Will types for a minute, then stops, then starts again.

U are (intellectually & spiritually) Sherlock Henry Cavill

Scarlett laughs, loud and giddy, then claps a hand over her mouth. She looks back down at the paper in front of her.

> I wonder what happened to her there.
> Sadie, I mean
> It doesn't say anything it just says women's hospital and when she was there.
> She had depression when she was younger (I think)
> Will what if it was something bad???

. . .

I'm on the case, Sherlock
watch this space.

Scarlett's cheeks are boiling hot. She just had an accidental, full-on conversation with Will Taylor. About Sadie. As soon as she registers it, the heat spikes through the rest of her. She stands up and pushes the window open so fast the hinges scream. Sea air washes in.

It's only when her breath comes back that she wonders why Sadie's hospital record was with the things Maggie left behind.

14.

On Friday afternoons Cinnamon drives her father to see Dr. Silva in town—usually.

This week Amy insists on coming. She and Cinnamon sit uneasily together in the front seat of the Jeep. Ian's legs are too long, so his jeans-covered knees jut into the console.

Amy hums along to the radio without knowing the song. She's wearing a black silk dress with spaghetti straps and approximately seven hundred necklaces, her hair and wrists filling the car with the scent of roses.

Cinnamon glares hard at the road.

They park in front of the powdery sand dunes of Main Beach, opposite the pub.

Knowing this week's schedule (because she did it), Cinnamon very pointedly doesn't look at who's on the register.

It's burning hot already. The sky looks almost *too* blue, she thinks. A bright, bragging sort of summer blue that makes her feel like nineteen is ancient, and she should maybe actually be doing something with the rest of her day.

Or her life.

She slams the car door and accidentally locks it with her parents still inside, then has to unlock and lock it again.

Dr. Silva's office is sandy brick like all the buildings in town, but with the street-facing wall made entirely of frosted glass. Brass letters above the door read *WELCOME*.

Cinnamon hates it here.

Amy fusses with Ian's shirt, straightening the collar on his moon-pale neck.

"I've got it," he says, with a faint version of the smile that's still only hers.

"You don't want to look like nobody owns you," Amy jokes half-heartedly.

"Nobody does." Ian winks. "Only my girls."

Cinnamon squints in the searing summer light. She makes a visor out of one hand, planting the other on her hip. "Do you want us to come in?"

"I'll be fine on my own, Bug. You two can hang out."

Cinnamon opens her mouth to protest the validity of both of these statements, but Ian is already slipping through the glass doors.

"So!" Amy says. Sunlight pools in the black creases of her dress. "Do you want to—"

Cinnamon stalks off down the scorched footpath, walking fast toward the beach.

"Cin," Amy calls, her quick steps sounding behind Cinnamon. "Come on, darling. I know you're angry with me, but we have to talk at some point."

Cinnamon spins around. "Do we?"

"Yes."

"Why?"

"Because we're family," Amy says. "Which means we don't have a choice."

Anger bursts through Cinnamon at the melodic tone of her mother's voice. It never alters, not unless she's properly angry. She has a sudden desire to try and make her mother that—angry. That's the only way they could be remotely similar.

"You did have a choice, though," she reminds her. "You left."

"You know what happened, darling heart. I went back to work, and we just . . . fell apart. I didn't *leave*—"

"Oh my god," Cinnamon says, more to herself than anything.

"I didn't leave *you*," Amy says with wide eyes. "That's what I was trying to say, if you'd let me finish, Cinnamon."

The best revenge is saying nothing. Cinnamon knows this, but rage is rising in her, unstoppable as the tide. Her mother knows exactly how to get her to talk.

"You literally did!" she shouts. The words come from somewhere deep in her stomach. "That's what a divorce is. When you plan it out for months, and save money and shit, and get a new place, then one day you're totally gone."

That was the worst part when it happened, and her parents told her. Not when Amy first took the job or anything else, but all the stuff she'd already put in place for After.

Amy looks stricken when Cinnamon walks away. Good. Cinnamon's still blisteringly angry—it stings in the tips of her fingers. She kicks up sand with her black-and-white Vans, taking deep, hard breaths. Eventually it gets too hot standing there in jeans, and she has to move under a tree. She tears apart skinny Norfolk pine cones in her fingers, one after the other until there's carnage all around her and she feels marginally calmer. Then she checks her phone for the time and heads back to the car.

Amy is leaning against the front passenger door like she's been there this whole time, even though the sun is fierce overhead. She holds her arms up in a surrender gesture. "I come in peace." Light bounces off her rings: brass craft-fair-looking ones, and the ancient diamond Prince wedding band she never took off.

Cinnamon sighs. "Whatever." She walks around the car to wait by the driver's-side door. When she flicks a glance, Amy looks unhappy, so Cinnamon looks away again, toward the pub. The lunchtime rush is starting up, tables filling with families for dine-in. She lets herself search—just for a second.

Just to calm her down.

Daisy is serving people in the outside eating area, wearing black bike shorts under her apron. Her hair's in a plait between her shoulder blades, the sun making it glow neon bright. Pieces of pink fall all over her face while a customer makes her laugh.

"She's very beautiful," Amy says, startling Cinnamon.

Cinnamon's chest is a record player scratch. She tears her eyes away. "It's not . . . I don't . . ."

"You know you can talk to me about dating."

"No thanks."

She made that mistake with Will. When they broke up and Cinnamon lay dry-eyed in the dark wondering what was wrong with her, Amy said, "It's for the best—you should never stay together just for the sake of it." At the time Cinnamon found it comforting, which made it worse—made her feel guiltier remembering it later—because it helped.

"You don't have to take so much on board, sweetheart," Amy says now in the sun. "That's why I'm here. You should be *living*."

"I don't care what you think," Cinnamon says coolly, staring at her shoes.

When they get home, Cinnamon employs her childhood avoidance strategy of being unassailable to her mum by seeking out the lesser of two evils—her conflict-hating, can't-shout-in-front-of sister.

She finds Scarlett in the front lounge room with a Christmas movie playing mutely on the TV. Usually that would be a straight-up no-go for Cinnamon, but it's *Home Alone*—her childhood favorite.

Scarlett is reading a novel by Sheila Heti. "God," she says when she looks up at Cinnamon in the doorway. "Announce yourself. You nearly gave me a heart attack."

"Heti and Culkin," Cinnamon says when she sits down on the floral-fabric couch opposite her sister. "The loners' afternoon companions of champions."

"*You* had the crush on Macaulay Culkin," Scarlett says. "I'm only watching because it's on, and like, for the feels."

Cinnamon smirks, pulling her legs crossed yoga-style underneath her to watch the movie. Unmutes it. Scarlett looks tense for a second, then she closes the book and sets it down on the coffee table.

It's not awful, Cinnamon admits to herself fleetingly, sitting here while the air-conditioning blasts away all traces of the earlier shouting-at-Amy heat, watching a white-Christmas movie from the nineties together, with the pulled-shut blinds and double doors blocking the world outside.

They stay like that, watching together until the credits roll.

"God," Cinnamon says afterward, tipping her head back. "A masterpiece, truly."

Scarlett shakes her head. "I don't get why you love it so much." This used to be their argument every Christmas.

"Um, because it's the best Christmas movie? In all of the ways."

"His parents literally lock him in an attic at the start!"

"Yeah, but it's Catherine O'Hara. I'd let her lock me up anywhere."

Scarlett rolls her eyes. "How'd you guys go today?"

Cinnamon makes a noncommittal sound like *meergh*.

Scarlett tries to hold her eyes properly—to talk about it, probably; Scarlett always wants to *talk about it*—so Cinnamon asks, "How're things going with Will?"

"What do you mean, how are things with him? They're fine. Great. I mean . . . What's he said?"

"He told me he's helping with the search for Sadie P., our mutual favorite maybe-murderess who can Houdini her way out of a grave."

"Oh!" Scarlett's voice is shrill. "Well, yes. It's . . . He's . . . We're . . ."

"He loves that stuff."

"*Mmm* . . . We found something about Sadie in Maggie's stuff, but we're not sure. He's looking into what it means."

"He'll figure it out. He's the smartest person I know."

Scarlett looks like she's deliberating something. "So why did you guys split up?"

Cinnamon sighs. "Will and me? Um. We just decided it was time, I guess."

"But you were in love with him," Scarlett presses. "Right?"

"I mean, yeah. Of course."

"So why did you stop?"

Cinnamon exhales through her nose. "It just, like . . . I don't know. We're just different. At the end we argued all the time about the stupidest stuff. And the whole dating thing, eventually we realized it wasn't making us *happy*. We didn't feel it anymore, the same way."

"But you stayed best friends."

"You can fall out of love with someone and still love them."

Scarlett digests this for a minute. "I can't imagine ever falling out of love with someone. But I guess I also haven't done it."

Cinnamon feels for a second how hard Scarlett always tries to understand, even if she can't. A confusing stab of protectiveness pulses through her. "It's weird," she agrees, biting on her thumbnail. "People say love's this fire or whatever, and maybe it is, but I feel like . . . sometimes it sticks, and sometimes it can't."

"Yeah." Scarlett nods quickly. "I think I get that."

They both sit silently for a second.

"What are you gonna do if you guys find her? Sadie, I mean." Cinnamon watches Scarlett's intense face.

"I just feel like it's the key to something," Scarlett says fast. "Her story. It's where it all started, you know? Us. The Mad Princes, et al."

"Why? It's not like it's really gonna change anything. They'll still all be gone, and we'll still be here." Cinnamon stopped believing in stories and legends around the time her parents stopped telling them. She stopped telling her mother when blue ghosts showed up in her dreams or what they said. Sometimes, she believes, the truth is worse than the lie.

"I think if I find her, then I'll know why."

Cinnamon chews her lip. "Maybe try not to get too hung up on it," she says, trying to be not too blunt but also not liking the tightness in Scarlett's eyes or what it will mean later if things go wrong.

"Why?" Scarlett asks. Snaps, really. "Because I can't ever handle knowing what's actually going on?"

Cinnamon backtracks. "*No.* Jesus, you don't have to be so intense about everything all the time."

"So don't be myself, you mean."

Cinnamon stands up and shakes her head. It's gone, whatever softness they had just before. "Be careful is what I meant, actually," she says from the doorway, and heads back upstairs before Scarlett can reply.

15.

Scarlett is maybe properly regularly messaging with Will Taylor. As in, her sister's ex-boyfriend.

It started off as scattered tidbits here and there after discovering Sadie's patient record—memes or occasionally reacting to a story, *Is this happening? Is this a thing? Maybe it's not* sort of things.

There are six notifications sitting on her phone the next day. Six times he was thinking of her; six reasons this is A Bad Idea bordering on The Worst Idea.

It's boiling outside. Scarlett pours a giant glass of water and plops fat ice cubes into it. Then she looks at the notifications again and makes an iced chamomile tea. She heads out the back door to the veranda and sprawls on the deck floor with the breeze washing her face. She clicks Will's name with her thumb and reads all the messages.

> **Pls tell me your day is more interesting than mine**
> **why is it necessary to contribute to the capitalist machine**
> **and yet so unnecessary**
> **WOW WOW okay I take it back**
> **are you sitting down? Bc I am like *99%* sure I just found**
> **something**

Scarlett's heart jumps. She clicks the photo attachment. It's a faded black-and-white picture from an old newspaper article. Grainy faces that he's zoomed in on. A boy and two girls in front of a piano, staring silently through her phone and fifty years. The girl farthest from the left has a sharp bob, pointed chin, and Scarlett's eyes. Underneath, Will said:

Kinda reminds me of you??

Goose bumps rise on Scarlett's arms. She looks from Will's messages to Sadie's eyes and back again. Her hands are numbing, but she's read the message now. She quickly punches in a reply so as not to be rude.

OMG yes, I think that is her—amazing! You're a wizard!

And even though it took Scarlett ages to reply to him, he's right there.

right?? There's more too
. . .
You should come down and see

Scarlett can't breathe.
Can't go.
Can't not.

If you want
. . .
Obviously no pressure or anything

just if you're a "client" I can go through this stuff for hours on the clock :P #cashmoney

Scarlett starts typing four different sentences, backspacing and rewriting. Briefly considers deleting the app altogether.

Sure!! Be there in ten.

She has nothing at all to wear. She spends way too long worrying over it, pulling everything out of her suitcase before finally settling on a denim skirt and vintage cream short-sleeved button-up blouse with roses stitched onto it.

Outside in the sun the skirt feels too short and too tight on her hips, and she starts to worry the roses draw attention to The Chest. She walks fast down the hill before she can look over at the lying graveyard or ask herself what exactly she thinks she's doing. The library is made of sandy brick, old as the town itself and tucked back from the ocean by a row of trees. It gives off nostalgia like perfume. Scarlett used to come here every week of her younger-years summer holidays.

Will is leaning, beaming and blond, against the front desk in a collared shirt when she walks through the doors. Sadie Prince is inside somewhere, waiting to be found. Scarlett can feel the hard beat of her pulse in her neck.

"Why hello, client!" Will calls. "Come on through."

Scarlett waves awkwardly, making a little claw-hand up near her jaw. "Hey."

Will leads the way, weaving them through aisles of books. Scarlett is grateful for the rows of bright spines crowding around them, folding everything in friendly dark.

"I found out another thing just before," Will says over his shoulder.

"Oh?"

Will stops suddenly in front of a door with RECORDS etched on a plaque. Too suddenly. Scarlett almost crashes into him.

"Did you know," he says, "that the first book Arthur Conan Doyle wrote Sherlock Holmes and Dr. Watson into was literally called *A Study in Scarlet*?"

"What?"

"Yep."

Scarlett's mouth makes an O shape. "You just made that up."

"Google it! It's true!" Will says with a laugh. "I mean, apparently the 'Scarlet' in that title is like a metaphor for the insidious red bloody thread of murder in general—which you, Scarlett, clearly are *not*, but—"

Scarlett shakes her head, hot-cheeked laughing too.

They're very close to each other. It's air-conditioned but not enough. There's a sheen of sweat on his face, darkening the stray strands of his hair that fall across his forehead. She realizes she *likes* this—seeing him up close. Much more than she should.

Will looks at her for a second, his expression indecipherable. Then he turns and twists open the door.

They stand in silence for a moment, staring at the computers and filing cabinets full of other people's lives.

Will clears his throat. "So, are you ready for me to blow your mind?"

Scarlett nods. "Show me what you've got."

"Right. Yes!" Will moves toward one of the cabinets against the wall. There's a table in the center of the room surrounded by beige leather chairs. He pulls one of them over to stand on, stretching to the highest drawer and yanking it open.

"These are a bunch of local newspaper clippings from over the years," he explains, thumbing through plastic-wrapped yellow papers. "Federation times, both wars, and . . . the sixties—the time of Sadie's alleged, um . . . you know. My boss keeps originals of *everything*. Like, to a worrying degree. I was on digital cataloging for him last summer too."

"That's so cool," Scarlett finds herself saying; her voice sounds slightly foreign, like when one of her ears is full of water. "To be able to look back over the years like that. And physically see them, I mean."

"*Mmm.* Not all my colleagues think so," Will says. "But I happen to agree. Why rely on foggy memories when you can have the real thing?"

Scarlett feels Will's words the way she felt his eyes in the hallway—warm, everywhere. *Sister's ex-boyfriend. Bad idea. Stop stop stop.* "So then, there was something in the paper about her? Sadie Prince?"

Will nods. "Yep. A few somethings, actually. Just give me a . . . gotcha!" He eases a tissue-wrapped, yellowed piece of paper out and steps back off the chair. Then he holds it out to her, faceup. "I repeat: Is your mind ready to explode?"

Scarlett looks down, expecting to see a headline about Sadie's death or the murder of Robert Hammond.

It's the photo Will sent her earlier, Sadie staring stoically at the camera with wide eyes, dressed full sixties, and sitting with the clean-cut boy and girls at a piano. The paper looks more modern than that, though. There's a byline dated in the nineties and then:

PIANO PRODIGY'S DISAPPEARANCE
HAUNTS LOCALS DECADES LATER

Sadie Prince, musician and daughter of Bill Prince, magnate of the now-sold Prince Wines Estate, was described by her contemporaries as an erratic genius.

Her moods were as legendary as her performance of Tchaikovsky's *Pathétique Symphony* 4th movement at the conservatorium in her teens, but locals in the pianist's seaside hometown still remember her for more sinister reasons.

"I'm glad it's stayed a mystery," said Christopher "Kit" Wembly (pictured, left, in 1965), who attended music lessons with Sadie, about her vanishing from public life in the late 1960s. "It was an awful business. They buried it, of course. But we know the true story. She had the looks but not the talent and underneath she was rotten to the core."

Sadie's nephew, Ian Prince, followed in her musical footsteps, allegedly penning the track "Paper Ghost" about his late aunt. The Princelings are currently touring nationally and refused comment for this story.

"Oh my god," Scarlett says.

"I know."

"'Paper Ghost' is about my *mum*. They wrote letters to each other when he was touring!"

At least, that's what they told you, a voice in her head says.

"And who is this Kit Wembly person? Why would he say, 'I'm glad it's stayed a mystery,' and 'We know the true story'?"

"From what I can gather, Sadie was a better musician than him. They went up for all the same concerts and stuff, and Sadie always won. So there's that. Clearly he took it really well."

Scarlett feels as if the world has slipped its axis under her feet. *Sadie was a brilliant musician, just like Ian. People were glad she was gone.*

Slowly she sits down in one of the chairs. Will pulls out the one opposite her.

"It didn't mention Hillbrook," Scarlett realizes suddenly. "Do you think that means nobody knew?"

"Potentially, yeah."

Scarlett doesn't know why, but she's glad about that. She feels protective of Sadie, or at least of her secrets.

"But the family knew," she says. "Right? They had to. What if they sent her there? Why would they *do* that? And there was no mention of Robert Hammond in the article either."

A confusing mixture of things is swirling through Scarlett, its intensity fuzzing her vision at the edges. Pianos and moods, curses and hospitals.

She looks right at Will.

Will looks at her intently. "You really want to find her, don't you?"

Scarlett slides the paper back toward him. "I have to," she says. "I can't explain it, but I just feel like she's the key to something. I need to know what happened to her."

"I get that," he says. "And I haven't even told you the other mind-blowing part."

"What do you mean?"

Will goes over to a computer in the corner. Scarlett hesitates, then follows.

He's typing something into a search engine. "After you sent me

the admission record from Hillbrook—that name is a misnomer, by the way; the wing where Sadie went was actually called Harmony Hill—I looked up their online records."

"They have those?"

Will turns around, an earnest sort of expression on his face. "Harmony Hill has a pretty sketchy history, especially in the sixties and seventies. They had patients with mental-health issues, but also unmarried mothers and palliative care."

Scarlett feels physically sick. History that shouldn't have happened. "None of that sounds good."

"No," Will agrees, "but it means the present-day Hillbrook Hospital made lots of their records available to the public to try and make amends."

"Did . . . did you find something else?"

Will clicks a link and waits for it to load. "Not exactly. More like, the rest of the thing you found."

"Wha—"

"There." Will points excitedly to the very bottom of the document. "See that signature? The paper copy didn't have the last page."

Scarlett reads.

Discharged into the care of
Elston Hammond

"Oh my god." Scarlett swallows. "Do you think that was a relative of Robert's?"

"I don't know. But I feel like the fact that a Hammond checked her out at all means the story of her murdering Robert on a cliff probably isn't true."

"Oh my *god*!"

Will holds her eyes for a beat. Something flickers between them. "So this is, like, a real-life mystery now," he says, "aka my kryptonite. And I guess what I'm saying is—if you wanna find her, I'm totally in."

Scarlett tries to ignore the bolt of happiness, despite everything she's just read, that spikes through her chest. "Where do we start?"

"WWSD," Will says. "What would Sherlock do?"

"I don't know," she admits. "What would he do?"

"Who was quoted in the article as a witness?"

Scarlett's face falls. "Kit the Misogynist."

"I checked," Will says, "and he's still alive. He lives by the bay."

Scarlett pushes her chair back under the table. "Okay. When do you wanna go see him?" she asks. "Tomorrow?"

Will looks suddenly self-conscious. "It's actually my birthday tomorrow. It sucks being born literally days before Christmas, so I'm kind of, um, having a thing. What about the day after?"

Awkwardness clamps hot hands around them again.

"Oh!" Scarlett trills. "That's fine!" She walks, rapidly, to the door. "You can just let me know his address and I'll go, or—"

"Do you wanna maybe come to it?" Will asks at the same time.

"What?"

"My party. It's at your house, actually, but I don't know if Cinnamon . . ."

Scarlett feels searingly awkward again. "No. She didn't."

"Well, *I'm* inviting you. And I'm the birthday boy. So now you have to come."

"The birthday boy?" Scarlett smiles despite her slippery heart.

"Yeah, as soon as I said it, I was like, no, I hate it," Will apologizes with a grin. "I am the guest of honor, though. So, will you?"

"I . . . Sure."

"Cool! We can plot our trip to Wembly's house then. It'll all be very Holmes and Watson, only with beer."

"Ha," says Scarlett, who's never had a drink in her life. "Okay. As long as I'm Watson."

"Please. You're Robert Downey Junior Holmes."

"I thought it was Henry Cavill."

"Right! Exactly. The point is, you're Holmes and I'm Watson."

"Disagree."

"Agree to disagree." Will's smile lights up his whole face, so bright it hurts to look at.

"Deal."

16.

Cinnamon's next shift with Daisy Leung is painful for different reasons than before. It's better in some ways. More comfortable. They greet one another when they clock in. They make small talk. It's fine, all of this is fine. Except Cinnamon can still feel white Converse tucked under her thigh.

Boys, for her, are a look across the room, a nod, and a warm rush of a feeling. Girls are an image she has to store to analyze later in phases—hair-hands-smell-smile. She can be friends with them, though. Even fascinating ones who wear overalls with no actual top underneath.

It's quiet tonight, customer-wise. Daisy is methodically putting the dinner plates through the dishwasher to prep for all the holiday bookings, while Cinnamon sits behind the counter folding cloth napkins into truly awful swans. Daisy's wearing the sort of dark, complicated perfume that sometimes makes Cinnamon notice people on the street, just for a second.

They're chatting back and forth.

So far Cinnamon has learned that Daisy really does love her parents, who met at university when her mum was on exchange in Hong Kong and her dad still lived there and then moved to Melbourne, where Daisy's mum's family lived in the nineties, and Daisy hates it when people ask her where *she* is from. Daisy drinks tea in the afternoons and never speaks ill of anyone ever, and in her final year of school, she got really good at painting stuff on the back of old denim jackets like the one she wears home from work sometimes on cool-clear nights that says *YES MANY AND BEAUTIFUL THINGS*.

Daisy has several exes in her hometown whom she mentions in passing, always good-naturedly and without being mean—or gender specific.

Not that gender isn't a construct anyway—it totally is.

Not that Cinnamon *wants to know.*

Daisy is telling her now that she's named by legacy of her grandmothers, because she asked Cinnamon about her name. Cinnamon told her how Maggie suggested it because Amy put it on everything when she was pregnant, and when they looked at her newborn raisin-face, they thought Cinnamon Margaret must be her name.

"Wait, both your grandmothers are called Daisy?" Cinnamon asks too emphatically, but whatever, because they have things in common and they're talking. She realizes, in a hyperpresent way, that her heart is beating very fast and maybe has been for several hours.

Daisy shakes her head. "My dad calls me my Chinese name, which my grandma chose, and then my mum kind of went all out on my other formal names. Daisy's a nickname for the first one, which was after Mum's mum, who died."

"Your *formal* names?" Cinnamon asks. "Shock. Intrigue."

"It's really not. And it's not even that bad, it's just kind of . . . Actually, you know what, I don't think—"

"D-Leung," Cinnamon cuts in, and uh-oh—weird nickname. "Chill. My name comes from a literal spice rack."

"Adelaide May Ling Elise."

"That's not even that long." Cinnamon repeats it back, carefully, to show she understands.

Daisy gets the strangest expression on her face. Happy-sad.

Cinnamon has a sudden urge to trace Daisy's features with her fingertips—the way a tiny shift of the smooth space between her eyebrows can mean an entirely different thing.

She's learning to read it.

She thinks.

"What?"

"I don't usually tell people my full name," Daisy says, like she's confessing something but isn't sure what. "It feels . . . weird."

"Oh." Cinnamon's insides drop. "Weird how?"

"Like, kind of an exchange of power, or something."

"Oh," Cinnamon says again.

"But I like you saying it."

All the heat surges back into Cinnamon's body. "Yeah?"

Daisy nods, and her face blooms. "Yeah."

They're interrupted when Tony walks in the back door, announcing, "I've decided what to do for my annual NYE party."

Daisy looks up, blinking. "Ooh!"

Tony nods. "Yep. And I want you both to come."

"That's so nice, but I don't know if I'm . . ." Daisy tells Tony.

At the same time Cinnamon says, "What? Why?" She didn't go last year.

Tony's eyes widen. He steps forward dramatically, until he's standing between the two of them with his arms around their shoulders. He smells like chicken salt and BO. "You guys are two of my best friends! Of course I want you there." He holds them there, leaning on their shoulders and watching their faces expectantly.

Cinnamon presses her lips together, not looking at Daisy. "Um. Thanks, man. We, uh, wouldn't miss it."

Tony lets them go, clapping his hands together and grinning. "Yes! *So good.* Okay. I'm gonna clock out early, and then I'm going to visit my pops for Christmas, but I'll see you guys at the party!"

Cinnamon waves the tea towel in her hand. "See ya."

"Oh!" Tony says from the doorway. "Bee-tee-dubbs—it's *Frozen* themed."

"Aw, like a winter wonderland?" Daisy asks.

Tony pulls a face. "No. Like the movie. Bye!" The heavy door clunks shut behind him.

"Don't," Daisy warns.

And Cinnamon says, "Don't what?"

And then they look at each other, and suddenly they're cracking up. Their laughter fills the room—brilliant and huge—until Daisy's eyes run with mascara and Cinnamon has to sit down again to breathe.

"*Frozen?*" Cinnamon asks.

"My *pops?*" Daisy demands helplessly.

Cinnamon shakes her head. "God, I love that guy."

"We definitely have to go to that," Daisy says. She doesn't even pause beforehand, says it like the "we" is nothing.

Maybe it is.

"*Definitely.*" Cinnamon smirks.

Daisy smiles back, eyes and cheeks and everything impossibly bright.

Maybe it's not.

"Speaking of parties," Cinnamon says, unable to stop herself, the brightness drawing her in. "What are you doing tomorrow night?"

"I invited her to the party thing," Cinnamon tells Will on the phone later.

"*My* party? Whomst?"

"Daisy. It just came out."

"You mean like you came out? Sorry, I couldn't resist."

"Did I officially come out, do we think?"

"Yeah! After the Beth thing, I said, 'Do you think maybe . . . ?' and then you said, 'Yeah probably.'"

"Okay. That doesn't count."

"It totally does! We had a beautiful moment. A moment that I *treasure*. I sent you the link to that T-shirt that said 'bi the way' on it."

"Can we circle back to the fact that I maybe asked Perfect Daisy out, please? I'm casually dying here."

She can hear the smile in Will's voice. "You did *what*?" he demands in mock indignation. "Also, sidenote. Can we talk for a second about how lucky you are that I'm—"

"Currently having a three-way with your PlayStation and your phone? Can your Discord bros spare you for a second? Don't think I can't hear that you haven't even pressed pause."

"*Awake*, is what I was gonna say. It's one a.m."

"Is it?" Cinnamon checks her phone screen. She's been sitting on the balcony for almost an hour. "God."

"*Mmm*. So, Perfect Daisy?"

She listens to the sounds of Will's game in the background and looks out ahead of her to avoid answering his question. The sea is silver underneath prickly stars.

"I mean. I don't know why I bothered," she says eventually. "I don't even know if she's . . . And, like, it's not as if she'll actually come."

"*Mmm.*" Something in Will's game goes *zoosh*.

Cinnamon pictures herself stuck to his shoulder while he kills ninjas or whatever, his ear going red from the heat of the phone. Then the image is replaced by Daisy's white shoes. "I just . . ."

Will's end of the phone crackles with movement, and she hears the ping of him pressing pause. "What?"

"I don't *know*," Cinnamon insists, because she does know.

Will just says, "Sure you don't."

"I—"

"Go to bed, C-3PO. Everything makes more sense after sleep."

"But—"

"I'll see you tomorrow."

He hangs up before she can protest. Exhaustion and years of habit prompt her to do as he says, pausing only to savagely brush her teeth and throw her work clothes into the laundry.

She crawls into bed and lies there shivering in her underwear, moon-cold air poking through the window. It's only because she's trying not to that she's still thinking about Daisy. There was a scuff on the toe of one of her white shoes today—a smudge on the logo and another mark on the tongue.

How did that happen?

Why does Cinnamon want to know?

17.

Scarlett dreams about Sadie. It's the sort of rolling nightmare she used to get a lot when she was at school. The kind that continues after she wakes up and falls asleep again, bringing her back to exactly where she left off, on a loop until she wakes up for good, all sweaty and gross and having forgotten what's real for a second.

In the dream, Sadie is surrounded by blue-green water. She's swimming, far out in the surf past the jetty—at the edge of the bay, farther out even than Maggie would go—but she has this look on her face like she doesn't want to be there. And the jetty is keys on a piano.

Then the scene flips, and Scarlett *is* Sadie, swimming and swimming but not getting closer to shore, and no one can see her. Then she's the one watching again, desperately saying *Look! There! Help her! Someone help!* Then Sadie's face switches to Maggie's—and back and back and back again.

When she finally gets out of bed and realizes none of it was real, Scarlett can't shake the false memory of swimming. She opens her blinds and lets too-bright light flood the room in a buttery tidal wave, taking no chances with letting herself fall back to sleep. Her phone is plugged into its charger on her desk—she picks it up and flops back down on the bed.

Niamh hasn't texted her all summer. The thought flits through Scarlett's mind, before she bats it away. Instagram is still open from before she went to bed last night. So is the online yellow pages, where she found an address for Christopher Wembly, piano teacher. She sent it to Will and said:

I don't know if I'm ready to see him

To which he straightaway replied:

yeah, fair.
we can talk about it @ party, if you want :)

After rereading their conversation and silently judging her own reply (**sounds good!!!**), Scarlett clicks on the story Will posted this morning. It's an intentionally bad photo of him holding coffee and pulling a weird Victorian-era-family-photo sort of face, captioned *BIRTHDAY BOI*.

She stares at the words, wondering-wondering-wondering what they mean. That was their inside joke, wasn't it? *Was it?* Should she wish him happy birthday? Have the straight two hours of nightmares utterly scrambled her brain?

Quickly, deciding it's too early to trust herself with anything else, she does a clapping hands react before letting her phone drop to the floor.

Amy is outside when Scarlett comes downstairs, walking along the back veranda and holding a gently smoldering bowl of flowers and herbs. Amy always makes these when she's at Halcyon. When Scarlett eases the sliding door open and walks out, eucalyptus and lavender and cedar and frankincense and sage waft over her.

Ian and Cinnamon are both still asleep. Amy and Scarlett were always the early risers—it comforts her for a minute, thinking that in this one and only regard, the Princes are probably just like any other family.

"Morning, darling heart." Amy smiles, turning to douse the top of Scarlett's head in sweet-smelling smoke.

"Morning. What are you doing?"

"Oh, you know. Cleansing." Amy gestures to a second bowl on the balcony railing next to her.

Inside the bowl are two little pieces of paper. On each, Scarlett knows, is a name. "Cleansing what?"

Amy tucks her hair behind her ears. The strap of her green maxi-dress is falling off her shoulder. She looks tired, Scarlett thinks, but in a regular way—not the Ian kind. Tired like she did when she asked both girls to come live with her in the city, and Cinnamon said no.

"Work stuff," Amy says, pulling the strap of her dress up and moving her smudge stick over the bowl. "One of my older authors is being a bit of a prick."

Amy is an editor for a new-age publishing house. She used to do it freelance, but then they took her on part-time. Scarlett has read a few of her books, even though she's not exactly the target demographic.

"What's the problem with them?" Scarlett asks, shielding her face from the morning sun. "The author, I mean?"

"Him. Just disagreements. Men. Heels digging in. Darlings refusing to be killed. Higher-ups getting antsy. The usual stuff."

Scarlett doesn't ask about the second name in the bowl. Instead she hands her mother the faded silver gas lighter from the table.

Amy clicks it with her thumb and puts the flame in the bowl.

Scarlett watches the papers catch fire, flaring orange and gray, then curling in on themselves until both the names are gone. She hears Maggie's and Amy's voices in her head from when she was small and they'd occasionally do this, and first taught her how. *Write the name of someone you want to break your emotional attachment to on a piece of paper, set fire to it in a bowl until it's ash, and blow the pieces away into the wind.*

It's not a spell, exactly—but it helps, in Scarlett's experience. Even if it's just a placebo kind of thing.

(There's a proper one that's worse, which Scarlett has never tried: *Put your enemy's name in the freezer if you really want to curse them; include a mirror, so the curse doesn't rebound.*)

"Can I do one?" she asks when Amy tips the burnt contents of the bowl into the air.

"Who?" Amy asks, turning back around.

Scarlett thinks about Niamh again. She did say she was spending Christmas skiing with her family, and they weren't exceptionally close friends, but still. She gets as far as writing Niamh's first and middle names, then feels petty and mean and even lonelier than before. She crosses it out and writes *Kit Wembly* instead, figuring she can use as much help as she can get with that one.

Really she should write *sister's ex-boyfriend Will*. Then maybe she'd stop thinking about seeing him tonight. Or getting anxious-excited about it already, even now.

Amy is watching her face intently. "Ready?"

"As I ever am," Scarlett says, and they watch the name disappear.

18.

The day of the party, Daisy texts earlyish and asks Cinnamon to go shopping with her to find a present for Will. Cinnamon deliberates for an hour, staring at her phone so hard she starts to get a headache. Then she replies:

👍

Ugh.

Daisy picks her up at ten o'clock on the dot, parking down the street like Cinnamon asked her to. She never brings people up to the house first go. Daisy is in a tiny yellow car that fits her perfectly and not much else. Her hair's gathered into two buns on either side of her head, brown-and-pink bangs falling into her eyes when she steps out. "Cinnamon Prince." She grins like they're partners in crime. "We meet again."

"Hey. We do."

Getting into the car is weird—stiff movements and smiles, Daisy opening Cinnamon's door for her, then letting her hands flutter back down to her sides. Cinnamon imagines Halcyon watching them from the cliff with black amused window-eyes.

Cinnamon folds her high-waisted-baggy-jeans-covered legs up near her ears in the passenger seat and watches the world flash past outside her window, yellow-gray-blue. She thinks in a sudden riot that she should have worn a better shirt. Her orange crop tee is plain, and there's a bleach stain on the neck that didn't feel like a big deal at home and now does.

Does that matter, if they're just friends?

Daisy is wearing jeans too, flared ones, with a watermelon-pink corset-y blouse on top and platform Docs sandals in shiny black. The drive is quiet. Cinnamon hates talking while driving; she wonders if Daisy's the same.

Downtown tapers off and there's a silent sun-soaked stretch of time when they're surrounded by trees. Daisy fiddles with the controls on the car radio until it lands on a Taylor Swift song from the new album that keeps repeating the word *daylight*. She makes a little *sorry* sort of face, and changes it.

Cinnamon wants to say, *No, I want to know what you like*, so forcefully that she can't say anything. She's never been good at this sort of stuff: feelings, friendships, other people generally.

Are they friends?

She's still thinking about it when they pull to a stop in the shopping center parking lot and Daisy reaches out to grab the ticket from the machine, then holds it between her teeth. Cinnamon has to silently admit she doesn't know what they are.

They walk inside to bright lights and air-conditioning blasting their exposed limbs.

Christmas shoppers jostle past and Cinnamon hugs her arms across her chest.

"So," Daisy starts, clearing her throat and turning to look at Cinnamon. "Your Will—what sort of stuff does he like? You'll have to guide me."

Cinnamon almost smiles. "It's Will. He'll like whatever."

"Okay, that helps me precisely not at all."

Cinnamon shrugs. "He prefers moments to things. It's one of his many mantras."

Daisy makes a soft scoffing sound.

"I'm very aware of how annoying that is," Cinnamon agrees. "In the context of a birthday."

"I mean, kind of. Yes!" Daisy laughs, and Cinnamon thinks, *This is fine, this is good*.

They're talking—she's making whole words happen.

Then Daisy says, "What did *you* do? When you . . . You dated him, right?"

Cinnamon looks up so sharply she gets the headache feeling again. This is the first time Daisy has asked her a question like this. She coughs, trying to gather the bolt of her thoughts before answering. "Uh—yeah. In school."

"And how did you give him *moments* for his birthday?" Daisy teases. "Is that, like, a euphemism?"

"No," Cinnamon says, too fast. She plunges her hands into her pockets. "We weren't . . . We just used to spend the day doing stuff he liked. Board games, etcetera." They still do all those things, but that doesn't feel relevant in this particular moment.

Daisy raises her eyebrows suggestively—they disappear behind her baby-pink bangs. "Sure."

The two of them walk past a department store and decide with a shared look not to go in.

Cinnamon feels weirdly exposed, under these lights, in her cropped top.

"So why did you two break up?" Daisy continues. "I wondered, just because—you know, it seems like you're still so close." She laughs self-consciously at the expression on Cinnamon's face. "Sorry! You don't have to answer."

"No, it's just . . ." Cinnamon sighs. "Everyone always asks me that. I never know what to say."

Especially to you.

Daisy hums thoughtfully.

"'Cause it's not like I can tell them the truth."

I don't want to tell you.

Daisy's forehead creases. "Why not?"

Cinnamon's chest is tight, and she realizes she's going to tell Daisy the full truth. "Um, because in a breakup there's always an arsehole, and it was definitely me?"

Daisy raises her eyebrows again. "Interesting. I don't think I can picture you being an arsehole."

"Seriously? I feel like that's the number-one word people use to describe me."

Daisy shakes her head. "Please. There's a big difference between 'guarded' and 'arsehole.'"

Cinnamon considers this. Thinks about Daisy thinking of her as "guarded." Thinks about Daisy thinking about her full stop, and then has to stop because it clogs up her throat.

"I wanted out first," she says. "I mean, I did love him . . . *do* love him, but after a while when we were dating it wasn't—we wanted really different things, life-wise, so it was all kind of a mess." *God.* She widens her eyes at herself. Thinks stingingly about the time she told him she never wants to be anyone's wife or anyone's mother or maybe anyone's anything. "And, yeah. That's why we broke up. So it was my bad."

"That must've been really hard," Daisy says eventually.

Cinnamon's eyebrows scrunch together. "That's it? You don't think I'm an evil hag?"

Daisy shrugs. "We can't choose who we love or how we love them. That's the whole entire point, surely."

Cinnamon just stares at her. For an inappropriately long time.

"What?" Daisy asks, laughing again.

"Nothing."

"I do feel a strange need to get him something really good now, though," Daisy says, grinning. "To compensate."

"For me being an arsehole?" Cinnamon says.

"For you being human," Daisy corrects her. "C'mon."

They're approaching the newer part of the center, where all the gift stores are, expensive and niche with their artisanal signs and sugary-diffuser smells. Daisy steers her toward one by linking an arm through hers.

Cinnamon freezes, then unfreezes. She's always found this practice try-hard and uncomfortable with other people—cementing something as wispy as friendship with trite PDAs—but when Daisy does it, it's just warm. Like, *Come here, look at this, walk with me.*

They stay that way through five whole shops, until Cinnamon's wrist is on fire, and Daisy picks out a thick Renaissance philosophy book for Will.

They drive back in radio silence. Daisy parks closer to Halcyon this time—daringly far up the big hill. The house always seems creepier in gray light. Daisy's bright artist's eyes gaze back at it differently from the way most people's do, though. Like it's a worthy opponent, or maybe a puzzle she wants to solve. It's not dissimilar to the look she gives Cinnamon sometimes.

"Jesus. This is where you live?" she asks.

"Uh-huh."

Daisy leans forward in her seat, squinting at the sea and then back up to the stark-white, giant-windowed house. "Do you *own* the beach?"

Cinnamon snorts. "No. You can't own a beach."

"Are you like . . . rich, Cinnamon Prince?"

She shakes her head. "My family used to own vineyards, but they sold them in the seventies. They built this house way back when we were rich-*ish*, and the town was just beginning."

"Can I see it?"

Cinnamon looks down at Daisy's hand resting on the gear stick. Impulsively, she lets hers brush against it as she leans over to open her door. "Come on."

The ocean is louder once they step out of the car. The clouds part, but the water holds on to their color, turquoise gray gleaming up from the waves as Cinnamon and Daisy crunch across the gravel to the edge of the cliff.

The two of them look at Princes Beach spread out below them.

Cinnamon watches a stray strand of bubble-gum-colored hair play along Daisy's jaw, then looks away again when Daisy catches her staring.

Storm clouds are brewing on the horizon, dark as a day-old bruise. Whitewash slaps at the rocks below. *The end of the world*, she thinks but doesn't say.

"Do you swim here?" Daisy asks.

Cinnamon's hands ball into fists at the painful memory, but then she's talking, letting it out. "My nan did. She used to swim every morning. Sometimes right out to the point. We'd always be scared that she wouldn't come back." She stops. It's too easy to do this when they're together: say too much.

Daisy smiles faintly. "My grandma hates ocean swimming. She asks why anyone would want to offer themselves up to a shark."

"Mine died," Cinnamon says bluntly, then cringes at herself so hard that it hurts. "Last year," she clarifies, her voice rough.

"Oh. I'm sorry."

"*Mmm*." Cinnamon nods tersely. She'll be lucky if they're friends at all, after today.

"You don't have to tell me about it." Daisy's face is soft. "But also, you can."

"Alzheimer's." Cinnamon says the word for the first time in months. She stares ahead at the bleed of blue into blue. "It was . . . I stopped swimming after that."

It scares her, all at once—the way Daisy listening makes her run her mouth off instead of running away.

The clouds over them move thickly, and it starts to rain.

"Ah!" Daisy looks at her, strands of hair turning darker pink around her wet, sympathetic face. The droplets splashing on their heads intensify into a full-blown shower, and the sea twists into a gray roar below.

"This is what we hardened locals call a squall," Cinnamon says.

"A *what*?"

Cinnamon imitates Tony's voice. "As in: *batten down the hatches, it's the squalls!*"

Daisy laughs and grabs Cinnamon's hand, and they walk-then-run back down the hill to the car.

Their shoes slip on wet gravel, and Cinnamon grips Daisy's fingers tighter, enjoying it suddenly—the heavens coming down on top of them, the carefree sound in her throat. She thinks that if she saw herself from a distance right now, she wouldn't know who it was.

Or maybe she'd know exactly who.

Maybe.

Daisy shuts Cinnamon's door, then crashes back into the driver's seat, laughing and slamming her own door closed. She's soaked through, water streaking her eyeliner, glittering down her throat, beading on top of her makeup like dew.

Cinnamon laughs too, even though she doesn't know why. She's breathless. And cold. She pulls her top unstuck from her skin.

Daisy is . . . also cold. Cinnamon very purposely doesn't look in the direction of the soaked blouse on her chest, because she's not the male gaze. She's not.

Rain batters the windshield, droplets trapping light and racing each other down the glass.

"Wow," Daisy says, leaning her head back. "You must love it here."

Cinnamon considers this for a second. "Yeah. But I always thought I'd leave as soon as I grew up. See the rest of the world."

Daisy tips her head to the side. "Why didn't you?"

It's more *tell me* than a real questioning of Cinnamon's (lack of) life choices. Somehow that makes the jump of her pulse even worse.

"Sometimes," Cinnamon says, trying to pull her thoughts into words, "I feel like if I want something, then that means I can't have it. Or shouldn't. Like I don't deserve it, or wanting it will push it away. But then I just end up doing nothing, and feeling like . . ."

"Like what?"

"Like I'm becoming the nothing."

Daisy makes a faint humming sound.

"I don't know," says Cinnamon. "Is that really weird?"

"No. I don't think it's weird at all."

Cinnamon takes a breath. "I think it's part of why I deferred my BA."

"Because you wanted it?"

"Yeah." Cinnamon watches two raindrops get stuck together, wrapping around each other and slipping down the windshield in a silver rush.

"Wanting something isn't a bad thing," Daisy says. "I mean, to know what you want is to be human, and all that. The happiest and bitterest part."

"Did you just hit me with surprise-attack Pablo Neruda?"

"Paraphrasing, but yes."

Cinnamon closes her eyes and briefly fights off what is potentially a stroke. She does want things, this second—in a sharp, devouring way—and uni is pretty freaking far down the list.

"So you know you deserve to have things, right?" Daisy says. The entire car smells like her—rose and amber and sandalwood and raspberry and cloves.

Cinnamon looks at her. Her cheeks are faintly pink, wet hair still clinging to them.

Daisy stares back—steely and bright. "Not to presume! But just, like, in case you needed to hear it. You deserve to have whatever you want."

Cinnamon wonders how such a person even comes to be. She'd like to climb into Daisy's head now. Run her hands over the lines of Daisy's thoughts to see exactly how they knit together. *Exactly*. She needs to know that.

She needs to know everything.

"Do you wanna maybe come inside?"

"Cinnamon Beach-Baron Prince." Daisy grins, and the full name thing is—yeah, Cinnamon might die. "I thought you'd never ask."

19.

Will's party kicks off at six. Scarlett spends most of the afternoon thinking she can't go. For one, she has nothing to wear. Again. All her clothes are what-was-she-thinking hideous.

Secondly, she's lying upside down on her bed holding a tattered copy of *Persuasion*, and it's getting too good to just stop (re)reading, even while listening to the sounds of her family moving around the house. Ian's voice is more prominent than usual today, a proper conversation rather than just one-word answers to Amy's prodding.

Cinnamon went out somewhere earlier, but she's back now, and there's a girl in her room. At first Scarlett thought it was Phoebe Mendis, but their talking is too close to a bearable volume for it to be Phe. Scarlett also thought she heard the unknown girl say "your sister" just now, but she was probably imagining it.

Thinking about Cinnamon makes her anxious, and the words on the page blur together and vibrate across her vision, meaningless, so she goes back to listening to her parents.

"Dinner!" Amy is saying. "And then I thought we could stay the night at the beach motel or somewhere."

"I don't know, Aimes."

"Dinner will be fun. I'll make sure of it. You know I will."

"I don't feel like going anywhere."

"She'll hate it if we're here. C'mon, it'll be—"

"Amy!" Ian says sharply. "Stop."

Scarlett freezes. They mustn't know her door is open, because then her dad says in a voice she's never heard, "Sorry, it's just . . . It feels *pointless*, Aimes. Like I'm weighing you all down."

Amy hisses, soft but firm, "Do not speak like that, okay? Ever. Because it's not true."

There's something blocking air from getting past Scarlett's throat. She pictures Doctor Marnie. *Look at three things.* The window, the walls, her hands. *Touch three things.* The bedspread, the wooden bedside table, her clothes on the floor.

By the time she's trying to smell three things, Scarlett's breathing has almost slowed back to normal. She closes her eyes, feeling air fill her chest for a few minutes and thinking like she does every time that she won't take it for granted ever, ever again—even though she knows she will.

As though she's mum-read Scarlett's mind, Amy appears in the doorway. "Darling, you're not even dressed! Cinnamon's gathering starts soon."

Scarlett sits up slowly. "Um. I don't know what to wear."

Amy steps into the room, closing the door behind her and clapping her ringed hands together. "Right, then. Let's strategize. What are the options?"

Scarlett tries to read whether her father is okay by scanning her mother's face. Amy absorbs everything but gives nothing away. When she sometimes imagines her mother as a teenager, Scarlett always pictures her determined and brilliant, and worries whether she would've been her friend or hated her.

Scarlett can be determined too. She wants to talk to Will about Kit Wembly. She has to go tonight—she *can*.

She can.

"These." She points to the outfits strewn beside her suitcase.

"Excellent!" Amy says, smiling. "I love the blue."

Half an hour later, Scarlett is dressed in a black turtleneck T-shirt and a navy velvet pencil skirt. It clings to all the places on her body.

Amy helps with her makeup, producing a dark-plum lipstick and violet eye shadow pot from her bag. "There," she says when they're done. "Perfect."

"I'm not sure if—" Scarlett starts to say. Then she hears Will's voice downstairs. At least, she thinks it's Will.

She stuffs her feet into the one pair of high heels that she owns—T-strap Mary Janes (also navy blue)—and stumbles her way toward the landing, holding on to the banister for support.

There's definitely a blond boy at the foot of the stairs. Other people are already here—it's after six, too far after. She took too long. Scarlett focuses on descending gracefully but wobbles on her heels. It's like the *Pretty Woman* makeover reveal, only worse.

"Hello!" says the boy politely when she's in front of him.

It's Will but not Will. This version is taller—older maybe, though not by much. His hair is the same as Will's, but his face is different in tiny but fundamental ways. More angular, a longer chin, longer nose, slightly wider mouth. He's also much better dressed than she's ever seen Will, in an expensive-looking button-up shirt over pressed black pants and tan-colored boots. His watchband matches his shoes.

"I'm Ollie." He smiles. "You must be Scarlett."

The music switches on around them, too loud, pulsing through the floorboards under her feet. Scarlett doesn't feel good. "Er," she says. "Yep!"

"I've heard a lot about you," he adds. His face is kind. His voice is deep and smooth. Will's brother. She's sure she's met him in passing before. But the room is warping around him, and she's wondering what *a lot* means. If he's mentally comparing her to her sister, like people sometimes very obviously do.

"Oh, thanks. You too!" Her lungs start twisting in on themselves, and Scarlett barely has time to politely excuse herself before she turns on her heel and goes back to her bedroom, falling backward on the bed with her shoes on and the door tightly closed.

She grabs *Persuasion* from her bedside table and flips it open to the good bit—Anne reading Wentworth's letter, when he says, "I am half agony, half hope." Her eyes sting. She reads.

20.

Will's party kicks off at six. Cinnamon spends longer than usual getting ready, changing her pants three times in the wardrobe.

Daisy Leung is sitting cross-legged on her bed.

"That is a lot of books over there," Daisy says of the shelves on the opposite wall when Cinnamon finally emerges wearing her black boyfriend-cut jeans.

Boyfriend—shit. She needs to write in Will's card.

"Ha. You should see my sister's room. Or my mother's entire apartment."

Daisy looks up from scanning the wall-to-wall bookshelves Ian built years ago. Her eyes run down the length of Cinnamon's legs—noting the change of pants and probably thinking it's weird, Cinnamon decides.

Probably.

"Is she here, your sister? I'd like to meet her."

Cinnamon feels her nose scrunch up. She turns away and rummages through her drawers for something to cover her arms if it rains more later.

"Wow." Daisy laughs. "That is a *face*."

"We're not close," Cinnamon says.

"I *see*. Interesting." Daisy comes over to stand by Cinnamon's side in front of the dressing table mirror, so close her breath hits Cinnamon's shoulder. "You should wear this." She picks up a black mesh shirt that's half hanging out of the top drawer and hands it to Cinnamon.

"I . . . thanks," Cinnamon says, and pulls it on without buttoning it up, so that it drapes over her hips.

"Cute." Daisy nods approvingly, smiling.

Cinnamon blinks at her and stores this away to die over later. Then they head downstairs. Daisy bumps into Cinnamon, their hips touching before she holds the ornate wooden banister and smile-bites her lip.

Phe wanted to decorate and Will didn't, so the downstairs entryway is bare and clean—but Amy, in her Amy-ness, has added a colored disco ball and pumped a few helium balloons, both left over from Ian's last big party.

It's after six—guests are starting to arrive, voices coming from the driveway.

Cinnamon is thinking about maybe gathering up some of the balloons and floating them back up the stairs when the doorbell rings.

"FOR HEEEE'S A JOLLY GOOD—oh! Hello." Will's eyes widen when the door swings open and he bounds into the entryway and sees Cinnamon and Daisy, but he recovers fast. "New friend Daisy! Glad you could make it."

Daisy smiles self-consciously. "I hope it's okay that I'm crashing."

"Oh, please," Phe says from behind Will, out of breath from the pile of presents she's holding. "It's more than okay. It's magnificent! And so are *you*, CP. My god. Who is this sexy mesh fantasy?"

Cinnamon rolls her eyes. "Very funny."

137

"I'm being one hundred percent serious, babe. Why do you never dress this well for me? Don't you love me?"

Shut up, Cinnamon says with her eyes. "Are you already drunk?"

Will laughs. "Somewhat. Doesn't bode well."

"I can hear you!" Phe calls from where she's moved into the living room to not-inconspicuously-at-all unravel multicolored streamers from her purse. "Pre-drinks don't count!"

"Happy birthday," Cinnamon tells Will, pulling him into a hug out of reflex. His long limbs wrap around her and squeeze. It's still weird—them hugging.

It still never feels like nothing.

"Thanks, C-3PO," Will says, warm into the crook of her neck.

When they pull apart, Daisy is watching them.

"We got you a present today," Cinnamon says over the silence and the breath caught in her throat.

Will digs his hands into his pockets. He's wearing checked pants, a white T-shirt, and white sneakers—effort, for him. "Oh yeah? Hit me."

Daisy holds one of her forearms with the opposite hand. "Um. I think it's still upstairs."

Will waves his hand. "Oh! Don't worry about it—I'll just go get it later." Pause. "Which is to say, uh, Cinnamon will. From . . . her room."

Cinnamon looks from Daisy to Will and back again. She feels as if she's miscalculated something important but isn't sure what. She desperately scans the arriving guests for a distraction and spots a familiar blond head. "You didn't tell me," she says in a dramatic voice, "that your godforsaken brother was coming."

"Oh. Yeah." Will does a strained little laugh and calls Ollie over from where he's talking to Phe with his arm around the waist of a dark-haired boy.

"Hey, hey!" Ollie says, smiling wide. His eyes flick over to Daisy very fast and then back again. "This is Luke. Luke, this is my little brother. The boring Gap version of me. And this is our host, Cinnamon Prince."

Luke waves. "Hi, all. Great house."

"Shame about the host though." Will's voice is joking, but still weirdly formal.

"So very pleased to meet you, Luke," Cinnamon says, then turns back to Ollie, who is standing beside Will and analyzing her and Daisy without looking like he is. He's going to text her about this later—she can see it in his eyes. "They really let you out of Canberra?" she teases as another distraction. "Just, like, let you have uni holidays like everyone else? Do they not know who you are?"

Ollie snorts. "Literally. It's like how they won't let you in?"

Cinnamon frowns and gives him the finger. Ollie gives her a one-armed *I'm kidding* hug while she tries to pull away.

"Someone has to stay here and keep the town's *thriving* café culture thriving," Will says mock-seriously. "Don't hate because that someone is us."

"It's not much," Cinnamon joins in when Ollie lets her go. "But it's honest work."

Ollie laughs again and rolls his eyes. "Be careful of these two," he says warmly to Daisy, who hasn't said a word since present-gate. "They're the worst."

Cinnamon suddenly needs a drink. Any drink, even water, because water is not *here*.

"Oi!" Phe calls from the living room. "Pull your heads out of your arses please, people. These streamers aren't gonna hang themselves."

"I thought I said absolutely no streamers," Will calls.

Ollie pats Will on the shoulder and walks into the living room, pulling Luke with him. "We'll help!"

🗝

Later Halcyon is a thudding pulse of lights and music.

People from school crowd the living room, dancing and laughing. People who moved away but are back for Christmas catch up with their friends over drinks in the kitchen. High schoolers drink too much too fast and then clog up the bathrooms.

The rain stays away, but clouds hang in threat, a curtain of humidity sheening everyone in sweat. Will holds a cider and plays host for a while, before hanging off to the side with Phe.

"He hates parties," Cinnamon tells Daisy while she's getting them drinks from the kitchen. She has to stop talking about Will, she knows that, but she also has to talk about *something*. They've been mostly quiet for the last thirty minutes—the easy atmosphere of the two of them in her room earlier is like-it-never-happened gone.

Her phone buzzes. Ollie.

ma'am that chemistry legit gave me sunburn back there pls explain

"Why have one, then?" Daisy asks.

where are you guys? you can run but you can't hide

Cinnamon shoves her phone away and thinks for a second, music spilling through her veins. "Nothing really happens here, so we all kind of take any opportunity to . . . gather? Especially Phe. This was mostly her idea."

Daisy looks outside, where Phe is trying to make Will dance to a song by a female rapper by forcibly moving his arms up and down. "You don't say."

Cinnamon stares at her in the half-dark of the kitchen. Daisy's hair dried differently after they got caught in the rain. She took it down a while ago, and it's sitting wavy on her shoulders. Pink-silver-purple-black-brown. "Um, do you wanna go for a walk, or something?"

"*Yes,*" Daisy says. "Sorry! I mean, I just kind of hate parties too."

Cinnamon's insides blanch. "God, sorry. You can go if you want."

"No, I want to be here! Just not *here*, here."

Cinnamon laughs. "Okay, a different sort of here, coming right up."

Daisy laughs too, and they disappear together out the door and down the set of stairs beside the deck.

Cinnamon leads the way through the backyard—across the wet grass and past the people clustered in groups by the side fence. The moon is stuck behind clouds, which makes things brighter somehow, like the sky is backlit.

"Wait, is that . . . are those *graves* in your backyard?" Daisy asks, stopping to look.

Cinnamon links their arms together—trying to be brave and make up for hugging Will earlier—and pulls. "Yep. Don't question it."

The sounds of the party are sucked away. They walk to the edge of the cliff, stopping almost where they did earlier, except now the horizon's flat black.

"Now what?" Daisy asks.

Cinnamon pulls her again, steering them toward the rickety stairs that lead down to the sand. An impulse fireworks its way through her—she drops Daisy's arm and reaches down to unlace her shoes.

Daisy looks wildly at her for a second and starts doing the same. "You totally do own this beach," she accuses in an undertone, holding her sandals by the straps together in one hand.

Cinnamon smirks. "It's not the kind of beach you *could* own, anyway."

"What do you mean?"

"You'll see."

In the dark, the walk down the stairs is a bit like stepping into thin air. Daisy weathers it easily, staying upright by pressing up against the side wall. Then when she slips a bit on the sand, she holds on to Cinnamon, fingers gripping into the mesh tail of her shirt.

It's high tide, rough water lapping almost to the bottom step as waves crash in.

Cinnamon steers them sideways until they're standing spaced apart on the rocks. They look out at the sea. A dozen or so ships are anchored for the night—from this far away they look like colored spots of light bobbing in the background of a rainy scene in a movie.

"Wow," Daisy says softly. "This is . . ."

Cinnamon looks at her. "I know."

Quiet envelops them again. Cinnamon's mind goes back to the car earlier, to Daisy's wet hair on her jaw and how she wanted to read her mind. She wants that again now.

She wants something else too.

"Can I ask you something?"

"Sure."

"You don't have to answer."

"Okay."

She's never known if it's a thing that you ask or hover on the edge of asking or just *know*, but Beth Fisher is her only point of reference, and Daisy Leung makes her want to be careful.

"The other day, when you were talking to Tone about your ex and you said 'them' . . ."

God. It wasn't the other day. It was like, her first week. Cinnamon was listening even then.

Daisy is still looking out at the sea, but one side of her mouth lifts slightly. "Emma. Her pronouns are she/they, but in Cantonese, like when I talk to my dad at home, there are no gendered pronouns. There's still gender roles, but gendering people in speech isn't a thing. Describing someone is always 'them.' I love that gendering people is just a nonissue in Cantonese when it's such A Thing in English, and I try to avoid gender-exclusive language to make a point."

Even with the wind coming off the ocean,

Cinnamon is so hot.

"I mean," Daisy continues, "I have a few exes—but the most recent was Emma."

Cinnamon can feel herself doing a weird expression with her eyebrows lifted high. *Words. Words are a thing that you say when your friend tells you things that are just things they're telling you.* "Oh! That's cool. I love that. So but then, are you, you're like . . ."

Daisy has the nerve to look amused. "I mean, I'm bi, if that's what you're asking. It's been a fairly even mix."

Cinnamon is on fire.

Cinnamon nods, rapidly. Swallows, barely. "Okay. Cool. No, yeah. Cool. That's cool. Um, me too."

Daisy turns to face her with a dancing look that's an echo of the one from carols by the beach. "You don't say."

"But my most recent is—" Cinnamon cuts herself off.

They keep looking at each other.

Something is happening.

Waves continue to crash on the shore.

Cinnamon bites her lip. Shakily, carefully—so carefully—she closes the short distance between them, rocks crunching under her feet.

"Hi, there," Daisy says when she's standing right in front of her.

Cinnamon suddenly worries she's misjudged it, this crackling whatever-it-is that's beaming through her like moonlight. "Um. Hey."

Then very slowly, without breaking eye contact, Daisy Leung touches her hand.

Cinnamon's breath hitches. She waits a second for her stomach to stop swooping like a bird of prey, then flexes her fingers. Reaches up toward the perfect face. Her hands are shaking.

She isn't sure she can touch it.

If it's allowed.

If she can bear it.

"Cinnamon?" Daisy whispers.

"Yeah?"

"You can have this. If you want."

"Yes," Cinnamon says. And then they're kissing.

She isn't sure who started it, only that their mouths are melding together, and the feeling she feels should be enough to shake the ancient earth under their feet.

There's purpose to this kissing. It's like inevitability and something else. Daisy tastes salty like lipstick, sweet like summer. Cinnamon whimpers, which should be mortifying, but there's no room for that. There's no room in her head for anything. Only Daisy, the soft slip and bite of her. Her shape and smell. The way she holds Cinnamon's cheek so soft but with her chin jutting forward, hard in a way that's shockingly nice. Her *body*—the one she's been thinking and thinking about. Cinnamon doesn't know what to do with it. But also she does. There's an instinct there, like the one that tells her to keep breathing. She skims both hands along Daisy's waist, which makes Daisy press forward and gasp-grasp the nape of Cinnamon's neck.

Cinnamon pulls back, her head swimming and hands still holding on tight. Daisy's eyes have the ocean lights in them.

After a beat she reaches out to poke Cinnamon's frozen face. "Wow," she says. "Hello."

"Hey." It takes Cinnamon two tries to get the one syllable out. She wonders if this is what it feels like to die and come back. So much world in one moment.

"Hi," Daisy says again. A giant smile tugs her kiss-red lips.

Cinnamon feels vaguely high. Not in a bad way, but definitely altered on a brain level. On the cliff above them, the lights of Halcyon House flicker and then go out.

21.

The blackout only lasts a few minutes.

"BLOWN FUSE!" someone shouts from the side of the house. The lights surge back to yellow life, and everyone cheers.

But Scarlett has The Feeling.

It started off so faint that she almost missed it, just a slight tightness in her throat she could try to rub away with reading or touching it with her thumb.

She feels it in earnest now—it demands that she does. Wet and heavy on her chest.

Latched to her sternum and making a lead ball of everything underneath.

She's in the front living room. All around her people are dancing and bellowing and living, their laughter racing across the floorboards and over her ears. Her brain flips through worries like songs.

- This party.
- Her parents.
- Cinnamon.
- Not being able to find Will to say "Happy Birthday" when she finished *Persuasion* and finally went downstairs.
- Kit Wembly and whatever "true story" he knows.
- SadieSadieSadieSadie.

- The hospital.
- The Mad Princes.
- Herself.

Scarlett is maybe about to be sick. She runs toward the back balcony door, pushes it open, and tries to do the breathing. In, out. Fill the chest, focus on the exhale. It's a fierce pressure in her chest now—the kind that consumes, hurts—but also the total absence of it, as though with each squeeze she becomes a tiny bit less real.

There's nobody out here—most of the people have gone either inside or out the front. Scarlett holds her throat with one hand, and the balcony railing with the other, and concentrates on not dissolving. That's what people would always tell her to do when she was younger. *Just try to hold on to something.* She does, hard and then harder.

This doesn't happen anymore, she thinks as the metal cools her fingers. She is not this person. They said it together, she and Doctor Marnie—months ago. She had "come a long way."

She is maybe not a person at all right now, just this sick sinking feeling and these jagged bursts of air. They're not enough—each breath makes her more convinced she can't breathe and maybe never will again. She tells herself, *Twenty minutes. The longest it can go on for is twenty minutes. That's a thing, isn't it?*

She closes her eyes and hears the sea's ebb overlay the pulse in her temple, like it's worried for her. After a while it starts to sound like her name, but as a question. *Scar-lett? Scar-lett?*

". . . Scarlett?"

She tries to hear over the feeling, but it's stronger than she is. *Of course it is*, she thinks like bitter vinegar.

147

"Wow, you look . . . Are you okay?"

Scarlett just shakes her head. Let whoever it is see her, the last Mad Prince, falling apart in technicolor. She doesn't care.

But then there's a hand on her back, the hesitant span of a palm.

"Hey," Will Taylor is saying, removing his hand but hovering it there so she can still feel its warmth. "What can I do?" His whole face is puckered. Scarlett doesn't know whether he's worried for her or by her.

"I can't do this," Scarlett says in a small voice that doesn't sound like hers. Then she whispers it to herself again, because saying it out loud feels almost good, for a few seconds. "I can't do this."

"Hey," Will says again softly. "You're okay. I'm here."

"I can't . . ." Scarlett covers her eyes with vibrating hands.

This is panic, Doctor Marnie's voice says in her head. She remembers and grabs the words, mentally throws them down at her body like sparks: *just panic, because see—there's the sea, and your house, and a breeze, and Will's face.*

For a minute they just stand there, his fingertips unsure at the small of her back and her hands over her eyes. Scarlett leans into his palm slightly, then focuses on making sure her breath is coming from her abdomen. In and out and in and out.

"Happy b'day," she says without looking at him when she can talk again.

Will laughs in a quiet, uneasy way. "A joke, wow. But you're definitely turning, like, green."

"*Mmm.*" Scarlett shuts her eyes again and holds her stomach. *Breathe breathe breathe.* "What are you doing out here? Shouldn't you be partying?"

"I needed a breather and a nonalcoholic drink. . . . Are you sure you're okay?" He still hasn't taken his hand away from the small of her back, but it's okay. It feels nice, like maybe she doesn't need to rip her own skin off.

"I'm sort of having a panic attack?" Scarlett's voice is squeaky. "Just . . . talk, maybe. Tell me something."

"Like, anything?"

"Anything. Something long. Just keep talking."

"Okay," Will says uncertainly, then pauses as though he's thinking hard. Scarlett wants to look up but can't yet. "Uh . . . have you ever heard of Orpheus and Eurydice?"

Scarlett huffs out hot air. Shakes her head. "No."

"Listen, are you sure I can't get you some—"

"*Will.*"

"Sorry!"

"Tell me."

"Okay. So I read about this the other day and basically, they were, like, these mythological star-crossed lovers." He pauses. "You're not gonna vomit, are you? I mean, you totally *can*, but if that's the case, we can, like, move you."

Scarlett presses her lips together and looks at him through her eyelashes. "I'd say there's at least an eighty-five percent chance I won't."

Will makes a sympathetic wincing face. "Cool. Love those odds."

"Orpheus and who?" Scarlett prompts. "I feel like I vaguely remember hearing about them."

"Right! Orpheus and Eurydice. So Orpheus was the son of Apollo, and like, a shit-hot lyre player. As in, nobody is supposed to have been able to resist his music. A lyre is like a—"

"Harp."

Will's voice goes a bit unsteady for some reason. "Y-yeah, exactly. So eventually Orpheus meets Eurydice, who was meant to be totally, uniquely beautiful. They fell in love and got married, but then she got bitten by a viper and died."

Scarlett is breathing in and out through her nose. "Right."

"Wait, it gets better, I promise. After Eurydice died, Orpheus sang about his grief for a bit and moved everyone with it. Eventually his dad was like, 'Bruh, you need to go down to Hades and get her.'"

"To hell?"

"Yep," Will says, talking faster now. "So that's what Orpheus did. He fully descended to the underworld to find her. Played his music and charmed everyone, even Hades, until they agreed to give him Eurydice back. But there was a catch: he couldn't look at her while they were on their way back up to the living world, or else she'd die again."

Scarlett feels the slowing of her heart, the tingles spiking across her cheeks. It's almost over. "But he was a fallible man?" she guesses softly.

Will grins. "But he was a fallible man. He knew he shouldn't— that he *couldn't*—but he also just *had* to look at her, so much that he didn't even realize he was doing it. While they were en route to the light, he turned his head for just a second. Eurydice was there, and she smiled. Then she vanished for good."

Scarlett's eyebrows pull together. "Seriously?"

"I know, right?"

"What happened to lyre guy?"

Will moves his hand from her back and leans both elbows against the railing, his hands clasped together and his body bent over them, so he's looking up at her. "I mean, there's two endings: ripped apart by dogs or KO'd by a lightning bolt via Zeus."

"Wow."

Will grins again—bright with relief that she isn't going to throw up on him, Scarlett assumes. "Right?"

Scarlett looks at the excited pink in his cheeks for a long moment. The measured close-far distance between them. Feels the blood rushing back into her hands. Somewhere between this balcony and the underworld, she stopped vanishing.

"What?" Will asks.

She smiles wearily, exhausted all of a sudden.

Relieved. Alive. "Just . . . of course you're into Greek mythology."

Will smiles back, self-consciously this time. "Whatever. Yes, I'm a massive nerd. Not exactly a surprise at this point. Oh! Also, here." He reaches into his pocket and hands her a literal, real, honest-to-god *hanky*. It's even monogrammed—*WT* stitched in silvery thread.

She wipes under her eyes with it, then turns the soft cotton over in her hands. "How do you just happen to have this? Are you a hundred and four years old?" Scarlett feels the leftover adrenaline making her bold.

Will's cheeks flush. He mutters, "Everyone should carry a hanky."

"I've never owned one. I can't even spell *hanky*."

"It's h-a-n-k-y."

"Really?"

"Yeah! I mean, you'd think if Chewbacca is shortened to Chewie with an i-e—which it *is*—it'd be h-a-n-k-i-e. But no."

Scarlett just blinks at him.

"Wait. I just looked. The Americans spell it h-a-n-k-i-e. I'm aware all this just took me from 'massive nerd' to whatever's worse than that." Will grimaces.

Scarlett laughs, wipes her smudged eyes again, and shakes her head before handing the hanky back. "Massively, life-savingly so."

Will scratches the back of his neck. "Well. You're welcome."

"No." Scarlett laughs again, but this time it's like air being let out of a bag. She catches the very edge of his sleeve when he turns away, still light-headed with relief. "Really. It's . . . cute. Very on-brand."

They both go quiet at that.

Even the sea waits while Will stares down at her hand. "*Is* cute my brand, do we think?" he asks lightly, but his face is deadly serious. His breath smells vaguely of alcohol, but not obnoxiously so.

Scarlett thinks it's seriously screwed up, how breathlessness can make you feel like you're dying one minute and like *this* the next. "Yes."

Will keeps looking at her. It's a very good look. His wrist turns over beneath her grip.

Slowly—the scrape of his watchband and then soft vein-filigreed skin—until his fingers are half-cupped around hers for a second before she pulls away.

"Okay," he says.

His eyes are still on hers. Scarlett's stomach flips with the giant dead-alive thrill of it.

"I'm going!" Phe announces loudly from behind them. "Cin's buggered off, and I'm tired and I need a liter of filtered agua down my gullet literally this second or I'm gonna have a monster hangover."

Will turns away from Scarlett to accept a hug from Phe. He clears his throat. "That's all good! Thanks for coming."

"Tell Cinnamon I said bye and to text me and that she's an arse-hole," Phe says. "But lovingly. Like, my arsehole. But not like she's literally *my*—oh, hello, Scarlett! I love the velvet. You look like the hot one in *Mad Men*."

"Go get your agua and go to bed," Will tells her.

"Okay, Dad." Phe nods mock-seriously and waves goodbye. "HAPPY BIRTHDAY TO YOU!" she yells, moving away in a line that's far from straight.

Will's eyes find Scarlett's. There's a lot going on in them. "I should probably walk her home," he says apologetically. "Sorry. I'll message you?"

Scarlett grips the balcony railing once more and nods. She doesn't know if his eyes are trying to tell her something, or just saying, *My ex's freak sister just almost threw up on me, gross g2g bye.* Or if what she thinks just maybe happened between them actually happened. If anything did. "Yep! Okay. See you!"

Cinnamon doesn't emerge even once the party's properly over—she's either run off or she's in her room, Scarlett thinks as she brushes her teeth an hour later after the world's longest shower. The warm water made her feel almost normal. Then she'd think of Will's hand hovering on her back again, and her insides would scramble like a dropped puzzle. *Is cute my brand, do we think?*

Why did she say literally any of the things she said? Is he going to think she's obsessed with him now? (Is she?)

She pulls on her cotton old-lady nightgown, feeling it fall over her like a hug, and crawls into bed under all the covers even though it's still hot. She hasn't checked her phone.

There's no point, she reasons with herself. He didn't mean it; there's no way he did. In no way is a *panic attack* a meet-cute. Sighing, she picks it up off the nightstand.

Hey, so sorry I had to go!!

are you feeling better now? I hope u are

It's after midnight, and he sent the messages forty-two minutes ago. AH. There's no way he's still awake.

Hi, all fine now—sorry was in the shower!

She worries that's TMI, so quickly adds:

Thank you for talking to me, haha (and sorry for being demanding!)

The light is foggy amber gold in her bedroom. Scarlett stares up at the dancing shadows on the ceiling for a while, then switches off the lamp, deciding this is fine—she isn't sure if she can handle it if he actually replies, anyway.

Her phone lights up the dark.

Not demanding at all!!!
Sorry if I was incredibly boring tho going on about Greece haha

Scarlett holds the phone close to her face, watching as Will types something else and then stops.

Noo, not boring at all!

She feels like Orpheus walking out of hell. What are they doing? Her body is full of it, and also with wanting more more more of it.

Will says:

good

. . .

. . .

I like talking to you

Scarlett pulls the sheets up over her head.

          I think I really am ready for us to go see Wembly

Then, before she can wuss out, she adds:

          What are you doing tomorrow?

. . . absolutely nothing

Yes

22.

The day after the party, Cinnamon is hungover. At least, she thinks that's what it is.

She wakes up in her room holding her phone—which is plugged into her charger without the charger being plugged into the wall. She vaguely remembers several strong drinks at some point, and not getting to catch up with Will much at all because so many people ended up coming.

She opens her phone to text him an apology:

happy night-I-barely-even-saw-you, Birthday Boi.

He doesn't reply, which is weird. But also probably not, considering everyone was here until after midnight.

A watery memory flashes through her mind, and she realizes she's not alone.

Daisy Leung is on the floor.

"Hi," Daisy says, amused, when Cinnamon peers over the edge of the bed. Sleepy Daisy looks cute, her eyes slightly puffy and her skin bare.

"Hey."

"I couldn't drive after those shots Phe got us to do. Your mum made me stay when she got back. She's nice."

Cinnamon remembers Amy ushering the two of them in here, late. She remembers they stayed up talking, passing a bottle of something back and forth between them. Daisy lying on her back looking up at the ceiling. At Cinnamon. Her painted-nail hands folded across an exposed sliver of her stomach.

She doesn't remember all of what they talked about, only that it was a lot, judging by the thumping in her head. It was easier in the dark than the way it feels right now. It's not an unpleasant feeling, but it does make her think she might float away through the roof unless she does something with her hands.

"I need coffee," she says, pushing herself and her blurry brain upright. "Desperately."

"Oh my *god*, I thought you'd never ask."

They walk along the beach into town. It's a cookie-cutter sunny day, warm but not hot yet, water lapping softly over their bare feet.

Daisy looks at everything: gentle morning waves and shells scattered in a line behind them, a family with a particularly cute dog. And she looks at Cinnamon.

She doesn't say anything about the kiss.
Cinnamon doesn't know what that means.
What any of this means.

It doesn't feel like the right moment for the *What Are We?* conversation or to mention that her only actual dating experience amounts to Will, a guy called Greyson (she's pretty sure) she met at a party, one dinner with Beth, and an assortment of mixed-up hot-feeling crushes on girls that she often didn't see for what they were until after.

Coffee first.

Frank greets Cinnamon warmly when they order at the café. "Cinnamon! I've missed you!" He says it in strong elegant syllables like *SEEN-AH-MON*.

"I've been working."

Frank *tsks*. "You're wasting yourself in that job. A pub, with your talents? *Pff.*"

Cinnamon and Daisy share a look. "This is Daisy," she says. "Who also works at said pub."

Frank pushes the grinder on the coffee machine, glaring at Cinnamon for letting him walk into the trap and muttering to himself.

"Love you!" Cinnamon smirks, cheered up slightly.

Frank says what, judging by tone, sounds like a bad word in Italian, but he's smiling.

"Interesting," Daisy says when Frank moves away to get milk.

"What?"

"You."

Cinnamon swallows. Or some unseen force swallows *her*—she's not sure which.

After Frank hands them their drinks—Cinnamon is secretly pleased with Daisy's order of a long black with almond milk—they walk back toward the beach. The heat kicks up a notch as the sun shifts higher into the sky. They finish their drinks quickly. Cinnamon feels hers go straight into her veins.

"It's so hot now," Daisy sighs, pulling sweaty hair away from her neck. "I'm still not used to it here."

"*Mmm.*" Cinnamon watches Daisy pile her hair into a pink hair-tie-less bun and drop it again.

"I think I might swim," Daisy says. "Is that okay? You don't have to."

Cinnamon chews on the lid of her empty coffee cup. She thinks of all the times she's felt this way before and run away. She did this last night too, and each time she stopped talking, Daisy just kind of . . . let her. Sat there quietly but stayed awake in case Cinnamon wanted to say something else later, which she did.

"Um," she says now. "No, I'll come."

Daisy smiles. "Yay."

There aren't many people out this early, but still they make their way to the very edge of the flags, where it's just empty sea.

Daisy strips down to her underwear and stands in the baking-hot morning gracefully, all legs and narrow waist and hips, her smooth arms hanging down the sides of a soft-looking triangle bra with pink and white stripes.

After a stunned-blinking moment, Cinnamon quickly pulls her own T-shirt off and crosses her arms over her black sports crop top. She hasn't been swimming since last year—was worried that going without Maggie would feel like a final goodbye. It doesn't yet, though. And she can *sense* something happening again, can tell it's about to be right from inside it. She doesn't want to stand still while it blinks past.

Daisy walks ahead, the sun on the backs of her thighs and setting her hair—and Cinnamon—alight. Cinnamon follows after a minute, standing at the shore's edge so that only her feet are wet. The sea hums all around them.

Daisy dives under the first wave that crests into her. She smiles when she surfaces, like maybe she's surprised Cinnamon is still there but in a good way. "Hi. You okay?"

"Yep." Cinnamon wades minutely deeper. The water is up to her knees now. It's cooler than she remembers. She remembers other stuff too, flashing pictures: swimming with Maggie, Maggie at her funeral in the blue dress, her dad collapsing afterward. She takes a breath, focuses on the soft decline of the sand underneath her, then takes a step forward, and then another, submerging her thighs, her arms hovering uncertainly.

Daisy moves back over to stand beside her. "Look at you, swimming."

"You're swimming," Cinnamon points out. "I'm watching."

Daisy tilts her face toward her. "Oh really?"

Cinnamon wades deeper, frowning. "That sounded less creepy in my head."

Daisy smiles. Cinnamon stares at the wet skin of her face, freckles scattered across her nose and cheeks. Her eyelashes are wet too, dark and stuck together.

"It's not creepy."

"What—" Cinnamon starts to ask, but Daisy dives under again. She watches the shape of her swimming body, blurring out of focus like art. Cinnamon dives under too. She used to love this part of swimming at the beach best—being covered completely in cold, right over the top of her head. Underwater sounds in her ears and the way the world looks when she opens her eyes, like she's doing right now: upside down and made of light.

When they both come up for air, Daisy flips onto her back. "I love this," she says.

Cinnamon thinks, *So do I.*

How is that possible? How is any of this possible?

"My art-galleries-tour trip at the end of the summer," Daisy says. "Part of it is to all these random little islands. I didn't really know why I wanted to go so badly, only that I'd never been before. But I think it's for this. You know?"

Picturing it makes Cinnamon feel like she's starving hungry for something but doesn't know what. She tips her head back, rewetting her hair. "*Mmm.*"

Daisy finds her feet again and turns to face Cinnamon. "Also," she says softly. Shy. Her pink hair is fanned out in the water around her, as though it belongs here. "Last night."

Cinnamon feels cold inside as well as outside. Then hot, when she lets herself remember their kiss: glowing lights on far-off ships and how the sway of Daisy's waist felt to hold. She waits for the Beth Fisher curse to strike the same place twice, though. "Yeah?"

Daisy pauses. "I don't know about you, but I kind of want to do it again. Like, a lot."

Cinnamon thinks about cupping Daisy's wet-cold cheeks between her hands. Thinks about it so hard it feels like she did do it.

"Should we get out now?" Daisy asks.

"Yeah."

23.

The day after the party, Will comes to get Scarlett midafternoon. He's awkward, but also remarkably chipper for someone who drunkenly educated a girl about Greek mythology while she was low-key–high-key mid-breakdown the night before, then texted her things at one in the morning that kept her awake most of the night.

Scarlett doesn't know how to pick up from that.

Kit Wembly's house is at the boundary of town, down the tail end of the beach where it's mostly holiday homes now. They're going on foot—Will rode to Halcyon on his bike—and they run out of small talk around the end of her street. It's bright and sunny, all cloudless robin's-egg blue. The sort of day that makes Scarlett understand why people say the light quality is different out here.

"I don't really know what to talk about," Scarlett admits after a while. She's glad she wore her green linen wrap dress with the ruffled trim and the good waist. She's not sweating, at least. Not yet.

"Right?" Will agrees gratefully, holding the strap of his backpack. "Same, even though it's like . . . we do it electronically all the time. We should be nailing this."

Scarlett laughs nervously. "I suck at small talk."

"*Same*," Will says again.

"We're letting the team down."

Something about addressing it makes walking side by side in broad daylight both easier and harder.

"No, come on," Will says. "I believe in us! We've got this. We can do a 5K walk. Let's just start with the basics. We were so busy with the case we fully skipped those."

Scarlett tries to pull an unimpressed face, but she's so nervous it's probably closer to a grimace. *He said he liked talking to you*, she thinks. *Talk. Now.* "Like what?"

Will stares ahead for a minute. They're following a path of sorts, worn into the overgrown grass beside the road. "Um . . . Do you want to know my zodiac sign?"

"Yes?"

"I think it's the horse one."

"The horse one." Scarlett laughs. "Good to know."

"One of the horse ones. The centaur one? With the arrow."

"Sagittarius," Amy Banks-Prince's daughter replies.

"Yes! Whatever that means."

"It means you're, like, optimistic, honest, and adventurous."

"Yeah? I guess that's mostly true."

"I'm a Scorpio," Scarlett says to keep things flowing and keep herself from thinking too hard, even though he didn't ask. "But Cinnamon says I'm the weakest one she's ever met. Which is actually an incredibly Sagittarius thing for her to say."

Will laughs in an awkward way, maybe because she mentioned Cinnamon. "Wow."

What are they doing? Should they stop?

"And my birthday is on Halloween, so weirdness was always my destiny." She knows she's rambling, but she can't stop herself. "I guess you kind of found that out last night."

Will's brow furrows. "What?"

"I'm sorry you had to see me, like, crazy spiraling or whatever," Scarlett apologizes with the words coming out fast. "It isn't an all-the-time thing, don't worry."

"Oh! God, don't even . . ."

Don't bring it up, she finishes in her head. *It's weird.*

". . . worry about it," he finishes. "I totally get it and don't think you're crazy. At all."

Now Scarlett is frowning. She stops walking to look at him, his face earnest and his hair bleached in the sun. "Really? Not even the almost-vomiting-on-you-on-your-birthday thing?"

"*No.*"

Scarlett hasn't had a panic attack in front of anyone for a long time, but it definitely doesn't go like this afterward. The last time she was with a teacher, she thinks. He kept telling her to *just breathe* but in an annoyed kind of way—like it was a choice to feel how she did, and she was choosing wrong. The only person who's ever understood *that* was Cinnamon. At least she used to.

"Why not?" Scarlett asks.

Will scratches the back of his head. He looks nervous. Or stressed. Probably stressed. Scarlett is a stressful person to interact with sometimes—she knows this.

"Um . . . I have OCD," Will says, his eyes straight ahead. It sounds almost like a question and almost like a declaration. "Like. Have had. Clinically. Since I was a kid. So truly, I get it."

"Oh." Scarlett looks at him again in genuine surprise. The sky over his shoulder is very blue.

"I take medication for it," Will says after a beat, "and sometimes it's totally fine and under control. But sometimes it's . . ."

"Not," she guesses quietly.

"Yeah."

Scarlett rubs her lips together, mind whirring. A car speeds past them, rustling her dress. "Thank you for telling me that."

"I don't usually talk about it. Just to Cinnamon and Phe and my brother. So it's kind of nice? In a horrific sort of way?"

"Yeah," Scarlett agrees.

They go back to small talk after that, but the awkwardness is gone.

"He seems great," she offers. "Ollie."

Will smiles. "He's the best. Like a young gay Obama but without the occasional questionable policy. And then there's me."

Scarlett understands this as well.

They walk and walk along gray asphalt so old and struck by sunlight it looks almost white, Will slightly ahead of her with the maps app open on his phone until they turn down Wembly's street.

"Okay," he says once they're in front of an unassuming white fiberglass cottage. "It's this one."

There's a neat front yard scattered with flowers, framed by a metal gate. Will eases that open with a squeak, the two of them stepping onto the driveway, and someone opens the door.

"Who is it?" A hunched-over man shuffles onto the concrete veranda. He looks like he's in his eighties, minimum. All traces of the clean-cut boy are as much vanished as Sadie is, save for the same bright-dark eyes. "Who's there?"

"Hello!" Will says pleasantly. "Mr. Wembly?"

The man squints suspiciously. "Maybe. Who wants to know?"

"My name is William Taylor, and this is my friend Scarlett Prince. We're working on a town history project and are wondering if we could ask you a few questions?" Will's voice is so courteous and his lie so smooth that Scarlett feels an odd mix of uneasy and impressed in a stomach-swoopy way.

"Prince?" Kit Wembly repeats flatly. His face pinches in on itself, making him look older still.

It's a familiar look to Scarlett, and nerves stab through her in darts. She tries to smile at the man, feeling gross for it even as she's doing it.

"That's right!" Scarlett says, trying to copy Will's assured historian voice. Hers falters. "We're researching my great-aunt, actually. Sadie Prince? You played piano together, right? I wondered if we could talk to you about her."

Kit Wembly's eyes flit over Scarlett. "I have nothing to say about her."

Scarlett's pulse picks up speed. She's not sure what she expected from this, exactly, but a hostile exchange in the driveway was not it. Still, Wembly is their only living lead. She physically bites her tongue and steels herself to try again, but Will is already talking.

"We understand it might be a difficult topic," he says, still all politeness. "But a lot of Sadie's legacy is conjecture at this point, so we're trying to piece together what actually happened, and it's important we have all the facts. It would help us so much if you were to tell us what you know."

They wait for a tense few seconds, Scarlett's face as red and hot as the sun over their heads.

Wembly looks at them both. He narrows his eyes again, before letting them rest on Scarlett. "All I know is, Sadie Prince and her father and her boyfriend argued up on that cliff, and only the father came back. Robert Hammond was stupid enough to get mixed up with her and is still casting a pall over this town from up in his grave.

It's not my job to tell you. I don't care what a mad woman's legacy is. All looks and no talent. She demanded attention enough when she was alive."

Scarlett stares at him in shock. She pictures those eyes, dark and searing, trained on Sadie half a world ago when they were both young. She wants to say something, run, yell, but her throat is suddenly blocked.

"Mr.—" Will starts. His voice sounds different. Not polite at all. He sounds like Cinnamon. Kit Wembly just walks back inside.

Will looks at Scarlett, stricken, when the door slams.

Talk, she instructs herself mentally, but even her internal monologue drips with disappointment, heavy as lead.

There's nothing to say.

After a near-silent walk back, they go to the coffee place next to the baths. Scarlett looks at the blackboard drinks menu behind the counter for a stressed second while Will asks the barista for an almond latte.

Her brain has moved from shock to shame to overdrive. She doesn't know how being alone with Will again can override the cruel spit of Mr. Wembly's words, but it does. She's intensely upset about that, but also convinced everything else is going to go wrong now too. That it'll ruin their vibe, or whatever strange delicate easy they had last night and earlier today.

She desperately wants a hot chocolate—a proper, comfortingly huge, syrupy to-go one—then immediately worries that's a weird thing to order. It's certainly not a cool thing. Is it *normal*, though? Normal enough?

Do other people drink children's beverages in the dead of summer because the nostalgia vibes of its sweet marshmallowy goodness soothe the bullet-beating of their anxious hearts?

"What do you want?" Will asks softly over his shoulder, pulling a crumpled ten-dollar bill out of his wallet. "I'll get it."

"Oh, no!" Scarlett says too loudly. Her voice is off from not talking for most of the walk back. *Chill,* she tells herself. *If you cannot be chill, at least project chillness.* Then she adds, "You don't have to do that!"

"I want to," Will says at a regular volume. "It's the least I can do."

He still looks unhappy. Scarlett wants to tell him it's fine, honestly, but half her brain is still stuck on the drink question. She shoots a panicked look at the barista, who is waiting impatiently to take her order with his hand on the till. "Just a large hot chocolate for me, thanks."

"Two marshmallows or three?"

"Three, please!" Scarlett says primly. *Ugh.*

Will doesn't say anything about her choice, just hands over the ten and takes his change, stuffing the latter into his pocket as they walk out the door to wait by the takeout window.

Dusk happened while they were ordering; the world is all smudged lavender and white and baby pink when they step back into it and lean against the outside wall.

The two of them look out at the beach, tilting their heads toward the late-afternoon-flat sea, as if out of habit. Will stares at it for a beat longer than she does, and Scarlett watches his face in profile for a flickering minute. She can't help it. The way his eyebrows drop down a little when he's stressed. The dip at the end of his nose, and again at his throat when he swallows.

"I am so sorry," Will says. "That sucked."

"It didn't . . . ," Scarlett starts to lie. "I mean, it wasn't *your* fault."

"It was my idea to go, though." Will looks sideways at her. Streetlights are switching on behind him, yellow beams casting their glow on the hazy salt hanging in the air like smoke. "Initially. I shouldn't have . . . I *thought* . . ."

Scarlett has been steadfastly doing what Doctor Marnie calls "worry postponement" about all the big, Mad Princes-ish stuff from today. She feels a flash of it rear up again for a second, picturing dark eyes, but keeps her face smooth.

"WILL!" the barista calls out, setting two mint-colored cardboard cups on the ledge behind them.

They head back along the footpath, sipping their drinks in companionable silence, Scarlett mirroring Will's steps so she's not too slow or too fast. She hasn't walked this much in years; her legs ache, but it's kind of nice. It makes her feel stronger. She takes big gulps of hot chocolate and is glad she braved ordering it. It's a warm sugary hug from the inside.

"It really is fine, you know," she tells Will when her drink is almost gone and she feels almost fine.

Will stops, giving her his full attention. "What is?"

Scarlett gestures with her hand. "Today. Kit Wembly being confirmed awful. Revelations, etcetera."

"Really?"

"Yeah! I'm not going to, like, go to pieces over it," Scarlett says, even though this is exactly what she plans to do when she gets home.

"He was totally, indefensibly out of order," Will says. "And I hate it. But I've been thinking—there was one thing he said that could maybe be A Thing."

It's nearly night now. Scarlett can make the lines of Will out in bursts under the salt-glittered light. Each time his eyes come into full view, a jolt of blue, the eventual end of her worry postponement feels slightly further away.

She swirls the last syrupy dregs of lukewarm chocolate. "What?"

"About Robert Hammond still haunting town from 'up in his grave.'"

Scarlett thinks for a minute. "Do you think he was being literal?"

"I think," Will says, "that Kit the Misogynist is incapable of literally anything else. Which means—"

"Robert Hammond could be buried somewhere nearby," Scarlett finishes. The three local cemeteries in the area blink through her head—all perched on hills. "Do you think that's possible?"

"I definitely think it could be," Will historian-hedges.

Scarlett looks at the beach, the water hissing black in the almost-dark. A wave of wind picks up her hair and sticks strands in her lip gloss. She tosses her head and tries to unstick it, thinking she needs to just cut it all off like Cinnamon. *God.*

"Oh! Here." Will pulls it loose easily. Then he tucks her hair behind her ear, his fingertips grazing the back of her gold earring with the little dangling star.

It happens in about five seconds total, and Will widens his eyes slightly afterward like it was automatic or an accident, but Scarlett almost dies.

Then Will shoves both hands in his pockets and coughs. "Um. Sorry, I was . . ."

Scarlett pretends to sip her hot chocolate even though it's all gone. "So what do we do now?" she says, because she doesn't know what else to say and his cheeks are turning red. "With the search?"

Will's eyes are moon-bright. "Well, we know what we're looking for now."

Scarlett shivers, thick nightfall rippling across her shoulders. "Another grave."

24.

When Cinnamon finally starts walking home from spending the day with Daisy at the beach, she feels sunburned inside and outside. Her nose is definitely pink, but she likes it. Her lips are too. Kiss-chapped. It's unconscionably sappy to like that, but she does. The rest of her is full of a happy-warm that she imagines—maybe—looks like layers of light.

She walks to the end of Main Street like a tourist, to the rows of towering Norfolk pines, and stops for once to look at the way the day bleeds away through the tips of them. She smiles at a passing tourist toddler already in their pajama pants, who promptly starts to cry. Briefly even considers getting a gelato, before deciding that's too far. Her life is turning on its rusty axis enough as is. Best not to push it for pistachio swirl.

The problem happens when the sunset powers down into purple, the moon hung in a mauve sky, and Cinnamon is still so scarily happy she forgets who she is. She pulls her phone out of her pocket, still feeling all-over and cozily hot. She dials her dad's number, like she did the last time she went on a first date that ended after dark.

She forgets.

"Bug?" he answers groggily.

"Hey, can you pick me up from town? I didn't take the car."

Ian pauses. She forgets to analyze it, forgets to call her mother instead, forgets that Scarlett could come get her in Amy's car.

"Sure. Where are you?"

She tells him dreamily, the way people on a train sometimes talk to their loved ones, content to sit and think for a while—*no rush, I'm happy to wait.*

He says something else before hanging up, but she forgets that too. She forgets-forgets-forgets until twenty minutes later when the two of them are driving home, and Ian misses the turnoff for Halcyon. It wouldn't—shouldn't—matter, not on a day like today, but Halcyon is built on the road out of town, so missing the turn means a trip right up to the highway to do a U-turn.

"That was the turn," Cinnamon says in her most patient voice.

Ian looks tired in his cheeks and under his eyes. "No, it wasn't."

Cinnamon takes a breath. "Yes, it was. By the tree? Back there."

"I think," Ian snaps hard, "I know where my own fucking house is, thank you very much."

Cinnamon closes her mouth and swallows. "Well, you drove past it," she tells him bluntly with her face very hot.

"Sorry," Ian says immediately. "Bug, I'm sorry."

They drive in silence to the main road. Then he swings sharply around, nearly knocking her into the door.

Cinnamon remembers then that she's sore from all the swimming, and tired from all the feeling and talking and making out, and so freaking starving in the close heat of the car that she could faint. Would faint, if she were a fainter. Then she wouldn't have to be *here*.

She remembers something else too.

The thing she remembers is this: When the Princelings celebrated twenty-five years, there was a tour. It was planned.

It just never happened.

Venues were booked. Dates were saved. People bought tickets. All the extras that make an idea into an all-caps THING—important backers, marketing, hype—all the pieces, were carefully put in place.

But Ian Prince was the piece that didn't fit. Not with his band of brothers, who understood that sometimes he got the blues but, man, they also had a job to do. Not with his ex-wife, who talked to flowers sometimes because she always had to talk to *someone*.

He fit best with his daughters, who he said in that one song were like the two halves of him. Brave and boisterous Cinnamon and Scarlett who felt like the whole world. They were that—the world. He told them all the time. Used to, anyway.

So it was them who picked up the pieces when it all fell apart during the first show of a hundred, and Ian collapsed.

Maggie had hung on as long as she could. Long enough to forget her son and the way light slanted through the drawing room in Halcyon House and the name of her favorite chocolate cookie (Tim Tam). Long enough that Ian wasn't expecting it, none of them were. The hospital called. Cinnamon first; she was the only one home. She called Scarlett, who cried at length and volunteered to tell Amy, who cried at length and volunteered to tell Ian.

Then Cinnamon drove his car to the venue two towns over to see him, boisterous and brave, because she wanted to. Drove and drove and didn't let herself think the question they always thought, his three girls, about what would happen, because they were his world and they knew.

It was very dark. She always remembers that part first.

The headlights on the car cut white, foggy shapes across the road. It was winter-dark, thick and quiet and midnight blue. So quiet. Like she was totally alone, and everything else was temporarily hiding from her.

Then there was security and the venue parking lot and the gray dirty backstage. People everywhere. Then the greenroom, which wasn't green, and the TV stuck to the wall where she watched Ian fall down and not get up.

She hated that night and hated herself even more for wanting to stay in it forever. Because after was worse.

After was a funeral organized by Amy and then waiting for her to leave again and being so angry when she finally did that it felt like the few seconds when a radio signal cracks and flickers out, and Scarlett saying *it's fine* over and over and over until Cinnamon wanted to scream, and then she left again too, and it was just the two of them, just Cinnamon and Ian, even though he didn't want her to stay.

⚷

When they get home, Amy is cooking something so spicy in the kitchen that Cinnamon's eyes water.

Amy looks at Cinnamon's face, the guilt on Ian's. "What happened?" she asks. She hugs Cinnamon, who receives it stiff as a board. Amy smells like wild basil from the garden.

Ian puts his keys on the hook very carefully, like he's never done it before. Cinnamon watches him, her anger at him and the Daisy-warmth from earlier leaking out of her fingers and leaving her cold. She shakes her head, bumping her shoulder against Ian's on her way upstairs, and he catches and gentle-squeezes her hand.

25.

Scarlett forgot to cancel today's appointment with Doctor Marnie. She only realizes when she wakes up to her alarm reminding her.

She clicks it off and opens Instagram. Will hasn't messaged her, but that's probably fine. Maybe he doesn't want to go grave hunting the week of Christmas. She lurches out of bed and hunts for today's clothing in the colorful mess of her wardrobe—she actually unpacked late last night.

After she's thrown on an oversized purple T-shirt, bike shorts, and her old white Nikes with frilled socks—god, she needs to do some washing, all her good stuff is suitcase-crinkled—she bounds downstairs with ten minutes to spare.

Amy is reading tarot at the kitchen table, a practice she's taken to doing every morning lately. Three cards on a good day, five for a bad. She's facing the window that frames the sky and sea, selecting card number four in a Celtic Cross spread.

Scarlett taps her on the shoulder tentatively. "Mum?"

"*Mmm?* Oh, morning, Scar." Amy turns around slowly, her face pale from stress or sleep.

Cinnamon and Ian are still hiding—never a good sign—but Scarlett isn't going to touch that one.

"Can I take the car? I have an appointment in the city I forgot about."

"In the city?"

Scarlett takes a breath. She's not the best at driving generally, let alone through traffic and tiny city roads, but it's too late to take the train. "Yeah. I forgot to cancel."

"Marnie?" Amy asks knowingly.

Technically *Doctor Marnie* is just Marnie. *Marnie Lindell, clinical psychologist.* Scarlett just called her "Doctor" when she had to discuss their appointments with students or teachers for logistical reasons at school, because it was easier, vaguer.

"Yeah," she says.

"Of course. The keys are on the hook."

Amy pays for the sessions; she found Marnie in the phone book after Scarlett arrived on her doorstep panicking one afternoon during year-ten exam block. No questions asked. Scarlett feels like she should say something to her mother now but doesn't know what, so she just goes with "Thanks."

Amy smiles. "Drive carefully." She never makes a big deal out of the sessions with Doctor Marnie, which is exactly how Scarlett needs things to be. It's funny, she thinks as Amy turns back to her cards and plucks out number five, how sometimes mums just know.

Outside is hot but breezy, so Scarlett winds both windows down in the car. It feels strangely odd to be driving *out* of town. Strange that it feels odd. She grips the steering wheel tight and heads for the highway.

Doctor Marnie's office is in an inner suburb that's easy enough to get to if you make the right turns. Scarlett watches the road and her mirrors carefully for the full hour and a half, trying to ignore the sparks of anxiety in her throat each time she has to merge. When the familiar buildings loom ahead of her, Scarlett misses the city even though she's here.

At an intersection near her old school, she stops at the lights for a few seconds too long, looking at the modular road-facing admin building and suddenly wish-wish-wishing she could go back there next year. Even if being the weird girl with a panic disorder who was the daughter of that redheaded rock star from the nineties *did* make her a social pariah.

The man behind her honks his horn so loud that she physically jumps and accelerates hard through the intersection. It takes until the GPS says "Destination on your right" for her hands to stop shaking. At least she'll have something to open with at therapy if she gets stuck.

Scarlett finds a parking lot outside the complex of doctors and dentists and climbs the steps. It always feels like her senses are slightly sharper here; she shouldn't recognize every layer of the smells and sounds as soon as the automatic doors let her in, but she does. Apple and disinfectant and a weirdly pleasant afternote like rubber gloves. The hum of air-conditioning and hushed voices behind thick doors in the other consultation rooms. It also shouldn't immediately relax her a little, but it does.

There's a woman in the waiting room with a walker and a shock of white hair who looks like she must be older than Maggie was when she died. She looks at Scarlett with *Hello, we are both in therapy* eyes— the same as nearly everyone she sees here.

"Scarlett!" Marnie says. She stands at the reception desk holding a clipboard. Scarlett is one and a half minutes late. "The woman of the hour. Come on through." She leads Scarlett down to the familiar room at the end of the hall. Inside is a gray linen armchair, across from a matching couch with mustard-yellow cushions by the city-view window.

Scarlett sits on the couch. She's anxious again now that they're alone. Or she's remembering being anxious here. A lot. Before school ended and she stopped coming.

This feeling, this remembering-bad-times feeling, is why she's been canceling appointments. She feels a rush of sudden fear that Marnie will be angry with her for that. But she just sits on her armchair with the clipboard on her smart pants-covered knees, smiles, and says, "It's lovely to see you."

"You too," Scarlett says. She swallows. "And I'm so sorry I missed our other appointments! I guess I just kind of thought I didn't really need to do therapy as much anymore."

Marnie *mmm*s sympathetically. "That's perfectly all right."

Scarlett takes a steadying breath. The familiar sight of Marnie's rose-gold glasses and warm brown eyes is splitting her open, like all the coping she's been doing lately is ice-cream-melting away. "Like I thought it was maybe . . . over? The panicking all the time and never being able to do anything, I mean."

Marnie has a clever, even-featured face. Like that famous portrait of Elizabeth I, but if she'd had a sensible chin-length bob. She frowns softly now and writes something down. "Have you been panicking all the time?"

Scarlett's hands are clammy where she has them clasped in her lap. She puts them on her Lycra-ed thighs and looks out the window at tall brown-brick buildings for a minute. "Well, not all the time. It's not as bad as it was before. But it's happening again."

"How was graduation?" Marnie asks gently. That was the last time Scarlett saw her—four emergency sessions in two weeks because her brain convinced itself she wouldn't be able to get through the ceremony without somehow making a fool of herself onstage.

"It was . . . okay, actually," Scarlett says. "Nothing bad happened, and it was nice to see everyone before I left. But now I'm back at home, and even though I'm not really doing anything, not like I was in school, I still feel like I'm anxious *all the time*."

Marnie tilts her head thoughtfully. "That's no good. Do you have any specific thoughts when you're feeling anxious, or is it more of a constant general hum of anxiety?"

Scarlett thinks for a second. "Both? Maybe I *think* about panic more, like worry about it happening, because there's less distraction—no study to do or people to talk to or whatever. And also, because . . ."

Marnie waits. "Yes?"

"Because of my family, you know. Because everyone used to say we were crazy. Maybe we are. My dad's depressed again—I don't think I told you that last time."

"I'm so sorry to hear that."

Scarlett pauses. "We're all there trying to *be* a family for a bit, but it's not really working."

"And do you think you're feeling anxious about that?"

"Maybe?" Scarlett takes a breath and lets her eyes dart to the window again. "I had a proper panic attack just the other day at a party—a bad one—and I've been trying not to focus on it, but it's . . . hard. It's the first time it's happened in a while."

"Of course," Marnie says. "I can imagine that must have felt scary."

Scarlett's eyes prickle. There's a staticky ache in her chest. She always cries in therapy—there are tissues ready. She takes one and scrunches it into a ball. "I thought I wouldn't be like that anymore," she says. "I thought I was better."

"What does that mean to you, being better?"

"Not feeling like life's an impossible series of things that terrify me?" Scarlett murmurs, but with a force that snaps.

Marnie frowns sympathetically. "We don't want you to feel like that," she agrees. "Let's unpack it a little. When you say things terrify you, what are those things?"

Scarlett chews her lip. "I just think doing life generally scares me, because when my anxiety is bad and I can't control it, I feel like it must be because there's something really, fundamentally wrong with me. And I'm going to end up like the rest of them."

"Who?"

Scarlett's eyes swim. She scrunches the tissue into a tighter ball and doesn't answer, because she isn't sure if what she's said is actually true or if she should've said it even if it is.

"The thing about anxiety, Scarlett," Marnie says kindly after a minute, "is to think of it more like a way your brain is wired, rather than it being a flaw or deficiency to overcome. It might always be possible for it to resurface when your surroundings change, or you're faced with situations that prompt a fear-based response—and that's okay. But it's never because *you* are fundamentally wrong. Your system of thinking works a certain way. And the key for us is to come up with strategies to work with it."

"Okay," Scarlett says with her breath stuck in her throat. Two tears roll down her cheeks. She wipes them away.

"It's really, really important to try to recognize how far you've come too," Marnie continues. "Going to graduation and a party are both examples of you acknowledging your fear and working through it to get to something that's important to you. You should be very proud of yourself. I know I am."

Scarlett starts crying in earnest, salty drops falling down her face and into her lap. "I'm sorry," she says reflexively, scrubbing her eyes with the back of her hand.

Marnie's expression goes unbearably soft. "Please. I buy the expensive tissues for exactly this reason."

Scarlett sniffles a laugh and looks out the window again. "I guess I kind of have been doing some things I never would've before."

"See?" Marnie smiles. "This is just an idea, but what would it feel like if 'better' looked a bit more like working with yourself to—safely, and as comfortably as possible—say, 'Well, I might be anxious, but I've got through all these other things, so I'm going to do my best at this too'?"

Scarlett wipes her eyes again and lets out a giant breath. "*How?*"

"Let's workshop it by listing some of those things together." And they do.

When there's fifteen minutes left on the clock, Marnie says, "Anything else?"

"Well," Scarlett says, "lately, there . . . there might be a boy."

"Ooh! A nice boy, I hope."

Scarlett blushes. "Very."

"That's amazing!" Marnie enthuses.

"It's kind of, like, a little bit complicated for a few reasons. But yes. It's been good."

"Tell me all about it."

Scarlett does.

When she gets home, she feels pleasantly worn out. Cinnamon is in the driveway washing the Jeep, partially blocking the space where Amy's car usually goes. Scarlett tries three times to turn in, twisting the steering wheel to hard lock, reversing, trying again. She's starting to worry about the loss of her therapy-calm when Cinnamon drops her sponge into a bucket and walks over to Scarlett's window, motioning for her to wind it down.

The outside air smells like soap and summer grass. "I'll back it in for you," Cinnamon says, squinting in the warm light.

"Really?" Scarlett asks, switching the engine off, relieved-surprised.

"Yeah. It's fine."

26.

Last January before Will and Cinnamon had a giant fight and finally broke up for good, they'd been fighting a lot. Will kept saying, *I just wish you'd* talk *to me*, and Cinnamon had lots to say about the fact that she had nothing to say.

Two Wednesdays later they went for coffee like they always did. They didn't plan it; they just both still showed up. Will looked sheepish and unwashed, or extra-washed maybe—his hair looked wet, and his eyes were pale pink at the edges. Cinnamon warmed him up after a while, like she always could. They small-talked for a long time about university and how he was going to accept his offer at the local one because he wasn't ready to move.

"I think I'm just going to defer," Cinnamon said as she tipped the last of her black coffee into her mouth. It was cold.

Will's eyebrows pulled together. "Because of me?"

Ian was at home asleep even though it was one in the afternoon. Cinnamon frowned. "No."

"Then why?"

"I just can't do it, okay?" she snapped.

Will looked like he wanted to argue, then remembered they were broken up, and the most he could do was politely object. She belonged only to herself again.

Cinnamon changed the subject to people from their graduating class, the shitty new Volvo Will's parents were thinking of buying, which classes he was excited about taking (all of them). All the stuff they talked about when it was good. Neither of them wanted to stop talking. It was sad but very nice.

"Do we just keep doing this? Can we?" Will asked when the café was closing. "Like, are we friends? Is that . . . I mean, do you want—"

"Yeah," Cinnamon said like an exhale, and they did.

She's thinking about that exact moment, in abstract circles with no end, when she drives to Daisy's house for the first time to pick her up.

She's thinking about Will's face, the way the sunlight from the café window lit half of it fuzzy gold. Then her mind skips back further, to after they got paired up in a group assignment in year eleven, and he asked her out by slipping a handwritten note in her locker that she dropped and didn't see, and he thought that meant no, and it took him three more days of them kissing after school with their uniform ties undone and her bedroom door shut to blurt out, "Why don't you want to go out with me?" and she poked his red cheek and told him she thought she already was.

She remembers how good it felt at the start—falling into him— because he was so good. And still she wrecked it, properly wrecked it like a ship thrown at rocks, and what kind of person does that make her? Is that what's going to happen every time with everyone she likes?

Daisy Leung makes her want to be careful.

She parks the Jeep outside the address Daisy sent when she texted:

good morning
what are we doing today?

Cinnamon cuts the engine and thinks of last night. The whip-crack of Ian's voice. The silence that followed when they got back to Halcyon, and the way he looked grimly at her for a few seconds with his face full of *sorry*.

The exact way she probably looked at Will last January.

Daisy taps on the driver's-side door. "Well, hello," she says through the window with a smile.

Cinnamon eases the door open, shaking her head to try and clear it. "Hi." She still feels bad thoughts surging like a pulse through her limbs and making them heavy, so she focuses on Daisy's pink-orange lips coming toward hers.

It's still very good when they kiss.

Too good.

There's a man in the front garden bent over a bed of herbs with his back to them. "Ah Ling?"

"Bye, Dad!" Daisy calls.

"Where are you going, Daise?" asks a woman's voice out the window.

Daisy chews her bottom lip, looking at Cinnamon. "Sincerest apologies in advance for what now has to happen," she says, grabbing Cinnamon's hand and pulling her toward an immaculate timber bungalow with a yellow door while the sun lights their backs and the tops of their heads. She's wearing a polka-dot minidress with a wide collar that's a different pattern and chunky sandals, and her toenails are painted bright red.

Cinnamon straightened her hair this morning. She tucks it behind her ears and pulls the legs of her black jumpsuit straight.

Daisy's house is small and welcoming and entirely the opposite of Halcyon. A tall blond woman opens the door. She has a wide face with big lips and dark eyes. "Hello!" she says in a deep voice, pulling Cinnamon into a very perfumy hug. "You must be Cinnamon. I'm Lydia."

"Must be," Daisy deadpans.

Daisy's mother releases Cinnamon and swats her daughter's arm reproachfully. "Where's Dad?"

"Weeding."

Lydia rolls her eyes. "Ed! Take a break! Daise's brought a friend!"

The middle-aged man with jet-black hair still holding sun from the garden appears in the kitchen, with a potted plant in one hand. He deposits it on the counter and smiles. It's soft and secret like Daisy's, like you have to really work for it if you want to see teeth.

"Hello," he says warmly. "We are so happy to meet you."

This, for some reason, makes Cinnamon feel very overwhelmed all of a sudden, like she needs to go away and process this moment in order to *be* in it, even though nothing's really happened yet. The lights in the kitchen feel too bright, the sea outside too loud.

She's going to ruin this.

She shakes Daisy's nice dad's hand woodenly and he jokes, "Good shake," and Daisy frowns at him.

"I just made cookies!" Lydia says. "Would you girls like to have tea?"

"Uh," Cinnamon says. "Sure."

"She's much nicer than Megan," Lydia says to Daisy in a loud whisper.

Ed laughs through his nose.

"Mum!" Daisy hisses.

"What? She is!"

Only because I'm not saying anything, Cinnamon thinks over the ringing in her ears.

"Megan was vegan," Ed tells Cinnamon.

"She was a vegetarian, Dad. You just think that rhyme is funny," Daisy says.

"It's very funny," Ed replies with a shrug.

They sit down at a polished-wood table with bench-style seats. Cinnamon's legs don't quite fit underneath—she keeps nearly playing footsie with Daisy's dad—so she tucks them sideways. The four of them crunch cookies and drink from a tea set with lots of parts.

Conversation tapers off, going slightly wrong in the way that is inevitable when all parties are anxious to get things right.

Cinnamon feels sweaty and fidgety and like she should really properly ask about what happened with Megan, but she also can't help staring at Daisy's perfect parents, and the perfect home around them. She doesn't think she's ever been in a house this neat before. Even Will's place always has papers in manila folders stacked on the counters.

When she met *his* parents for the first time, they looked at her like, *Oh god.*

"So, you work with Daise?" Lydia asks. "Is that right?"

"Yes." Cinnamon nods, swallowing a shard of pistachio cookie with an audible gulp.

"That's nice," Lydia says.

Daisy isn't playing along with said awkwardness. She's as warm as ever, with her knee nonchalantly resting against Cinnamon's. "She's technically my superior, actually."

"Oh, is that right?"

"I mean, kind of. Not really," Cinnamon stumbles, tapping her foot under the table. "Everyone likes her better."

"Somebody has to," Ed says with a smile, and Daisy slides her calf over Cinnamon's shin to kick him under the table.

"And are you in uni?" Lydia asks.

"Um." Cinnamon picks up another cookie but lets it hover in her hand. "No, not at the moment."

"Gap year, is it?"

"Sort of, yeah." Cinnamon can feel herself shrinking into being slightly rude, but not in a way she can stop.

"Your dad is that singer, from that band," Ed says suddenly with interest. "Are you a musician too?"

"Um," Cinnamon scrambles. If this were a school speech, she would've failed already. "No, not at all."

"She's an artist," Daisy puts in when Lydia's eyebrows rise.

"No, I'm not," Cinnamon says automatically. "I mean, I do stuff with Photoshop sometimes, but that's not really . . ."

"Oh," Lydia says, nodding.

"I'm taking a gap year too, Mum," Daisy points out.

"Of course, darling," Lydia says. "What do your parents think, Cinnamon?"

"Is it all rock and roll at your house?" Ed asks. His face still looks kind, not slightly concerned like Lydia's.

Cinnamon thinks about last night again. About the cold emptiness of Halcyon and how the Princes belong there. What is she doing here with these people? Why would they even want to meet her at all?

"Yeah," she says, smiling tight without looking anyone in the eyes. "Actually, I'm so sorry, but I just remembered I have to get home and help my mum with something."

"Oh! That's a shame," says Lydia genuinely.

"I'll walk you—" Daisy starts to say.

But Cinnamon is already standing up and saying, "No need."

She's ruined this.

"Come back soon," Ed says.

"Absolutely," Cinnamon says to her feet. "It was really nice meeting you guys."

Daisy follows her anyway. "Hey," she says when they're back on the doorstep, which feels different now than it did just before.

Cinnamon turns around without looking at Daisy properly. "I'm really sorry, I just have this thing—I totally spaced."

"Okay. But hey," Daisy says again. "Are you okay? They really like you, my mum's just . . ."

"Totally. Yeah," Cinnamon says. She wants to keep this, to stay with Daisy. A lot.

She has to get away.

Daisy reaches out slowly, one small cool hand tickling Cinnamon's neck, and sweeps her hair back off it. "What's happening right now?" she asks softly, like, *Tell me and I'll help.*

It feels nice, the touching.

Too nice; nice in HD.

"Nothing," Cinnamon says. "I'm fine. I'll see you later."

Message from D-LEUNG, Monday 7:56 p.m.:

thanks for a truly lovely 48hrs
I had to buy a new chapstick on the way home from the
beach yesterday btw.
you owe me $5.99.
:p

everything ok at your place? how come you had to leave?
X

Message from D-LEUNG, Tuesday 8:10 a.m.:

this painting reminds me of you
like how you look sometimes when you're thinking
like you're somewhere else
i've been thinking about it (you) all night is that weird
Open multimedia attachment.

Message from D-LEUNG, Tuesday 9:42 a.m.:

I'm still thinking about you now tbh

Message from D-LEUNG, Tuesday 1:19 p.m.:

my parents loved you dw abt mum she keeps saying she
loves your hair
& apparently, I seem "smitten" which is gross but also true

Message from D-LEUNG, Tuesday 5:55 p.m.:

what's up?
You alive?

Message from D-LEUNG, Tuesday 8:36 p.m.:

Cinnamon?

Message from D-LEUNG, Tuesday 10:59 p.m.:

?

27.

Ian has a Very Bad Day on Christmas Eve. It's the hottest day of summer so far, and the air conditioner is screaming, and his ex-wife can't coax him out of bed.

Scarlett lies on the floor in her bedroom below the window all morning reading Maggie's *The Bell Jar* because she's already scanned every page of *Ariel*. She's listening to her parents, and the squawking of seagulls, and people down on the beach, and her parents.

She allows herself twenty minutes of worrying that the Very Bad Day is her fault for digging up buried things, before she closes the book and closes her eyes the way Marnie said to, and tries to remind herself she has no proof to back up that thought.

She worries that she's making the situation about her. Does she do that about everything? Then she thinks about the fact that she hasn't seen Will since the trip to Kit Wembly's and hasn't spoken to him because she's too scared to be the one to message first.

Her mood is unstable—that's the only way she can describe it. Not in a way that's particularly dramatic or worth interrupting her parents. More that she can physically feel it, twisting and heaving inside her chest like a thing caught in the wind.

She gets out of bed at eleven and turns on the shower. The mirror is steamy, and the air feels thick.

Scarlett turns the tap to cold and stands still under the freezing water until her skin adjusts. She pushes her hands through her hair methodically, icy droplets running the length of it down her back. *No proof, no proof, no proof.* She washes her hair twice and leaves it wet to keep her cool, wrapping a towel tight around her chest when she's done.

The only clothing option in this heat is a loose cotton shift dress with a yellow-and-pink sixties floral pattern. She pulls it over her still-semi-wet body, then sprays on enough deodorant to make her feel a flash of guilt about climate change. *Are aerosols bad?* She thinks probably yes. By the time she's fully dressed and lip-balmed, it's noon and Scarlett hasn't spoken to anyone yet, but she's exhausted.

When she and her mother and sister congregate in the sweaty kitchen to assemble individual salads for lunch, Amy clears her throat and asks Scarlett and Cinnamon to go grocery shopping together.

"Not a chance," Cinnamon says immediately.

"The Christmas shop? Mum, that's our thing." Scarlett pouts. *And also, no.*

Amy waves one hand, dismissive and irritated. "Someone's got to do it, and it should really be sooner than later, otherwise there'll be no free-range pork left."

"We can just have a shitty little ham," Cinnamon says.

"Cinnamon," Amy says.

"What?"

"We're not sacrificing tradition. Not this year. Now go get the list and my wallet."

Scarlett's chest flips and then falls. *You are sacrificing tradition,* she wants to say. *We go together, you and me. It's been that way every year we've had Christmas here.*

Cinnamon returns to the kitchen, reading the list. "Jesus Christ Superstar Esquire," she says. "It's gonna take us ages!"

Amy pulls her credit card out of her wallet and thrusts it at her. "Good. You two don't spend enough time together. Use this as an opportunity to bond."

"But—"

"Cinnamon," Amy says again warningly. Both girls look at each other and sigh. Scarlett pulls the car keys off the hook.

"Uh-uh," Cinnamon says. "Give me those. If I have to participate in this Hallmark-movie bullshit, I'm not also being killed by your driving."

"I know that!" Scarlett snaps, handing them over. "I was getting them for you."

"Sure you were."

"I *was*!"

"Sounds convenient."

"I literally was just about to—"

"Girls!" Amy calls wearily from the kitchen. "Go."

When they get to the grocery store, Cinnamon wants to split up straightaway.

Scarlett shakes her head. "I think we should stick together. Otherwise, we might double up or miss stuff."

"God forbid." Cinnamon wraps her hands around the cart handle and restlessly pushes it back and forth.

It's air-conditioning cold and pre-Christmas busy inside, purposeful people weaving around them with packed baskets and crumpled lists and stressed expressions.

It takes a long time for Scarlett to calm down enough about not being here with Amy and get into the shopping zone. "Did you hear them today?" she asks after a while. "Do you think he's okay?"

Cinnamon doesn't ask who she means. She just chews at a loose piece of skin beside her thumbnail, then makes a face. "I dunno."

"It feels stupid to prep for Christmas," Scarlett continues in a rush, daring to hope that this might be it, the moment they actually talk about it. "When he might not even want to . . ."

Cinnamon wipes her thumb on her cut-off shorts. "*Mmm?*"

Scarlett drops her voice low so only her sister can hear. "I'm scared he won't get better this time."

Cinnamon's eyes flick up. "If we say shit like that, then he definitely won't," she snaps, looking pissed off. But also, for a second, scared too.

They wind through the harshly lit aisles silently after that, Scarlett methodically tossing vegetables, snacks, and tubs of pasta salad into the cart while Cinnamon mostly just squeaks her burgundy Docs on the linoleum floor.

When they get to the dairy section, Cinnamon picks up three different brands of camembert and says, "Let's just get these for nibbles."

Scarlett looks at her, aghast.

"What?" Cinnamon demands.

"You can't just get *one* type of cheese."

"Why not?"

"Because people want different types of cheese!"

"Do they? We all like camembert. We don't need anything else." Cinnamon speaks with such conviction that Scarlett starts to feel properly stressed.

"You have to have *variety*! That's the whole point of Christmas."

"Cheese is the whole point of Christmas?"

"Yes!" Scarlett's voice goes high, and she wishes Amy were here, who never questions her system. "The cheese sets the tone for the *entire day*."

Cinnamon gives her a look that's impressively derisive, given her hands are full of wheels of soft cheese. "Well, fuck. I must've missed that bit of the nativity story."

Scarlett exhales sharply. She can already feel heat rising in her cheeks, and they haven't even been here an hour. She can feel herself looking like some sort of cheese-obsessed freak too. Nobody can infuriate her like Cinnamon. She snatches one camembert out of Cinnamon's hands and deposits it into the cart on top of the leeks. "Just grab those." She points out three other cheeses—two more than she would usually get.

"You're the boss," Cinnamon says, chucking the cheeses in, then holding up her hands in mock-surrender. "The big guy. The big . . . cheese."

Scarlett glares up at her. "*Stop.*"

28.

Christmas is a nonevent.

Scarlett and Amy try to make a thing of it, decorating the tree with the family's kitsch ornaments and baking enough gingerbread cookies to fell a horse. There's presents—little things in stockings that nobody really wants. They used to do secret Santa, one person each—now they just do secrets. Like how long Amy is actually staying, and the new meds Ian is on because Cinnamon saw the bottle in the kitchen, and what the hell Scarlett is thinking all the time behind her giant gray eyes.

Then there's the food: breakfast is Amy's pancakes that she thinks are good but really use too much flour; cheese and nibbles (so much cheese; too much cheese); pork and roast vegetables and heavy wine-flavored gravy for the big four o'clock dinner; pavlova with warm fruit on it for dessert. Everything is topped off with several festive movies, the four of them crowded in the lounge room watching depictions of northern-hemisphere white Christmases to try and feel something. Ian sleeps, mostly.

Cinnamon doesn't blame him.

She retreats to her room too. She loads up interviews of her dad in his band glory days and watches them back-to-back. The MTV special where he got his arm tattoo, a spiraling image of Amy he's not yet removed. The performance at the flood-relief concert where he did an acoustic cover of "Cloudbusting" by Kate Bush in the pouring rain. The time he brought baby Cinnamon onstage with baby headphones on. Him sweaty-laughing-kissing his drummer, Stan, on the lips after a festival show.

She reads words of his too. He fascinates her, this version of her dad it feels like she never met but must've.

"I get very down sometimes," he told *Rolling Stone* in 1998. "I've had some dark periods for sure. It's not a secret and I don't think it should be—there should be more conversations about that. But I do okay."

Cinnamon can't bring herself to reply to any of Daisy's messages.

She tried to, at first.

She wants to.

She picks up her phone and stares at the words. But her mind is doing a thing it sometimes does where it can't deal with everything and so it just . . . shuts off. It's easier, better, to get away before the inevitable happens.

Later she goes to sit on the sand dunes. Cold grains stick between her bare toes. The night is thick and humid, and the sea looks untouchably black. She's sad in a way that feels so big it's hard to breathe around, as if she's floating somewhere much higher up—space, maybe Mars—watching someone who isn't her hug their knees to their chest and cry so hard they feel sick.

Her phone keeps ringing, but that feels like it's happening to a different person too. A person worth caring about. Cinnamon is just this blank moment—cold arms and the waves echoing in her ears.

The sound of the phone ringing is annoying, though. She wipes her eyes angrily and yanks it out of her pocket. Presses the button without checking who it is—only who it's not.

The feelings she feels confuse her, but Daisy's face keeps flashing through her mind, no matter how hard she tries to stop. A collage of different versions of it—smiling, laughing, frowning, puzzling her out—all layered on top of each other. Eventually she just gives up and traces mental fingers over them one by one.

Cinnamon is not a philosophical sort of person, not even when she's drunk. She is a realist. She's read books on nihilism, skimmed them, anyway, but enough to get the gist: *Nothing matters and then one day it's gone.* She prides herself on this fact so much that having to admit it isn't true—even just to herself—makes her cry harder. Big, hoarse sounds that she's embarrassed are coming from her even as they do.

She wonders briefly if this is what her dad feels like. Sometimes, all the time. How *hard* it is. To let people close. To let things happen. To be alone with yourself afterward.

This.

This.

Her phone is still ringing-ringing-ringing in her ears. It's making her dizzy. She slides her thumb over the button. "*What?*"

"Where are you?" It's Will.

She closes her eyes and doesn't answer him.

"Cin. I know you're there."

"I'm fine," she says eventually.

"Right. Well, you don't sound fine."

"Well, I am. Sorry to disappoint."

"Come on. It's Christmas. Everyone's worried."

"Everyone who?"

"Your mum. Me."

"You?"

"Of course! She called to see if we were together. You've been gone for ages."

"You don't sound worried," she says snarkily.

"Where are you?" he asks again, more urgent now. "Just tell me where you are, and I'll come. No questions asked."

This strikes her as incredibly annoying. That he automatically assumes she's off doing something exciting or dangerous or wrong that she doesn't want to tell him about, instead of just being here, feeling.

This. This. This. This. This.

"I don't need you to save me all the time, you know," she says. "You're not, like, my savior."

"*Jesus*, don't—"

"What?"

"I'm not trying to be that!"

"Aren't you?"

"No. I'm trying to come get you."

Cinnamon is crying so hard, and she doesn't even know *why*.

She does. She ruined it.

Will exhales into the phone. "I'm trying to be your friend."

"Well, stop," Cinnamon replies, and hangs up. Hot droplets roll down her numb cheeks. She thinks about him standing in his front hallway holding the phone with his puppy-dog look and his keys on the key ring he bought while she was with him.

Time slips into the blue-ink horizon. She doesn't know how long she sits there for. But eventually she sees someone coming up the beach. Running and calling her name.

"Thank actual god. You fully scared me for a minute."

Cinnamon glowers up at Will. She feels entitled to glower at the first person she loved when they still don't let her bolt in a crisis, ages and ages later. "I told you I was fine."

Will pulls a disbelieving face. "Is that . . . You're *crying*."

Cinnamon sucks her teeth. "So?"

"So, I've literally never seen you cry once in five and a half years."

She shrugs. "Guess this year's just my peak."

"Cin, come on. Tell me what happened."

Looking at him is like eating toast with butter when she has the flu.

Why did she lose him too? Why did she want to?

"We don't do anything anymore." Cinnamon's voice is toneless. "You're always busy."

"That's not . . . So are you!" Will bites his lip, like he regrets being defensive. She must really look bad. "I mean, I'm here now."

"I didn't ask you to come."

"Do you want me to go?"

Cinnamon knows as soon as he asks that he means it; if she asks him to, he'll leave. She can't bring herself to say no, so she says nothing.

Will runs a hand through his hair. For a minute he seems to be deliberating something, and then he sits down beside her with a sandy thud. "What's wrong?" he asks. "At my birthday you seemed fine."

"I was," she says. "That was the problem."

"Tell me."

Cinnamon doesn't think she can. The words have officially left her brain. All of them. Pac-Man is chilling in there in the void alone. She thinks of her dad sleeping through Christmas. Daisy's parents wanting to know her. All those unanswered texts on her phone.

"I just think maybe I'm not capable of being happy?" she says finally. Two tears fall down her face, neat and one after the other. She can't make them stop. "And that maybe I don't believe in good stuff anymore."

Will sighs deeply. He gets his deliberating look again, and then he shuffles closer to her, until the sides of their bodies are touching. Cinnamon wants to rest her head on his shoulder, but also, fuck the patriarchy, so she settles for resting it against the side of *his* head.

Will leans into it, his temple and her temple pressed tight together, warm.

"Ew," Cinnamon murmurs, but she doesn't pull away.

"So I'm listening," Will says after a long time of them sitting. Just that.

29.

Christmas is an event.

Between baking, basting, frying, decorating, curating entertainment options, and trying to ignore the fact that everything feels different and weird this year and maybe it'll never be the same again, Scarlett barely stops all day.

She's determined to tick off every festive thing she can: nibbles and cheese, roasting of meat and potatoes (Amy), festive carols through Ian's sound system, stuffing and salads (Scarlett), red-and-green table decorations and the plates with holly on them. There are variables this year: stony silence as they eat (Cinnamon), sleeping until noon and then rubbing her shoulder appreciatively and retreating upstairs halfway through the planned Bad Netflix Christmas Movies marathon (Ian), leaving too soon after (Cinnamon).

"Well, that went well," Amy jokes when it's just the two of them.

Scarlett laughs back. It did, relatively, is the sad bit.

She feels a rushing sense of wanting to solve the mystery of Sadie so she can figure out the rest of them.

"Mum," she says.

"What is it, darling?"

"Do you know anything about Sadie Prince being sent to a hospital?"

Something flits across Amy's face, but her overall expression is polite-concerned. "What's got you worrying about this?"

"Nothing," Scarlett lies. "Just, I found something weird in Maggie's stuff and it looks like Sadie went to a hospital."

She doesn't know why she leaves out everything else:

- the fake grave,
- the name of the hospital,
- the misnomer,
- the newspaper article.

She feels protective of it all, of Sadie, and worried that if she tells an adult before she has all the facts, even her mum, they'll think she's making it up.

"Do you think they sent her away?" Scarlett pushes dangerously. "Would Great-Grandpa have done that, do you think? And why? If she was . . ."

Amy licks her lips. "Ask Daddy about it in the morning." Then she retreats too.

Scarlett deflates like a balloon watching her go, and thinks, *What is it about Christmas that it either glitters or highlights how bad things were before?*

Once it's finally Christmas night, Scarlett lies down on the couch looking at the stockings on the fireplace mantel: *Amy, Ian, Scar, Cin, Maggie, Charles.* She tries not to think about the fact that two of them are empty.

Her parents are upstairs napping. Cinnamon is out, no one knows where—Amy is worried. *Elf* is on the TV, which feels like the single most depressing thing to watch by yourself, so she switches it off.

She scrolls around on her phone for a while, looking at family snaps posted by people from school. Niamh's look like something out of a Ralph Lauren catalogue, and her boyfriend from the boys' school, who bought her a Pandora ring, looks like a model.

Scarlett thinks again about how they haven't spoken all summer. They were only really friends in a convenient sort of way, lunch and homeroom and usually sitting together at dinner. But still.

She scrolls aimlessly through more stories and accidentally clicks on Will's. Scarlett whole body flushes hot. She's been avoiding thinking about him the last couple of days. Definitely hasn't overthought the hair-tucking in the salted dark a hundred times, and has taken instead to googling graves in some of the local cemeteries late at night, so that at least if she finds something, she'll have an *excuse* to message him and it won't just be the desperate move it is.

There he is, in her phone and still out there existing, which frankly feels rude. Cute too. It's a picture of him and his brother playing soccer, a ball stopped under Will's foot while the sky behind their matching blond heads blooms orange watercolor dusk. But mostly it's rude.

She thinks of him seeing that she's seen it. Wonders why she *swears* she remembers temporarily anxious-muting him when she clearly Did Not. Then she clicks one of the apps on her home screen until they all start to jiggle in fear, finds Instagram, and swiftly deletes it.

She gets up and goes into the kitchen to inspect her earlier cleaning job, leaving her phone wedged between two cushions on the couch. She runs her hand along the countertop. It doesn't feel sticky exactly, but it's not *un*-sticky. It's in the sticky family. A derivative of sticky.

Who took that picture of Will?

When did it say it was? Yesterday or today?

Not important. What's important is that they should change whatever they clean with. She wants to Google cleaning products and list them in terms of effectiveness and sustainability, but that would mean getting her phone.

Since when does he play soccer?

30.

"Do you wanna go to the sales?" Scarlett asks Cinnamon on Boxing Day.

Cinnamon rolls over in bed. She's still wearing her outfit from last night, mascara stuck to the creases at the edges of her eyes. She'd rather do literally anything else.

"We can split up when we get there," Scarlett offers pleadingly. *She's* fully dressed: gingham shorts and a red top with puffed sleeves, wet-red lip gloss.

Cinnamon thinks about spending the day with Ian and Amy and her phone instead (last night Daisy texted: **okay I get it, sorry. bye**). "Whatever. Sure."

"Great! We can take mum's car. I've already asked."

"I'm driving."

"*Yes.* Obviously. God."

In the car Scarlett asks Cinnamon if they can play Christmas carols on her phone. "Christmas is over," Cinnamon snaps. "And when are you gonna get your own Spotify account?"

"That's not true. It's Christmas the whole week!"

Cinnamon taps her fingers on the steering wheel. "Says *who*?" She can feel Scarlett watching her.

"Everyone! Why are you in a mood?"

"I'm not."

"You've been in one for days. That's your in-a-mood face."

"I just didn't bring my phone, okay?" Cinnamon's voice wavers. She hates it. This. But staying home is worse.

Scarlett hesitates, then clears her throat. "What . . ."

Cinnamon shakes her head. Daisy's last text flashes through her mind again. Then Christmas in a montage. She feels, unforgivably, as though she might *cry*. Again. "Don't."

"Are you *okay*? Is there something . . . Because you look—"

"I don't wanna talk."

"But—"

"Just leave it. Okay?"

Scarlett sighs. "Okay."

Cinnamon has never been the type of girl who goes to shopping centers. When she was younger, twelve maybe, she used to worry about it vaguely—her disinterest in clothes or shoes or makeup. It made her different from her mother and sister, something else. To her credit, Amy never made her go to the shops. She went with Scarlett, and Cinnamon got clothes the way she liked: when she needed to and by herself.

Being at the shops today makes Cinnamon think of linking arms with Daisy Leung. Her perfume. What was it called? She told her once.

Roses. Something roses.

Cinnamon can smell it in her nostrils now if she concentrates. She reasons with herself even as she's doing it that she is not this person. The broken one, who sits at home sad. The jilted girl in a freaking Sylvia Plath poem. The type to be soppy enough to be obsessed with someone's goddamn *smell*.

Except she is.

Roses and cloves.

All she can think about are roses and cloves.

She remembers Daisy saying you can only get it—the perfume—at some big makeup store. She finds it on the glaringly bright electronic map of stores—it's in the middle of the center, stretched across three shop fronts. There used to be a place people bought stuff for horses there, Cinnamon recalls. She thinks about texting a picture to Will and captioning it *Alexa, play "Ironic," by Alanis Morissette*, their joke for when something is only ironic in the vaguest sense of the word.

Everyone she walks past on the way there is a couple, she decides. All of them. Happy couples who are happy, unlike her, who ruins everything because everything she touches gets worse.

When she enters the megastore, the fluorescent strip lights and colors are confusing, but Cinnamon eventually finds what she needs lined up on the back wall. She remembers the perfume brand when she's looking at the bottle, though the one Daisy had was smaller.

Cinnamon picks up the big tester bottle now. It's heavy in her hands. Not physically heavy, but just . . . weighty. She watches the pale-gold liquid inside slosh back and forth for a minute, before spraying some onto one of the cardboard stubs on the shelf labeled *FOR TESTING*.

It leaves an oily crater in the middle of the card, and she must have sprayed too close, because the smell is all wrong. Acidic and chemical-y, even when she hurriedly fans it through the air.

Cinnamon suddenly feels sick, as if she's being drowned in this smell that isn't right, not whatever she wanted when she came here, if she even really knew.

She glances at the cheery salespeople closest to her—a dark-haired boy not much older than she is standing by the colognes, and the woman with a neat doughnut bun who greeted Cinnamon when she first came in—before spraying two more pumps over her neck and collarbones. *It just needs some heat*, Amy always says when she does this exact thing.

It is better. It's everything, and this is maybe the most desperate thing she's ever done or will do, but Cinnamon sprays more—all down her T-shirt and the legs of her jeans. The boy shop assistant watches Cinnamon with a sardonic-amused sort of expression that gives her insides a tired jolt.

"Excuse me," Doughnut-Bun barks, and the boy smirks. "What are you doing?"

Cinnamon sets the bottle back down so sharply the shelf wobbles. "I don't know," she replies. She is drowning in it—roses and raspberry and spice—and it just makes her sad. "I'm sorry. I don't know."

When she meets back up with Scarlett to eat something, her sister says, "You smell nice. What perfume is that? You hate wearing perfume."

Cinnamon just shrugs.

Scarlett looks at her for a long time, twisting her mouth to one side. "I got you sushi," she says eventually, pushing a paper bag across the table.

"Thanks."

The lights are too bright, but the air-conditioning is nice. Neither of them buys anything.

31.

Will messages Scarlett at seven o'clock that night.

> **Fully not trying to be weird**
> **But**
> **I need you to meet me at the headland cemetery.**

It's been a weird night already—she caught Amy crisis-burying wishes in the garden and Cinnamon and Ian both stayed in their rooms through dinner. It's almost eight by the time Scarlett has:

- showered,
- deodorized,
- submerged her face in tinted moisturizer,
- thrown a denim jumpsuit and yellow sandals on, left her mother a note, and barreled into the car she technically *did* say Scarlett can borrow for emergencies.

She has to turn on her map app to get to the cemetery up on the biggest hill at the other end of the beach. When she pulls up, Scarlett remembers she's here because Will is here, and that means she's suddenly so nervous it might kill her. *Can your heart beat so hard it cracks a rib?* She hopes not. There's also the fact that this is a literal creepy graveyard that looks very real up close—not small and familiar like the one at Halcyon.

More like how she pictures Hades's hell.

Her hair is still wet from the second shower. She can feel it leaving a sweat-cold mark down her back.

The headland cemetery is the oldest in town, so old that even a couple of Scarlett's distant ancestors were buried here pre-house. It's huge, all green-steep-sloping hills, intricate memorial statues, and rows of grayish headstones that vary in stone, size, color, year. Far ahead of those are the white war graves, then a stone wall that brackets a cliff where the sea stretches out dark and endless beyond. Some people think the Princes have the best beach view in town, but really that belongs to the dead.

Will is perched on the wall. His jeans-clad legs are dangling in front of him, and there's a notebook in his lap. When he sees Scarlett, his face lights up and breaks into this *grin*, and Scarlett wants to shout at her thunder-heart to please have some respect.

"Sherlock! You came."

Scarlett shuts the car door and double-locks it, just in case. "Of course. You said you had a lead."

Will shakes his head slightly, like he's remembering something. "Right. Yes! I do. Come with me." He jumps down from the wall and starts striding into the cemetery proper, neatly weaving them between rows of graves.

As in, they're walking over people's graves. Actual dead people. Scarlett keeps her eyes fixed straight ahead and holds her breath, focusing on Will.

They're in what looks to be an older section; the stones around them are sand colored with family names and crests, spaced far apart across stretches of overgrown grass.

"Wow. You really know where you're going," she comments, mostly to let some of the adrenaline flowing through her out.

Will holds his chin in his hand for a second, his palm covering half his mouth, then quickly moves it away. "So, okay. You know how there's no digital record of this cemetery, right?"

Scarlett had Googled this. "Yeah."

"Well, I've maybe been, like, charting it?"

"*What*? When?"

"Sort of. I mean, it's massive. But I realized the second night I came back that there's a *tiny* bit of order to it, if you really look. Edwardian-era graves down the left side at the front. Families sticking to the same area over generations—stuff like that. Then I started making a map." He pulls it out of his notebook with a flourish.

"Of course you did," Scarlett says. She tries to sound teasing but can't quite manage it.

Will gives her a lopsided smile. "If you mock my system, I might pull a disappearing act and leave you here."

Scarlett genuinely shivers. "Oh my god, don't even joke."

Will's smile gets wider. "I walked here, so I actually can't, but also as if I would."

"So then, wait. What are we looking for now, exactly? What did you find?" Scarlett asks, trying to keep her voice even.

"Ah, I'm so glad you asked. One hundred percent did not bring you out here as part of some sort of nefarious Shelleyian fantasy or just to show you my map, but rather in search of . . ." Will consults his map for a second, brow furrowed in concentration, takes two steps to his right, looks up, and points. ". . . this."

Scarlett walks over to stand beside him. She's wearing what are maybe the worst possible cemetery-recon shoes. Grass pokes sharply through the holes.

Will turns on his phone flashlight.

They're facing a grave that's more like a tomb, dominated by a statue of a middle-aged mustached man holding an ornate sword. It's the name, though, that's the thing. It explodes in Scarlett's brain like a bomb.

R. Elston Hammond III

15 May 1946–26 August 2002

Forever Remembered, Beloved Son

Her heart stops and starts again. "What the fu—" she starts, energy zinging through her body. "*What?*"

"I know," Will says. "I also feel like the 'remembered' is *quite* rich."

"This is *him*? *The* Robert Hammond?"

"Yep. The names on his birth certificate are a perfect match."

Scarlett feels weird, like she's swaying on the spot even though she hasn't moved at all. "But 2002—how is that even *possible*? It's not. Is it?"

"That's what I wondered. Hence why we're here."

Scarlett reads the dates again rapidly. "If this is right, then not only did Sadie not—I mean, we knew she didn't—but he probably *outlived Sadie*. And wait. He's—"

"Elston Hammond. He must have signed her discharge form from Harmony Hill with his middle name. And he's been sitting up here this whole time."

It takes Scarlett a minute to identify the hot liquid emotion running through her for what it is. She's furious. "So Wembly, everyone, just blamed Sadie—blamed *us*—for this made-up, massive crime without even checking the *main cemetery* in this godforsaken place?"

Will watches her in the way Scarlett watches thriller movies: excited and scared. "I mean, to be fair, I only found it because I noticed a pattern of where most bigger families had their ancestral plots and literally stalked him—but otherwise, yeah. That's pretty much it."

"I can't believe he's just been right here! That's insane!" Scarlett bursts out, feeling marginally vindicated by using the word people used to describe Sadie and on them. "Why would people say Sadie pushed him off a cliff if he was still alive?"

Will folds his map carefully, tucking it back away. "I don't know. Maybe someone did see something that day but didn't really know what. Or they just lied."

Scarlett rubs her hand over her forehead to try and unfog her brain. "I just . . . I can't even *process* that. It's so wrong."

It fits, though, with everything she already knows. That's the worst bit. All the things Amy has said to her over the years about women and history—fair and unfair—but it still makes her feel punched-in-the-gut sick.

"How did you know to look for him here? Like at this cemetery, at all?"

Will shrugs. "I didn't, really. I just kind of *kept* looking, and then . . . I had a hunch."

"Some hunch," Scarlett says, still feeling close to tears or screaming. She blows out a breath.

"Sometimes—rarely—I'm kind of useful," Will says, smirking.

"Thank you so much," Scarlett says. Her thoughts are coming in fits and starts, sadness and surging injustice punctured by adjusting to the hugeness of this new development and then, suddenly, by the knowledge that Will Taylor tried really quite hard to bring it to her.

"Oh, I mean, don't mention it. I owed you one, really. That's mostly what it was."

She focuses on him properly, pale in the star-scattered night with his black backpack straps on his shoulders and his hair falling into his eyes. "Mostly?" Scarlett thinks she sees his cheeks flush, before deciding she must be more scrambled by Hammond Gravegate than she realizes.

"I . . . yeah. That's what it was."

Scarlett lets it drop, staring again at the blue-gray grave, rising out of the dirt proud as a lie. "What do we do with it? This? What do we do now?"

Will lifts his shoulders a fraction. "Same thing we've been doing. We keep looking for Sadie. Like, we know she didn't kill anyone now, which feels like a pretty good step."

Scarlett hadn't thought of it that way. "That's true."

It's strangely cold, and feels dangerously late now compared to when they arrived.

They start to turn away from Robert Hammond's headstone.

Scarlett feels sad in a way that's so hopeless it doesn't even hurt. She takes one last look, the stone blurring in her eyes. The light from Will's phone darts across different parts of it as he turns away. Cracks and weather marks, smudges. Then she sees something she didn't notice before.

She steps back toward the grave and turns on her own phone flashlight.

Haphazard, tiny letters. Two words, scratched into the stone.

Like someone did it as an afterthought, perhaps with a knife. Next to where it says *Beloved Son*.

"What's up? Are you okay?" Will asks.

Scarlett shakes her head, the nearby sea hissing through her ears like static on an old phone. "Look."

Will leans closer, squinting in the dark, the flashlight streaming over the scratched words. Then he says, "Holy crap! *And* . . ."

"*Father*," Scarlett finishes reading. "*Beloved Son and Father.*"

"Holy crap," Will says again.

Scarlett gets the same buzzing in her blood as when she found Sadie's hospital record, but more. As if she's so *close* to something, something so important she could burst with wanting to know what it is. Her brain plays it through rapidly, drawing on every mystery story she's ever read.

- Elston Hammond.
- A secret grave.
- The argument on the cliff.
- The hospital. The . . .

"Will," she says urgently. "That's *it*. It has to be. That's why Sadie left! Because she was *pregnant*."

Scarlett stares at Will.

Will stares at the grave. He's thinking too. They both scan the etched words, over and over.

And father. And father. Whose father?

"Sherlock, I think you might be right," Will says.

"Harmony Hill." Scarlett remembers with abrupt, searing clearness. "Didn't you say it wasn't just a hospital?"

"Yes!" Will agrees. "Oh my god. It was also a mothers' and babies' home. You're exactly right."

Scarlett blinks under the weight of everything clicking into place. Of this, their first proper Sadie-discovery. Of what it *means*.

"That means I have a secret relative," she says aloud.

"Potentially probably yes." Will nods. He's looking at Scarlett as if she's the sun.

She's almost (almost) equally impressed with herself. The one time jumping to conclusions has proven useful. Doctor Marnie would be so proud.

"This changes everything," Scarlett says, because it feels like it does. Her head swims. "Can . . . can we sit down?"

"Absolutely! Halftime break to process the history-altering discovery."

"Should we go back to the car?"

"Um. I know a place, from my fully not-creepy wanderings here, if you want some air?"

"Air," Scarlett repeats. "Yes, please."

Will leads the way, steering them to the edge of the graves and through a line of trees.

"Why are we entering a haunted forest," Scarlett asks, "and why do I feel like you hang out here a lot?"

Will laughs. "Because I'm brooding and mysterious?"

"Ha."

"Is that meant to be you laughing in the face of danger?"

"Obviously, yes."

They reach a parting in the trees. Will does a *ta-da* gesture with both arms.

"Is that?"

"Yeah."

Scarlett can feel a laugh bubbling in her throat. In front of them is a park of sorts. It's got monkey bars and a metal slide and a sad rusty swing set with no swings. "That's the most depressing thing I've ever seen!"

"I know. It's glorious. It's my favorite thing."

Scarlett raises her eyebrows. "Why?"

"Because someone spent actual money putting a *park* in here, steps from a literal graveyard. One that looks like the Huns from Disney's *Mulan* have recently been through it—who, to be historically accurate, weren't actually Huns at all but an entirely different nomadic tribe. It's completely bizarre."

Scarlett shakes her head. But she does feel cheered up. "Amazing." She feels laugh-drunk and shivery. Is this how actual Sherlock feels, when he solves part of a case?

Will is looking at her again; it's a look that she can't figure out or doesn't want to. Or *does* want to.

Scarlett chews her lip and something flashes in Will's eyes that isn't just blue. She can see the headstones behind him and *oh, god*— she gets it. She's never going to be blasé watching biopics of Mary Shelley ever again.

Then Will loses his balance and slips sideways, his knee hitting the bark of a nearby tree. "That was on purpose!" he jokes. "I'm that dedicated to cheering you up." He recovers fast, batting at the stained right knee of his jeans ineffectually and frowning. "But. Definitely burning these when I get home."

"Are you okay?"

"Why, how do I look?" Will asks.

And Scarlett accidentally honestly says, "You look like a bad idea."

As soon as she says it, regret pours over her head.

Will digs his hands into his pockets and clears his throat. "Oh yeah?"

Scarlett squeezes her eyes shut for a second because *what is she doing*? They just had a major development about Sadie. Weird sexiness of cemeteries aside, she should go home right now, and quit while she's ahead.

But. She wants to feel something, for once—something besides afraid.

"Yeah," Scarlett somehow says.

"How bad are we talking?" Will asks, the two of them moving fast into the kind of heart-pounding moment Scarlett was pretty sure didn't really exist outside of books, until right this second.

"Um." She swallows. Her heart *is* actually pounding, but it's not like it normally does. It's laced with something else. Sugar, maybe. Acid. Gold. "Very, very bad."

Will looks up at her then. He takes a step closer. Scarlett feels it like an adrenaline shot licking heat through her blood.

"Huh," Will says, all breath. "What'll we do about that?"

He's different like this—the way she's seen musicians like her dad be different once they're onstage. Switched to full wattage. Confident, she guesses, in the knowledge they know what they're doing.

"Um," she says again, struggling to keep up with the shift in mood. To know what she's supposed to do and also hold back while everything she *wants* to do is thundering through her.

Will steps closer again, and Scarlett doesn't move. Not even when he comes to a stop so close that their shoulders touch.

For a minute they stand still. Scarlett's pulse is trying to escape her wrists, neck, temples.

She can't do this. With Will—*Cinnamon's* Will, now and maybe always. She pictures her sister in a flash and sees it all stretch out in front of her—the world afterward, if she does do this. The same, but fundamentally changed forever, the same slipping-under-your-feet kind of way it feels right after somebody leaves or dies.

She can't do this.

She can't not.

"I mean, *I* can think of a few things we could do." Will's voice isn't entirely steady. "But it's . . . it's your call."

Scarlett's breath hitches. *How* do people do this? *Feel* this way? So good she almost can't handle it. Did Sadie feel this way for Robert? All this *energy* just running through her, electric like she's stuck her hand in a socket.

She gulps. Screws her adrenaline into a ball. "Okay. If we kiss in this graveyard right now, it absolutely didn't happen. It's as friends."

"Understood," Will says immediately, and then they look hectically at each other, and Will hesitates like he's nervous or unsure. Then his chin bumps hers whisper-soft, and Scarlett does kiss him.

Will is gentle at first, but there's a heat underneath that burns. Scarlett's jaw drops with it. After a minute his hands wrap around the thick straps on the front of her jumpsuit, gently tugging her in closer. His fingers curve the denim to rest, tentatively, against her chest.

Scarlett gasps.

"Is this . . . ?" Will asks straightaway, pulling back. "Are you . . . I don't want to . . ."

"Yeah," she whispers. "It's . . . Don't stop." She doesn't know how else to voice the feeling in her except to kiss him again, crushing their bodies together hard.

He makes a groaning sound against the side of her lips, and

she does it again. She can do this. *Is* doing this. His chest feels hard against hers. His mouth is so warm. One palm slips up to cup her neck, her collarbone, her jaw below her ear.

Her fingers chart a path up his shirt to touch his cheeks. Will's mouth opens wider, movements becoming faster and less precise. She likes it—him as blurry-urgent as she is, everything else forgotten— much more than she should. The way his hand falters when he skims it lower over her chest.

Will is the one who has to end it. He holds her there, though, close but at a safer distance and with one hand still in her hair. "Holy shit," he whispers. "I should point out geographical similarities to Disney's *Mulan* on our doorstep more often. I mean, if it's this hot."

"Shut *up*. Oh my god," Scarlett says. She buries her face in his shoulder, because she wants to hide. Because she doesn't.

She feels full of a bright-clear sense that she's really *here* for once. Here in her body. Standing next to Will in his. It's so big she thinks that the dead can probably feel it too, and finds she doesn't mind at all.

32.

Cinnamon is avoiding Daisy Leung.

That's where they're at. Or where she's at, at least. She can't show up at work while her insides are still jumbled Christmas lights tangled in a ball. That's not happening.

Where she's at is home, technically. She cashed in her work leave up until the end of the week. Tony said, "Absolutely fine, Cinnatron!" He wasn't even mad, or wasn't surprised. Maybe he knows.

Will knows, because she told him. Some of it. But he also knows not to text.

At least none of them know she hasn't left her room in forty-eight hours. It's the hazy time between Christmas and New Year's anyway, everything slightly unreal and suspended and *hot*, days bleeding together, then away. She isn't sure if she likes it—this temporary ceasefire of living—or hates it. Her opinion changes every year.

She's sitting at her computer, steadily ignoring the fact that last year, not far off this time, she was avoiding Will and becoming not-his-girlfriend. At least they properly *dated* first. Whatever *this* is has to be a breakup personal best.

What's happening right now?

None of that exists here in her slope-roofed, sea-facing room. She has always been good at compartmentalizing. Had to be. The compartment she's chilling in for now has nothing but the glow of her computer and her index finger clicking things alive.

What she's making is unclear, but so far involves pulling stock images from online and lifting colors and shapes from them, then layering in Photoshop to form a silhouette in the middle, in the approximate shape of a girl's face in profile. A flat strip of sea from somewhere in Greece for the background. Rainy-gray sky. A bunch of foxgloves in soft pastel pink.

She's sitting on the ergonomic chair Ian bought her when she aced graphics in school, back when she'd sit for hours at her computer in the dark making-making-making, sometimes with nothing to show for it at the end, but never with the sliding feeling currently in her chest that life is water rushing past, and she is wasting time.

One of her legs is tucked up so that her chin rests on her knee. She clicks her jaw every now and then, up and down, when she can't think what else to add to the background, so it contrasts but isn't *busy*. Cinnamon hates busy designs. Art shouldn't look like it's trying to be anything.

A ceramic purple mug with daisies on it.

Delete that.

Save it though.

She finds a painted picture of a wave crashing, its white meringue tongue licking sand. She adds that to the sky behind her silhouette, along with a slice of purple gloss ceramic with yellow-centered flowers.

It's been hours of this already, Cinnamon clicking her jaw and thinking only of which tool to use, and clicking her jaw, and manipulating colors and layers, and clicking her jaw. It's still not perfect, but it's reached the point of not-perfect where she also feels like it's almost done.

There's a shitty-quality photo of the full moon she took in 2017 that'd make good cut-out eyes, if she can find it. She clicks around, searching, but it's hidden deep in the folders she never labels properly. She takes a break, because several hours when you're graduated and nineteen feels like a long time.

It's late when she zones back into the buzz of Halcyon. She can't hear anything except birds and the beach—probably because everyone else is asleep. Cinnamon should go to bed too. The shape of the facing-sideways-girl's eye isn't right yet, though.

If she gets the eye right, maybe she'll know what it is.

She decides to make coffee. Just a dirty instant one. When she creaks downstairs, the house is all dark blues cut with the gold glint of the lights on the Christmas tree in the entryway. She thinks about switching those off but doesn't.

Cinnamon starts when she sees Amy in the Christmas-lights glow, sitting at the table and cradling a mug under her chin carefully, like it's an infant. Then she nods curtly in greeting, flicks the kettle on. She doesn't have the energy for this.

For anything.

Amy doesn't seem to want to talk either. She watches Cinnamon mixing powdered coffee in milk with a tired expression on her face, as though she's deep in thought. Her short, dyed hair is pulled into the world's smallest ponytail, and her crimson Christmas nails look black against her cheek.

The kettle clicks off.

"You up late making something?" Amy asks.

"Kind of. I mean, maybe."

"It's nice to see you in the art-zone again."

Cinnamon was expecting Amy to be annoying, but not this . . .

interested. It gives her a feeling in her throat for a second like she has a cold. "Thanks."

"You know, we need someone to make graphics for the new website, at work," Amy says.

"Don't you have a designer for that?"

"We did. He left. It's mostly done—it just needs a couple of visuals to fill the gaps."

"I don't know how to do website stuff," Cinnamon says.

"I've seen you make animations, which is mostly what we need. And you could learn."

"Maybe," Cinnamon says, like *no*.

Amy shrugs easily. "All right. Just a thought. Night, darling."

"Night."

When she gets back upstairs, Cinnamon reads through all her text messages from Daisy to check if they still hurt.

Spoiler: they do.

Then she opens her archived emails from the university and stingingly reads those too. *Please let us know if you accept your place for Semester One.*

Or if you'd like to mess this up too.

Lastly, she opens YouTube, types *Ian Prince interview* into the search bar, and looks at the results—tiny thumbnail tiles of his face stacked on top of each other. She hovers over the first one and presses play.

"Oh, life is amazing right now," her dad's voice tells ABC in 2001 while she reopens Photoshop and tries to get the eye right. "Everything's moving really quickly, between the album being number one and becoming a parent, but I love that. So far, fast has been the only way I move."

33.

A few days after Hammond Gravegate, and it's raining again—fat droplets drumming along the roof of Halcyon and gray-green clouds clustering the sky. There's a breeze misting up off the water that almost feels cool.

Scarlett is sitting with Sadie in the drawing room to stop herself from thinking about Will. It's working great. (*It's really not.*)

When she thinks of The Kiss, guilt flares through her fast as a fire. Guilt and something else, something scary low down in her stomach. They haven't talked about it. Or talked much at all. They've talked about the *case*, briefly, but the rapid-fire messaging is no more.

Scarlett doesn't know what that means. He's probably treating The Kiss as a just-friends thing, as she stupidly—*no, rightfully*—said to, and it's made things horrifically weird. *She* has. Like always.

She brings her focus back to the painted portrait of Sadie in front of her. It's a triumph from an artistic point of view. Scarlett thinks so, anyway. Her grandpa created lots like it, always insisting that they were a hobby more than anything else.

She used to have a sketch, now lost, of her and Cinnamon as little girls. Cinnamon's surly face peering off the paper and her fat toddler hands cupping Scarlett's potato baby head. She didn't think to keep it back then. Grandpa Charlie scattered sketches like footprints.

The portrait of Sadie is his best, though. The colors behind her—navyblueforestgreendarkplumgold—are careful and chaotic at the same time, making the pale oval face with its giant eyes even more striking. It's so realistic it looks like a photograph, but it's better than a photo too. More.

Scarlett can't stop wondering if it's also a clue. She's sitting on the rug staring up at it every few minutes, sorting through the final box of Maggie's things.

Three of the other boxes were books, the last of which Scarlett finished on Christmas night when she was soft-sad like she is now and trying not to think about Will for different reasons. She kept most of Maggie's books—added some to the bookshelves downstairs, packed some up to be repaired. She kept all Maggie's clothes too, even half-finished sweaters and vests Maggie knitted with missing stitches. She thought she might repurpose some of them, but really she just likes to look at them, the small pieces of her grandmother that still exist.

The last box is full of miscellaneous things—a crystal jewelry box, an old smudged mirror, a VCR, clip-on earrings scattered like sequins and no longer in pairs. When she's almost finished sorting through it, thunder cracks in the distance. It starts raining hard, and water whips in through the open window.

Scarlett stands up and closes it, then walks back over to Sadie. She studies the portrait closer, traces the swirl of her granddad's signature, the half smile of the mouth, the black-blue ribbon in Sadie's hair. The portrait has always hung there, for Scarlett's entire life. It's always looked to her as though it wants to tell the viewer something.

What, though?

Thunder cracks again, and it could be the storm, or the force of trying to do this without—*off-limits-off-limits-stop*—Will, or Maggie's mismatched earrings on her ears, but Scarlett does maybe the most impulsive thing she's ever done. She grabs the gold edges of the picture frame. It's heavy and stuck fast from hanging there for decades, but after a minute and a lot of jiggling, Scarlett lifts it off the wall. Gingerly, she lowers the canvas to the ground and looks back at where it was hanging.

She's not sure what she expected. A safe or something, maybe. That would be the movie version of this moment. Instead the part of the wall where the portrait hung is a different color than the rest of the room—years of paint preserved like a lemon—but that's it.

Scarlett runs a frustrated hand through her hair. She's officially the worst at this. Sherlock-ing. Detective-ing. Will Taylor—however good he is at confidently kissing girls in cemeteries and then playing it infuriatingly cool—is wrong about her.

She hoists the portrait back into her arms and wonders/worries if she's going to be able to get it back on the hook, or if she's going to have to risk the wrath of Cinnamon or the sadness of Ian. She loses her grip, and the frame slides down the wall.

She blows her hair back from her face, gearing up for round two, but then there's a muffled sound of something hitting the floor. With one hand still on the painting, she crouches down, feeling until her fingers grip something that isn't carpet.

Another sticky note, Scarlett thinks, like the ones all through the cookbooks. But the paper is cardboard-hard and the handwriting on it smaller and more precise: *Sads & me, '72.*

Scarlett turns it over, trying to breathe normally. She studies the faces of the two women standing with their arms around each other's shoulders.

A long-haired and infinitely younger but unmistakable Maggie, tall like Cinnamon, with her dark hair and dark eyes crinkled at the edges by a wide lipsticked smile. And next to her, short hair and gray eyes that gleam even in black and white, is Sadie. It looks like the origin of the painted portrait. She's wearing the same white blouse tucked into polka-dot cigarette pants, only they're rolled up over her shins in the photo version.

On her other side is a dark-classic-handsome man who must be Robert Hammond. On her hip, fair-haired and smiling, looking over at Maggie: A child. A boy. A son.

Scarlett remembers Maggie's face when she talked about the Legend of Sadie Prince. *Nobody knows.*

And what if that always meant, *Because I didn't tell.*

She props the portrait against the wall, pockets the photograph, and runs downstairs to the hook to grab Amy's keys.

Fifteen minutes later, Scarlett is in Will Taylor's bedroom, soaked with the second storm of summer still dripping from her hair.

"Okay. I only have this," Will announces from the doorway, offering her a (very) threadbare white towel. His voice is a shade too loud.

When he answered the door, he looked fresh out of the shower, no shirt on and his hair wet. He's wearing a gray T-shirt now. He smells clean, like soap and sherbety laundry detergent.

"Thanks," Scarlett says, her insides shivery, both from the cold and from being inside his room. Boy paraphernalia is dotted all around her—space-themed bedding, jeans folded in a pile on a desk near the door, two tall wooden bookshelves with glass doors, bluish walls tacked with posters of bands she's only half heard of. She dries her hair quickly, throwing the wet length of it back over her shoulders and rubbing excess droplets off her arms.

It's so awkward once she's done. She wishes she'd thought to just message him the photo. She wishes she could message him now instead, so they could talk and still be a safe distance from the giant swallowing feeling currently clogging her throat every time she looks at him.

She looks at the towel, turning it in her hands. "Don't," Will warns.

"Willie," she reads the embroidered cursive letters out loud, then looks up quickly.

Will makes a soft wincing face.

"Wait. Is that *you*?"

He takes the towel back and scrunches it into a ball. "If I tell you that's an unfortunate yes, will you tell me why you're here?"

Scarlett shifts away from him, turning back toward the window. Something in her chest flips, then twists into all the reasons he probably (*definitely*) never wanted to see her again after what happened.

It's wet gray everywhere outside, punctured by blurred splashes of yellow streetlight. His room faces the empty slick road and, beyond it, the sea.

"Is it bad that I'm here?" she asks quietly, without turning around.

Will is silent for a moment, then says, "No." His voice is closer than it should be, right next to her shoulder.

Scarlett's eyes squeeze closed for a second in a flash of relief. "Glad to hear it—*Willie*."

Will laughs. She can feel his breath fan out onto the back of her neck.

She breathes in some air of her own, trying to get it to go down into the knot in her chest, then turns around. It's not easy to make words happen with him here-right-here. She inhales again. "I found something. Something big."

Will's eyebrows rise, but he still looks reserved. "Yeah?"

Scarlett can feel the photo burning a hole deep in the pocket of her pink corduroy skirt. She pulls it out and thrusts it toward him.

He studies it, his eyebrows shooting up higher.

"Right?" Scarlett says, trying to sound friendly and normal. "Read the date on the back."

"Seventy-two. And that's the kid, right? Sadie and Robert's. There's definitely a kid."

"*Mmm*," Scarlett agrees. "He even looks like us, sort of—it's so weird."

"He *does*! Where'd you find it?"

"I maybe pried a fifty-year-old portrait off the wall in the drawing room, and it was stuck to the back."

Will looks up at her: dead-on, wide-eyed. Then away again. "Wow. I'm impressed."

Scarlett shrugs. "Blame it on New Year's Eve eve."

Will stares at the photo again. "We can totally use this. The stuff in the background, all of it. I'll scan it through the work computer tomorrow."

Tomorrow.

He wants her to go.

As in leave.

"Oh!" Scarlett nods, heart twisting, turning, spitting fire. "Of course, I'm interrupting your night. I'll go."

Will looks stricken. The kiss must have been bad. She's a bad kisser.

"That's not what I . . . You don't have to go!" he stammers, cheeks turning pink.

Scarlett recognizes that look. She's burning with the need to ask him what he *did* mean, but instead she hands him a lukewarm joke to put him out of his misery. "Why is everything of yours personalized?"

"Wow, okay." Will laughs. "Why must you come into my room and speak such truths?"

And suddenly she does have to know. "I'm here because . . ." Scarlett screws up every ounce of courage she's maybe ever had. "I found a thing. But also, I was thinking about you."

Will's cheeks pink even more. "Um. That's . . ."

Weird, Scarlett waits for him to say. *Leave my house and never come back.*

He doesn't say that. He looks at her for a beat with his mouth half-open, then, "Yeah. Same."

A hot feeling washes over her skin. She pictures Sadie and Maggie staring down the camera and how they're so close to figuring it out, and tries to be brave. "I feel like that sometimes happens when two people kiss."

Will takes a step back. "Scarlett . . ."

The heat on her skin freezes. She's said too much, Scarlett thinks in a crash, just like always. But she can't stop. "Are we not going to talk about that? Or not talk anymore at all?"

"*No*, I . . ." Will rubs his hands through his hair and then down his cheeks. Scarlett tries not to notice the way the heel of his palm skims the side of his mouth. His face, when he drops his arms back down, is pained.

Her chest flips again, waiting for the worst.

"Okay. Obviously, this is really complicated," he starts after a few seconds. "And entirely my fault. I was so stupid that night, and I'm so sorry. Truly. For like, ruining a friendship that was good."

Scarlett blinks slowly. "You were stupid," she repeats.

"Not that you aren't—" Will says in a rush. "Not that I didn't *want* . . . but we can't, and you've been clear about that, and I—"

"What?"

"Am the worst," he finishes helplessly. "It's well known."

"I was there too," Scarlett says, trying to sound breezy like she does this all the time and not like how she feels: gut-dropping disappointed.

"Oh, I'm not trying to, like, take away your autonomy or anything! God. You must be pissed enough at me already."

"I'm not angry at you."

Will's eyes flash with something like disbelief, but brighter. "You're not?"

"Apart from the semi-communication blackout with no warning? No."

He winces, swallowing hard. She watches the way his Adam's apple moves under the pale skin of his throat, waiting for him to tell her to go. Instead he reaches into his pocket and pulls out his phone. The blue light of his lock screen illuminates his face. He slides his thumb over it, then holds it out to her with the Notes app open.

Scarlett squints down uncertainly. Her eyes take a minute to adjust to the light before she can read what he's showing her.

Hey! So, about,
So yesterday was kind of
Are you thinking like
Sorry if you now feel massively weird, or
God wow!! I'd totally understand if now
Was that . . .

"Shitty conversation starters," Will explains. "There are seventeen of them written during various points of desperation in the last twenty-four hours. This afternoon I felt like I nearly cracked it. That last one? *Phwoar.*"

Scarlett looks back up. She doesn't know whether to jump on him, or cry. "*Will.*"

His eyes are wide, pupils almost entirely swamping the blue. "I so, so don't want to do the wrong thing here," he whispers. "And it is undoubtedly a really bad idea, as you rightly said. But I feel like it's *just*—"

"Inevitable?" she says, giving the phone back. Her hands are shaking, pounding, like her heart's beating inside them maybe, and his too.

Will swallows again. "Yeah."

Scarlett's limbs are still blooming with a weird electricity. She thinks about Jane Eyre running bravely across a field to Mr. Rochester, despite everything. One foot in front of the other. "How bad are we talking?"

"Okay. If quoting me back to myself is meant to turn me *off* . . ." Will shakes his burning-cheeked head.

Their foreheads touch. Will's breath is on her mouth. His hand is on her waist. A wave crashes across the road. It hits Scarlett's ears quick as a shock.

They stare at each other, close-up. For so long. *Have* been staring at each other for so long.

Then there's a different kind of crash—glass. The window caves in, which doesn't make any sense, but suddenly there's bits of it and the rain all over the rug.

Scarlett grabs her throat and spins sharply around to face the street again.

Will swears.

There is a jagged hole in the glass.

Cinnamon is standing outside.

Scarlett knows, in the few seconds their eyes meet right before her sister hurls a second rock through the window, that both were meant for her.

34.

Cinnamon is running home.

The branches on all the trees of Main Street are still wound with lights that look, in the dark, like rain made out of gold. Cinnamon hates them. It's not even the lights themselves—it's the way they look. And the way the way they look makes her *feel*.

Hollow.

They're mocking her, those trees, tonight. Just like the rest of her life.

It's not Will or her sister that's the problem either, necessarily. She doesn't think, anyway. It's the way watching the two of them made her feel. The way that, lately, everything makes her feel—the kind of angry that makes you feel like if you scream, pieces of you will fall out.

And you kind of want them to.

Will's house was a mistake—she hasn't gone to his house after dark since they did lots of stuff after dark. Leaving her room was a mistake. Possibly her entire life is a mistake.

She runs and runs, along the ocean, past the navy rippling surface of the baths, strokes of yellow on their surface under a waxy waning moon. The waves are heavy on the beach beside her, thudding like her footfalls on the path.

"Cin!" shouts a voice from behind her.

"Leave me alone!" she roars.

The sea roars too, crashes, booms. "Just stop! Please."

She doesn't stop.

Will doesn't catch up to her until they hit the promenade. One of the gates is shut, and Cinnamon decides to spin around and let him have it.

His face is drawn in the dim light, lavender bags under his eyes like he's already rubbed them over and over.

She's properly furious, seeing him look at her like that, his familiar face tinged bright red. She can't speak. Only glare.

"Really?" Will says, out of breath. "You really woke up and chose rock-through-the-window, and we're not even gonna discuss it?"

"It's all fairly self-explanatory. Betrayal of the most basic kind. No further discussion required, ever."

Will's expression shifts from sad to pissed off. Up close he looks even worse, his hair wet and falling all over his forehead. "Wow."

"What?"

"Just, the hypocrisy of it," he says. "It's pretty incredible."

"Whatever." She can feel her face curling into a sneer. "You know everything, right? You win."

Will rubs his hands over the bottom half of his face. "Jesus. There's no *winning* here, Cin, not if—"

"If what?" Cinnamon spits.

His mouth works, stops, works some more. Then he tips up his chin and says, "If I lose you."

"You don't have me!" Cinnamon shrieks. "I'm not, like, *property*."

"I don't think that about you! I've never thought that about you. But judging by this reaction, that's exactly what you think of me."

"Oh my god. I am not doing this right now." She turns and walks toward the beach.

He follows. She kicks up rocks, watches them bounce down the sand slope and into the water. Will watches, bottom lip caught in white teeth. Waits.

"Look," Cinnamon says eventually. She's still so *angry*. Full of it. But she's also so tired. Full of nothing. "We broke up ages ago. Objectively, it's fine for you to tongue my sister. I'm just being an arsehole about it because . . . I don't know. I'm just an arsehole, probably." She expects his face to relax a bit. For him to start calming her down, or at least trying to.

He doesn't. Instead Will stares out at the beach for a stretch of time. Then he says unsteadily, "Do you think it was easy for me?" His eyes are still on the awake night sea. "Us breaking up?"

Cinnamon flinches. Remembers the way back then he said, "No please, it's *fine*," to all her reasons it wasn't.

They don't talk about this, as a hard rule.

"No," she says too fast.

"Because it wasn't," Will continues. He interlaces both hands behind his head and leans back into them, elbows spread out like wings. "It was totally, utterly shit. All of it. But I sucked it up . . ." His voice cracks. "Because having you as my friend was worth it."

"Will . . ." She doesn't know how to explain this giant feeling to him; she can't explain it to herself. There's no word for it, the desperate-sudden clawing in her stomach and missing him when he's standing right here.

He finally looks at her. "What do you *want* from me, Cin?"

The worst part is that he means it. *Tell me and I'll do it.*

"What do you mean?"

240

Will never yells, but he's yelling now. "Because we've been breaking up for literally an entire year! So, what? *What do we do?*"

"I don't know!" she yells back at him. "I just . . . everything's so . . . I hate this." The worst part is she can't tell him the truth.

I didn't want to keep you, and I don't want to let go.

"Hate what?"

"Everything! All of it!" she screams even louder, and it's *good*, the sound of it ricocheting off the faraway rocks, until it feels horrible again. "Nothing's like it was. I don't know what I'm doing, ever, or what's going to happen next."

Will looks properly pained. "Come on—you're you. You'll be fine."

"Everyone always says that. But it's kind of up to me to decide whether I'm fine or not, isn't it? And I say not. And now it's like you're leaving too."

"What did you think would happen when we ended it? That things would stay like school forever?"

"No," Cinnamon says again.

It sounds like the lie it is.

Will sighs. "They just can't, Cin. I mean, some things can, but we were always going to have our own lives, you know?"

"Yes, I *know*. Thanks." She's snapping again, thinking of Scarlett's stupid shocked face, her long wet hair.

"Don't do that."

Cinnamon feels cold, even though the air is soupy summer. "Do *what*?"

He comes closer to her instead of answering. He exhales, reaching out to touch her arm with just his index finger. "Look. I'm sorry, okay? *Really* fucking sorry. I should've . . . I should've said something sooner."

She folds her arms tight across her chest in agreement. "But this whole summer's been weird with us."

"*Mmph*."

"I feel like I never really know what's going on with you anymore." Cinnamon folds her arms tighter.

"And . . ." Will bites his lip. "Scarlett, she . . ."

Cinnamon sucks in a breath that cuts her chest. "Yes?"

"We just kind of . . . accidentally clicked? I don't know! Or *I* did, at least, and I've been feeling like such a *dick* about it, the whole time, but I just . . ."

"You like her." Cinnamon tilts her head up toward the rained-out sky and uncrosses her arms. She thinks, inexplicably, of Daisy's white shoes. "I like someone too. As long as we're being honest."

"Daisy?"

"Yes."

"I know."

"I think maybe I really do, and that's why I messed it up."

"I know."

Cinnamon thinks it's those two words that finally make the fury start to flicker out.

They don't say anything else. They just stand with their fingers gripped messily together, watching the tide leak away.

Will lets go first. "I can't be yours anymore," he says. Very quietly.

For once, Cinnamon is the one crying. "I *don't*—"

"But that doesn't mean I won't be here."

She feels it again: hot-sad-sick. The moon slips behind the clouds, spilling dark in its wake. "I think maybe I need you to not be, for a while."

Will looks like he does when he's going to cry—chin tipped up, mouth turned down.

If he does, she might punch him.

Or hug him.

"Okay. That's . . . yeah. That makes sense."

When she looks back, he really is leaving. And she's alone.

35.

Scarlett can't go home.

After the window-smashing, Will kept saying *Oh god* over and over.

Cinnamon ran off without saying anything, then he looked at Scarlett with a sad, desperate, honorable sort of expression on his face and went after her.

She can't stay in this room, after that.

Can't go.

Can't not.

Guilt claws at her throat. Thick, hot tears blur her vision. She sits on Will's floor and counts her breaths. Out for five, in for four. No, that's wrong. In for five, out for . . . She can't keep count. Into her abdomen—that's the important bit. *Deep breaths, not shallow. Panic can't kill you. Panic's technically partly in your mind.*

Guilt is in your body, though, wet like rain or dread. She breathes and counts and counts and forgets while the sea crashes and heaves outside, for almost an hour.

It's windy when she finally manages to walk to the car and drives home shaky-handed. Town is fairy-lit and eerily still. The car lurches through it slowly, her heart pounding so hard it feels like it's between her ears.

"You can do this," she says to herself. "You can do this, you can do this, you can . . ."

It's even windier once she gets to the top of Halcyon's hill, heavy humid air that tosses her hair and fills it with salt.

Cinnamon is out front, on Princes Cliff.

Scarlett clicks the lock on the car keys just once, and tries to remember every brave thing she's ever done. Rocks crunch under her feet. Her chest tries to rip its way free of her body.

"Don't," her sister hisses like the sea, once Scarlett's behind her.

"Cinnamon . . . ," she tries gently.

"Stop talking."

"But I can—"

"You actually can't."

"Please will you let me—"

Cinnamon turns around to face her. Her features are hard and beautiful, only the red of her eyes and the wet of their lashes giving away that she's a thing that can be hurt. "You can't rationalize this with your stupid Sensitive Scarlettisms so you're not the one who's in the wrong. You are, for once. Deal with it."

Scarlett's mouth falls open.

Cinnamon turns back to the ocean again.

"I'm sorry, okay," Scarlett bursts out. "I'm sorry! I'm sorry!"

Cinnamon pulls her knees up to her chest and leans her folded arms on them. "Don't care."

Scarlett walks closer and stands in front of her, sea breeze blowing hard against her back. "We didn't mean to upset you—I swear. I would never try to hurt you. It was just . . . It was an accident. And it's not Will's fault, okay. Don't hate him."

Cinnamon looks up at her, slow and cold. "Jesus—it's not even about that."

Scarlett throws her arms up in exasperated desperation. "Oh. Then what *is* it about?"

Cinnamon stands up, brushes dirt off the backs of her thighs. "It's *you*."

"Me?"

"Yes."

Scarlett's brain is scrambled eggs. "But you don't even *like* me anymore. What do you care what I do? I thought Will—"

"Will can't hurt me like you can!" Cinnamon shouts. "He's not meant to be my *sister*."

Scarlett blinks. This is so opposite to where she expected the conversation to go that, for a minute, she can't process it. At all.

"I am your sister!" she snaps back.

Cinnamon's top lip curls. "Right. My sister who's literally never here."

"I couldn't be here! I'm not like you! I couldn't handle living here when—"

"My sister who comes home and ignores our dad and me," Cinnamon continues. "And just goes after the one person I've ever lo—"

"*I'm not ignoring Dad!* He's ignoring *me*! Like everyone ignores me!" Scarlett is shrieking now, heart pounding hard in waves against her ribs. It's always like this when they fight, though never this bad.

What Cinnamon really thinks is a complete mystery, right up until the second she wants to let you in. The worst part is the shock of it.

Cinnamon shoots Scarlett another dark look and drops her voice low. "Yeah? Because you're the one who left."

Scarlett's hair is blowing all over her face. She sweeps it away angrily. "I went to *school*. You're being awful. I'm going."

Cinnamon's eyes are stony. "You left me here."

"I thought you *wanted* to stay!" Scarlett gasps, stricken. "How was I meant to know—"

"I wanted a life that wasn't only here!" Cinnamon screams at her. *Screams.* "One that was mine!"

Something snaps inside Scarlett. She feels it like a rubber band come apart, everything it was holding together spilling messily out. She pictures quickly again the world spreading out in front of her, different afterward if she does what she's about to do.

She doesn't recognize her own voice when it responds, "You think I don't want that?"

"Are you kidding me? You *have* that!"

"No, I have *your* shadow!" Scarlett says in the same strange cruel tone. "That's what I have. This whole entire argument is literally because that's the only place I ever get to be."

Cinnamon shakes her head, scowls. "That's . . . You're ridiculous."

Scarlett's ears are ringing. She's fuming. She's shaking. She's done. "Cool. Yeah. Glad we cleared that up."

"And what, because you think you're my shadow, you have to take Will?" Cinnamon counters meanly. "Is that it?"

"YOU DIDN'T WANT HIM ANYMORE! You had him, and you didn't even want him!" Scarlett screams back so loud and inhuman that it drowns out the roll of the sea. "You're just mad that the world doesn't revolve around you for once. Admit it."

"Admit that I hate you right now? Easy."

"Whatever, Cinnamon." She spits the full name, exactly the way

Cinnamon used to do when they were younger to make her crack. "Hate me, then. I honestly don't care." The knives twisted in her throat tell Scarlett that this is mostly a lie, but only mostly.

Cinnamon stares at her like she's looking at a stranger, or an enemy.

Every fight the Prince sisters have had has followed a pattern: Cinnamon rages and Scarlett follows after her and placates, they're quiet for a few days, and then it's over.

Scarlett always gives in. She wonders now, wind whipping through her ears, if that's just because she's never had anything real to fight about before.

They're standing far apart now, both breathing hard. Both thinking that the real cliff's edge they're looking at is whether to walk toward each other or away.

Scarlett jumps first, spinning around and storming into the house.

"What happened?" Amy asks frantically.

Scarlett swallows. "Ask Cinnamon."

36.

Cinnamon drives off into the night.

That sounds more dramatic than it is. More like something *Scarlett* would do. What really happens is she takes the keys to the Jeep while everyone's asleep because Ian never uses it anymore anyway, and she drives to the city until she's nearly calmed down, and she manages to find Phe's street.

Phe's house is pale-green clapboard. Outside is green-green-green too, with a sweet floral smell hung on the air like an old lady's bathroom. The sky is that late-evening color that looks like it would feel thick if she ran her fingers through it.

Mattie greets Cinnamon in the doorway and ushers her inside. The Other Roommates—two guys who study engineering—are nowhere to be seen.

"Sorry to just rock up," Cinnamon says.

Mattie shakes her head. She's wearing a black hoodie tied ironically under her chin, her angular face with its power-brows dewy from a day's worth of sweat. "She'll be happy to see you. Everything all good, though? You look kind of . . ."

Cinnamon is still bursting at all her seams with the screaming feeling from the beach. She likes Mattie, but she doesn't want to unleash it yet. "Yep. Totally."

They sit on the couch watching a cooking channel on TV, waiting for Phe to come home from the theatre where she works. Phe's parents didn't ask her to move out, didn't want her to, but she was insistent (prior to accidentally falling for Mattie) on Starting Her Life As a Woman Alone. Whenever they talk on the phone, Cinnamon is struck by how much Phe actually likes it—her life. Her job and going out to dinner with Mattie, or staying in and waking up when she wants and coffee on her back veranda.

It sounds nice.

Each time Cinnamon has visited Phe here, she's taken a picture of the hallway. It's an old house, so the ceilings are high, and the hallway opens with an arch that's decorated with flowers surrounding a cross. Cinnamon doesn't know why she takes these photos (she's taking one now, on her way to use the bathroom), but she thinks it has something to do with the way, when the front door is open, the hallway draws her eyes right out onto the street, where you can see the city rising up with its beaming skyscraper-window stars.

It looks like—possibility. Or something.

Phe comes home a little while later, looking tired and grown-up.

"Babe." Mattie stands to kiss her cheek. "Look who's here."

Cinnamon feels out of place suddenly in this old-smelling house full of people starting their lives, like she shouldn't be here but also doesn't know where else to go, but Phe yanks her into a bear hug.

"What are you *doing* here, my love?" she asks, pulling her sticky blouse off and standing there just in her bra.

"Oh, you know," Cinnamon says, "home troubles. Etcetera. Etcetera."

Phe scrutinizes Cinnamon's face, throwing her shirt on a hat rack in the corner. "Uh-oh."

Mattie moves discreetly into the kitchen, turns the tap on, then hands Phe a glass of water, which she gratefully drinks.

"So, what is it?" Phe demands between gulps. "Don't give me that face! I'm only asking."

"I'm fine," Cinnamon says.

Phe is unconvinced. "Your fam? Your dad? And . . . William? How is the dear old boy?"

"I don't want to talk about Will," Cinnamon snaps.

Mattie's eyebrows rise.

Phe lowers her glass slowly. "Ooh. Okay. I smell discord. What's happened?"

"*Nothing.* I was just in the area. You're always telling me to visit."

"This is true. But you're also here because your soul is troubled."

"Don't have one, so . . ."

"Cin."

"*What?*"

"You usually come to me when you can't talk to Will about something." Phe shrugs.

Cinnamon wonders quickly if that's true. "That's not true!"

Ugh. It is.

"I mean, I don't *mind*!" Phe says genuinely. "It's sweet, your whole codependency thing, in a low-level probs-unhealthy kinda way."

"We aren't codependent," Cinnamon says. "We're just . . ." She doesn't know what they are.

Phe mouths *ookay*.

Mattie looks between them and clears her throat. "I'll just be in the bedroom watching *Gilmore Girls* if you need me, y'all," she offers, and melts away in the direction of their room.

"Don't go past where we're up to!" Phe shouts after her. "*RE*watch."

"Oh, so skip ahead?" Mattie teases with a languid smile over her shoulder as she goes. "You want me to tell you how it ends?"

"*Re*watch, Matilda! I mean it. They style Rory's hair utterly differently every three episodes. I'll know!"

Once they're alone, Cinnamon says, "I take it she's not dumping you, then?"

Phe's arched dark eyebrows pull together. "What? Oh, no, I was just on my insecurity bullshit. We had big talks about it the other week. But don't try to change the subject!"

"There is no subject. I just . . . didn't want to be there anymore, so I came to see you."

"So that is it, then, my love," Phe surmises, voice overly gentle like Mr. Rogers. Then she speeds up again as she leans into the drama. "Something *has* happened. And you've run away. I am harboring a fugitive. I'm here for it, but also I'd like to know what I'm harboring."

"There was no *crime*, so how are you harboring a . . . Ugh. Never mind."

Phe chugs more water like she's pregaming for something huge. "No, no. Come on. I want the tea. You can't just show up on my door as a *fugitive*—"

"Again, how am I a fugiti—"

"And not spill that sweet sweet tea."

Cinnamon chews the inside of her lip, looking toward the frosted window to avoid answering and listening to the faint sounds of the city. It's constant here—a steady hum in the background like the sea, except it's more of a buzz than a roar. Then she looks at Phe's beloved worried face, sighs, and tells her everything.

"You are"—Phe blows out a breath once she's done—"genuinely joking, right? Scarlett? Scarlett *Prince*?"

Cinnamon shakes her head. She falls backward into the green velvet couch Phe and Mattie saved from the curb the last time she was here—she helped them drag it a mile in eighty-five degrees—and lets its soft, musty, slightly sagging folds catch her.

"My sweet little love," Phe says, setting her glass down on the kitchen counter to come sit next to Cinnamon. Phe's still wearing just jeans and a bra, gleaming brown skin pooling in familiar little rolls over her high waistband. "Let it out. This couch has seen all manner of things."

"Don't say that when I'm literally sitting on it." Cinnamon wrinkles her nose, then sighs again. "It's not even that I, like, have a problem with them," she says through her teeth.

Phe nods sagely. "Oh, I mean—clearly not. You're fine."

Cinnamon scowls at her.

"It's just that my own life is an absolute garbage fire right now."

Phe makes a *hmm* that still doesn't sound as though she's convinced. "And Will?"

A bolt of heat lances through Cinnamon. She curls her legs up to her chest and holds them there. "What about him?"

Phe gives her a leveling look. "Babe."

"*What?*"

"Okay." Phe holds up her hands. "I won't get involved. At least I know why he messaged me so desperately for my entire shift trying to see if I'd heard from you, though."

"He did?"

Phe holds up her phone as evidence. "Desperado."

Will is notorious for double-texting, but there are so many messages crowding the screen that Cinnamon can't hold them all in her eyes at once.

"I'm gonna tell him you're here, and you're fine, and then I'm gonna tell him to keep it in his *incredibly* unstylish pants," Phe says. "And you are going to tell me all about you and Ms. Daisy Leung."

"Are you gonna put clothes on first?"

Phe makes a face. "I can't strategize your love life *and* care about arbitrary societal rules at the same time. I'm not that kind of lesbian."

Cinnamon smiles slightly. "You can't use that joke as an answer for everything."

"Sometimes I sub in 'but I'm gay'! And also, it works for everything. Now, tell me. William's been infuriatingly cryptic. I don't have the patience to wait. I'm not that kind of—"

"Okay! God. So you know how I told you Daisy and I kissed at the party."

"Yees."

"It was all going fine, and then after that . . . Then I kind of . . ."

"I've got a bad feeling."

"Freaked out and maybe ghosted her?"

Phe sits up and rounds on Cinnamon, face animated in exaggerated faux-rage. "WHAT?"

"Accidentally!" Cinnamon says. She leans her head against the back of the couch, her eyes on the ceiling.

"*Why*, in the name of our lord Kristen Stewart, would you do that? You literally used to call her Perfect Daisy!"

"She's like . . . even better, now that I actually know her. It's . . . That's the problem."

Phe *tsks* in the way she does that makes her look like her mum.

Cinnamon wrings her hands. "It felt different with her," she says. "And, I don't know. I couldn't deal."

Phe frowns. "Because she's a *her*?" she asks gently, like she wants to understand.

Cinnamon shakes her head and tries to think. "Because I kept feeling like when she looked at me, she, like, really saw me. Or wanted to, anyway, and . . . I didn't want her to."

"Why not?"

Cinnamon shrugs and looks up at the ceiling again. "I don't know. In case she didn't like what she saw?" When she looks back down, Phe is frowning deeply.

"Oh, babe."

"What?"

"That would never happen. You are, like, a magnificent phoenix, and we're all lucky to witness you."

"*Pfft.*"

"Excuse me! It's true."

"Plus there's also the whole me-not-having-any-real-world-idea-how-sapphic-sex-works thing, which is not *not* an issue," Cinnamon continues fast.

Phe waves a dismissive hand. "Oh, it's easy! I mean, it's not, but you just do what you do to yourself slash what they ask for slash what you like other people to do to you. I literally tell you about it all the time."

"Super clear, wow. But that's just another *thing*, though, that's like—what if I'm a disaster bi but not in a cute way? What if I can't do it right, and just disappoint her in all the ways?"

"Do you *want* to do it?"

"Obviously."

"Then you will do it, and it'll be great."

"But what if I'm completely shit at it and get it wro—"

"Then you'd talk about it with her, and try again, and it'd be fine! But I don't think you're gonna be shit at it. I have a feeling. And you'll have a feeling. And the feeling will tell you, in the moment when it's happening, what to do."

Cinnamon shakes her head. "You're actually getting low-key wise in your old age, you know that?"

"I know. I'm like a sexy owl. Also, I think you should call her right now."

"*Mmm.* I don't know. I really think maybe I've messed it up for good."

Phe pulls Cinnamon into a hug so hard she has to unravel her legs, and their cheeks squish together. "Call her. *Talk* to her. You cannot ghost Perfect Daisy and remain my friend. You cannot."

"Get off me, you animal!"

"Call her. *Tonight.*"

"Maybe."

⚷

Two hours later, when she's tucked up in Phe's spare room after herbal tea Mattie made and three episodes of the most dialogue-heavy but oddly compelling show she's ever seen, Cinnamon pulls her phone off the rickety stack of books by the bed.

She opens up the multimedia message, finally, from days and days ago and looks at the painting Daisy sent. She thinks it's impressionist, though she spent most of high school art class in detention with Phe, because she fundamentally disagreed with most of the stuff they were taught.

It's by Mary Cassatt—*Portrait of a Young Woman.*

Cinnamon scrolls her up and down, zooming in and out on the

fingers splayed on her cheek and the night-green-blue of the background, until after one in the morning. She stares at the racks of Phe's and Mattie's clothes shoved around this room, its chipped-paint walls glowing by the light of her screen. Then looks back to the picture of the young woman. Stares at it and stares at it until her eyes sting.

She holds down on the corner of the photo hard with her thumb, and reacts to the message with a heart.

37.

New Year's Eve is a hundred degrees. It's a fire-and-brimstone, going-outside-before-sunset-is-impossible sort of day, the fan above Scarlett's bed whirring its wings to no discernible effect.

She alternates between watching the blur of its spinning, and checking and rechecking the zero new notifications on her phone, generally feeling sorry for herself.

Through her window she can see almost up to Main Beach, distant people already setting up to watch tonight's fireworks. Later Amy and Ian are taking the boat out of the shed to bob in the bay and watch, like they did every year when she was small. She's invited, but in a way that suggests they know she'd rather ring in midnight here, curled up alone in the dark.

Cinnamon hasn't spoken to her since their cliffside argument. Scarlett's shifted between being fine with this to being categorically Not Fine several times over the last twelve hours.

Her sister's bedroom is silent; there haven't even been any footsteps echoing across the hall for Scarlett to analyze the estimated level of sadness/anger by the heaviness of their tread. Maybe Cinnamon's not even there.

Ian is quiet like he always is at the moment. Amy's been silent too, except to repeat the need for *time. Time heals everything.* Except if that were true, the Prince girls should be best friends by now.

Scarlett throws an arm over her sweaty face. She hates this. Hates that she did it and can't fix it. She has no plan, and it feels like falling, like all the summer heat in the world is swallowing her or maybe just holding her still, in powerless purgatory.

She sighs hard and drops her hand away from her face, focusing on the fact that right now, this second, she's just in her room. She tries to read—three different print books and one on her e-reader that everyone at school said they loved. *Emma* sucks her in for a while, but then the blond Mr. Knightley in her head starts to look like Will.

The daylight finally starts to turn watery when she's halfway through a reread (Joan Didion recommended by her sister, ages-ages-ages ago), shadows feathering their way across the room to hide parts of it from view.

The thing with Cinnamon is you can't make her come to you. And for the first time ever, Scarlett isn't going to try.

Amy's busy getting ready, so it's just her dad sitting at the kitchen table when Scarlett finally slinks downstairs to go for a walk.

"Scar?" he says when she's almost at the front door.

She sighs and turns around. "Yeah?"

He's drinking coffee even though the day's almost done. He looks freshly shaven, though. "Where you off to?"

"Nowhere really."

"On New Year's Eve?" Ian quirks an eyebrow and smiles faintly.

"*Mmm.* Just grabbing supplies to take up to my room. Because . . . you know. I had a fight with Cinnamon."

"You really upset her," Ian says.

She winces at the guilt in her chest. Of course Amy told him. But he sounds so unjudgmental that Scarlett is sure he doesn't know the full story.

"Yes," she admits. She's been working on this alone in her room. Admitting she was in the wrong, because Cinnamon spat that she couldn't.

Scarlett looks at Ian's faded red hair. His faded face that looks more like his face right now than it has in a long time. Her mind runs over the sharp edges of the rest of Cinnamon's words. *Leaving. Ignoring him. Left. Left. You left.*

When Maggie died and Ian fell down afterward, she wrote him a very long email while she was on the train back to school. She never sent it. It's still saved as a draft.

"Daddy?" Her voice is small.

"What is it, love?"

She walks over to him, shoes sticking to the wood on the floor, and hugs him awkwardly, him sitting and her standing up. "I love you," she says, like she should've then, should've all summer, should already say again.

"Oh. I love you too," Ian says into her cheek.

Scarlett pulls back and looks at him, forcing the words out. She can admit it. She *can*. "I'm so sorry I left. I'm sorry I wasn't here. I was scared you wouldn't come back. Sometimes I still am."

Ian frowns. "I would never *want* to leave you," he says seriously, emphasizing the *want*, as though it's important and he wants her to understand. "You know that, right?"

Scarlett kisses the top of his head. She keeps looking at him even though he's sort of crying and the sight of it is jagged in her chest.

"Do you want us to stay home?" Ian asks when she straightens up. Something like mischief lights in his eyes.

"I think I should be on my own," Scarlett says. "Go with mum. Have fun."

"I don't know if 'fun' is the right word."

"Mum will make *sure* you have fun."

Ian smiles faintly again. "That's very true."

Cinnamon crashes through Scarlett's door later like thunder, shouting, "What the hell does Olive from *Frozen* look like?"

Scarlett sits up on her bed. Something subtle and sisterly passes between them, ephemeral like how a beam of light shines on motes of dust. Not forgiveness. Armistice.

"I . . . What?" Scarlett asks.

"I have to go to a fucking *Frozen* party in an hour, and I don't know any of the characters. You do, right? I know you do."

"Um . . . okay. A, why?, and B, how is it even possible that you've never seen *Frozen*?"

"Because I was cool in high school," Cinnamon snaps. "Are you gonna help me or not? You owe me."

Scarlett stares at her sister. Cinnamon is wearing old leggings and her Nikes under a white ribbed singlet with a coffee stain above the right boob. Her bare face is red and blotchy. It's as close as she's possibly ever gotten to looking properly bad.

She also looks decisive, though. For the first time in weeks. "Does this have something to do with your moodiness?"

"*Do not* try to therapize me while I still have you hooking up with my ex-boyfriend seared into my retinas."

"*Fine!* But on the off chance"—Scarlett decides to throw caution to the wind—"you are maybe going to see a person for sexy reasons at this party, are you sure you want to go as Olaf?"

"Why?"

Scarlett wonders wildly who the person Cinnamon's going to see is. "Um, because he's a snowman," she says. She doesn't push, for the sake of preserving the armistice, instead pulling up a picture of Olaf on her phone.

Cinnamon swears again.

"It's fine. There are lots of characters to choose from. It just depends whether you're going for, like, shock factor or hot."

Cinnamon's eyes flare and then flick away. "Hot, obviously."

"Right." Scarlett swipes around on her phone again and holds out a photo. "Well, Mum's got like a million doublet-y looking blouses, so I feel like your best bet is this guy."

Cinnamon squints. "*Ew.* Is he dating that donkey thing?"

"That's a reindeer. And no! It's a children's movie."

"*Kristoff*," Cinnamon reads. "Jesus H. Christ. Fine."

"So, you just need a blouse and some corduroy pants and then you should be good," Scarlett says. She's enjoying this. Not just because it's funny—and they've stopped hating each other for a brief, shining second—but also the fact that Cinnamon looks genuinely flustered over something, or *someone*. It makes her seem more human. Makes Scarlett feel sympathy and hope and like hugging her, and like they might eventually *actually* be okay.

Scarlett does Cinnamon's makeup with more care than Niamh for a date, her pinkie finger resting against her sister's soft-warm cheekbone while she fills in her brows and paints on eyeliner.

When she's done, Cinnamon says, "Sweet. Later," jumps up, and stalks out the door, leaving it hanging open behind her, letting in the breeze.

38.

Cinnamon finds a place to park very effing far away, rosy dusk on the horizon and New Year's Eve crowds thick. When she finally pushes open the wood-and-stained-glass door, the pub has been transformed into a kitsch winter wonderland.

It's beautifully horrific—sequins and fake snow dusted on everything and the air conditioners blasting so hard she shivers. There's a piñata shaped like a donkey with antlers, a lot of long red or blond wigs, and an obscene amount of white cardboard cut into the shape of snowmen with speech bubbles that say WORM HUGZ in Tony's handwriting, though the man himself is nowhere to be seen.

There are also more people than Cinnamon anticipated—most of the regular customers are clustered around tables of sparklers and tipping their heads to her as she passes by them fast. She's on a mission.

Daisy's standing alone by the bar underneath a pulsing disco ball, wearing a white T-shirt with a light-blue silk dress that slips down her hips like water. Her hair is pinkly plaited over one shoulder, multicolored strands twisted in on themselves like the tail of a fish.

It takes Daisy a few seconds to see her.

They look at each other.

Cinnamon thinks about grabbing Daisy's wrist and kissing her, and also maybe about running away.

"You're here," Daisy says without much inflection. The words still sound like more than that.

Cinnamon isn't sure *what*, though.

She forces her tongue to come unstuck from the roof of her mouth. "I . . . Yeah. Hi."

Daisy looks like she's deliberating for a beat. Disco-ball light glances over her face in glittery spots. "Hi."

Everything is loud and bright around them. Tony's party is like Tony—too much, but in a strangely comforting way. There's a TV blaring and a fancy stereo playing a song by Harry Styles that isn't on the charts anymore, and several people dressed up as literal trolls. Nobody seems self-conscious.

Cinnamon is. She can already feel it, between them—the hazy scratchy-surface tightrope she's been walking since their first shared day at work. Like standing on the edge of a tall building and looking down. Lean forward or run away. Stop-go-stop. Since the first frigging day.

She takes a breath. "Do you think we could, like, talk?"

Daisy looks up, little black flecks around her bright eyes. "I don't know—can we? You haven't seemed particularly interested in talking to me, lately. Apart from one *very* belated and solitary heart react."

Cinnamon flushes. She pushes her hands into her pockets and nods. "Okay. I deserved that one."

Daisy just smooths down her dress with fingernails painted electric blue. Because it's Daisy, there are lots of tiny details. Snowflakes in her ears and berry lipstick. Smudged whitish eye shadow like maybe she did it in a rush, mesh socks poking out of the tops of her Docs. In the context of both this party and everywhere else in the world, she looks very good.

Cinnamon swallows. If it has to happen here, then fine. "Listen. I'm . . . really sorry. For what went down with . . . us. For everything. I didn't mean to bail on you; I swear to god. I just—"

"Ghosted me anyway?"

"*No.* At least, not deliberately."

Daisy raises her eyebrows. "Wow. That's worse."

Cinnamon runs a frustrated hand through her hair. She's never been good at this. Talking. Feelings. Even if said feelings are all she's thought about every second for the last however many days—she can't make words to match them.

"I ghosted everything for a bit, okay?" she tries again. "Not just you. You were like . . ."

Daisy folds her arms across her chest. "Like what? If you wanted to just stay as friends, and not . . . I would've been *fine* with that. Eventually. You didn't have to disappear."

Cinnamon can feel the pulse of the music in her blood. "I don't want that."

Daisy makes a face that's like: angry-confused-pleading. Cinnamon looks at it for a minute, then she grabs Daisy's wrist and pulls until they're both standing outside in the clear last night of December.

"What are we doing, Cinnamon?" Daisy asks. "I don't understand."

"Wait, I'm not saying it right."

"What?"

The darkness is warm and flat, just empty space and the two of them and a strip of a crescent moon. Cinnamon lets it fill her, carry her, thrillingly fast.

Stop-go-*go*.

"What I mean is that there were a lot of things going on, at Christmas. My dad kind of isn't well. He's depressed. He had a breakdown. We don't really talk about it, but he's still not okay. Maybe I'm not either. Maybe none of us are. But you were like this really, *really* good thing that just came out of nowhere, and made all the shit things better. And I got scared, so scared it would end up wrecked, because sometimes it feels like *everything* does. And you don't even have to say anything. I know, okay. I screwed it up. But I just really wanted to say that. So you wouldn't hate me as much."

It's the longest stretch she's spoken for in maybe forever. When she's finished, her breathing is all weird, and she can't look Daisy in the eyes.

"So I wouldn't *hate* you?"

Cinnamon shuffles her shoes. "I know I don't deserve anything else." Her voice is betraying her, swaying and wavering like the leaves in the wind above their heads. "But I couldn't stand it if you hated me."

"Cinnamon . . ." Daisy doesn't sound like she hates her.

Cinnamon still can't look at her. She just stands there, with her eyes fixed on the gravel by her shoes.

There's a crunch of footsteps. And then blue-painted fingers slipping into the spaces between hers.

"I'm sorry," Cinnamon says for the tenth time. "You must've thought I was fully awful."

They walked to the ocean baths, the faint chatter of people moving farther up the beach to watch the fireworks flitting in and out on the breeze. They're sitting side by side at the bottom of the stairs now, near the beaming yellow light that glances over the cement at their feet and plays on the surface of the water in lane one. They're Not Touching, but the space between them buzzes, electric, with *maybemaybemaybe.*

Daisy looks thoughtful, crossing one leg over the other. "I think I knew when I met you that you'd probably break my heart a little bit."

Cinnamon frowns. "God. Why?"

Daisy shrugs. The cooler air coming in from beyond the rocks blows her hair off her face. "Just did," she says. "But I also thought it'd probably be worth it."

"I'm sorry," Cinnamon says, again again.

"Thanks," Daisy responds, sarcastic but soft. Then she leans forward, moves one hand up to hold the back of Cinnamon's neck, and kisses her on the dark steps of the baths with their knees touching while salt wind washes over them both in a sigh.

The second time Cinnamon goes to Daisy's house, she properly appreciates it. Daisy's parents are away visiting friends, but traces of them are everywhere. Triptych frames all over the walls—Lydia always smiling and Ed with his thoughtful look. Daisy at various ages, from toddler to primary school to braces to now. Cinnamon stares at each of those to store away for later. The evolution of D-Leung as seen through The Face. The way it was always beautiful.

They sit together on stools in the kitchen, drinking ginger beers from fat-lipped stubby bottles that sit cold and dewy in their hands.

"Is this okay?" Daisy keeps asking, tucking her hair behind her helix-pierced ear. "I can make something, like, cooler. I think we have gin." She sounds nervous.

"This is fine." Cinnamon is nervous too.

They talk more. Some, and then a lot. Great winding tangents that somehow find their way.

It's not scary or wrong when she tells Daisy about Ian—all of it. Maggie. The tour. Then Scarlett and Will. How sometimes she wishes her family weren't her family, but also she'd die for them. It isn't hard to think of things to say or how to say them.

It's not annoying when Daisy occasionally sits up straighter, gasps, and interrupts her to say something. It feels like collaboratively making art—all their thoughts exhaled up into the high ceiling to fall down again, mixed together, and fill up the room.

"So, what went down with you and Megan?" Cinnamon hears herself ask at one point. She doesn't think about it beforehand; it just comes out.

She wonders how long she's been wondering about that.

Daisy's mouth opens for a minute, surprised. "Um. Megan was just . . . intense. We were in the same friend group—she was my best friend, really, until I came out in year ten and she was just kind of *convinced* it was a phase?"

Cinnamon winces. "Ugh."

"*Mmm.*" Daisy nods. "My parents couldn't stand her. She got sort of . . . possessive, I guess would be the word. Like she had this idea of who I was allowed to be. And then once she said . . ."

"What?"

Daisy looks uncomfortable. Cinnamon knows, without knowing how she knows, that it's probably because Daisy doesn't want her to *think badly of Megan*, rather than uncomfortable at whatever the deal was between them.

"She was mostly joking, but we were in legal studies once talking now, near the beaming yellow light that glances over the cement at their feet and plays on the surface of the water in lane one. They're Not Touching, but the space between them buzzes, electric, with *maybemaybemaybe*.

Daisy looks thoughtful, crossing one leg over the other. "I think I knew when I met you that you'd probably break my heart a little bit."

Cinnamon frowns. "God. Why?"

Daisy shrugs. The cooler air coming in from beyond the rocks blows her hair off her face. "Just did," she says. "But I also thought it'd probably be worth it."

"I'm sorry," Cinnamon says, again again.

"Thanks," Daisy responds, sarcastic but soft. Then she leans forward, moves one hand up to hold the back of Cinnamon's neck, and kisses her on the dark steps of the baths with their knees touching while salt wind washes over them both in a sigh.

The second time Cinnamon goes to Daisy's house, she properly appreciates it. Daisy's parents are away visiting friends, but traces of them are everywhere. Triptych frames all over the walls—Lydia always smiling and Ed with his thoughtful look. Daisy at various ages, from toddler to primary school to braces to now. Cinnamon stares at each of those to store away for later. The evolution of D-Leung as seen through The Face. The way it was always beautiful.

They sit together on stools in the kitchen, drinking ginger beers from fat-lipped stubby bottles that sit cold and dewy in their hands.

"Is this okay?" Daisy keeps asking, tucking her hair behind her helix-pierced ear. "I can make something, like, cooler. I think we have gin." She sounds nervous.

"This is fine." Cinnamon is nervous too.

They talk more. Some, and then a lot. Great winding tangents that somehow find their way.

It's not scary or wrong when she tells Daisy about Ian—all of it. Maggie. The tour. Then Scarlett and Will. How sometimes she wishes her family weren't her family, but also she'd die for them. It isn't hard to think of things to say or how to say them.

It's not annoying when Daisy occasionally sits up straighter, gasps, and interrupts her to say something. It feels like collaboratively making art—all their thoughts exhaled up into the high ceiling to fall down again, mixed together, and fill up the room.

"So, what went down with you and Megan?" Cinnamon hears herself ask at one point. She doesn't think about it beforehand; it just comes out.

She wonders how long she's been wondering about that.

Daisy's mouth opens for a minute, surprised. "Um. Megan was just . . . intense. We were in the same friend group—she was my best friend, really, until I came out in year ten and she was just kind of *convinced* it was a phase?"

Cinnamon winces. "Ugh."

"*Mmm.*" Daisy nods. "My parents couldn't stand her. She got sort of . . . possessive, I guess would be the word. Like she had this idea of who I was allowed to be. And then once she said . . ."

"What?"

Daisy looks uncomfortable. Cinnamon knows, without knowing how she knows, that it's probably because Daisy doesn't want her to *think badly of Megan*, rather than uncomfortable at whatever the deal was between them.

"She was mostly joking, but we were in legal studies once talking about historical marriage structures, and she said it shouldn't matter to me really because I wasn't actually queer enough to be affected and could just flip back to being straight."

"Nooo! What the *fuck*?" Cinnamon says with feeling.

"And I kind of had a crisis about it. I'd liked more girls than boys at that point, but I was still like, maybe she's right, and I am making this up, or not committing, or not being honest or whatever."

Cinnamon frowns. "If you're queer, then you're queer enough." This is something Phe says a lot. She's never really thought of it as lucky or anything, that she's been orbited by loving planets like Phe and Ollie ever since it mattered, but she feels it now.

Daisy gives a weak little smile. "I mean, it *is* just as well I didn't retract my status as friend-group bisexual, because I was very in love with our other friend Alice, who moved, and then I started to semi-seriously see Brandon Innes for most of year eleven, and he was great. Before Emma." One side of her mouth lifts higher. "God, sorry, I didn't mean to, like, rattle off a comprehensive list of all my exes!"

Cinnamon shakes her head. "I don't mind. I did creepily ask you about it once."

It really doesn't bother her. She's already stalked Emma on Daisy's Instagram, a soft-featured emo type with a cute flippy short-back-and-sides and dark-rimmed glasses.

Cinnamon wants to punch *Megan* in the throat ASAP, but the rest just interest her, as extraneous parts of Daisy.

Daisy laughs, awkward but with her cheeks bright pink. "True."

Cinnamon looks at her for a minute. "Megan sounds like a socio-path," she proclaims. "Tell me more about your grandparents."

"Well, my granddad hates to travel, so we mostly see him when we go back, but my grandma visits every year and goes on these massive hikes—like super far—but she loves . . ." And they're talking again, Daisy lighting up and Cinnamon storing away each new expression to think about in a totally appropriate manner when they're apart again.

It feels good in the way talking to someone you really like always does—exactly the same as sitting contented-quietly alone. They don't kiss again, though, even as midnight inches closer on the bright-colored cuckoo clock in the hallway.

Cinnamon wonders a few times whether this is their first date or their second or if it's a date at all, then Daisy says something else and the moment pulls her back in, and she tries to just be here for whatever it is.

39.

After Cinnamon leaves for the party, Scarlett goes downstairs to make tea. Usually after so much conflict, she'd feel drained like a bath with the plug left half out, but she's almost . . . not *calm*, but somewhere in that ballpark.

Her parents are out on the boat. The house is silent aside from the kettle boiling slowly.

It's dark but not in a scary way—more warm and enveloping.

At the start of summer, Scarlett felt like Halcyon was a person she hated. When she was small, she thought of it as endless—all that space with all its history. She remembers roaming the dusty rooms with floral wallpaper and stately high-backed furniture, looking at the Princes of the past picture-framed everywhere, and wondering where it all went wrong.

Now she wanders back through the kitchen cradling her tea and switches on the hallway chandelier just to watch it cast shapes on the scuffed-hardwood floor. Looks at the ornate banister, thinking of all the years it's seen, and feels weirdly content that the last person she watched walk down the staircase was Cinnamon, looking so good she almost *grinned*—they both did, before her sister snapped, "It's just makeup. Shut up."

Scarlett's mind relaxes and wanders through multiple tangents like river forks.

Cinnamon.

Sadie.

Princes.

Hospitals.

A baby. *And father.*

She's still standing in the hallway when she hears a knock on the door.

Her peace-feelings shatter around her, and Scarlett's rabbit heart jumps into her throat. She concentrates on slowing it, before she goes to answer.

The door swings open with a creak on its ancient hinges.

There's no one there. She holds her tea warm and reassuring against her chest and cranes her neck out into the blue-black night. Switches on the pearly veranda light until it washes across the front steps and grass.

Nothing. Then her foot nudges something—a white envelope. She bends down to pick it up, spilling tea on the wooden slats underneath her.

She looks out at the night again quickly. Still nothing. No one. Just Halcyon's overgrown front yard moving in the night wind like a breathing thing.

Scarlett turns the envelope over in her hands. It's the industrial kind you can get only at a stationery shop like the one Amy used to take her to in the city each term. She holds it up to her face so she can read the white sticker on it with printed black text—as though someone made it with a genuine label maker.

They probably did, she realizes as soon as her eyes scan across what it says.

He probably did. Only Will Taylor would use a literal label maker to say goodbye.

She looks out at the empty clear night again, but there's still no one there. Just her and Halcyon and a stuffed envelope in her hands that reads:

FOR S.

(HOLMES)

W

🔑

She's not sure why she goes to the drawing room to open the envelope. It feels creepy again, running through the house, even with lights on. Like when she was a kid and she'd be convinced, every time she got up to pee, that the monster under her bed would grab her ankles if she didn't get back in fast enough.

It's surprisingly easy though, to think of Will Taylor maybe standing on her doorstep, to let the adrenaline bass-beating through her body drown out the rest of her thoughts. To get dressed in a navy skirt and a mustard band T-shirt of Cinnamon's from the hamper, because this feels like the kind of occasion where you don't want to be in your ratty pajamas, and wearing her sister's clothes and her sister's smell has always made Scarlett feel inexplicably brave.

There must be something. Or he must at least *think* there's something, to give her this. He must be trying to show her something big. *Or maybe he's just trying to say he's sorry.*

She locks the drawing room door behind her and shakes her head, ripping the envelope open.

It's not a sorry or a goodbye. It's the photo she found, the one she left in Will's room of Sadie and Maggie in 1972. Or fragments of it, at least.

Scarlett goes over to her grandfather's dark-wood desk, sits down, flicks the lamp on, and empties the envelope's contents out. Sadie's all-seeing unseeing gray eyes watch from the portrait on the wall behind her.

Seven fragments in total—different sections of the one image, magnified and *annotated*. Scarlett makes an involuntary sound at the incredible Will-ness of that. His handwriting is neater than she expected, little thin slanted letters. Labels next to where he's circled things in the background behind Maggie and Robert and Sadie.

She spreads the images across the desk like a puzzle, trying to figure out the answers. Most of the annotations are labels for the plants in the bush backdrop behind Maggie's and Sadie's heads:

Banksias—bush plant

She-oak—bush plant

Grey gum (?)—bush plant

Weeping roses—<u>*introduced.*</u> *Also grown at Halcyon House.*

The last three fragments are magnified even further, cropped closer in, only showing the section of the building the two women are standing in front of. It's blurry, in black and white, even on the original—let alone zoomed in. But there's a placard above the door, the kind there often is on old houses because people used to give them names. Will seems to have focused on that, zooming in, closer and closer.

On the last image, he's traced over the letters in careful pencil.

W   D   L   ND?

"*Holy crap,*" Scarlett says to nobody. Because she's think-think-thinking it in her head, even before she reaches for a pen and fills in the letters and underlines the word in ballpoint black.

<u>WONDERLAND.</u>

40.

They're on a date.

It's definitely—probably—a date. Cinnamon is at least ninety percent sure. They're sitting on Daisy's tiny balcony facing the reserve and beach, waiting for the fireworks.

Mismatched plain wax candles Daisy brought up are placed in random spots around them, the only source of light besides the sky. The air smells of vanilla and smoke, like the shivery moment right between "Happy Birthday" and *make a wish*.

Cinnamon's legs are folded underneath her. She shaved them rapidly earlier, when she decided it was too hot for corduroy pants and grabbed shorts instead. She even stole weird moisturizer from Scarlett's room with some kind of oil in it. They gleam.

And Daisy's hands are sort of on them.

Daisy was brushing them with her fingertips when they first moved out here. Seemingly accidental touches when she gestured, while they were talking. But they stopped talking a while ago and her palms are warmly there. Daisy looks like she's waiting for something, brown eyes transparent in the dark.

Cinnamon's gaze flicks over Daisy's small, elegant wrist, following the line down to her hands where they are unequivocally still on Cinnamon's legs. Then back up to the waiting eyes. Then away again, because *AH!* Cinnamon physically feels her heart, when she looks down at those hands. So big she can't pretend not to know what it means.

She clears her throat. "So, hey, listen . . ."

Daisy smiles. She seems to like Cinnamon best when she's slightly a mess—which is all the time, when they're together. "Yes?"

Her smell should be illegal, even more illegal than her cheek dimple, better-worse the closer they get. Floral-citrus-soap.

"I kind of haven't done this with a girl before," Cinnamon says in a rush into the space between them.

She regrets the words as soon as they're out, feels shitty about them, hopes to every deity she knows that they come across more as a warning than because she's unsure.

Daisy blinks. "Oh! But you're so . . ."

"Gay?" Cinnamon fills in, still talking too fast. She plucks at a loose thread on her shorts. "Right? It's tragic."

Daisy shakes her head. "I was going to say confident."

Cinnamon can't decipher from her tone what Daisy's thinking, and *oh god, oh god, oh god.* The smell of her *hair.* She keeps her face even.

It's very hard to do.

"I said I hadn't done it before, not that I'm not a top." She's not sure if such a joke is the right thing to say—is pretty sure it's not, actually, but she feels awfully vulnerable suddenly, like she's just split open her stomach and showed Daisy all of what's inside, so that's what comes out. She can't look at her. Might never meet her eyes again, actually. Never ever ever. Amen.

"Me too," says Daisy quietly after a beat. "What a shame. Our love's forbidden."

Cinnamon does what is possibly the most embarrassing accidental laugh of her life, the kind that'd make her want to die if someone played it back for her. "Really?"

Daisy snorts. "No, I'm kidding. I feel like there's not always a one-size-fits-all kind of way to type people."

Cinnamon's insides rinse themselves with cold water. "No, right, I know. I'm just . . ."

Nervous.

So nervous it feels like her head might explode.

"But," Daisy says softly. "If needs must . . ."

Then there's one of her hands, small but firm, touching Cinnamon's chest just below her sternum. Gentle pressure pushing her slowly backward, until her legs unfold and she's lying under an inky ceiling of stars.

Daisy Leung is on top of her.

It's careful and loose, but—there are *thighs* straddling either side of her hips. Hands resting on top of said thighs, the same way moments ago they were on Cinnamon's calf. Careful, but tight with energy. Like they're asking her permission. A question. A dare.

Cinnamon is maybe going to black out.

"I don't want to push you, Cinnamon Prince," Daisy whispers. Sitting back all powerful-respectful like a pink-haloed angel, and staring down at Cinnamon like a gift. Like a challenge. Like a *blaze*. "Okay? We can do absolutely whatever you want."

Cinnamon gulps. Daisy's warmth spills down her throat. "I want," she says, grabbing for the words. "I want . . ."

She can't get anything else out, so she reaches up to hold the back of Daisy's shoulders and kisses her hard, but careful. Just once.

Daisy makes the *hmm* sound she made earlier at the baths, but more, leaning down to kiss back with her ginger-beer mouth cool and soft. One hand follows Cinnamon's arm up to touch her jaw, her hair, tucking it back from her face—then scrunching in it, when they stop being careful.

With Will it was unhurried and planned out, his researcher's hands making her gasp in the dark, her reciprocations making him say, *We'd better stop*, until the night he didn't, and they didn't. He wasn't her first, but she was his. She still remembers watching him right at the moment, chewing his lip and not moving. Looking at her like she could do whatever she wanted.

Daisy is different. And the same. And different.

Cinnamon sits up more. Daisy's legs wrap around her waist, the two of them kissing like they want to absorb each other, kissing hard and soft, kissing with tongue, holding on tighter and tighter.

Everything is so close, hot, high-definition. She bites Daisy's lower lip and earns a sigh. Daisy shifts and pushes one knee between hers, and Cinnamon holds on to it with her entire soul.

This balcony isn't big enough for the need she feels.

It still feels zoomed-in intimate, holding a body with all the same parts as hers. She badly wants to be good at it. After a while, slowly and more deliberately than the very first time on Princes Beach, Cinnamon palms Daisy's hips—until she finds the hem of her T-shirt.

"Okay?" she asks, pulling back.

Daisy laughs against Cinnamon's chin, out of breath. Her fingers are still twisted up in Cinnamon's hair, two soft elbows framing her face. "Yes."

Oh. Cinnamon likes that word. The way it comes out like an exhale and makes Daisy's mouth open wider when she kisses it. She wants it again.

"This?" she asks.

Under Daisy's T-shirt now, her fingertips following the shape of Daisy's waist where it dips inward.

"Yeah," Daisy says like another sigh.

Cinnamon traces the lines and curves of her, the ones that've lived rent-free in her head for months. She doesn't want to miss any details.

Up, up. Over smooth warm skin. The notch of collarbones. A thin cold necklace chain. Then along the killingly fascinating seam of her soft cotton bra.

Under that too.

Daisy exhales and kisses her harder, arching under Cinnamon's grasp like something blooming alive.

It goes on like this, more, more, for a long time, until the sky is on fire or maybe it's fireworks but who even cares, and Cinnamon's bones are halfway incinerated, or maybe just under-oxygenated from swallowing shared air, and it's an entirely new year.

Then Daisy is moving—reaching, down, kissing her. Murmuring something that starts with, "Please can I?" and Cinnamon hears herself say, "Uh-huh," and her head is rolling back, her mouth falling open, and her eyes close, firework-light painting the lids gold.

41.

Scarlett spends the rest of the night in her room looking at the photo fragments, trying to keep her thoughts in list form so she can hold on to them.

Wonderland lives very deep in family lore, though Halcyon's falling-down glamour always eclipsed it in her little-kid brain. Wonderland was the wild bush cottage by the vineyard where her great-great-squared grandfather first lived. Maggie and Grandpa Charlie lived out there too for a while, when they were newlyweds and Great-Grandpa Bill was still a recluse living at Halcyon—Scarlett remembers them telling her that. She tries to focus on Sherlock things (details). Not Scarlett things (feelings).

- The photo was taken at Wonderland.
- Robert and Sadie were at Wonderland.
- With Maggie and their baby.
- They definitely had a baby.
- They definitely went to Wonderland.
- With *Maggie*, her favorite grandmother.
- Maggie, who lived there. Maggie of the cups of tea on the veranda. Maggie, who told her everything, but not this.

Robert and Sadie. She types them into Google on her phone, then again on the laptop on her desk. *Sadie Prince Hammond. Robert Elston Hammond.* Robert Hammond's obituary comes up when she adds his middle name. He was a writer.

Wonderland, she types after that; she remembers the cottage but doesn't know what's up with it now.

Wonderland Cottage, she tries.

Wonderland Princes.

Arthur Prince.

Arthur Prince Wonderland.

Prince Wines Estate. It's called something different now.

Sadie Prince cottage.

Scarlett tries everything she can think of. She can't find the names of any lost Princes, no matter which words she uses in what order.

She has to find them. She has to know what happened. For Sadie and Cinnamon and Ian and herself and for all of this, so she can finally understand.

She searches and searches until her hands cramp and she has a headache from not wearing her glasses with the blue-light filter.

Scarlett's eyes grow heavy. Her thoughts stay awake for a while, though: a kaleidoscope of Sadie and Robert and Cinnamon and armistice and Will and Sherlock Holmes and were things simpler when Holmes was alive or at least when he would've been if he was real but is anything ever simple or does it just look like that from afar and what's real anyway what is a story if there's truth in all the stories and most of the stories are true is that what Grandpa Charlie's painting was trying to tell her what Maggie was what Will was too the truth the truth it's right here it's somewhere *there must be something* if she just keeps going over . . .

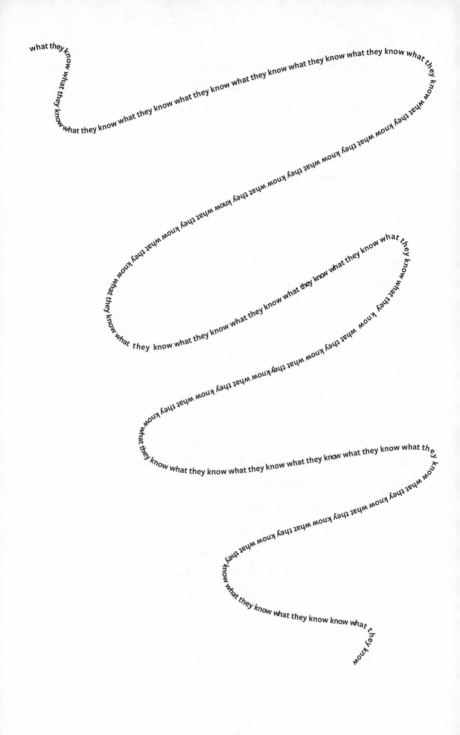

what they know know what they know

42.

When Cinnamon shows Daisy her art the next morning, Daisy looks at it in the way she looked at Halcyon, the way she looks at strangers who interest her, the way last night—after—she looked at the stars—eyes lit with an everyday kind of wonder.

"Oh, I love this," she says.

They're alone in the house. Last night they slept here. Cinnamon's parents aren't back, and Scarlett went out early this morning, leaving a scrawled note that said something like *Gone to library to look for Wonderland*, like they're supposed to know whatever the hell that means.

Cinnamon looks back at Daisy in her room—Daisy with no makeup on, Daisy in a white pinafore and bare feet, Daisy's toenails painted dark-dark blue, Daisy after last night, still here—with a lump in her throat. She blurts out the thing she's thinking. "Hey. When do you leave?"

Daisy's eyes flick over from a sketch of flowers coming out of women's faces. She looks unhappy. "The eleventh."

"As in just over a week from today," Cinnamon says, trying to sound brave about it. She doesn't want to ruin this already by being weird and needy.

She doesn't sound brave about it.

"Come with me," Daisy jokes whisper-soft. She comes over to stand in front of her, puts her hands on Cinnamon's cheeks. "It's not for that long."

Cinnamon pouts; it's hard to do while Daisy's got hold of her face, but she just about manages. And maybe they will—manage.

Maybe they won't.

"Six weeks is like a hundred years in early-dating time," she says.

Daisy lets go of Cinnamon's cheeks but moves one hand across to rub her thumb over her bottom lip. "Says who?"

"Phe. Everyone." Phe was joking when she said it, but Cinnamon's mood feels too dark to mention that part.

"Well, then we've already had like"—Daisy thinks for a second—"seventyish years. We should be fine."

"What if you realize I'm an arsehole while you're sipping dranks in Greece?"

Daisy's thumb slips down to Cinnamon's chin. She kisses her once, soft but firm. "I won't."

"What if—"

Daisy kisses her softly again. Again. Again. "I won't. I won't."

"But—"

"Cinnamon, I won't."

⚬━O

Later they decide to go down to the beach. The tide is low and the water is postcard-pretty, sparkling clear and turquoise at the foot of the cliff.

For Cinnamon, this means retrieving the one bathing suit she still owns that isn't serious black wet suit–style. For Daisy, it means being the first non-Prince to see the attic of Halcyon House.

They climb the creaky stairs to the third floor, Cinnamon pulling Daisy along by the hand. She's forgotten how creepy it is up here— the steep, scratched dark-wood stairs and tiny circular windows like portholes on a ship make the attic feel as if it's a whole other dimension, which in a way it is. Maggie always said the past was a place in the same way the future is, only backward.

"You're sure there's a *bikini* up here? Totally sure?" Daisy asks once they're surrounded by boxes and furniture and dust. This high up all they can see out the window is sea upon sea upon sea. The end of the world.

The high ceiling arch above them is coated in spiderweb chandeliers and the walls seem to breathe—strange running-water noises that can't be heard anywhere else in the house.

Cinnamon smirks, pulling Daisy forward. "Yes. C'mon. It won't hurt us as long as I cut open my hand to show I'm of the right blood."

"If you . . . ," Daisy starts, looking aghast. "Oh. You're joking."

Cinnamon smiles again and nods. "So *easy*, D-Leung, god. It's like you've never lived somewhere haunted before."

"Don't." Daisy laughs, folding her arms around herself.

Cinnamon starts rummaging through the nearest box. She's pretty sure she's seen a bunch of old clothes in boxes . . . somewhere here, by the door.

There's a wooden chest full of baby things: creamy lace turned yellow by years, lonely socks with frills on the ankles, blankets embroidered with hopes and names. Cinnamon tries the smaller one next to it. Photographs. Ugh. She flicks through them anyway, looking for Lycra or a drawstring shoved at the bottom.

The walls make their humming sound again, like a waterfall that only drips whispers. Daisy's eyes slide around the room in alarm.

She moves closer to Cinnamon, the tops of their arms touching. Cinnamon briskly digs through belongings in varying states of decay.

Daisy's eyebrows pull together. "You really are just mostly fearless, aren't you?"

"That's hot," Cinnamon says mildly. "Say that to me again when I'm not under the watchful gaze of my ancestors."

She finds old things of Ian's in nineties prints, the things her mother left when she left, and then lastly, far up against the wall, a ragged-looking box labelled *SP*.

"Bingo," she says. "My sister'll have something. She's obsessed with clothes. I mean, it'll be old as shit, because she hates coming up here, but . . ." She rips open the masking-taped cardboard.

The top layer of the box is a bunch of old documents, musty and tea-stain-colored like the assignment she did on the Gold Rush in year four. Most of them are indecipherable—all flowery penmanship with some of the letters rubbed off. Cinnamon can feel her heart beat-beating in her throat. Daisy kneels down beside her. Carefully they pull more pieces of paper out. There aren't any bikinis, but Cinnamon keeps looking.

The last thing folded into the back of the box is an official-looking document, faded yellow. She can just make out the first few lines.

DEED OF TRUST

24 August 1974

between SADIE GRACE PRINCE & MARGARET LUCIE PRINCE

The Cottage at 162 Filigree Road,

hereafter referred to as

"Wonderland"

Cinnamon turns with wide eyes to Daisy. "Holy shit."

Cinnamon and Daisy run down to Scarlett's empty room, then down the stairs two at a time, but Scarlett still isn't back. Cinnamon yanks her phone out of her pocket and calls her, but her sister—follower of rules—must have it switched off for library quiet.

"What now?" Daisy asks.

Cinnamon thinks for a second. "I don't . . . god. This is big."

She has a feeling. It pulls her downstairs, through the kitchen and hallway to the hook on the wall where Ian's keys hang. The one for the house. The one for the Jeep. And one more, made of brass.

"I have a fully harebrained idea," Cinnamon tells Daisy, who says, "Perfect. I love those."

Will answers his phone on the second ring. "Hello?"

Cinnamon coughs. "You won't believe—"

Will's already talking. "Hey. *Hi.* How are you?"

"This is not a social call," Cinnamon says flatly.

Daisy frowns and swats her gently on the arm, like, *Be nice.* They're sitting next to each other on Cinnamon's bed and holding the deed after mutually deciding that this discovery requires serious backup.

"Okay." Will pauses, and Cinnamon can picture his face exactly just from that pause, and then she does feel a little bad.

She sighs. "Fine. It's not *just* a social call."

"Right."

"We have a proposition for you."

"Okay. Who's we?"

"Daisy's here too. You're on speaker."

"Hi, Will!" Daisy pipes up, leaning forward to shout into the phone and wave a bit. It's so distractingly cute that Cinnamon doesn't even point out the fact that Will can't see them.

"Hey, Daisy," Will says. "So what's up, y'all?"

Daisy chokes on a laugh.

"No, god—minus the 'y'all,'" Will says. "Sorry. That was weird."

"Incredibly so." Cinnamon chews her lip to suppress an almost-smile. "Okay. I'd like to preface this by saying that I'm still in the process of forgiving you."

Daisy swats her arm a second time.

"Right," Will says again.

"But you're proving extremely difficult to hate," Cinnamon says. "And also we need your help with something potentially massive."

Will laughs, awkward and grateful. It crackles through the phone like warm air. "Yeah. Thanks for that. So are you, as it happens. Incredibly so. So, what do you need?"

Daisy leans forward again, tucking her hair behind her ears. "I'm glad you asked," she says.

Cinnamon leans forward too. "Do you happen to know why Sadie Prince would've left Wonderland to Maggie in trust?"

Will hisses something that sounds like *the secret Prince* and then says, "Wonderland? You seriously found it?"

"I think maybe yes," Cinnamon says. "How do you feel about a road trip?"

Twenty minutes later, Daisy drives them down the road in her car. Will is waiting on his front step dressed in baggy blue jeans, forest-green

Converse, and sorry, and he's bouncing his hands on his knees.

"Want me to come?" Daisy asks when she cuts the ignition. Cinnamon shakes her head and steps out of the car.

Will walks over to her quickly. "So a collective road trip, huh? That's the plan?"

Cinnamon thrusts the mortgage deed at him, then plunges her hands into the pockets of her black denim skirt. She's crackling with a weird feeling she can't name. Wariness, maybe. It makes her angry; she's not used to being wary of Will. "I mean, Sadie Prince gave Wonderland Cottage to my grandma to hold in trust for some secret Prince, which is a low-key earth-shattering discovery that also probably means she lived there for a bit, and I've got what I think is the literal key to Wonderland, and you're the only one with 'budding historian' in their dating-app bio, so."

"C'mon." Will's face softens. "Can we press pause on the ice freeze for the sake of the mission? Please? This *is* huge. You have to be nice to me if you want me to come."

Cinnamon looks at Will's infuriating blue eyes. "You realize my sister will also join us on this mission—the one who you literally made out with?"

"Together with the girl you made out with at my literal birthday party?" Will counters. He flicks a brief apologetic glance at Daisy in the driver's seat with the window down, who waves a *fair enough* hand. "Yeah. That mission."

Cinnamon folds her arms and frowns, the way she always does when he's right.

"Shall we get going, then?" Daisy asks cheerily. "I feel like we should get going."

"I'm in if you are," Will says to Cinnamon.

"Of course you're in, this is, like, detective porn for you," Cinnamon mumbles, but she walks beside him.

Daisy makes a careful five-point turn to back out of Will's driveway without hitting the stone wall, then she follows the ocean, cerulean water and sky spreading out alongside them, before stopping at the service station across from the pub. She fills up the gas tank, then walks sunlit across the concrete and through the automatic doors to pay.

Cinnamon watches one leg of Daisy's jeans tuck into her Docs sandal strap, before turning around to face Will.

"Well?" Cinnamon says, ignoring the ghost of a lurch in her chest. She gestures in the direction of the library, two doors down from the pub. "Go get her, then."

Will widens his eyes in an exaggerated show of innocence. "Go get who?"

"William."

"No, okay, I just—"

"Chill. It's fine."

"*Is* it?"

"I mean, it *will* be. Probably."

"You're still a really bad liar, you know that?"

"No, I'm not. Watch this: those pants look really good."

"Ha. Okay."

"I love them. You should wear them all the time."

"Fine, I'm going!" Will gets out of the car all smiling, careful-slamming the door shut behind him.

Cinnamon is struck by how strange it is to be laughing with him and still feel this way. It's still strange *between* them, but no longer awful. And that feels like—something.

Hopefully.

She leans back against the headrest. It's still warm from being parked outside Halcyon earlier.

Daisy opens the driver's-side door. "You okay?"

Cinnamon considers this properly for a second, rolling her neck from side to side and mentally scanning the rest of her body for signs of pathological rage. "Actually . . . kind of. I think. Like I hate him a bit but he's also still my best friend?"

Daisy smiles. "I'm glad to hear it."

"Are you?"

"Yeah. He's important to you. And that"—she leans forward and kisses Cinnamon on the cheek—"is important to me."

Half of Daisy's face is covered in sunshine, illuminating the different-colored flecks in one eye. Chocolate-gold-black-green. The whole car is her smell, and her things, and Cinnamon is a lightning bolt of glad to be one of them.

"I'm sort of obsessed with you," she tells Daisy softly. "Just as, like, a general warning."

Daisy turns the key and the car roars to life. "Big ditto energy, Cinnamon Prince. Huge."

43.

"Just hear me out for a second," Will Taylor says far too emphatically for a library.

Scarlett glares at him and glances at the half-dozen other people scattered around them—all of whom are clearly listening to every word. They're in the nonfiction aisle. He looks so good, and she's still wearing last night's clothes. She's been here since opening trying to locate Wonderland and the Lost Prince Baby in newspaper slides and physical census records, but still hasn't found a single solitary thing.

"I prefer to remain *un*murdered," she hisses at him. "And also—no."

"Because of Cinnamon?" Will says, still too loud. For someone who works here, his grip on the concept of an inside-voice is decidedly loose.

"*Yes!*" she whispers back. "I shouldn't even be talking to you."

"Sherlock," Will says, stepping toward her fast like something made out of pure energy, until Scarlett's back is almost pressed up against the spines of the books. "She's the one who sent me."

"She *what*?"

"*Shh!*" a woman hisses from the next aisle over.

Will twists his mouth to one side. He takes her hand (!) and leads her down the aisle to a deserted spot by the back window.

"Cinnamon sent you?" Scarlett asks.

"Yeah."

"To find *me*? Seriously?"

"Yes."

"Did somebody die?"

"No, it's—"

"Is my dad okay?"

"Yes! Sorry! Everything's fine, promise. It's nothing bad. It's just…" He takes a breath.

They're standing very close—Scarlett can see each strand of blond hair falling over his eyes. She looks at a fixed point over his shoulder to try to stanch the hot drop in her stomach. "What, then?"

"Cinnamon found her."

"Her?" Scarlett blinks at him. "You mean, as in—"

"Sadie Prince." Will nods. "Well, her house, anyway. She left it to Maggie. Wonderland. Cinnamon knows the address."

"So this is awkward," Will says once the mission has been explained, and Scarlett's brain has partially (hectically) adjusted to incorporate the concept of a *spontaneous road trip*, and the four of them are stuffed into Daisy's car hurtling out of town and onto the highway.

"Really?" Daisy Leung jokes from the driver's seat, eyes fixed on the road. "I hadn't even noticed."

Scarlett and Cinnamon are silent.

Scarlett is carefully thinking about nothing. Underneath that, she's trying not to get her hopes up. Underneath that, she's trying not to notice Will's familiar smell permeating her nostrils.

She's also trying not to panic. Or think about panicking. Or move, in case her sister remembers to be ragingly angry with her.

When she got in the car, she said, "Thank you for this. Really. It means a lot to me."

Cinnamon looked at her kind of thoughtfully for a long minute, then nodded. "It's okay," she said quietly. Then her eyes flicked over Scarlett properly, and she said louder, "Is that my fucking shirt?"

Now green countryside swirls summery past the window as Daisy (who said, "I'm so glad to finally meet you!" over the top of Cinnamon's crack about the shirt) drives them all farther and farther away from the coast. Daisy is gorgeous in an unassuming, sneaks-up-on-you sort of way. Scarlett thinks of how Cinnamon's been the last few weeks, rapidly comparing it to how she looks right now, looking at Daisy. And she understands.

The cottage address is five and a half hours away. Scarlett leans back in her seat restlessly and sighs. Her arm accidentally brushes Will's elbow, and *agh*.

"Sorry," he murmurs, looking at her quick and guilty. "I'll just . . ." He rearranges his long legs so that he's tilted away from her, toward the window on his side. He shifts again so that one leg is crossed over the other, discreetly adjusting the middle seam on his jeans by pulling the cuffs.

He widens his eyes suddenly then, like something's gone very wrong down there, before huffing, uncrossing, and settling back the way he was before—with his forearm still pressing against Scarlett's shoulder.

"Ow!" Cinnamon snaps from the front. "Knee my seat again, and you're going on the roof rack, Willie."

"Sorry!" Will says again.

Daisy turns the radio up. It's playing "New Year's Day," by Taylor Swift, the pleasant piano strains of which are almost enough to stop

Scarlett worrying about carsickness. She focuses on the music. The seat beneath her. The fact that the car is crowded, but with people who are safe.

Bar Will, she thinks tetchily, feeling the burn in the spot where their skin's touching. *Not safe. Danger. Turn back.* She settles her thoughts on imagining Wonderland up ahead of them somewhere and the fact that, for better or worse, they are finding Sadie Prince.

Daisy presses a button on the radio, and the same song starts again. "Really, again?" Cinnamon asks in a soft voice.

"*What?*" Daisy laughs. "I'm not ready for the vibe to change!"

Cinnamon just shakes her head.

Scarlett doesn't think she's ever heard her sister speak softly like that to anyone. It kind of makes her feel like crying, but in a way that's not at all bad.

Hours and miles blur together as they drive, and the weirdest thing happens—Scarlett falls asleep. It's been at least ten years since she's allowed herself a slip in control like that—in a *car*, no less. But sleep she does—a blink and then warm dull red nothing—and she doesn't wake up until they stop for food and fuel.

Daisy cuts the ignition, and Scarlett's eyes fly open. She looks out at the night through the windshield while her vision adjusts. A streetlight nearby washes its pale glow over Cinnamon's hair, which is scraped into a spiky ponytail at the base of her neck.

There's a spot of drool on Will's left shoulder, and his cheeks are bright red. *No. God, no.*

Scarlett sits bolt upright, pulling her skirt down over her knees. It's chilly. "Where are we?" she asks groggily.

Cinnamon looks down at her phone, ignoring her.

Quietly and without making eye contact, Will tells her the town they just passed, and . . . far really is far.

Scarlett can feel the distance and the knowledge that it's dark, and they're trapped here, just the awkward four of them, pumping her fully awake. She opens the door and steps outside.

The service station lights cast an eerie halo around the building that fans out like a mirage into the indigo nothing stretched in every direction beyond it. Other than one truck outside and a surly-looking cashier inside, their car and its occupants are completely alone.

The air hangs with gasoline, but it also smells, faintly, like the smoky-cold of winter, which should one hundred percent not be possible, Scarlett thinks, in literal January. Has time stopped? Is this a time loop? Is she dead and this is purgatory?

Scarlett can feel her heart beating wrong. Her hands ball into fists, nails digging into the palms. Breathe breathe breathe.

"Hey," a voice says from behind her.

Scarlett turns around and Will is standing there, one hand in his pocket and the other scratching the back of his pale car-messy hair. "Uh. You okay?"

"I'm fine," she responds in her clipped voice from years of running out of class so she could get to the bathroom before the tingling totally took over her skin.

Will presses his lips together. "'Cause I mean, it would make total sense if you were maybe a little bit freaking out."

Scarlett brushes one hand up her chest to rub under her throat, trying to look like it's a chill thing to do and not so that she can reassure her brain there is definitely oxygen going in. She wonders how long he's been there. How he knew to wait for the falling start of it to be over before offering to help. It's annoying. It's nice.

"We're not, like, mental-health besties just because I told you one thing one time," she snaps, more snappily than she intended to. "And I'm not—"

"*I'm* kind of freaking out," Will continues like he didn't hear her.

Scarlett looks up, instantly sorry. "Why?"

Will shrugs. "New place. Vague *Cabin in the Woods* vibes."

Scarlett laughs unwillingly. It sounds like a bark.

"Also," Will says, "like more than half my brain is on what the sleeping arrangements are gonna be tonight. Where we'll be, bathrooms, sheets, showers, time since last human inhabitant and/or dustpan, etcetera. Just OCD things."

"Oh."

"So, I'm just gonna stand nearby-but-farby, and we can freak out separately together, if that's cool with you."

Scarlett just nods. She can't control what her face is doing.

Her pulse is slowing again. She tries to focus on the kiss of cold over her cheeks. That open-air smell. The fact that Will is here, and she doesn't have to say anything for him to know not to either come any closer or leave.

"Will, why didn't Maggie tell us about Sadie and Wonderland? Does my dad know? Should I call him? I know Cinnamon left him a note, but . . . Do you think he knows, whatever we're here to find out?" she asks in a rush, looking up at so many scattered silver stars. "What happened to the baby? Who were they? Are they? What if we do find out and it's really, really bad?"

"Well," Will says. "Then we'll know."

When Scarlett's body is shivery-spent but her own again, they walk silently inside to where the other two are in the chips aisle gathering snacks. Will gives her a complicated look that makes her feel the same way she did watching Cinnamon and Daisy in the car. Radiating warm.

44.

"Okay," Cinnamon says when they finally arrive at the end of the mile-long winding dirt driveway, the four of them stepping out into the navy-frosted late night. "So, it's a dump."

"Noo!" Daisy says. "Not a dump. A . . . rustic abode."

"Which is a polite way of saying haunted cursed rat palace shithole," Cinnamon says. "Yeah."

It's not *that* bad, true—but it is bad.

There's a lot of night to look at, all the way out here. It feels like being swallowed by it, taking in the giant star-dotted sky and waiting for their eyes to adjust. What reveals itself is a sizeable front yard that's full of gnarly bushes and trees that even Daisy would have to describe as "chronically overgrown," in the dead middle of which stands the cottage. A-framed and lemon yellow, half taken over by a climbing something, like roses or ivy or weeds. Will would know exactly what that is, but Cinnamon can't bring herself to ask him, because he's staring at Scarlett like a lost dog while he shakes the drive off and pulls down the legs of his jeans.

Sadie's runaway bungalow does look like it used to be a safe haven. Even Cinnamon can see the appeal of its faraway-ness, the tiny veranda and low-hanging trees. But in true Prince fashion, things ended in ruin.

She pulls the brass key she stole from her dad's key ring out of her back pocket. Daisy comes to link their fingers together, and the two of them walk through overgrown grass toward the front door.

This part of the house, at least, isn't boarded up like something out of *The Purge*.

Granted, the entryway does have a canopy of slick gray spiderwebs covering it that Cinnamon has to karate kick out of the way, but the door is still a door, red painted wood and stained glass, that swings creakily open on rusty hinges.

Cinnamon turns to look for her sister. For some soppy reason she can't name even to herself, she feels like they should step inside together. "Oi. Come on."

Scarlett is still standing by the back door of Daisy's car. "Y-you go!" she calls back in a high-pitched voice. "I'm good!"

"Hurry up and get inside!" Cinnamon's voice bounces out seemingly for miles. They didn't see any other properties for the last half hour of the drive. She and Daisy switch their phone flashlights on at the same time, two milky beams illuminating the gloom.

"Do you really think it's haunted?" Daisy asks.

"We'll be fine. I definitely used to talk to ghosts when I was a kid, but everyone kind of thought that was a me thing and not an our-family thing." Cinnamon gets an embarrassing emotional heartburny feeling as soon as the words are out. She's never told anyone that before, not even Will.

But Daisy just smiles and says, "Oooh. Intrigue."

The two of them walk through the entryway and look around, lights glancing out of their hands and over everything. The front door leads to a hallway, with dark-wood floors and floral cornices on the ceiling that cast creaturelike shadows over the walls.

"I mean, it's not *not* haunted," Cinnamon says, dropping her voice when Scarlett and Will come up behind them.

"Are we all fully sure we should stay here tonight?" Scarlett asks shrilly. "I definitely think I saw a hotel a while ago. We could come back in the morning."

"*Two hours ago*," Will says.

Scarlett's eyes blow wide. "I . . . Still!"

Will pats her shoulder awkwardly, then retracts his hand as if it's on fire. The two of them are standing carefully apart, but Cinnamon is still annoyed, in a way that's white-hot, by the thought of having to allocate where they sleep.

"Let's look around," she says.

The four of them walk across the cold slate floor of a kitchen, with sugar and tea jars painted with pictures of bees on the coral-colored counter. A white stove with metal hot plates that are well worn and covered in dust. Then a hallway where there's art all over the walls—a sketch of a bird, a beach drawn in pastels that looks like Princes except it's flipped and it's not. Cinnamon walks closer, holds her phone right up to the signature. Her grandfather's initials, the same as hers.

Scarlett's face is shock-pale when Cinnamon's phone light passes over it.

Wonderland is different from the way Cinnamon imagined it. Familiar even though it shouldn't be familiar at all.

They walk farther, Will and Daisy respectfully quiet while the Prince girls' eyes fill with things they didn't know, but did. Chesterfield chairs with a chessboard in front of them. A velvet sofa in bright burnt orange. Dusty timber bookshelves, rows and rows of them. A desk painted sage green facing a window. Wallpaper like at Halcyon, except wilder, brazen patterns that catch and trap light. All the furniture faces the garden. All the tables have lacy runners.

Tiffany lamps are placed haphazardly around the room like they're there for color as much as light. Impulsively Cinnamon walks to push the switch on one. It turns on. Scarlett yelps with surprise.

"There's power," Will muses. "I wonder . . ."

In the corner guitars lying down like they're asleep with less dust on them than everything else in the room.

Cinnamon's eyes linger on those; she grips the key in her fist.

Scarlett clears her throat. "It's late. Maybe . . . Should we conserve energy and look at the rest in the morning?"

Cinnamon is staring transfixed at the lamp. She wants to turn them all on, see the way the room looked when it was living. But she's tired.

"Yeah. Fine. Whatever. Dibs on the biggest room!" she says, taking Daisy's hand again and pulling her down the hall. "We'll reconvene in the morning. Don't get possessed before then. Night!"

"*Cin*—" Daisy giggles, but she lets Cinnamon pull her through the musty dark.

"C'mon."

Cinnamon can hear Scarlett and Will politely arguing over who gets the smaller bedroom and who'll take the couch. She twists open the gold doorknob of a room in the very back and finds a bedroom with a wall of more windows, cathedral-shaped and facing the trees.

"Oh," Daisy says from behind her, so close that Cinnamon can feel her breath ruffle the hair on her neck.

She smiles, leaning backward so that their bodies connect. "Jackpot."

"*Mmm*." Daisy finds her in the moonglow.

Then they're pressed together, Daisy's hands on her hot-soft skin, and both of their hands skimming over faces and chins and neck napes and the bases of spines like air. Kissing like they want to wake the house back alive. Like they're drinking each other in so fast and so slowly, they'll never be done.

When they finally fall into the quilted bed, Daisy yawns in Cinnamon's ear, and they laugh.

"Oh my god," Cinnamon murmurs. "The sheer number of things we could do on this bed, and I am literally so tired."

"What things?" Daisy teases innocently. Her mascara is smudged under tired-wide eyes, and she pinned her bangs back a while ago with two mismatched pastel clips on either side. Seeing them gives Cinnamon such a weird squeeze of affection in the base of her spine that she loses focus for a few seconds.

"I mean . . . Just like . . . Not that, like, I'm too tired to think about—" Cinnamon stumbles.

The bed is deliciously soft. Being in it together is too.

"It's okay." Daisy curls up against her, one warm cheek in the crook of Cinnamon's neck. "Me too. I genuinely can still feel the steering wheel in my hands."

"*Mmph.*" Cinnamon frowns unhappily and grabs Daisy's hand on her chest, half-asleep massaging her fingers.

Daisy shifts her head farther up and smiles against Cinnamon's throat. "Tomorrow," she says, yawning again.

Something about the word—or this sad safe house, or Daisy's bare leg hooking through both of hers and how oddly frigging perfect the two of them road-tripping together was today, despite everything else—makes Cinnamon's mind flash to the date of Daisy's flight next week.

"Tomorrow," she murmurs a beat too late, closing her eyes.

45.

Things are always worse once everyone is asleep.

When Scarlett was very small, the night was a battle. She'd spend every day in terror of it, and when it finally arrived, sleep would elude her. Her thoughts would go into a burning overdrive that was mostly just *alone-alone-alone*.

She'd spend hours prowling the silent house. Reading. Watching late-night TV. Sometimes she'd become convinced of her parents' deaths and stand outside their door trying to hear whether they were still breathing. Other times she'd get so anxious that she'd have to run outside and throw up, or try to, and then she'd just lie in the yard staring at the moon. Eventually she'd crawl into bed with Cinnamon, who'd whisper *What?* all annoyed, and they'd both sleep. But that was then.

She's never been sure what exactly it is—the *reason*—though Marnie says that feelings don't need a reason to be valid. But surely there must have been a moment Scarlett's forgotten, where something happened to make her this way.

Wonderland isn't a terrible place to be, she thinks now, as far as terrible nights go. The room she's in is small and cream-colored and smells like pine. It's the window over her head that's the problem—

Scarlett can't shake the idea that someone, anyone, could be standing outside, watching her. The springy old single bed creaks underneath her. She pulls its seventies-looking checked wool blanket right up to her chin.

You don't need eight hours of sleep to function, she reminds herself in Marnie's voice. Lying here is still resting. Five hours, even, would be enough. And if her brain needs to talk to itself for a while first, that's theoretically Fine.

She wishes the window had a curtain on it.

Her body is pressed as hard into the thin mattress as she can get it, but Scarlett still suspects that a person could see her vulnerable blanket-covered legs from the driveway.

If they looked. (Which they wouldn't.) But if they *did*—

Scarlett hears a scratching sound that makes her jump. "Ah!" She claps a hand over her mouth.

Then there's shuffling footsteps on the grass outside, the creak of the rusty loveseat swing she saw out in the yard before she lay down. She's going to die here. That's that.

She throws the itchy blanket off, crosses the bedroom, and opens the side door that leads to the yard. Her pulse is thudding so hard she can feel it in her hairline.

Outside is cold, like stepping through a wall of water. She stays holding on to the threshold, blinking out at the green-leaves dark.

"Hello," Will says from where he's sitting with his legs stretched out on the swing in the backyard.

"Ohmygod," Scarlett exclaims. "You scared me!"

"That's me." Will smiles slightly. "Terror Taylor, they call me."

They definitively shouldn't be talking to each other right now. Still her feet are moving, walking toward him. Just to get away from the house, she tells herself. So they don't wake up the others. "What are you doing out here?" she asks.

Will shrugs. "Couldn't sleep. You?"

He's still wearing his jeans, but his feet are bare. Scarlett thinks about the fact that she's never seen his feet before and has to look up at his face so as not to stare at them. That's worse, though. His hair is caught by the light of the moon, so bright it looks almost silver.

"Same," she says.

Will pats the spot next to him, frowning slightly when his hand touches a questionable-looking stain.

Scarlett looks over her shoulder at the stoic silent cottage, blending into the landscape as though no one's ever lived there and maybe never will. Then she sighs and sits down.

Will leans his head back against the striped canvas swing covering. Scarlett feels nervous, so she focuses on what's in front of her, like that his hair is glowing because it's wet, slicked back from his face like something out of actual *Downton Abbey*.

"So," he says. "What is it for you?"

Scarlett leans back too, accidentally swinging them both. "I kind of have an anxiety-insomnia, fight-or-flight thing. Sleep and I are not friends."

"Aw, man. Brutal."

"You?"

He swings them more deliberately back and forth for a beat before answering. "I may have showered for forty-five minutes."

"Is that bad?" Scarlett asks. It's easy to do this with Will: talk and keep talking, and actually want to.

Will stares hard at the aged canvas stripes of the swing. "Not in itself, I guess. Sleeping somewhere random is sort of my worst nightmare, though, and . . . it just freaks me out, when I lose track of time like that. Like, I'm counting it, obsessing over it, but also . . . losing it."

They're swinging in earnest now. Scarlett's feet are off the ground, giving her a lifting feeling in her stomach, as though she's suspended in night. "*Hmm*. Why'd it freak you out tonight?" she asks, because she wants to know.

Will pulls the corner of his mouth into his teeth, then lets go of it again. "Because it hasn't been that way for a while, but it used to be . . . anyway! Not making things about me."

"You can't just say that after I revealed my anxiety-insomnia!" Scarlett says only half-jokingly, stopping the swing softly with her feet. "It used to be what?"

Will's legs are still moving even though the seat isn't. Scarlett has the sense that there's something happening, between them, just for right now, that she has to grab on to.

"Bad, I guess," Will says eventually. "It happened a lot. I used to fully dissociate, like, all the time."

"*Will*." Scarlett recognizes the word from conversations with and about Ian.

"Yeah." He nods. "But it's fine now. Mostly. Everything is fine. Just stress, etcetera."

Scarlett frowns.

"Seriously," Will says, smirking weakly and shifting so that he's facing her. There's a hectic splotch of pink on both of his starlit cheeks. "Aside from the incredibly depressingly abnormal bits, I'm totally normal."

"Normal is overrated."

"Really?"

Scarlett shrugs. "That's what my therapist says."

"Snap. Mine too. I have to say that having a brain that's not on fire or eating time with intrusive thoughts still looks pretty appealing, though."

"Right? Mine always says at least I *have* a giant imagination, even if it does sometimes severely work against me."

Will tilts his head sideways. "That's . . . true, actually, I guess."

Scarlett pushes her feet off the ground to start swinging again. "But sometimes I feel like life is just this . . . massive thing, and I'm not big enough to match it."

"*Same,*" Will says. "Hard, hard same."

Scarlett's never had anyone nonaccredited she could talk to like this, about this. For a minute she just holds that shining fact tightly in her mind and lets her feet trail back and forth through the cool of the grass. It's probably past midnight now, she thinks, judging by the depth of the dark, but she's not as worried about those eight hours of sleep.

"So what do you usually do?" Will asks.

"What do you mean?"

"When you're stuck being anxious-insomnia-awake."

"Oh! Usually I kind of . . . lie there and go through a highlight reel of all my sins."

Will looks doubtful. "What, all three of them?"

Scarlett laughs and elbows his arm. "I have sins!"

"Sure you do."

"I do!"

"Oh really? Like what?"

"Like kissing you," she shoots back without thinking about it, and *oh no oh no oh no.*

Will stops the swing.

Scarlett internally explodes. Why can't she hold a conversation with another human being without it turning everything to complete and utter crap?

"Sorry!" She scrunches up her face. "That was . . ."

"No, you're right." Will clears his throat. "I forgot about the whole me-being-your-one-great-sin thing for a sec."

"You're not the *only* bad thing I've ever done!" she rushes to reassure him, before realizing that came out entirely wrong. "Not that it was *bad*. I mean, it *was* bad, but not for me. Just bad generally. In . . . the moral sense."

Oh god. Now she's thinking about it—the kiss, the cemetery, his room, Will's forehead on hers—and her hands are getting all sweaty. So is the rest of her.

Will shifts again next to her. "Not bad for you?" His tone is unreadable.

Scarlett covers half her face with one hand, wishing the grass would split open and swallow her whole. "Oh my god, don't. We were going so good, and we're all stuck here together, it's . . . We don't have to—"

"Wait . . ."

"I promise I didn't mean to say that. Just ignore me—"

"No, I'm just really curious about the 'for you' part."

"Let's please move on."

"Does that mean, like . . . Do you think it wasn't good for *me*?"

Scarlett isn't sure how she got from deciding to not have this conversation at all costs on this trip to directly bringing it up herself. She can feel the beginning of pins and needles in her hands. She moves the one covering her face away. Will is sitting very close, looking at her with rapt attention.

"I don't know!" she whispers. "I mean, we haven't really discussed it."

"*Sherlock*," Will says. Even though it's dark, his eyes are lit like all the light of the moon. "What've I been telling you, this whole time?"

Scarlett looks back at him in confusion. "What?"

"Trust the evidence," he says, fast. Then he looks at her mouth and leans in slowly, one hand cupping her jaw, and kisses her.

Scarlett flinches in surprise, at first, and then her body moves forward of its own accord and her mouth opens, and she's kissing him back, melting into kissing him, fingers gripping the neck of his T-shirt.

They kiss hard and fast like Mary Shelley with Percy in the graveyard.

Like Rochester and Jane, fiery-warm right after she comes running back home. Soft like Knightley and Emma, once it's finally time. Hot like Lord Byron and everyone.

Then they kiss like Lizzie Bennet and Darcy in the 2005 movie version—her favorite—the part just before the credits roll. Careful and slow with intention.

Scarlett can feel the entire line of Will's body pressed sideways into hers. The knock of his teeth. The beat in his neck where it bashes away underneath her thumb. She experiences a moment of cognitive dizziness that it's for her—with her, that *she* can make him do all that—before becoming incredibly distracted by his tongue.

By the time she pulls away, Scarlett's skin has meshed with her heartbeat to the point where it feels like she's made of it. Heat pools in her cheeks and there's something in the very bottom of her stomach, heavy like an ache.

"Fuck," Will whispers, his breathing uneven.

Both of their breathing is uneven.

Scarlett replays the kiss in her head, even though it only just happened. She doesn't think she can physically walk away this time.

"Maybe you'd sleep better in my room," she says like a reflex, because Will's eyes are on her in something like wonder, which is exactly the feeling swirling through her chest.

"As a friend?" Will asks in a low voice.

He's different like this, again. *Confident.* Hot. It makes her stomach flip over.

Scarlett can feel herself blushing. *Brave, be brave.* "Obviously yes."

Will swallows. "Are you sure?"

Scarlett looks at him. She thinks about him losing time, and how she doesn't want to lose *him.* Not yet. "I think very. Like, the most sure."

Will makes a sound like *ungh*, and kisses her again.

Inside Wonderland's tiny gabled guest bedroom, Will's shirt ends up bunched under her head. Wherever was cold before is soon full of gasps, laughs, whispered questions, and twisted-together limbs falling into quiet dark. She's glad she took her cardigan off to sleep, especially when his lips carefully slip over her shirt on their way to her neck—*AH*—before coming back to kiss her mouth again.

Something about how self-conscious they both are in daylight makes it easier here, together, like this. She lets herself trace his shoulders, feel the jut of his hips between her thighs, his fingertips on her back and her shoulder blades, breathy kisses at her jaw and underneath her ear.

Scarlett forgets that her body is a thing she agonizes over. She forgets to worry about her stomach or her upper arms or her clothes bunching up, or smudged raccoon mascara or the softness of her hips. Forgets everything but Will and how increasingly desperate this feels—lips, this, that, there. Each new piece of him she gets to seetouchfeel. She wants every single one.

He's urgent beside her, closer than she's ever been to another person. She almost can't breathe, but in the best way. Breathless like a cold morning. Breathless as thrill. She's also very aware that the only thing between her skin and the hard press at the fly of his jeans is the thin fabric of her skirt.

Then Will Taylor looks at her shining and serious until she nods, and (as a friend) he runs both of his hands up underneath it, and then everywhere.

46.

Cinnamon is too tired to sleep.

Her body is exhausted, bone-tired lead limbs sinking into the old mattress. But her mind is prismatic. Mostly it keeps thinking of the child in the photo Scarlett showed her, the long-lost Prince this house was meant to go to. She wonders if her sister is right, and some stranger is the key to all their problems. If he even exists.

If Sadie even ever did, here.

She's scrolling on her phone absently, the brightness turned low. Daisy's eyelids flutter beside her, like she's not asleep either but at least halfway there. Cinnamon clicks until she finds her favorite video, the interview where her dad is young, all animated eyes and long red hair and an unlined face. No albums yet. No Amy. He looks like a different person and also exactly like himself. She turns the closed captions on and clicks play.

I guess the thing with music is, Ian Prince, aged twenty, says on the screen, mouth moving excitedly too fast the way Scarlett's does, *it has to tell the truth. If you're doing that, the work will usually be good. Not straightaway, but eventually, if you can represent truth, in all its glory and grossness, it'll be good.*

Cinnamon drags her index finger to rewind and play it again. What's the truth, here?

And what happens if they don't find it?

What happens if they *do*?

"D-Leung," Cinnamon says, stark and sudden into the dark.

Daisy shifts. Moves her head out of the crook of Cinnamon's shoulder to look at her. Midnight light on her face, "*Hmm?*"

Cinnamon takes a deep breath. She can't stop thinking a certain thought. She thinks that not thinking of it—not *doing* it—would maybe probably be a colossal mistake. And she's done with that being her thing. "So, like, what . . . What if . . ."

"What?"

"I mean."

Daisy watches her steadily. "Yeah?"

Cinnamon reaches out and touches Daisy's cheek with her thumb. "I've never been overseas."

"No?"

"No."

"*Hmm.*"

"I've never been anywhere. Or seriously wanted to. Till you."

Daisy rolls slowly onto her back. Looks at the ceiling, then back at Cinnamon. "Are you . . . Is this . . . Are you saying you want to come with me? Is that what's happening right now?"

Cinnamon is made of want. "Are you saying you'd genuinely want me to, if I was?"

Daisy rolls back toward her, shifting closer, until their breath mixes and Cinnamon can see the shine of her eyes. "Don't say it if you're not sure."

They're whispering. Cinnamon doesn't know why. She thinks maybe she is someone else for a second, someone full of velvety hope, and the old her is watching from somewhere far above. "Are *you* sure? Seriously. I don't want to just, like, crash."

Daisy makes a soft scoffing face. "What kind of a question is that? Am I *sure*?"

"I haven't figured out what I'm going to do with the year yet. I might be starting uni in March, but I could come for a bit," Cinnamon whispers even quieter. "The first bit, maybe."

"I'm going to New York first."

Daisy in New York. In a coat. Something with pockets for her always-slightly-cold hands. A fluffy wool hat. The two of them talking at night, a conversation that doesn't finish, just picks up the next day, and the next.

Cinnamon swallows. "Okay."

"Brooklyn." Daisy smiles.

"I've always wanted to go to Brooklyn."

Daisy's giant night eyes look so serious. "Are you actually saying you want to come with me? As a proper thing?"

"Yeah."

Cinnamon runs her nose along Daisy's. Daisy's mouth is on her chin, her hands holding Cinnamon's face.

It's maybe the best thing ever.

"What if we kissed, in Brooklyn?" Cinnamon murmurs in her ear. "In front of Dan Humphrey's loft?"

Daisy grins and rolls her eyes. Then she looks serious again. "What if we kissed *now*?"

Cinnamon moves, feather-soft, until Daisy's underneath her. "What if we . . . but this time I . . ."

It is the best thing. The truth.

"Whatever you want."

"Okay, but you have to tell me if it's—"

"*Shh*."

47.

"Was that . . . ?"

"*Mmm.*"

"I mean, are you . . . ?"

"Yeah, no, I'm good. It was good."

"Good?"

"*Very* good."

"Okay, but like—"

"What?"

"Are you ever gonna look at me again, or . . . ?"

Scarlett is lying on her back with both hands covering her eyes. At first she was just rubbing them, but then she stopped to look past the happiness spinning like cotton candy through her to actually *think* about the stuff that just happened for a minute, and all the things she might've done wrong, and then her heart started beating very fast and she couldn't move her hands away.

Will shifts slightly. "Did I do something wrong?"

Scarlett pushes the heels of her hands harder into her cheeks, fingertips cold on her eyelids. "*No.* Not at all. It was . . ." *It was wow wow wow, AH.* "This is just . . . me." She can't explain it. Marnie is always telling her to try to be vulnerable sometimes with people who deserve it, but this is so hard.

"Hey." Will lets out a breath and she can smell it: sugary-sweet from a dusty gas station packet of gummy worms.

After a beat, she feels his hand gently encircling her wrist. He pulls, but still gently. The choice is up to her.

She rolls slightly onto her side so she's bodily facing him, but otherwise doesn't move. Can't yet. Ever. He keeps holding on to her, though, adjusting his fingers so they're wrapped around her hand.

Scarlett thinks she might cry. Being here like this with Will Taylor is a whole blazing sun's worth of *a lot*. "Sorry. I'm just . . ."

"What, out of all the things right now, is stressing you out the most?" Will asks.

Scarlett squeezes her eyes closed tighter under her hands. Thinks about it for a second. "Um. Facing you, probably?"

"Cool. Okay. Easy fix." He pulls her hand lightly away again, and this time she lets him. Her eyes take a minute to adjust to Wonderland huddled warm around them. Will propped, furrowed-browed and shirtless, on his elbow beside her.

"Listen," she says to his patient, wide-open face. His eyes are like *stars* or something, up this close. "I know that probably wasn't . . . So, you don't have to . . . It doesn't have to mean anything. I mean it does to me, obviously. But I get why it doesn't have to, to you."

Will stares back at her without blinking. "Right. And if I said it did?"

Scarlett can't breathe again. Not in a bad way, though, she doesn't think. "Will . . ."

"Do you want me to go?"

Scarlett shakes her head so fast it surprises her. "No!"

Will smiles and tips his face just slightly closer to hers. Air chases its way over her nose and lips as he breathes out. "Okay."

"But I don't know what we do now," Scarlett admits.

His bright close-up face is mock-thoughtful. "Maybe sleep?"

Scarlett chews her lip. *Right.* "Okay."

"Everything always makes more sense in the morning."

"Sleep," Scarlett repeats.

"I mean, you did kind of promise I could," Will points out. "And you did say it was goo—"

Scarlett punches his shoulder and he grins.

"We don't even have to be touching," Will says more seriously. "If you don't want." He tries to retract his hand, but Scarlett holds on to it. Holds on to him.

Carefully, she runs one hand up the length of his arm to cup his cheek. Kisses him bravely—once. Softer than before.

Will looks at her.

Scarlett thinks that she wouldn't mind lying here awake all night, if it meant she got to keep that look. "Okay," she whispers. "Let's sleep."

It is easier in the morning—kind of.

Will is asleep when Scarlett wakes up. The room is full of pale morning light, and there are so many birds chirping outside that it sounds like a symphony.

His arms are wrapped around her, and she's leaning into them. His chin is resting on her shoulder, and her back is pressed against his chest. He breathes softly, in and out, and it tickles her ear.

They're *spooning.* And she *likes* it.

There's movement outside the guest room door. Clanking kitchen sounds, Scarlett realizes after a heart-shattering few seconds.

Cinnamon. If Cinnamon comes in here, they will both be quite genuinely dead.

"Will," she whispers, trying to untangle herself.

Will makes a sleepy noise and tightens his grip for a second, before wriggling his head back onto his own pillow and waking up. "Hi. Hi. Hello."

He lets her go, and she turns around.

He looks grinningly happy to see her. It makes her think of last night. Hands, cold and then warm, lips, scratchy blankets. Will in the dark, huffing and closing his eyes and actually looking like kind of a mess, for a second.

They didn't do *all* the things, but they did a few of them.

"We should . . . ," she says, sitting up.

"Oh, yeah. I mean. Totally."

Scarlett stands up and tries to smooth her impossible hair in the foggy circular mirror behind the door. It's standing up in staticky orange fuzz all around the part. Her head is rushing.

"You okay?" Will asks.

She turns around. "Y-yeah. I'm just . . . I can hear Cinnamon, and my heart is, like, doing this thing where it feels like it's flipping over. Which is just a thing it does. It'll stop in a second."

Will nods. He's already got his shirt and jeans on and is standing up. He points to the outside door in the corner of the room; Scarlett shoved a chair under the doorknob to ward off potential intruders. "Exeunt Will."

Everything is moving too fast for Scarlett to figure out what the swirling feelings in her chest mean. "Wait," she says. "You don't have to—"

"What?" Will stops with one long hand resting on the threshold of the door. When he looks at her, Scarlett thinks that maybe Marnie had a point somewhere in all that stuff about vulnerability.

She doesn't think she's ever seen this much in a single expression before. His face is puffier and younger-looking when he's half-awake. There's a tiny crease between his eyebrows. His bottom lip is gripped in his teeth, like he's asking her something but neither of them knows what. Or maybe she does know, because maybe she's thinking the same thing.

How bad are you gonna hurt me?

"So I really like you," Scarlett blurts out. "As in unplatonically. I have this whole summer or maybe even before. And that probably makes me not a very good person, but this, with us, is . . . good, I think? Or at least it could be. I feel like it could be good. So I just wanted to tell you. So you know."

Will's face flickers brighter, like when the switches on the dimmer lights at Halcyon turn right up to full wattage sometimes on their own. It's hard to keep looking at him, intense in a whole-body-shiver way that's more, somehow, than just kissing in the dark. But Scarlett manages to, even after he says, "I really like you unplatonically too."

"Um. So let's maybe talk about that properly, at some point?"

"That sounds good."

They're still standing on opposite sides of the room. She looks at her feet, then back at Will's face like a room full of light. "*Stop!*" She laughs self-consciously.

Will grins and doesn't look away. "No."

"You can go now."

"Nope. I wanna to hear you say 'unplatonically' again."

"*Go.*" She shakes her head, another laugh bubbling out of her when he does go, and trips slightly getting through the door.

It feels good. Her cheeks and ears are burning hot and she's pretty sure she wouldn't entirely recognize herself right now if she looked in the morning-lit mirror again, but it's good.

When she enters the musty kitchen a few minutes later, Cinnamon is sitting tired-eyed at the table.

Guilt rushes over Scarlett monsoon-fast.

"You look like crap," Cinnamon tells her. "Did you sleep at all?"

Scarlett's cheeks are still hot. She combs through the knotty fall of her hair. "Thanks."

Daisy is in the bathroom, splashing water on her face; the house is so small that Scarlett can see the backs of her legs where she's leaning over the basin.

"Good morning!" she says warmly to Scarlett when they're both in the hallway. "Bathroom's all yours. I'm done."

Will appears then, from the front living room with the couch where he didn't sleep. "Morning, kids," he says.

"William," Cinnamon says curtly.

Will looks at Scarlett once, quick and heavy, and her face blooms hotter. He turns back to Cinnamon. "You look chirpy."

"Hardly. We forgot to bring breakfast stuff. I'm so desperate for coffee I could push someone off a cliff."

"Cinnamon!" Scarlett admonishes before she can stop herself. "That's not funny."

"It's very funny."

"No, it's not. She didn't actually do that!"

"I never thought she actually did it," Cinnamon says.

Scarlett shakes her head. She and Will don't look at each other again, but for all she knows that might be normal. Maybe you *don't* look at each other, after you . . . and then they . . .

Scarlett wouldn't know. (Will definitely would, though.)

Unplatonically. She really said *unplatonically.* Her cheeks burn even more, the cogs of her brain overthinking so much it feels like they might actually start a fire. She water-splashes her face at the bathroom sink, rubbing it roughly with a threadbare towel.

Daisy comes out of the master bedroom with her pink hair scraped back from her pretty, bare face in a plait. "There's a McDonald's forty minutes away, according to maps," she says brightly.

"Really?" Will asks. "Mine said there's nothing!" He leans over her shoulder to nerdily squint at the phone. "What app do you use?"

Both Prince sisters roll their eyes.

"We could go get food. Coffee," Daisy offers, looking up. Her eyes are pretty too, Scarlett thinks. Especially the way they find Cinnamon and then light up and stay there.

"Oh my god, yes." Cinnamon tips her head back and groans exaggeratedly. "Let's go now."

Scarlett's heartbeat picks up speed quietly at the thought of being left alone with Will again.

"Weren't you going to try calling your dad?" Daisy asks Cinnamon.

"Ugh. That can wait. My stomach is eating itself."

"I'll go with you," Will offers suddenly.

Scarlett looks up; he's addressing Daisy, hands in his pockets. Casual. Trying. His eyes flick toward Scarlett and then away. Her heart goes: *boom-boom-boom.*

"Oh," Daisy says. "That would be . . . Sure."

"Cool," Will says, "I need to, um . . . I guess I can shower when we get back. Just let me grab my shoes."

"Hello?" Cinnamon snaps. "What do we do while we wait?"

"Start looking around," Will says. "We've got a lot of ground to cover in this secret nonmurdery bungalow if we wanna unlock its secrets by sundown."

"*Ugh!*" Cinnamon disappears back into the master bedroom to finish getting dressed. Daisy smiles slightly and follows her.

As soon as they're alone, Will looks at Scarlett properly.

She looks back and swallows. *Boom boom boom.* "Why are you . . ."

"I'm a simple man interested in simple things, Sherlock," Will says. "Like the fact I'm starving, and also, your heart staying still."

He's giving her space to think, Scarlett realizes. She also realizes that she wants to kiss him again maybe more than she's ever wanted anything.

Then Will hesitates the way he does, walks across the kitchen, and kisses *her*, quick but purposeful, hard but soft. He feels solid under her hands. His shoulders and his teeth and the sweet smell of his boy-deodorant. She feels it in her whole entire body.

Scarlett pulls away, and Will rests his forehead against hers for a few smiling seconds before he's gone.

There's guilt again when Cinnamon rejoins her to watch him leave with Daisy. Scarlett wonders if she *is* a bad person. How do you *know*, if you are?

She looks at Cinnamon looking at Daisy, her face like Scarlett has never seen it before. Peaceful. Almost. Then she waves goodbye to Will and thinks of the four of them fitting into this strange runaway house. She doesn't regret him.

"God," Cinnamon says, irritated, watching Daisy and Will turn around in the driveway. "I just know he's already telling her about that time I threw up down the side of an Uber, without even giving any context."

"I doubt it," Scarlett says. "I mean, he wouldn't." She really hopes that *is* what they're talking about and not the other, more recent, things Will might talk to someone about on a long car ride. Really really.

323

Last night when she sat up and turned away from him to take her shirt off, Will touched the small of her back absently with one featherlight fingertip. He called her beautiful at least once. It feels *incredibly* cringe and like she's maybe lying just by thinking about that now, in broad daylight.

But he did.

48.

"Did you guys hook up last night?" Cinnamon asks Scarlett bluntly. She doesn't know what makes her ask. She just has a feeling.

A hot and cutting feeling.

"Um," Scarlett scrambles, eyes even wider than usual. ". . . A bit? Yes. Yeah."

Which bit? Cinnamon wants to throw at her, just to see the look on her face. She keeps her own face impassive, though. She doesn't know how she feels about that yet, so she tables it for later.

Scarlett hovers there, waiting.

"Okay," is all Cinnamon says, because she's trying, but she's not a frigging saint.

"Okay?"

"I'm processing," Cinnamon snaps. "But . . . I guess thanks for not lying."

"Okay," Scarlett says squeakily, then clears her throat. "So where do you wanna look first?"

"Study," Cinnamon decides curtly.

The study is like the rest of this place: dusty—but doesn't seem dusty enough to be abandoned. The books on the floor-to-ceiling shelves are arranged in neat rows—(by *whom?*)—and Cinnamon's mind flashes to Ian and then away; empty-eerie—and there aren't any photographs on the wallpapered wall, just the giant window framing the overgrown backyard, under which sits a desk with three silver-handled drawers.

Scarlett tries to pull the top drawer open, but it doesn't budge. "It's locked," she says, looking stressed.

Cinnamon rolls her eyes. "Move."

"But we can't—"

Cinnamon rattles the top drawer with both hands and then her knee, then releases an annoyed *hmph* and leaves the room.

"What are you—" Scarlett starts to ask.

Cinnamon ignores her, combing through the drawers in the kitchen until she finds an old silver knife that's satisfyingly heavy in her hand. She heads back to the desk.

"Cin, don't . . . ," Scarlett says.

Someone saying the word *don't* to Cinnamon has always gone into her ears as *do it*. She slips the tip of the knife under the crack between the top of the first drawer and the desk and leverages her hands against it, pushing until the knife starts to bend and the drawer squeaks and shifts. Then it bursts open and Cinnamon falls backward, the knife clattering to the ground beside her. "Ta-da."

Scarlett's mouth drops open. "Do we think that was a priceless antique?" she asks in a small voice.

"Ingrate." Cinnamon peers into the drawer, which is entirely empty, and feels heinously disappointed. "Ugh. Dead end, anyway."

The two of them move through the house, upending vases and shaking out books and looking in every chest or cupboard or drawer that's been here for however long, until they're both red-cheeked and desperate and hot.

Scarlett rubs her forehead. "Maybe try somewhere else?"

Cinnamon turns toward the window, looking out at the bush. "Outside?"

Scarlett nods.

So they wander out the front door. It's overcast—the summer kind that somehow makes it even hotter and brighter, rather than colder and gray. Both Prince sisters frown under the glare.

The bush is a hug of humidity, blurred somehow as if they're walking through a dream. Any breeze from last night is gone, and everything looks ancient—tall trees rising ghostly white out of dry dirt. Cinnamon's phone vibrates in her pocket, but she ignores it because it's probably Will.

Or possibly Ian.

Scarlett is walking ahead of her along a dirt path that cuts through the trees behind the house, her hair messy and hanging down to the small of her back in little red waves. She's not wearing shoes.

Left them somewhere, probably, when she hooked up with Will.

Cinnamon shakes her head and forces herself to think of the mission. They don't have time for another Prince-Sister Blowup. Her Docs crunch on twigs and rocks as she follows.

"I feel like sometimes at old houses like this, there's an external shed?" Scarlett says like a question.

Cinnamon nods. She thought of this too. She looks ahead of them: pale-gray tree trunks grown tall and scarred by age, red-brown dirt, clumps of unruly grass. "Yeah," she says. "Let's try up here."

They walk farther in until they're properly surrounded, the scattered light-struck leaves at the top of the trees forming a canopy. Birds hoot in the distance, the only sound besides the movement of rough earth under their feet.

Scarlett looks more worried the more they walk, starting and stopping several sentences under her breath, but Cinnamon keeps going, taking the lead, until she comes to a clearing. In front of her is a corrugated-iron structure that looks even older than Wonderland.

"God," Scarlett says.

Cinnamon is already moving toward it as if pulled. "C'mon."

Whether it's because things are still weird between them or because she's being tugged by the same strange instinct, Scarlett does as she says, and suddenly the two of them are standing at the door. Cinnamon pushes it open.

Inside smells like dirt, is the first thing Cinnamon notices. The second is that there isn't actually much dirt, because it's less a shed than it is, like . . . a *cabin*.

There's a wrought-iron bed pushed up against one wall, a giant bookshelf on the other, and an old-fashioned dressing table directly across from them, and the smudgy mirror reflects back their own flummoxed faces.

"God," Scarlett says again. "How many secret houses does this family need?"

"It's not a house," Cinnamon hears herself counter dazedly, walking farther inside and looking around.

The floors are covered in at least an inch of dust. The bookshelves are stacked with dozens of thick, very old-looking books. Leather and canvas spines. There's an acoustic guitar and a giant stereo with the CD drive sticking out. A bulb hangs from a cord on the high ceiling; when she flicks the switch near the bed, it turns on.

There are no filing cabinets here, though. No letters or photographs. Nothing that could remotely resemble a record of Sadie. It's tiny, like the stuff was moved here. Or moved *back*. It looks like a hiding place, but with nothing to find.

"What *is* this place?" Scarlett asks. She stands by the dresser and moves artifacts gingerly around on the doily in front of the mirror.

"I don't know," Cinnamon says, flicking the switch on and off just for something to do besides think.

Her phone vibrates again, and she takes it out of her pocket. It *is* Will. She watches it ring, then sees there's a missed call from Ian too. She feels stupid for running off now that it doesn't mean anything, and, nonsensically, like she might cry.

Scarlett walks over to her slowly. The light from the bulb hanging above their heads illuminates her makeup-less face so that she looks like she did when they were kids: soft and unsure. It feels like the Sadie question is one they've waited their whole lives to know the answer to, only to find out it's not even a question at all.

"Maybe we should just go."

Scarlett nods sadly, her bottom lip trembling. "I really thought there'd be something here. We can check the house more. Maybe there's a Sadie Prince biography in there."

Cinnamon rolls her eyes. "Because that's likely." Her phone rings again.

"You should probably get that, so they know we're not dead," Scarlett points out. She goes back to the dressing table and starts absently searching through the drawers.

Cinnamon answers and presses the phone to her ear once she's back in the hot air outside. "What the hell is it, Will?" she snaps. "A McMuffin is a McMuffin is a McMuffin, just get us whatever the hell looks good!"

Something is happening to Scarlett behind her: she shifts into a higher gear, starts clawing through the dresser harder. Objects—old coins, a painted-faced doll, thin blue envelopes, lipstick containers—make scraping noises as she does. Cinnamon watches her while Will reads the entire breakfast menu out over the phone.

Scarlett crouches on the floor by the bottom drawer, face set, hands blurring, all the stuff in it flying everywhere. She says, teeth gritted and intently, something like, "There has to be something *here*."

Cinnamon slowly moves to stand next to her. Will is still talking on the other end of the phone.

Then Scarlett looks up at her in a shining flash with a piece of paper in her hands, and says, "Look."

49.

December 5, 1973

Dearest Darling Maggie,

I hope you and Charlie are keeping well. It really has been horribly humid lately, hasn't it? R and I were sweltering. He said it was too hot even to write before all the rain last week.

To answer your first question, of course we'll visit again, once the weather dies down. And thank you for the pictures you sent. I appreciate them and you, and hope you know that, even though I probably don't say it often enough.

Truthfully, I do wonder whether he's better off. I know you'd say not, dear Mags, and he really is a most beautiful child (particularly adorable is the photograph of him in the flower bed). But sometimes these things have a strange way of fitting together. Often now, I think that the only good thing to come out of those days is that now he has you as his mother. That's awfully philosophical of me, isn't it, darling? I'm not made for it the way you are, and perhaps it's because of what happened, or perhaps that's just my lot. But I think, Mags, I made him for you.

I've been married to a poet too long, writing pretty words about ugly things. It's a lot of time to think out here. I hear so many songs. They taste different in the bush, clear like running water or this rain. I've sent you one, enclosed.

You asked in your last letter how I really am, and I suppose what I want to tell you is: happy and sad and peaceful and maudlin and good.

I'll come and see you all soon.

All my love,

S.

"What the fu—" Cinnamon closes her mouth, drops to her knees.

Scarlett, next to her, with a face like she's thinking and thinking and thinking, flips the florid-cursive-covered letter over. On the back is a collection of music notes, also handwritten, in almost-neat lines.

Cinnamon traces the notes with the tip of her finger, the dips and twists of them, because they look so alive.

The song is called *Ian*.

She thinks of the boy in the photograph Scarlett found.

And then she knows, now that she knows, that he's like Ian in the videos, different and himself and always with his hair red and his eyes gleaming all-seeing gray.

Outside birds scream and the wind rustles and the trees move above. Cinnamon looks at Scarlett for a long drawn moment, in which the world shatters and knits back together again.

They're holding hands: one sweaty and one shaking.

"Grandma Sadie," she says out loud, because in her head it just sounds *unbelievable*. "Holy, actual shit."

50.

Scarlett explains everything to Will over McMuffins and lukewarm milky tea in the yard. She still feels faintly frantic, like when she'd get picked for an award at school and it took her body a while to realize it was over, her goal done.

Will cuts her off by kissing her. His mouth is hot and soft. "Sherlock, you *cracked it*," he says when he pulls away.

Scarlett touches her bottom lip where he just scraped it with his teeth. Her heart is vividly awake. "And that's . . . sexy? That my family is even more complicated than any of us thought?"

Will nods, eyes very wide. "That is some Dan Brown *Da Vinci Code* sexy shit." He leans forward and kisses her again, holding her chin with his thumb and moving his lips with such enthusiasm that Scarlett giggles against his mouth.

"I didn't crack it. Technically Cinnamon cracked it by bringing us here."

"You cracked it together. Of course you did. Prince power. Princes squared."

"Nerd," Scarlett teases warmly.

Cinnamon and Daisy are walking somewhere in the trees. Talking it through. It's sunny now, clouds parted, citrus summer glow making the landscape look like a home.

Scarlett and Will walk back through the house—*Sadie's house*—after a while and look at her things, her life, the blankets and the wallpaper and the lace curtains in the living room and the windows that are everywhere.

Scarlett shakes her head in soaring disbelief. Her brain is adjusting, and it feels like a betrayal of Maggie in some intangible way, how quickly Scarlett's thoughts registered Cinnamon's *Grandma Sadie* as true.

"We kissed on my biological grandfather's grave," Scarlett realizes and says aloud. "Robert's. Near it, anyway. Grave adjacent."

"We totally did." Will reaches out to touch her hand. She leans her head on his shoulder.

"I don't know what we do now," she admits when they pull away.

Will looks at her, like she's a code he'll never crack. "Me neither."

When Daisy and Will both walk to the car, the Prince sisters stand inside Wonderland one more time holding hands.

They turn to go, and then they see it out of the corner of their eye, like Cinnamon did when she was small and everyone told her it was nothing (and maybe it was): a shimmering blue outline like a reflection in water rippling so quick it's there-and-gone, that almost looks like the face of a woman.

51.

Cinnamon drives them home.

Scarlett is quiet. Will is genuinely *asleep*, leaning against the window with his face and hair splashed in sunlight, mouth-open snoring. Cinnamon shakes her head and tweaks the rearview mirror away from him.

Scarlett flicks into it, briefly. The sisters' eyes catch. Hold on quick and habitual, the way they held hands when they found the letter, sitting on Sadie's floor. Then Cinnamon swallows and stares hard at the road.

Daisy puts on Bleachers's "Wake Me," her hand on the back of Cinnamon's seat. (Not like it's *around* her. Like: *I'm here.*)

Cinnamon doesn't say much, the whole drive back. She just watches the countryside whirl by and grips the steering wheel like she's drowning. Steers Daisy's car down the open gray highway.

Home.

Getting there feels as though it takes a lot less time than leaving did. Town looks different, Cinnamon thinks. She can't decide if it's because she hasn't left it for so long, or if a place just changes for you once everything else does.

Both, maybe.

Neither.

It's hot in a way that flattens the world into a haze, the horizon hung with dusty blue-gold humidity. She follows the bay to Will's house.

"Oi," she says to the back seat once they're there.

Will doesn't move.

Cinnamon turns the car off. "Will. Willie. Will.i.am."

Nothing. Scarlett sighs beside him, gently nudging his shoulder.

Cinnamon leans farther back and claps in front of his face. He stirs but doesn't wake. She pinches him on the chin.

Will's eyes fly open, limbs unfolding everywhere and knocking into Scarlett and the roof. "Cin?"

"We're back."

Will blinks sleepily and smooths his hair. "Oh. Okay. Yeah."

He looks at Scarlett briefly. That still aches faintly in Cinnamon's chest, but it doesn't burn. Then he pushes open the car door and steps out onto the baked asphalt. "It was nice hunting with you," he says, leaning down through the open door with one sun-pale arm hooked around it. "I hope . . . Call me, if you need."

Which one of us? Cinnamon nearly asks just to be a rhymes-with-witch. But she's trying not to do that anymore. Maybe because of the whole nothing-being-what-she-thought-it-was thing. Maybe because she's pretty sure that she and Daisy could have, like . . .

Rhymes-with-dove.

"Robert that," she jokes instead.

Scarlett rolls her eyes. "*Cinnamon.*"

"What? It's funny. If you don't laugh, you'll cry, etcetera."

"It's aggressively unfunny."

"You're aggressively unfunny."

Will is watching the two of them intently.

Cinnamon knows the meaning of that look, without knowing how she knows. "Oh, for god's sake," she mutters, unclipping her seat belt. Feeling both Daisy's and Scarlett's eyes on her, she steps out of the car.

"What's wrong?" Will asks warily.

Cinnamon puts her arms around his waist and hugs him.

It takes a minute, but then he haltingly hugs back, his Will-arms coming up around her and his hands resting on her shoulders and his chin pressed against her cheek. She hugs him tighter, until he makes a sad strangled noise like a sigh. They hold on to each other for a long long time.

It feels like letting go.

🔑

They get back to Halcyon while the sun's still high in the air. Daisy kisses Cinnamon, properly, before she leaves. She lets her. She likes it. Daisy. This. Her brain is *doves-doves-doves*.

She walks with Scarlett up the familiar gravel driveway to the towering light-and-shadows house. It doesn't look any *less* now that it's not entirely full of secrets.

H

It's still too big and too white with too many windows that drop straight off into the ocean if you stand in front of them and stare.

O

It still whispers in the salt breeze like it's trying to tell them something.

M

There are still over a dozen graves in the backyard, and maybe some of those are liars too.

E

Scarlett is mirroring Cinnamon's steps around the side of the house to the rusty old gate. The sisters are molded together now in a way that they haven't been in maybe ever. Or maybe they always were.

Through the gnarled garden. Along the rain-stained edge of the house. Into the backyard with its swaying trees and lavender bush and the looping constant roll of the sea.

When they get to the back deck, their parents are sitting there. Waiting. Amy jumps up to hug them. Scarlett goes first, then Cinnamon. There are tarot cards splayed out behind her on the table like they live out here. The Empress. The World. She smells like patchouli and salt air and chamomile tea.

"Sweet darlings, you're back!" she says. "Your dad just wrote a new song."

Cinnamon hugs Ian record-breaking tight, until he pulls away and pinches her chin once and soft, like he always did before she stopped letting him.

"You stole my keys," Ian says softly, joking and just for Cinnamon.

"Deal with it, old man," she says.

Scarlett asks, "A song?"

Ian smiles sheepishly, all hair and history and hope. "Just one. But I think it could be the start of a new record. Maybe."

Scarlett smiles. Cinnamon sits down beside him and stretches her feet out on the table. "What's it about?"

"I'll tell you," Ian Prince, fifty-one years old, says, "but I want to talk to you both first."

52.

The Mad Princes started with Sadie.

Allegedly.

Her son is the one who ends it.

Scarlett will remember later the way the wind whistled, and her sister's face softened in attention beside her. For now she's in the moment so much she forgets that she's here, instead following the dulcet sound of her dad's voice back through the heaving past.

He tells them first about Sadie Prince in the painting. Young and short-haired and sharp as a tack. She wore trousers and red lipstick and made jokes that made people blush. She shone like *brilliant.* The apple of her father's eye.

She played piano so well that who knows—*they do, her family knows*—how far it could have taken her?

She fell in love with her beloved brother's best friend Robbie Hammond, bright and wild and by accident, and then there was a child. So Great-Grandpa Bill sent the apple of his eye away, to keep the child a secret.

Maggie, Scarlett's favorite grandmother, Sadie's beloved brother's wife, took care of the baby. Took care of Sadie when she went to Wonderland, when she remembered the past and needed the dark.

Ian had two sets of parents until 1976, when Sadie Prince drove over a narrow river bridge and another car crashed into her.

Robbie Hammond never recovered from losing Sadie, but he also never missed a visit with his "nephew."

Maggie and Charlie and Great-Grandpa Bill recovered better. And also, not at all.

"Mum told me the whole story, just before . . . when she knew she didn't have much time left to do it." Ian's voice is wet. "It was a lot, on top of everything. I couldn't cope. I know that. Couldn't tell you, this whole year. But I'm telling you now. I'm so so proud of you both, and I'm so sorry."

53.

Cinnamon helps Amy wash the dishes later, after dinner. Her thoughts are still fairly frenetic-ish, and she doesn't know what else to do. She wants to text Daisy, but she's waiting until she knows what to say; and knowing she can, whenever she wants, is enough.

It's a full moon outside or maybe it's just a bright night, the kitchen fully lit up by it and the dining room chandelier. Everything feels different but everything around them is the same.

"I'm staying," Amy tells her while they pat Maggie's porcelain plates dry. "At least for now. Most of my work can be done remotely, and I want to be here for him. And you."

"I'm leaving," Cinnamon says. It's the first time she's said those words out loud. "On a trip. Overseas. With Daisy."

Amy's face spills over with a gleaming smile. "That's *wonderful*, darling."

They finish the dishes. Cinnamon watches her mother watching the moon. She remembers being small. Back when every cycle Amy would tell both girls to make sure they give all their wishes to it. Bury them in the dirt. Say them out loud. Whisper them on the breeze.

It's worth a shot.

"When I get back, I might be able to help you with that work website stuff. If you want. If I'm not too busy with uni or anything, I mean."

"I would love that," Amy says.

"Okay. Cool. Um . . . me too."

54.

Scarlett can't sleep again.

She's so tired her eyes burn, but her body is wide-wide-wide awake.

Her stomach is full of a Prince family dinner that didn't end in shouting or tears. Her mind is a rush of everything that's happened, all the things she knows.

- Sadie's family sending her away.
- Is it enough that they found her again?
- Will's fingertips last-night this-morning last-night.
- Her sister.
- Sadie and Grandma Maggie—sisters too.
- Her dad.

She pads downstairs barefoot in her nightgown, Halcyon sleeping around her, and eases open the back door. The summer night sits comfortingly on her skin. The sea is calm, silver moonlight playing lazily on its surface.

Ian is leaning against the banister.

Scarlett turns to go at the same time he turns around.

"Can't sleep?"

Scarlett shakes her head. "You?"

Ian smiles. "Nope." He gestures for her to join him, and she does. They watch the sea lap black against the shore. Ian bumps his shoulder into hers.

Scarlett hears herself ask, "What do you think she was like?"

Ian puts his arm around her. It's giant and soft and crushingly warm. "A bit like you, probably. A bit like me. Like your sister."

"Why didn't you talk to us sooner about it?" Scarlett asks again.

Ian lets her go so they can face each other. The circles under his eyes are lighter today. His face can close off in a way hers can't, but it's wide open now. "Because I wasn't doing well and I didn't know how," he tells her honestly.

"How about now?"

"It's a little better now."

"Is it?"

"Yeah."

Scarlett thinks of all the Mad Princes glittery-scattered through the past. Sadie, Great-Grandpa Bill, Grandpa Charlie, and MaggieMaggieMaggie. What they left behind.

She thinks about Will and how long it took her to talk to him, how time is a thing you can't get back, but it's kind of okay, as long as you remember that. That *better* sometimes maybe looks like making space for how you are.

Mostly she thinks about her dad. How she loves him, how her sister does—so much. She looks at him, reaches and holds on to him, and thinks: when someone gives you everything they can, it's enough.

Watson,

Well done on a case solved. (Well done on . . . other stuff

too. We make a pretty good team.) My sister told me when I dropped her at the airport that you're going to try uni in the city this year. I think that's a great idea—you don't get to be the next Attenborough by standing still. I don't know what I'm going to do now that offers are here. I'm thinking of maybe trying to be a book editor. Stories, you know? You might run into me, whatever I choose.

There's a coffee shop down an alleyway I used to go to that I'll pin-drop after this, if you reply. I get why you maybe wouldn't want to though. Truly.

I've always wanted to write a long dramatic letter, even if it is aggressively uncool. You make me like that. I do things I want to instead of being terrified of them. Instead of *just* being terrified. *While* I'm terrified. I know you know how much that means.

I thought a lot about what I wanted to put in here and now I can't even remember most of it, even though it's allegedly easier to organize your thoughts in writing. The main thing I want to say is thank you. For this summer. The case. For all of it. I hope when you look back—not often, but sometimes, maybe—it's good.

I guess what I'm also saying is I hope I haunt you a little. (Feel free to tell me if that's incredibly cringe.)

S. xxx

It's not. (Don't worry, you)
Will
X

Scarlett is sending a location.

Hmm Looks v nice
Maybe I'll see you there
sometime

preferably soon
v v soon

Maybe you will.

55.

Cinnamon Prince is getting on a plane.

Author's Note

I began properly working on this story in 2021, when my mental health (like many people's) was the worst it had been in years. Mental ill health has been part of my life for all my life, but still I always thought that if I worked or pushed hard enough, I would be "fixed." It took a lot of time, panic attacks, and heavy dark to admit I wasn't coping—longer for me to tell people I wasn't and ask for help.

Then I started to write, because writing and books have always been the things for me that make all other things make sense.

I've done my best to carefully and respectfully represent *a* person navigating anxiety, depression, or OCD based on my specific set of experiences, rather than try or presume to ever speak for everyone. Every single one of the many, varied experiences on the broad spectrum of mental health is so very valid, and every story matters so much.

If you found a little piece of yourself in these pages, I hope you feel from-afar loved and seen. I hope you know that you deserve to ask for—and get—whatever help you need, and I hope you do. I hope, whatever "better" looks like for you, you feel a flash of it today. Or tomorrow. Or soon.

RW

X

Resources to Help

In case of crisis, you can contact the United States Suicide and Crisis Lifeline, which is for anyone in emotional distress of any kind, by calling 988 from any US phone (similar to how 911 works). The call is free and someone is available 24/7. For more information about depression and anxiety and other resources to help, visit the Anxiety & Depression Society of America at www.adaa.org.

I wholly recognize that therapy as described in this book is a privilege, and it's one I fervently believe should be freely available to all. Mental-health treatment plans have been key to my ability to pick myself up after numerous falls since I was nineteen. You can talk to your doctor about a referral to a counselor or psychologist, and check with your insurance to see about coverage, which is better now than it used to be. If you're a student, many universities have mental-health services on campus.

Please never be ashamed of thinking or saying, "I'm not coping" or "I'm not okay." Talking to someone when you're suffering is the bravest hardest thing, and it's often the saving thing too.

Acknowledgments

Thanks to my Australian publisher, Clair Hume, who combines uncommon warmth and support with an uncanny ability to always imagine the big picture. That's twice now you've seen and believed in a story of mine before even I was entirely sure what it was. I'll never forget it.

My AU editor and dear friend, Felicity Dunning—I'll never stop going on about how good you are. Please gently highlight all the things in my life I don't need one day. Thank you for stepping on the roller coaster with me again, loving these characters as much as I do, two-hour Zoom Zooms, and for being the voice in my head now when I write or read. Nearby, far-by, wherever you are-by.

Deepest gratitude to my US editor, Karen Boss, for another dream of an international edit. Thank you for being so in tune with the heart of my stories, your cleverness and kindness, and for how much our "Wait, what? What do you guys call that over there?!" comments make me laugh.

Thank you to my parents: Mum for teaching me tarot cards and everything else, and Dad for telling me to trust in my stories and myself.

To my brilliant, blazing sisters (who are not like the sisters in this book)! Caits, who's been ordering me to write stories pretty much since she was born, life is good because I always know I have you. The *Titanic* theme just started playing in my heart because I typed your name. Mia, my sounding board, tiny bestie, and favorite random driving-conversations partner, I'm so proud of you I could cry.

V sorry I borrow your stuff without asking (a **lot**). Loves of my life: I love you both to the moon.

To my wonderful friends, of whom little golden pieces are scattered all through this like magic (by which I mean, lifted verbatim quotes).

Heather Ovens, who cries over my books more and often knows me better than I do, you are the best thing a university group assignment where you can't pick partners has ever brought into anyone's life, and I love you.

Sophie Morrison, the best queer fairy godmother / garden witch for coming into my life right when I needed it.

Izzy Harrison, for a conversation when we got lost in the dark on the way home from Loch Ness, which helped early-spark the idea for the girls and the road trip in this story.

Rachel Partridge and her Amy, for being one of the reasons I wanted to make this about sisters.

Tom O'(slim)Shea(dy), the Dan Brown of Griffin, for making sure my nerdboi characters wear watches and many other Token Man Friend Things.

Thank you to Holstein Wong, future prime minister and generous friend, for her invaluable and insightful help in making Daisy the best she could be. And to her mum for her name.

My sincere gratitude also to Dini Peiris for her warm openness and wonderful notes on Phe.

Thank you to Team UQP, for another marvelous round of publicity to launch another project so close to my heart. How lucky am I?

To Christopher Cyr for this stunning cover and to Jon Simeon for your wonderful design. Cinnamon and Scarlett are thrilled to be in the USA.

To every single reader who sent me kind messages after the publication of my first book when I was writing this one: I appreciate them all so very much.

To Henry Hamlet, for making me an author.

And last but never least, James—for building a life with me and always being the one who pushes hardest for my dreams, even (especially) when I "no worries if not!" You're simply the best. All my, all my love.